Almost To Eden

OTHER BOOKS BY JUNE HALL McCASH

Jekyll Island's Early Years:
From Prehistory through Reconstruction

The Jekyll Island Cottage Colony

The Jekyll Island Club:
Southern Haven for America's Millionaires
(co-author William Barton McCash)

The Life of Saint Audrey,
a Text by Marie de France
(co-editor and translator Judith Clark Barban)

The Cultural Patronage of Medieval Women
(edited by June Hall McCash)

Love's Fool: Aucassin, Troilus, Calisto,
and the Parody of the Courtly Lover

Almost *To* Eden

JUNE HALL McCASH

TWIN
OAKS
PRESS

ISBN 978-0-9844354-1-8

Printed in The United States of America

Twin Oaks Press
twinoakspress@gmail.com
www.twinoakspress.com

Cover images from the Jekyll Island Museum
and the author's private collection.
Cover and Interior design
by Gwyn Kennedy Snider

For all the special Dannys in my life—

Eric, Noah, Nick, Gabe, and Luke.

And for Dallas, my bonus Danny.

Chapter One

9 SEPTEMBER 1911

"THERE IT IS! I SEE IT!" The breathless cry came from a towheaded boy perched on his father's shoulders. Hands clenched tight beneath his father's chin, he bounced with exuberance as he pointed toward the west. The man gripped the deck rail with one hand and held firmly to the boy's legs with the other as he strained to make out the speck on the horizon.

"There it is!" the boy cried again, louder this time. A cheer went up from the passengers, who rushed toward the rail to peer into the afternoon sun, their faces shining in the reflected light.

They had waited many days for this sight—the lady Liberty. They were here at last, on the verge of this land where they felt sure all their dreams would come true.

Maggie stood on tiptoe, stretching her five-foot-two frame in an effort to see over the heads of other passengers. Her heart pounded with excitement and apprehension, banishing the queasiness she had felt ever since they had left Queenstown on the Irish coast more than a week ago. She didn't know what to expect upon landing. She had sent her cousin Eleanor the date of her arrival and the name of her ship—the *S.S. Arabic*—and trusted her cousin would meet her at the dock, for she had no idea what to do or where to go on her own. The idea of a big city in a strange land was terrifying, as she had never been anyplace larger than Galway.

Maggie loved her steamship's name. It made her think of a magic carpet carrying her to places she'd only dreamed about, though it certainly didn't look much like a magic carpet with its four masts and enormous smokestack belching thick gray smoke. For those in steerage like herself, cabins were crowded, and the bunks were hard and uncomfortable. After the first few days, the public areas took on a pungent smell of vomit and body odor, disguised with antiseptic. But nobody seemed to mind. They were on their way to America—the whole eager, noisy lot of them.

Like the rest of the passengers, she was awed by the tall, bronze statue of the broad-shouldered woman, a book held against her body with her left hand and in her right the torch of freedom. In the distance toward the right Maggie could see the island of Manhattan. But the *Arabic* veered left instead, toward the Hudson River Pier. It was there, the sailors told them, that they would be allowed to debark at dawn and wait for ferries that would take them to their final point of immigration, a red brick building with four ornate turrets and white limestone tracings that made it look like a palace, the magic gateway to America—Ellis Island.

Nothing in its outside splendor prepared Maggie for the congestion of the dingy detention center and long lines of weary people awaiting medical examinations inside rows of small, green rooms. Men in uniform herded the passengers up a long flight of stairs, which opened into a barn-like room where children were crying, people milled about, and a perpetual babble of voices droned in myriad languages.

Maggie sat with the others, her green duffel bag perched on her knees, to wait her turn in the examining rooms. She watched the people on the benches around her. Several old men on the next row were setting up a card game, using the bench as a table, and a stocky blond man, a Finnish stowaway, someone had said, played wistfully on a harmonica. She wondered what would become of him.

More than an hour passed before her group was finally called to take their places in line for the examining rooms. Two women, gripping their bundles, stood in front of Maggie. One was young and pretty, wearing a gray-checkered kerchief tied under her chin and pushed back from her brow to reveal dark curls. The other, toothless and wrinkled, wore a plain brown scarf pulled so far forward that Maggie couldn't see even a tiny strand of hair. They were speaking a language she did not recognize. A Slavic tongue, perhaps. Or Turkish.

Behind Maggie was a man with a dark scraggly beard, curly sideburns that hung below his chin, and a black hat. He carried himself with a quiet dignity and spoke in a courteous and precise English as he urged her to go ahead of him in line.

When her turn finally came, it was difficult to maintain her dignity as the medical staff unceremoniously probed and poked at her body, examining her skin and scalp, peering into her ears and throat, and listening to her lungs with their stethoscopes. One doctor peeled back her eyelids, and when she winced, he said, "Sorry, miss, we've got to check for trachoma." She had no idea what trachoma was, though she gathered that if she were infected with it, they could detain her or even send her back to Ireland.

She proved to be one of the lucky ones who passed through fairly quickly. Others, she noticed, had large chalk letters scrawled on their backs to designate the need for further examination. Thus branded, they looked guilty and vulnerable as they were instructed to make their way down the hallway toward which the nurse was pointing. Among them was the pair of women wearing scarves who had been with Maggie in the examining room. One of the inspectors had chalked a large E on the back of the older woman's coat, indicating a problem with her eyes. Both women looked frightened and clearly understood nothing of what the nurse was saying to them as she pointed to the left.

"You'll have to go that way," she was saying to the older woman.

The younger one seemed to be asking a question, but the nurse ignored her, pointing toward the corridor. "You go that way," she insisted more loudly, but the girl kept shaking her head no.

Maggie wanted to help, but she didn't know their language either. The nurse kept repeating the same words again and again in ever more exasperated tones until finally a man in a blue uniform arrived to lead them away. The older woman was crying now. Maggie watched as they disappeared down the hallway.

"You'll need to move along, miss." An agent tugged at her sleeve, urging her toward the bright opening into a large room called Registry Hall.

At the far end of the hall sat an inspector on a raised platform. He was wearing a cap with a shiny eagle and the initials USIS on the front. Again she waited in line. When her turn came, she approached his desk, feeling like a child before a schoolmaster. He peered down and began to pepper her with a series of questions. *How much money do you have? Are you married or single? How old are you? Have you ever been arrested? Do you know anyone in America? Is someone waiting for you in America?*

Maggie dug in her pockets and counted out twenty-five one-dollar bills, the amount she was told new immigrants were required to have upon arrival. Then she produced from her other pocket a tattered letter from Cousin Eleanor stating that she would be responsible for Maggie's welfare. Maggie trembled as she answered his questions, knowing that this man could keep her from entering the country.

"I'm eighteen, nearly nineteen, unmarried," she informed him, "and I've never been arrested in my life." The inspector gazed at her with indifference through his round wire-rimmed glasses.

"I didn't think so," he said, stamping a card with a grand gesture. Finally he smiled broadly and announced, "Welcome to America, miss. You have to pin this to your jacket."

Maggie gazed at the simple card. She wanted to kiss it. At last she held in her hands the precious tag, the ticket that would allow her to pass through the final gates and board one of the launches bobbing at the water's edge to take her to New York harbor where her cousin would be waiting. She gave a sigh of relief and stepped outside to breathe the air of her new country.

The docks along the Battery teemed with people. Maggie searched their faces eagerly for that of her cousin. She hoped they would recognize each other. It had been nearly ten years since Eleanor's departure from Ireland with her husband, Darren, and their daughter, Kate. But none of the faces looked familiar.

Maggie found a spot to wait where she could be seen from several directions—near the street corner under a big round clock, its hands pointing to twelve-thirty. She had Eleanor's address pinned inside her coat. It was also on the letter tucked in her pocket where she would be sure not to lose it. Gripping her duffel bag so tightly that her hands chafed, she gazed about the unfamiliar surroundings. And she waited.

By late afternoon, the air was growing chilly, and she was increasingly aware of how hungry she was. She had not eaten since breakfast, served at six a.m. on the ship. She was weary, but she dared not sit down for fear Eleanor would not see her. Never in her life had she seen so many people in one place. Vehicles clogged the streets, and the noise from horns and hawkers assailed her ears. She found herself beginning to shiver—not so much from cold as from anxiety.

The sun was getting low in the sky. What should she do? She had no idea how to find her cousins. Perhaps there had been some kind of mix-up. Perhaps Eleanor wasn't really expecting her at all. Perhaps… But what difference did it make? She must do something before darkness fell. She couldn't stand here alone after dark.

Finally her eyes fell on a guard, a *policeman*, they called them here, directing traffic in the middle of the busy street. Maybe he could help. It would be difficult to reach him through the seething tangle of "horseless carriages" and horse-drawn buggies. But she had to try. Drivers of the horse-drawn rigs cursed and shook their fists at the drivers of the motorized vehicles, who tooted their horns repeatedly. Thank God it was still light, and the drivers could see her trying to cross toward the little concrete circle in the center of the street where the policeman stood.

Suddenly she froze in place as she saw a vehicle bearing down on her, not slowing at all. But the policeman quickly stepped in front of the oncoming automobile and blew his whistle. The driver slammed on his brakes, stopping just inches away.

"Let's not be in such a hurry, old boy." The officer shook his finger at the driver. Then he put his hand on her elbow and guided her back to the safer side of the street.

"That's a good way to get yourself killed, lass, stepping into the street like that. Some of these folks won't stop even for me," he said, helping her onto the curb. She was trembling.

"I'm so sorry, officer, but I needed directions. I've just arrived and I don't know where to go or what to do. I've been waiting here for hours." She was on the verge of tears.

"Well, that is a bit of a problem. Perhaps if you had an address …"

"I do, but I have no idea how to get there."

She pulled the tattered letter from her pocket and handed it to him. He scrutinized it, ignoring the blaring horns in the street as the traffic became entangled once again.

"Fifty-two Barrow Street. That's on the lower west side of Manhattan, miss. But it's too far to walk, especially now. It's getting dark. I suggest you find a cab to take you."

She looked nervously at the endless stream of vehicles. She had not seen many "horseless carriages" in her life, just those few noisy machines that had occasionally passed her family on the road as they made their way from Doolin to Ennis on market day. They always startled the horses and made her father curse under his breath. She preferred a horse-drawn cab if she could find one, but she had never in her life hailed down a carriage.

"Thank ye, officer," she called after him as he blew his whistle and raised his hand to halt the traffic so he could cross the street once more to take his place in the center.

But how could she tell which hansom cabs or hackneys were for hire? She waved her small hand at each one as they passed, only to realize that they already had passengers, or perhaps their owners inside. Even the ones that were empty passed by her without noticing her effort to signal them.

After several minutes the policeman became aware of her futile efforts. He stepped out in front of a cabbie he recognized and blew his whistle. The cab stopped, and the policeman motioned for Maggie to come.

"There you go, miss—good luck to you."

"Thank ye again, officer." She smiled at him, her face flushed as she got into the hansom cab.

The policeman smiled back. He watched intently as the cab pulled away.

He must think me such a dolt, unable even to get a cab for myself.

But for the first time since the docking of her ship, Maggie sat back and tried to relax, despite the noisy traffic. Looming buildings cast their darkening shadows over the streets. It was all so unlike the rural green and sweeping vistas of the cliffs of Mohr in Ireland that she had left behind. She gaped with wonder at the multitude of people swarming about, the vendors at every corner shouting about their wares. *This must indeed be a wonderful city*, she thought, *for so many to want to live here.*

The ride to her cousin's address took nearly twenty minutes. When she finally caught sight of a sign that said "Barrow Street," it was almost dark, and Maggie felt a wave of misgiving. It had been so long since she had seen Eleanor Brennan and her daughter Kate. She could barely remember what they looked like, and she knew that Kate would have changed from the ten-year-old gangly girl, all knees and elbows, she knew as a child.

They were her mother's cousins, who had left Ireland a decade earlier to come to New York, and, like so many who went away, never returned. Her father told her how they used to hold wakes for people about to depart for America, because those left behind in Doolin knew they would never see them again.

"Of course," he added with a twinkle in his eye, "the 'corpse' would join in the fun, and, as ye well know, we Irish know how to hold a wake."

Her mother would not let them hold a "wake" for Maggie, refusing to acknowledge that she would never see her daughter again. There was a lively family party, but that was all. Maggie, too, was sure that she would go home someday, that this was just an adventure.

"Ye've always been my most passionate child," Maggie's mother had told her with a wistful smile. "You lead oft-times with yer heart, not yer head. But ye're a good girl, ye are, and I think ye should go and follow yer dream." It was not really a hard decision, for Maggie knew it was a chance that would not likely come again.

The carriage pulled to the curb before a rundown house with the number 52 attached to its facade. It showed signs of once being a handsome brownstone residence, but it had surely seen better days. Maggie noted with interest the stone carved woman's face over the downstairs left window and a man's face over the right one and wondered who they were—portraits of the original owners perhaps? Mythological figures? The paint was peeling on the ironwork railing, and the building was in a frightful state of neglect, but it was a house of character nonetheless, and Maggie was relieved to be there.

"Here you are, ma'am," said the cabbie. "That'll be thirty cents."

Maggie handed him one of her dollar bills and waited while he counted out her change. It was part of what she had held out to the official on Ellis Island now wrapped in her handkerchief. As she stepped down, she grabbed her duffel bag just in time, for the cabbie was already flapping his reins and pulling away from the curb.

Maggie rang the bell, but no one came to let her in. She peered uncertainly through the glass doorway into a narrow, dimly lit corridor. A group of six black mailboxes were arranged just inside the dark hallway. She tried the knob. It turned and the door opened. The bottom mailbox on the right bore the label "Brennan, Apartment 1." It was obvious that the brownstone was now a subdivided multiple dwelling. Finding the number 1 on the apartment to her right, she turned the bell in the center of the oak door.

The door opened almost immediately in response to the jangling sound. On the threshold, a cheerful light behind her, stood a young woman with nut-brown hair and fair freckled skin, smiling brightly. When she saw Maggie, her face fell.

"Cousin Kate?" Maggie ventured, having no recollection whatsoever of the face of her cousin Eleanor's daughter.

"Yes?" said the young woman. "May I help you?"

"I'm Maggie," she said. "Yer cousin, Maggie O'Brien, just arrived from Ireland."

"Oh … well, do come in," her cousin said with little enthusiasm. "I'm sorry. I thought you might be someone else. I'll get me mam."

An older woman, a shorter, heavier version of her daughter, hurried in from another room, a dishtowel in her hand and her ruddy face splotched here and there with flour.

"It's not Patrick, Mam, It's your cousin, Maggie O'Brien," said Kate.

"Maggie," the woman said brightly, spreading her arms in a generous embrace. "Begorry, 'tis good to see you. You look like yer mother, ye do." She smiled, looking Maggie over from head to toe. "Ye must be tired and hungry after that voyage. Katy, take her bag to your room and set her a place at the table. We were just about to have a bite o' supper."

"Oh, thank you. That sounds wonderful." Maggie yielded her bag without protest.

"I'm sorry we didn't meet you at the dock, but we have no way to get there, and we didn't know just when your ship would arrive," the older woman said, leading her toward a table in the kitchen. "Now sit yourself down right here, and tell me all about yer mam and yer dad and yer big brother, Brendan."

"He got married, y' know," Maggie said smiling.

"Yes, yer mam wrote me about that. And how is she?"

"She's been a bit tired of late, what with the spring shearing and the wedding and getting me packed off to America. Perhaps she can get more rest now that I'm out from under foot."

Eleanor stirred the wonderful smelling pot on the stove as she reminisced about people and places she remembered from her youth in Ireland.

"Y' know we lived in Doolin for just a little while before coming here," said Eleanor. "It's like the end of the world—Doolin—but I loved that view of the Cliffs of Mohr and the great sea. Ah, but I do miss Ireland. 'Tis so good, Maggie, to hear the mother tongue spoken as it should be." She laughed. "I think I've near forgot the music of the language."

In truth, Eleanor's Irish-English was far more like that of Maggie's parents than Maggie's own. The younger woman was already aware that she needed to learn to say "you" more consistently, not "ye." But it would take a while to get used to it.

The pot on the stove proved to be a delightful Mulligan stew that Eleanor served with fresh-baked wheat bread.

"Cousin Eleanor, This is delicious. You do Ireland proud, you do."

Her cousin smiled and blushed. "Aw ... go on with ye." She hesitated for a moment, then asked, "Has Kate told ye about her young man?"

"No, not yet," Maggie replied, giving Kate a quizzical look. "Well, may I hear all about him?"

"That's who I thought you might be when you rang the bell. Sometimes he comes by after a day's work," Kate said. "He's a perfect fellow if one ever existed. We're going to be married in January, and we're moving to Missouri, where we're going to get some land and farm it."

"Missouri? Is that far from New York?" Maggie was stunned at the news. She thought that Kate would be here, someone near her own age who could help her meet people and find her way. January was only three months away. "Will ye ... you stay here alone, Cousin Eleanor?"

"My land, no, child. I'm going with them. I can do me needlework anywhere," she answered cheerfully.

With her words Maggie's sense of security in her new land vanished abruptly. She knew no one else. Eleanor and Kate were her only contacts with home. They had mentioned none of this in their letters.

"I had no idea," Maggie said softly.

Eleanor laid her hand on Maggie's arm. "Now don't fret yerself about it, dearie," she said. "Surely you didn't think you'd be staying with us forever. By then you'll have a job, and ye'll know lots of people. And if ye don't ... well, something will work out, I'm sure. Ye have to earn yer way in this country, y' know."

"I'm sure I'll be fine," Maggie said, not feeling fine at all, but managing a smile nonetheless. "Tell me more about your husband-to-be," she said to Kate.

By bedtime she wished she hadn't asked. Kate babbled on about him, hardly pausing for breath, for more than an hour. Maggie stopped really listening after a while, once she had heard the most important facts. His name was Patrick Fitzgerald. He was handsome, according to Kate, and hard working. Born in England to Irish parents, he had lived here in Manhattan since he was four, and he now worked as a typesetter for a newspaper, the New York *World*. "Patrick's a really wonderful man," Kate assured her. "Perhaps you'll meet him tomorrow."

Maggie raised her arms in weary surrender. "I feel as though I know him already."

When Eleanor finally suggested they all go to bed, Maggie gratefully inserted her exhausted body between the clean-smelling sheets of the pallet her cousin had laid on the floor of Kate's room. As she lay in the darkness, she pondered her unexpected situation. The news of Kate's impending marriage and the departure from New York of Maggie's only kin was more disturbing than she cared to admit. It cast an uncertain pall upon her first night in the city.

As she closed her eyes, she could see stretching before her only shadows around a sharp curve in the road she had not expected.

Chapter Two

MAGGIE LAY AWAKE much of the night despite her weariness, until finally exhaustion overcame her. She slept so hard in fact that, when she awakened the next morning, the clock on the wall indicated that it was already past ten. The thought of facing the day was not appealing, but she could hear traffic going by in the street outside and knew she must get up.

Dragging herself to her feet, she poured some water in the basin on the dresser and splashed her face. She pulled her wrapper about her, put on her slippers, and opened the door. The apartment was quiet. Making her way to the kitchen, she found Eleanor rolling out dough on the counter top.

When she saw Maggie, she said heartily, "There ye are, darlin'. Sit yourself down, and I'll pour ye a nice cup of breakfast tea."

"Thank you, Cousin Eleanor. I'm sorry I overslept this morning."

"Not a bit of it. I decided to let ye sleep. Kate wanted to wake ye so she could take ye to the Hibernian meeting and introduce ye to Patrick, but I'd have none of it. Ye need yer rest." She poured a steaming cup of tea from the blue flowered teapot.

"What's a Hibernian meeting?" Maggie asked.

"It's an Irish secret society, though not so secret if y'ask me. Some of the younger folk have informal get-togethers on Saturdays just for fun and to help new folks get settled in America, find jobs and places to live, that sort of thing."

"Is it too late for me to go? It sounds as though I might need such help."

"I don't think so. Kate's got something already in mind for you."

"Really? And what is that?"

"I'd rather not say. I think she'd like to tell you herself."

Maggie waited impatiently for Kate to return. She felt annoyed that no one had awakened her in time to go to the meeting. It might have been just the thing she needed to get her started in New York. And she could meet other people there. She fidgeted throughout the morning, writing a letter to her parents and washing the few clothes she had brought with her, all of which she had worn several times during her journey.

When Kate finally returned, it was past two. Maggie was in the bedroom when she heard the door open and voices and laughter in the parlor.

"Maggie!" she heard Eleanor calling her. "Maggie, come and meet Katy's Patrick."

In the parlor stood a burly and awkward-looking young man—nothing like the debonair fellow she had expected from Kate's description. His face was as red as his hair, and his collar looked too tight.

"Hello, Maggie," he said when Kate introduced them. Maggie was aware of his eyes studying her. She smiled at him and returned the greeting. Then he said, "I see that beauty runs in the family."

Well, Maggie thought, feeling herself blush, *perhaps he's not so awkward as he appears.* Kate was watching the two of them, and Maggie sensed her annoyance at Patrick's favorable appraisal of the new arrival.

"I'm glad you're back," Maggie said, focusing her attention on Kate. "I'm so sorry I didn't get up in time to go to the meeting. But your mam tells me that you have something already in mind for me."

"That's right," Kate said. "Interviews are coming up soon for positions at the Jekyl Island Club in Georgia, and I think it might be just the thing for you."

"Kate worked there for the last three seasons and loved it," Eleanor said.

"Tell me more about it," Maggie said.

Kate motioned Patrick toward the sofa, sat down beside him and slipped her hand into his, as she spun out the virtues of the Jekyl Island Club, a club for millionaires on the coast of Georgia.

"They bring their wives and children, their servants and chauffeurs. Some of the families even have what they call 'cottages' there. Pretty fancy cottages, if you ask me, more like mansions." She laughed. "It's like a fairyland. And it's so warm and sunny there that some folks even swim in the ocean in the winter. Flowers bloom all year long. And they grow oranges and lemons on trees."

It sounded like nonsense to Maggie as she listened to Kate babble on about the "good salary" and the "opportunity" to be a chambermaid to New York's elite. Maggie was getting the uncomfortable feeling that her cousin would tell her anything to get rid of her. The place she described sounded like Eden and too good to be true. But, even if some of it were true, it was entirely unacceptable because the "season" Kate described lasted only a little more than three months—from January to early April—and then she'd be on her own again.

Its only advantage, as far as Maggie could see, would be to relieve Cousin Eleanor of any further responsibility, and it would get Maggie out of their hair before Kate and Patrick's wedding. She listened politely to Kate extolling the joys of emptying chamber pots for New York's wealthiest families. But she had already dismissed the idea. It simply wouldn't do. She must have something more permanent.

"My employer, Mr. Pulitzer, is a member of that club," Patrick interjected. "He's been my inspiration. He arrived here as a poor immigrant like me and now he owns the New York *World*. Did Kate tell you I'm going to open my own newspaper in Missouri?"

Maggie was glad to have the subject changed. "She only mentioned your buying land and farming. Tell me more about your plans." She had already forgotten Kate's "fairyland" and was determined to begin her search for permanent employment on Monday morning.

When Patrick brought by a copy of the *World* on Sunday afternoon, Maggie sat down to scan the newspaper for job announcements. Only a few were for women—mostly domestic jobs of maid, nursemaid, laundress, and cook. Other ads called for seamstresses and typists. Although she had learned to sew from her mother, she could hardly meet the description of "skilled seamstress" the job called for, and she couldn't type at all.

Some of the ads even said, "Irish need not apply," which made Maggie's temper flare. Still she dutifully took down all the names and addresses for posts she thought she could handle, and on Monday morning she set out with determination to apply for jobs. Finding a position, however, proved not as easy as she had hoped in this so-called land of opportunity. There were few jobs for women, and many people applied. Those without experience and references were seldom hired. *How does one get experience?* she wondered.

That first week she applied for nine positions. It was always the same story. "Please list your references, miss, and write down any previous posts you have held." She had worked hard since she was twelve, helping her mother in the kitchen, with the housework, and in the parish church. She had even worked alongside her father and brother at lambing and shearing time. But New York seemed to have no need for any of that, and she could hardly use her mother as a reference, though she did try once. The interviewer only laughed at her.

For two weeks she went out every day, rain or shine, to look for positions. She knew she could qualify for nothing more than a domestic post, and there were already thousands of young women in New York seeking jobs like that. Finally the second Friday afternoon, she trudged back to the apartment, completely discouraged.

As always Cousin Eleanor was there with a cup of tea and a lot of unwanted advice. She suggested that, if Maggie got her own place, she could take in laundry. But since she had no job, she could not afford her own place, and how would she find customers since she knew practically no one?

"Well," Eleanor said in exasperation, "if ye want to meet people, ye'll have to find a place to meet them."

"What about the Hibernian Society? When does it meet again?" she asked.

"Formally once a month, but the members in our parish get together every Saturday at ten-thirty, I believe. Perhaps Kate and Patrick can take you there tomorrow."

This time Maggie was up before eight o'clock and ready to go long before ten. Kate had agreed to take her, and they would meet Patrick there.

The gathering was held in a large warehouse-like building. As they entered, Maggie could see dozens of people standing in small clumps, chatting with one another, and milling about.

"Patrick," Kate called, waving toward a group of three young men. He pulled away from the group, making his excuses, and hurried over.

"Hello, ladies," he said. He gave Kate a kiss on the cheek and shook Maggie's hand. "Did Kate tell you, Maggie? This is where we first met. I was assigned to help her and her mother almost eight years ago."

"Just after my father died," said Kate.

"Katy was just a wee twit of a thing then. But she grew." He grinned broadly, his eyebrows raised in enthusiastic approval.

Maggie laughed. "Why did the two of you decide to move to Missouri?" she asked.

"My brother is already there, and he's found us some good land to farm. We'll never have to depend on anyone but ourselves, and our children can grow up close to the land. I've never had that," Patrick said wistfully.

"What do you know about farming?" Maggie asked.

"Oh, I've been reading the almanacs, talking to people, learning what I can. But my brother has his farm going already. What I need to know I'll learn from him. Then I plan to start up a small weekly newspaper where I can be my own boss."

Maggie noticed his pride and thought his enthusiasm quite attractive.

The sound of a gavel cut into their conversation. A short, bespectacled man at the front of the assembly hall was banging on a table.

"We'll call to order this meeting of the Ancient Order of Hibernians," he said loudly, pausing to give people time to shuffle to the nearest chair.

"Now then," he began again, "let's see how many of you are new today. Will all those of you here for the first time please stand up so we can have a look at you." Seven people stood, including Maggie.

"Well," said the speaker appraisingly, "a fine looking bunch, the lot of ye."

Before she sat down, a man three rows away caught Maggie's eye and waved at her. She flushed. He looked familiar. Who was he? Someone from the ship? But he had not stood up with the newcomers. Finally it hit her. He was the guard, the policeman who had directed her to the Brennan address. She almost failed to recognize him without his cap. A lock of sandy hair had escaped his efforts to slick it back and tumbled over his forehead.

"A welcome to you all! My name's Seamus Kelly," said the man at the podium, "and I'm here to offer friendship and assistance. The Order was founded in America in 1836 to help our people. And when you have been here for a while and know the ropes, then you can help us to welcome other newcomers from the Motherland. *Dia's Muire dhuit!*" he said jovially, and the crowd echoed his words.

"*Dia's Muire dhuit!*" Friendship, Unity, and Christian Charity.

Seamus Kelly adjusted his glasses and peered out at the room. "I need not remind you that the Order includes only those who are Catholic and Irish. Membership is secret and not to be discussed outside the group. But we are happy to welcome newcomers, and if you want to join, we meet more formally on the first Friday evening of the month. As ye know, there's plenty of food to share in the back of the hall, and we have tables set up against the walls with information to help you get settled."

He went on and on about the help the Order provided—housing, job opportunities, classes and activities, study groups, legal aid, and understanding American customs.

Finally after ten minutes or so, he concluded, "We're always looking for new ideas, so remember this is your Order too. If you have suggestions, please let us know. Are there any questions or announcements?"

A woman on the second row raised her hand, and he gestured to her. "Mrs. O'Hara?"

She turned toward those seated in the rows behind her. "Father Molloy will hold a special mass at St. James at ten o'clock tomorrow, and he'll be baptizing the new Flannery baby, so all of ye come if ye can."

"Thank you for the news," Seamus said, smiling. "Now, let's all relax and get to know the newcomers. Welcome to New York!"

A fiddler and a tin whistler began to play, as the crowd rose to its feet again and started to jostle about. Maggie had barely gotten up when the man three rows away made his way toward her. "Mornin', miss. I trust you found the address you were looking for the day you arrived."

"Yes, thank you, officer ...? I don't know your name," she said.

"Stuart O'Neil, at your service." He leaned forward slightly in a mock bow.

"Officer O'Neil, this is my cousin, Kate Brennan, and her fiancé, Patrick Fitzgerald."

"Pleased to meet you," he said, shaking hands with them both. Then he turned back to Maggie. "And you?" he asked. "Who might you be?"

Kate laughed. "Let me present my cousin, Maggie O'Brien. Maggie, Stuart O'Neil. There now, you've been properly introduced."

"I'm glad to see you here, Miss O'Brien. I thought I might have to wander Barrow Street after my beat one afternoon so I could find you again."

"That's amazing. You two have already met twice by accident in only two weeks in a city the size of New York," said Patrick. "It sounds to me like the fates have taken a hand." They laughed, and Stuart blushed, peering out from under his wayward lock, and grinned.

Maggie left the three of them chatting like old friends, while she perused the job announcements on the table. Most were the same ones she had already found in the newspaper. But she finally drew up a list of six additional posts. Three of them were domestic positions—two in private households and one as a chambermaid in a hotel—two were in garment factories, and one was for a salesgirl at Macy's, which sounded the most exciting to Maggie. As always, most of the jobs listed were for men.

No matter, she thought, surely sooner or later something would work out, and she would be independent for the first time in her life.

Finding a position, however, still proved elusive. "Please list your references, miss, and write down any previous posts you have held." Whenever they said that now, she just laid down the application form and gave up, for she'd already learned that it would do no good.

She trudged each afternoon back to the Brennan apartment, her shoulders slumped with discouragement. What was she to do? Time was growing shorter, and she had been in New York now for almost a month. Still nothing—not even a nibble.

"Maggie," Kate said one evening over supper, "why are you being so stubborn? Why don't you go ahead and apply for that position at the Jekyl Island Club we talked about? They'll want to know your prior experience too, but at least there I can vouch for you. I was a good worker, and Mr. Falk will remember me. It might work."

"I don't know," said Maggie. "Maybe something will turn up soon."

"Maggie, they've already been interviewing for a week. If you wait much longer, all the positions will be filled."

"Do you really think they might hire me?"

"All you can do is try," Kate replied.

The position *would* have the advantage of providing her with room and board at just about the time Kate and Eleanor would be leaving New York. That way she could save a little money and look for something more permanent when she got back. It was worth a try.

"The best thing about it," said Kate, "if it does work out, when you come back to New York, if you've done a good job, you'll have letters of recommendation from Mr. Falk, Mr. Grob, and even Mrs. Clark, who's head of the housekeeping staff. If you succeed at Jekyl, you should have no more problems."

"I hadn't thought of that," Maggie admitted.

"Then it's settled. We'll go and see Mr. Falk tomorrow morning."

The next day, Maggie and Kate, dressed in their very best clothes, walked the few blocks to 512 Washington Street, the office of Baker and Williams, the firm of a Mr. Frederic Baker who owned a large number of warehouses along the dock areas of Manhattan. The office, Kate explained, also served as the New York office for the Jekyl Island Club, where Mr. Baker had served for a long time as treasurer. Now, though, in light of his advanced age, he was only an honorary vice-president with less responsibility. But he still allowed his offices to be used two weeks out of every fall for interviews.

When they reached the office, Kate explained to the secretary that they were here to interview for positions at the Jekyl Island Club. He nodded, took their names, and asked them to sit against the wall to wait their turn.

Maggie, seated beneath a fine painting of a hunting scene, had a chance to look around the room. Five people were there ahead of them. Two young women about Maggie's age sat opposite, reading small books. An older woman fidgeted nervously in a wing-backed chair. And two men in their twenties sat at the far end of the room, talking quietly to one another.

"What are the men here for?" Maggie asked.

"Waiters mostly, though they could be bicycle men, carpenters, grooms for the stable—that sort of thing. Those two definitely look like waiters." Kate was obviously enjoying her position as one-who-had-been-there. But it was comforting to Maggie to have her here. Perhaps Kate would help change her luck.

Finally the secretary called Kate's name.

"Please, sir, can the two of us be interviewed together? I'd like to introduce my cousin."

"I'll need to check with Mr. Falk," he said. He stepped into the inner office for a few moments and then returned. "Mr. Falk said that would be all right since you were at the Club last year."

Maggie walked with Kate into one of the most sumptuous offices she had ever seen. An oriental rug lay on the floor in front of a large mahogany desk. A glass-front bookcase in matching wood held a collection of ledgers. Sunlight poured in past the heavy, maroon, velvet drapes of the partially opened windows.

"Kate Brennan," said Julius Falk heartily, rising to greet them. "How are you? I'm glad to hear that you've decided to join us for another season." He gestured for them to sit down in the two upright chairs facing the desk.

"Ah, Mr. Falk, I'm afraid I'm here under false pretenses," she said. "I won't be able to go to Jekyl this year, though I shall surely miss it. I'm getting married."

"Why, that's wonderful, Kate. We'll miss you though. Please give the groom my congratulations and tell him he's a lucky man."

"I'll do that, and my thanks, sir."

"Tell me now, if you're not here to apply for a position, what can I do for you?"

"Well, Mr. Falk, I've brought along my substitute. My cousin Maggie O'Brien. She's recently arrived from Ireland. She's a hard worker, clean as a pin, and most agreeable to be with. I can vouch for her, and I hope you'll give her a chance, even though I'm her only reference, I'm afraid. She's only been here a few weeks and is staying with my mam and me." Kate paused, trying to gauge Mr. Falk's reaction.

"Well … this is highly unusual," he said. "Tell me, Miss O'Brien, have you done this sort of work before, the work of a chambermaid?"

Maggie sat forward on the edge of her chair, her hands clasped in her lap. "I've always helped me mother, and back in Ireland, I helped clean the church in our village. The parish was too poor to hire a proper sacristan, and me mam and me, we took on the task to help out. Perhaps I could write to the priest for a reference."

"I don't think there'll be time for that. We do make a point of not hiring anyone without references. Perhaps we ..." He seemed to be hesitating in his decision.

"Oh, please, sir," Maggie said, "I will work extra hard. And I surely know about housekeeping. My mother taught me well. Can't you make an exception just once?"

"As I was about to say," he said firmly, while Maggie reddened with embarrassment at her outburst, "I may be willing, on the word of Kate Brennan, who was our very best worker last season, to make an exception just this once."

Maggie beamed with gratitude.

"What do you know about the job and about Jekyl Island?" he asked.

"I know it's a position as a chambermaid, with all that implies, and I know that the club members are very wealthy."

"It's also on an island where there are only limited medical facilities. I assume that you're healthy, Miss O'Brien."

"They passed me right through all the medical examining rooms at Ellis Island, sir. I don't think that should be any problem."

"And we want our girls to be clean and proper. We don't like to have any ... ah ... problems among the staff."

"Oh no, sir."

"Well, Maggie, if I may call you that ..." She nodded in acquiescence. "I'm going to stick my neck out for you. If Ernest Grob, our superintendent, doesn't overrule me, which is unlikely, you have a job at Jekyl for the coming season. You will leave for the island with the others on December 26th and stay until one week after Easter. The wages are thirty dollars a month plus room and board. There may be tips as well. I think you'll like Jekyl. It's very beautiful, not at all like New York in the winter. We have palm trees and Spanish moss in the live oaks. It's quite a sight."

"Thank you so much, Mr. Falk. You won't be sorry," she said.

Maggie hoped that she would not be sorry either. But she would keep her promise to work extra hard, even though she was certain the island couldn't possibly live up to the Kate's fairytale description. In fact, she was not sure what she was getting herself into. But for now it would have to do.

Chapter Three

IN THE BRENNAN APARTMENT, Kate and Patrick's wedding was uppermost in everyone's mind that fall. It would be a simple affair, to be sure, although Kate was to have a new dress, flowers for her hair, and a bouquet. And there would be a modest dinner afterwards for a few friends. Patrick was helping with the expenses, and Kate used whatever money she had saved from her work at Jekyl Island. She wanted a wedding to remember forever.

Maggie tried to earn her keep until she left for her new job by helping Cousin Eleanor with the housework and cooking during the day. In the evening they sewed together on Kate's satin wedding dress. Maggie was learning to make decorative stitches from Eleanor, whose handiwork was meticulous and creative and earned her a reasonable living. For nights on end they embroidered cascades of delicate white flowers on the bodice and the hem of the skirt. Maggie limited herself to the hem, where her mistakes would be less obvious.

Their routine was interrupted occasionally by visits from both Patrick and Officer O'Neil, the latter of whom had taken to dropping by on a regular basis to "check on Mrs. Brennan and her girls." He rarely stayed long and appeared uncomfortable in the Brennan parlor, as he tried to balance an unaccustomed teacup on his knee. Though it was obvious to everyone that he was smitten with Maggie, he seemed unable to bring himself to ask her out for a walk or to one of the newfangled picture shows that dotted the city. Thus, on many late afternoons when he was off duty, they sat in the fading light of the room until Eleanor felt obliged to ask him to stay for dinner.

"Oh, no ma'am, I couldn't impose," he would respond, brushing back his sandy hair and taking the invitation as his cue to leave.

Maggie liked him well enough. He was older than she by perhaps seven or eight years, and he appeared to be a gentle soul. He was a large-boned, quiet man who took his duties seriously. Occasionally his plain and honest face flashed with humor, but, despite his affability, he seemed more relaxed in the streets of New York than in the confines of the Brennan parlor. And he was clearly inexperienced at the art of courting.

On October 30, Patrick came by the apartment at noon, bringing with him the latest copy of the New York *World*, which carried news of Joseph Pulitzer's death the day before.

"Wouldn't you know," said Kate. "He was on his way to Jekyl Island when he died on his yacht, the *Liberty*. I remember he used to anchor it off the south end of the island. 'Twas too big to come up the river to the dock. Sometimes you could hear the sailors singin' in the evenin'. Folks said they were Russians."

This time Pulitzer had anchored in Charleston harbor to wait out a storm, and it was there his heart finally gave out.

"They say at the end he was completely blind," Patrick said.

"He was a strange bird at Jekyl, to be sure," said Kate. ""He was different somehow, with all his liberal ideas and always siding with the poor. It was hard to see how he fit in with all those millionaires, though they say he was one himself. I guess money is always a common bond."

The Brennans had never paid much attention to the celebration of Thanksgiving, which meant nothing in Ireland, but this year in honor of their newly arrived cousin, they decided to make it a festive American-style holiday.

For the first time Eleanor invited both Patrick and Stuart to dinner, and the three women baked for days in preparation. They had found a *Women's Journal* that listed the ingredients of a typical Thanksgiving feast and were trying to emulate it in every detail. Eleanor and Maggie went together to the markets along Second and Third avenues to find a turkey, squash, and a pumpkin for a pie.

Neither of them had ever made a pumpkin pie in her life, but Maggie took it as her special project. "I can't imagine how it could possibly taste good," she said, "but I'll try anything at least once, I will."

In fact, it was delicious, as was all the other food they prepared, and they ate until they could eat no more. After dinner, Patrick suggested a walk in nearby Washington Square. "Ye young folks get along now," said Eleanor. "I'll stay here and tidy up the kitchen."

"Oh, no, Cousin Eleanor, we can't leave you here to do all that work alone," Maggie protested.

"I'll just stack the dishes and leave them for ye and Kate to do later. How will that be?"

"Well ... all right. If you're sure," Maggie said.

Kate kissed her mother on the cheek, and the young people quickly gathered up their coats and hats and headed outside. It was already cold, and there was the crisp smell of snow in the air.

Patrick gave his arm to his fiancée, and Stuart and Maggie walked side by side, not touching, feeling a bit awkward together.

"How long have you been a guard—a policeman, I mean?" Maggie asked.

"About seven years. I was twenty-two when I joined the force."

"Have you always lived in New York?"

He looked at her and laughed, surprised by the question. "No, of course not, I was born in Dublin and lived there until I was eighteen. I came to New York with my brother Robert. He's married now and lives in Newark."

"Your English is so ... American. I hear a trace of Ireland here and there, but it's so very slight. I just thought you'd lived here all along."

"Not many of us Micks have, Maggie, except for the children of those who came way back during the potato famine. And that was a long time ago. I've worked hard to blend in."

"I think half of Ireland must be living in America now." She laughed.

"You're probably right," he said soberly. "As for me, I'd like to go back to Ireland."

"But why? There is so much opportunity here."

"Not as much as you might think. As someone who had to look for a job you must know that. You have to know the right people. And someone is always trying to take advantage of somebody else. You see a lot of things in my line of work."

The sun was getting lower in the sky, and the air was taking on a penetrating chill. They walked briskly around the park, since it was hardly the weather for a leisurely stroll. By the time they returned to the apartment, red-cheeked from the wind, a light snow was beginning to powder the sidewalks. Eleanor had already cleared the dining table, put the food away, and washed every dish.

"Well," she said, at Maggie's protest of her broken promise, "at least now we're ready to start planning for a cheery Christmas dinner!"

The holiday season did not take on the festive spirit that Eleanor hoped for. On December 12 a letter arrived for Maggie from her brother Brendan. It was dated November 25.

Dearest Maggie,

It is with the heaviest of hearts that I write you this letter to tell you that our dear mother passed away yesterday morning about 6 a.m. Doctor said it was a growth in her belly that could not be removed. Our father tells me she suffered for many months. She did not want us to know for fear we would worry about her or change our life plans in some way. She had been tired for a long time, as you know, and about two weeks after you left she took to her bed and never found the strength to rise again.

Don't try to come home, Maggie. There is nothing you can do here. Just get on with your life in America. Papa will continue to live on the farm near Doolin, though I have tried to get him to move to Lochrea to live with us. He's a stubborn man, as you well know, but I'll keep asking. We all love you and hope you are well. Send us a word now and then.

Your faithful brother,
Brendan O'Brien

Maggie could hardly believe it. Her mother. Dead? There was no sense of reality about it. She sat numb after reading the letter, staring straight ahead. Eleanor picked it up and scanned the crumpled page that Maggie let slide to the floor as though she had lost control of her muscles.

"Oh, Maggie," she said, taking the girl in her ample arms. "What dreadful news! I'm so very sorry."

Feeling Eleanor's arms around her, so like the arms that embraced her before she left Doolin, the tears came suddenly, and her body was wracked with sobs. She had been closer to her mother than anyone else in her life. Why didn't her mother tell her? How could she be gone? Maggie rushed to Kate's room, threw herself onto her pallet, and wept until she wore herself out and fell, exhausted, into a fitful sleep.

For two days she focused on nothing but her grief and her fury with God for taking her mother. Finally, when they were alone, Eleanor said to her, "Maggie, I know that ye are deeply hurt that ye weren't there to say goodbye to yer mam. But, child, ye'll feel grief many times in yer life. Ye mustn't let it take control. Focus yer mind on work, on something productive. It will help, I promise. Learn to master the pain."

She let the older woman's words sink in for a moment. Then she picked up the hem of Kate's wedding dress and began to make stitches, angry stitches at first, until she felt calmer. Eleanor was right. The work did soothe her, and she felt less agitated than she had before.

She didn't know that at night Eleanor ripped out her furious stitches to sew her own gentler, loving threads in their place. Or that she understood so well her young cousin's need to jab her needle into the cloth, for she too, in losing her husband, Darren, not long after their arrival in America, had felt that same anger and need.

As the days passed and Christmas approached, Maggie lost herself once more in the ritual of cooking, Kate's wedding plans, and her preparations to leave for Jekyl. Once again, Eleanor invited Patrick and Stuart to Christmas Eve dinner. Neither of them had other family members in New York, though Stuart planned to visit his brother in New Jersey the following week. For such a special night, however, he preferred to be with the Brennans, Patrick, and especially Maggie O'Brien.

With the exception of that brief, light snowfall on Thanksgiving Day, the snows had held off until Christmas Eve, when dry, powdery flakes began to fall in earnest. Eleanor placed a burning candle in the window to welcome carolers who roamed the neighborhood streets. The city took on a kind of magic that reminded Maggie of her childhood. She missed her parents, especially her mother, that night more than in all the other days since her arrival in New York. Her sorrow hung heavy and silent throughout the day, and it had begun to irritate Kate.

"Come on, Maggie, try to cheer up a bit. It's Christmas, for heaven's sake. You've been moping about all day."

"I'm sorry," Maggie said, though Kate's annoyance depressed her all the more. She tried hard to affect an outward sense of gaiety, for she didn't want to spoil the holiday for everyone else. Trying to get into the spirit of the season, she pasted on a smile and greeted the guests as they arrived with the merry Irish Christmas greeting, "*Nollaig Shona Dhuit.*"

She tried to join in the conversation over their sumptuous dinner of roast goose and plum pudding. Then, to her relief, Patrick brought out his fiddle and began to play. She maintained her smile and even helped in the singing through a rousing rendition of "The Twelve Days of Christmas." She managed to keep her feelings under control as she listened to Stuart's Irish tenor rendition of "*Oíche Chiún,*" or "Silent Night" in the Irish language.

Her determination did not crumble until Patrick began to play her favorite carol, "Once in Royal David's City," and the singers reached the words about the "lowly cattle shed, where a mother laid her baby in a manger for his bed." Then it all spilled over. Remembering the times she had sung those simple lines, her voice harmonizing with her mother's, Maggie felt tears welling up, despite her efforts to blink them back.

"I think a brisk walk in the snow would do us both good," whispered Stuart in her ear. To the others, who had not noticed Maggie's quickly dabbed eyes, he said, "With your permission, Mrs. Brennan, I think Maggie and I will take a bit of a walk to settle dinner."

Maggie was grateful to him for finding a way to get her out of the apartment. She had felt that the walls were closing in on her, that the world was collapsing around her. Now she took a deep breath, and the rush of cold air into her lungs helped clear her head.

"Thank you, Stuart, I'm so sorry. I must have ruined the evening for everyone."

"No one noticed," he said, "except me, and I notice everything about you." He took her hand.

"It was good of you to take charge. Cousin Eleanor worked so hard to make it a happy occasion, and here I go, spoiling it all."

"Maggie, you didn't spoil anything. I'm just glad to have a chance to be alone with you. You know that tomorrow I'm going to my brother's for a few days, and I won't see you again before you leave for Georgia."

"That's right. My steamer sails day after tomorrow."

He stopped under a streetlight and turned to look at her. His blue eyes searched her face. "Before you go," he said quietly, "I just want you to know that I have come to ... to care for you a great deal in these recent months."

"Oh, Stuart." She had feared this was coming. She was fond of him in a brotherly sort of way, and she relied on his friendship. But she feared that any sort of declaration on his part, which she could not reciprocate, could destroy their warm friendship. "Ye know I like you very much—"

"I know that you don't care for me the way I care for you, Maggie. But perhaps in time ..." His voice trailed off, lost in a sudden gust of wind.

Maggie drew her coat tighter around her.

"I can't promise anything, Stuart. You know I'm fond of you, but I'm just not—"

"I'm not asking anything of you. I just want to be your friend, a special friend."

"You will always be my friend, Stuart." She touched his arm.

He looked earnestly into her eyes and gently pulled her toward him. "May I kiss you goodbye?"

She tilted her face upward and nodded quickly. He leaned down to place a tender kiss on her lips.

"Thank you, Maggie," he said huskily. "I shall treasure that kiss. I'll miss you while you're gone, but I'll be here when you get back."

She felt a sense of loss, for she knew she could never love him as he wanted. *Affection can be so bittersweet*, she thought. She knew little of life, so very little, yet she was learning more rapidly than she liked.

Chapter Four

AT NINE O'CLOCK IN THE MORNING—an hour ahead of schedule —the Mallory steamer sidled up to the landing, gentle waves slapping at its side, to disgorge its cargo of club workers onto the wharf of Brunswick, Georgia. The club launch was not supposed to pick them up and transport them to the island until ten-thirty, so the passengers, still wobbly from their unaccustomed three nights at sea, had an hour or so to roam through the streets of Brunswick.

Maggie felt a wave of weariness and wondered if this was all a horrible mistake. She had slept little during the nights on the steamer with its unfamiliar chugs and lurches on the open sea. And she had been seasick during much of the voyage, just as she was on the S.S. *Arabic*.

The night before, she had tossed and turned for hours before she finally dozed off. Her bunk was uncomfortable in the cramped cabin she shared with three other club workers, all of whom were coming to Jekyl for the first time.

Her cabin mates were chatty and eager to share their stories. Dolores, the Yugoslav woman with the Spanish name and dark, sunken eyes, had been orphaned at an early age and scrimped for more than a decade to pay for her passage to America. Olga, a fleshy Austrian, had heavy blond hair tightly braided and piled high on her head. She knew less English than the others and responded to almost any comment directed to her with a "Ja, ja," her flat open face begging to be liked. She had been hired as an ironer for the club's laundry, where her language deficiency would not be a problem, but where her obvious strength and penchant for neatness would be an asset.

But it was to her own countrywoman, Deirdre Callaghan, who had the bunk over her head and whose infectious giggles and impertinent comments could make her laugh, that Maggie was especially drawn. Deirdre's voice held the rhythms of Dublin, and her eyes, like Maggie's, had gazed upon those steep Irish hills. She was the sound and smell of home. A saucy girl with light brown hair and the devil in her dark eyes, Deirdre's bold and earthy humor could draw Maggie up from the deepest doldrums. The two had first met on the docks in New York, even before they discovered they were cabin mates, and Maggie was captivated by her new friend's lively spirit and refreshing candor. They had been almost inseparable since their first day at sea.

In spite of Maggie's weariness and misgivings, the Georgia sun felt good on her back, and it was wonderful to be off the steamer stretching her legs in a stroll about the town with Deirdre. It was the first southern town Maggie had ever visited, and it couldn't have been more different from New York. The Brunswick dock stood at the end of the main avenue, called Gloucester Street. The railroad lines and Bay Street, which ran alongside, were all that separated the dock area from the bustling shops and main center of the little town.

It was next to impossible to get lost, for the town had been laid out in symmetrical squares, the captain said, when Georgia was still an English colony. The streets bore the names of British lords or generals—Albemarle, Egmont, and Amherst, and some of the residences bordered on neat little squares with names like Hanover, Hillsborough, and Halifax.

A few blocks past the rows of shops on Gloucester Street, Maggie and Deirdre discovered an elegant tree-lined avenue named Union Street, flanked on both sides with large Victorian houses that looked inviting with their deep, shady porches.

"Deirdre, look at those trees. I think that's what Mr. Falk called Spanish moss. Kate described it to me—'like an old man's beard,' she said."
"And look at these flowers! I've never seen anything like them," Deirdre said, pointing to the huge camellia bush with its bright pink blooms beside the *porte cochere* of one of the houses. "Begorry, flowers in December and palm trees! I've died and gone to heaven, I have."

For the first time since she had received news of her mother's death, Maggie's heart lifted with the joy of her new experience, with health, with youth, and even a sudden surge of enthusiasm. *One* could *be happy in such a place,* Maggie thought, enjoying the winter sun on her back as she remembered the icy chill left behind in New York. They had walked almost to the end of the street, admiring the houses and huge live oak trees that lined the way, when they heard the boat whistle—a fifteen-minute warning before departure.

Turning back reluctantly toward Gloucester Street, they hurried toward the wharf. It would not do to miss the boat.

The club launch, its name, *Jekyl Island,* painted on the bow, was waiting for them at the dock. The captain stood beside the gangplank to help them aboard. Bales of sea-island cotton ready for shipment dotted the wharf of the deep-water port, and two little boys, dark as midnight, sat atop one of the bales, dangling their legs over the sides and watching with curiosity the workers boarding the vessel that would take them to their final island destination.

As each passenger crossed the gangway, the captain touched the brim of his hat and said, "Cap'n James Clark, at your service." It made Maggie feel like one of the Vanderbilts who, she had been told, sometimes came to the island.

Even the short delay as the launch stood in port waiting for everyone to board was delicious. The harbor was tranquil and quaint, after the noisy, teeming docks of New York three days earlier. Maggie drank in the simple beauty of the place. They had left behind snow and icy winds that would freeze her ears should she dare venture outside without a scarf or hat. Here the sun shone warm on her face, and she closed her eyes and felt its rays soak into her.

Finally they were under way. The excitement was contagious, and for the first time in a long while, she felt a renewed sense of adventure. The waiters in their ill-fitting suits grinned and joked, as they held onto their fashionable derby hats, while the chambermaids clutched their cloaks or shawls around them a bit tighter as they moved into the breezes of the cooler open water.

The trip to Jekyl took about thirty minutes over a choppy inlet that led out of Brunswick harbor and into the Turtle River, where they finally headed into a tidal creek that cut through the marshes toward the Jekyl River.

"Captain Clark told me that these are the famous Marshes of Glynn," Deirdre said.

"Famous? Why?" Maggie asked.

"There's a poem about them written by a bloke named Sidney Lanier. You mean you've never heard it? You can't have been to Jekyl before," said a voice at Maggie's elbow. "Everyone there knows that poem almost by heart."

The voice belonged to Bert Stallman, one of the waiters who came to Jekyl every year. Everyone knew him, and he knew no strangers. Throughout the voyage he brandished his brand new Kodak Brownie camera, taking picture after picture. Apparently he had no qualms about eavesdropping on the women's conversation.

"My favorite lines," he announced, "are:

'Somehow my soul seems suddenly free
From the weighing of fate and the sad discussion of sin,
By the length and the breadth and the sweep of the marshes of Glynn.'"

"That's beautiful." Maggie smiled at his overly dramatic recitation.

"The poem is really about the greatness of God, but I like the part about being free 'from the sad discussion of sin.' That's how I feel here," Bert said, basking in his authority.

It was easy to understand why the poet had been so taken with the marshes and why they would make him contemplate God's greatness. They gave Maggie the same feeling she used to have standing on the edge of the cliffs of Mohr, looking out over the vastness of the sea. Here the marshes stretched to the horizon, the cord grass swaying gently back and forth in the rising tide as their boat swept by.

At the water's edge a snowy egret high-stepped through the shallow waters along the bank, peering below the surface for his breakfast. Maggie pointed out the egret to Deirdre, and together they marveled at the soaring gray pelicans and the blue herons flying over the waters that sparkled like multi-faceted diamonds.

The marsh grasses stretched for miles, so even in height that they looked as though they had been trimmed by some divine gardener and trained to stop just at the water's edge. Maggie felt her anxieties drain away as the little vessel sliced its way through the water toward Jekyl. The island lay before them, a solid mass of green, looking as though it were uninhabited.

A dark-haired man the waiters called "Hector the Greek" was staring across the glittering marshes at the same snowy egret that first caught Maggie's eye. He watched its jerky mechanical motions with amusement. It looked as though it were being manipulated by the strings of a puppeteer. But it was not the bird that really held his interest. He had been watching the pair of young women ever since they left New York, trying to get up the nerve to strike up a conversation with the one whose wide, blue-gray eyes were shining as she pointed to the bird.

His new pal, George Harvey, who like Hector had been hired as a clubhouse waiter, goaded him on in his strong Liverpool accent. "Give it a go, old boy. She won't bite, you know."

But Hector held back. He was not usually so reticent. He knew that women found him attractive, though for the life of him he couldn't figure out why. He thought his eyebrows were too heavy, and his mouth was irregular with its lopsided smile. He could not see the fire in his own dark eyes that drew women like moths to a candle. He just enjoyed the results. This woman, however, was different. A sad cast about her eyes, even when they sparkled with excitement, seemed incongruous with her fresh-scrubbed innocence.

She was like new dawn, fresh, guileless as a kitten, and showed utter indifference to the playful flirtations the other chambermaids seemed to enjoy. Her long hair was piled on her head in a graceful Edwardian twist, though stray pieces had come undone in the wind and curled in tendrils at the back of her neck. The flashy, flirty one—Deirdre they called her—pretty as a black-eyed Susan though she was, held no appeal for him. Instead, it was the one with the upturned nose and porcelain skin sprinkled with pale freckles that drew him like a magnet. Yet she clearly had no idea of it and made no attempt to lure him with coyly lowered eyelids and secret smiles.

When their glances had met, all too briefly, one day in the steamer dining room, the gaze of her large eyes was steady. She smiled in a friendly, disarming manner as she might have smiled at a fond cousin, then turned away and went on with her conversation with the blonde, braided woman seated next to her. She seemed completely unaware that, in that tiny moment, that split second it took for their eyes to meet, he had fallen off the edge of the world.

Never since his voice had deepened had he felt shy like this, until now. For the first time, he didn't want an easy conquest, for he sensed that any entanglement with Maggie would be deeply serious.

She was completely different from the dark-eyed girls he had wooed so casually in his homeland, girls with sensuous moves, smoldering glances, and warm sun-browned skin. Maggie's hair was a blond of many shades that shone like gold in the winter sun, and her cheeks looked as though they had been lightly brushed by the colors of the sunset. She was not pretty in the usual sense of the word, but there was translucence in her eyes that came from something within, a deep beauty he had craved since the day he was born.

Deirdre intercepted his gaze and watched him with some interest, much more than she showed in the egret on the water's edge. She recognized the dark hunger in his eyes and something else there she couldn't quite fathom. But she knew attraction when she saw it, and she knew it was not directed toward her.

"That Hector the Greek is watching you," she said to Maggie.

"What?" Maggie was peering over the marshes for other wild birds and following the flight of the gulls that pursued the launch. She could barely hear Deirdre over the vessel's engine's chugs.

"The Greek!" Deirdre spoke louder. "He's watching you! He has been, I think, for the whole voyage."

"Oh, Deirdre." Maggie laughed. "Don't be silly." But she couldn't resist looking around to see if it was true. She had noticed him before, and their glances had met a couple of times during the trip, but he had not spoken to her. Nevertheless, she was already well aware of his strong chin and his intense eyes.

He sat on the metal locker where life jackets were stored, gazing in her direction. When she looked at him he averted his eyes toward the little blue flag on the prow that was waving wildly in the wind. Maggie turned back to the railing, flustered, and tried to focus her attention on the marshes.

"Beautiful, isn't it?" She was startled to hear the sound of a deep, gentle voice just behind her and feel his warmth almost touching her elbow. She turned to look up into the dark eyes of Hector and felt a sudden flush creep up her neck. He moved beside her and leaned on the rail.

"Yes, very beautiful," she said. "I can hardly believe it's real."

"Ah, yes, it's real. It almost reminds me of home."

"And where is home?"

"Smyrna," he said. "I am Greek. That's where my real home is, though now I live in New York. What about you?" He leaned easily on the deck railing, and the wind blew carelessly through his hair. He held his bowler hat tightly in his hand so that the wind wouldn't catch it and sail it out onto the water.

Maggie could hear the unfamiliar cadence of one who had recently learned English and still flavored it with the rhythms and phrasing of his native tongue, though he had mastered his new language very well.

"Ireland," she answered, "though I, too, now live in New York. 'Tis my first trip outside the city."

"Ireland." He grinned. "I thought so. It's my first American adventure too." She was amazed that he echoed her thoughts about the adventurous nature of this trip. "Perhaps we shall see each other again?"

Remembering what she had learned about the size of the club from Kate, she smiled. "I don't see how we will be able to avoid it."

Hector leaned his head backward and laughed with unfeigned joy. "That's good. That is very good."

The launch rounded a bend in the river and sailed within sight of a round ochre-colored tower that rose above the trees. It topped a large building, the upper floors of which were dotted with narrow balconies. The dark roof of the turret pointed upward, where, at its peak, a small flag, identical to the one on the boat's prow, waved merrily in the breeze. Little by little, as they approached the dock, the entire structure came into view. Maggie could see more balconies and balustrades and deep rounded porches that formed an almost whimsical design.

To the right stood another large edifice covered with mossy green shingles, with three main stories and balconies on every floor at both the south and north ends. Both buildings looked like palaces to Maggie, as she remembered her family's four-room wattle house on the Irish coast.

At the wharf stood a dapper man of medium height and build, in his mid-forties perhaps, holding a large bouquet of deep rose-colored camellias. Once the boat docked and was secured by spring lines to the pilings, Captain Clark strode across the deck to tap the chef and his wife on the shoulder and lead them through the crowd so that they could be the first to debark. His mate put out the gangplank. The captain climbed off and held out his hand to help the chef's wife to the dock.

He gave a nod to the gentleman with the bouquet of flowers, who stepped forward and said, "*Monsieur Larivette et Madame,* I presume." The chef nodded, and the gentleman who had spoken made a slight bow and held out the dazzling bouquet to the lady.

"I'm Ernest Grob," he said, "*à votre service.*" Although he had not clicked his heels together, something in his manner was equally brisk and ceremonious, and he gave the distinct impression of having surreptitiously done so. Clearly he considered the chef the most important among the seasonal employees.

Mr. Grob raised his voice and directed his words to all the newly arrived who had yet to set foot on the island. "Welcome to the Jekyl Island Club. May we all provide a fine season for the club members. Welcome to you all!" He spoke with a European accent, Swiss or German perhaps, and gave a courtly bow to the newly arrived.

Deirdre giggled. "A real gent, that one. I could fancy a bloke like that."

Maggie ignored her and picked up her green duffel bag. All her possession in the world were in that bag—a little notebook where she recorded her thoughts and daily activities, a Bible, two small books of poetry, her hairbrush, a nightgown, and three changes of underclothes. She had only two dresses—a cream-colored lawn fabric for dressy occasions and a smoky-colored muslin for less formal activities—one shirtwaist blouse and a black skirt. But she felt set for any occasion, possessing all a young woman of her class would need to get along in the world—or at least at Jekyl Island.

When it came her turn to step off the little vessel, she held her bag with her right hand and stretched out her left to accept the reassuring assistance of Captain Clark. "Watch your step, miss," he said jovially as she put her foot for the first time on the Jekyl wharf. It was a long dock, and Maggie shifted her bag to her other hand as she set out.

"May I help you with your bag, miss?" a deep, familiar voice said at her elbow.

"Oh, thank you," she said gratefully, yielding the burden to Hector. They fell into step side by side as they followed Mr. Grob, who was leading the chef and his wife down the dock toward the clubhouse.

"It's Hector Deliyannis, at your service," he smiled and lifted the hat he had put on as the boat pulled into the dock. He had paused briefly on the deck for Bert Stallman to snap his photograph with the other waiters before rushing forward to help Maggie with her possessions.

"You haven't told me your name," he said.

"It's Maggie—Maggie O'Brien."

"What a perfect smiling name," he said with a grin. "It sounds like Ireland."

Yes, thought Maggie, as she walked beside Hector toward the imposing clubhouse. *This does look like a place where one could be happy.*

Chapter Five

THE CLUBHOUSE WAS MAGNIFICENT INSIDE, with its carved oak woodwork, high ceilings, and graceful archway, hung with heavy drapes, that led into the brand new dining room. Mr. Falk in New York had described its atmosphere as one of "simple elegance," though Maggie saw nothing simple about it. Even the boar's head over the fireplace in the foyer seemed awesome to her.

She had little time to take in all the well-appointed details as she followed Minnie Clark, head housekeeper and wife of the boat captain, up the wide stairway to the upper floors and finally to a narrower stairwell that led to the servants' quarters on the fourth floor. As Mrs. Clark showed the new chambermaids to their rooms, she reminded each one that there would be a meeting at two o'clock in the help's dining room, right after the midday meal.

Maggie's room was small but cozy. From the window she could look through the trees, heavy with Spanish moss, and out over the wide stretch of marsh and the river by which they had come. The view left her breathless. The tiny room, its walls a creamy yellow with dark, oak woodwork, would have been stifling in the summer months. Now it was warm and cheerful. The furnishings were sparse—a narrow bed, an oak chest with a round mirror atop it, and a small writing table with a sturdy oak chair—but all she could possibly need. The only other item in the room was a wooden coat rack, where she could hang the few items of clothing she had brought.

She unpacked her clothes and hung her dresses on the coat rack to shake out the wrinkles. Everything else she tucked in the drawers of the chest, reserving the top one for her hairbrush and toiletries. On her desk she arranged her little journal-notebook, her Bible, and her poetry books, one by Emily Dickinson and one by Elizabeth Barrett Browning.

Last of all, she took out a framed picture, which she had carefully wrapped in tissue paper, of her mother and father sitting together on a stone wall in Galway and holding hands. It had been made at the time of the races two summers before she left Ireland. Her mother looked so pretty in the picture, her head tilted toward her husband, and a tiny smile playing about her lips. There was no hint of the disease that only a year later would begin to ravage her body.

This was the image Maggie wanted to remember—her proud and smiling father, shoulders back and head tilted toward the sky, and her mother beside him, her dark blond hair streaked with silver, but faded to sepia in the photograph, pinned neatly behind her head. Her mother had seemed delighted for her when Maggie had made her decision to go to the United States. Chattering with excitement about the wonderful future her daughter would surely find in New York, she had helped Maggie pack. She had smiled and said, "You must always remember your homeland and give me grandchildren."

Maggie could not deny she had been eager to go. Had she been foolish to sail off to an unknown land where her only acquaintances were cousins whom she had met only a few times as a child? She still wasn't sure, though she had felt a renewed sense of hope since arriving in Brunswick. She'd thought she could help her family by working in America and sending money home from time to time. Although that was her self-justification, she knew in her heart that she hadn't wanted to miss the opportunity to travel and see more of the world.

And now, here she was—Maggie O'Brien—in a spot that seemed closer to heaven than she had been since she left Ireland, a place she never could have imagined. She tried to shake off any lingering negative thoughts.

"I *will* be happy," she said with determination. Still, she thought of her father, alone now in the little house where she grew up. She would send for him, she decided, as soon as she could save enough money—if he would come. He must be lonely, for the cliffs could be bleak in winter. And it would fill her life to have him here.

Maggie heard a rustling and footsteps in the hallway and then a little tap on her door.

"Yes?" she answered.

"Maggie, are ye there? It's me—Deirdre. It's time for lunch and the big meeting. Are you ready? We can walk over together."

"Yes, I'm ready." She took a quick glance into the looking glass, patted her hair into place, and opened the door.

Other young women were streaming toward the staircase, chatting as they went. Some, those who had been to Jekyl before, knew where they were going. Maggie and Deirdre allowed themselves to be swept along with the tide, outside the clubhouse, across the lawn and down a white road covered with crushed seashells toward one of the frame buildings that lined each side of the roadway.

"That's Mr. Grob's house, the superintendent's cottage," one of the girls said as they passed by a large cottage on the left. "He's the one who met us at the dock. And over there is the Clarks' cottage, where the boat captain and his missus live." She pointed to the house to the left of Mr. Grob's.

"And there's the commissary," said another of the girls leading the group and gesturing toward an ochre building just behind the superintendent's house. She was obviously vying for status among the chambermaids, for she had been to Jekyl the previous season and knew the ropes. "That's where you can buy whatever you need in the way of supplies, talcum powder, combs, that sort of thing," she said importantly.

The new girls followed along, gaping at the graceful ghosts of Spanish moss that waved from the live oak limbs and the splash of winter sun that filtered through the tall pines.

The help's dining room, unlike the main clubhouse, was a simple affair, but lunch, though brief, was delicious and welcome, for they had not eaten since breakfast at seven. The dining room was noisy, as the new chambermaids began to get better acquainted with one another. Two young black women, efficient and unobtrusive in their movements, brought in the food and set it on the tables, where it was served family style.

When lunch was over, Mrs. Clark appeared, looking cool and crisp in her gray uniform and white apron. "I'm Minnie Clark," she announced, "and, as you already know, I will be your supervisor. I assume Mr. Falk told you a great deal about the club at the time you were hired for the season. As you know, the salary here is somewhat higher than what most of you would be earning in a similar post in New York, particularly if you factor in room and board. That is because we demand the best and we expect the best.

"You will be serving society's elite here, people who are accustomed to good service and who demand it. Employees are expected to do their jobs skillfully, cheerfully, and efficiently. As a domestic you will be unobtrusive, speak only when spoken to by a club member or guest, and never disturb guests in their rooms. If they wish to sleep late, they pay well for the privilege of doing so. You will be required to clean the guest rooms, change the bed linens, and perform whatever other duties a guest may require."

She went on to tell them where linens were located, where they could pick up their uniforms and supplies, how often linens would be laundered, and what precise activities would be required in cleaning each room daily.

"Be aware that I will inspect *each* room daily and will inform you of any deficiencies I may find, either in your work or in your character. We expect our young women here to be clean, hard-working, and modest in their behavior. I don't expect to have to repeat this admonition," she said firmly. "Now plan to work hard, but enjoy the club season. Jekyl Island has much to offer."

Suddenly Minnie Clark relaxed and smiled. "We're glad you're here." Maggie felt from that moment that she would like to be her friend. She certainly knew that she would like to live up to her high standards and do a job that would have made her mother proud.

The first days at Jekyl passed in a frenzy of preparatory activity as the chambermaids scurried about dusting all the rooms, airing feather beds, beating rugs, getting ready for the winter guests who would start to arrive within the week. It was a festive time for the young domestics who worked hard, but were compensated by having the run of the clubhouse for this brief period. All too soon, however, preparations were complete, and the first club members and guests began to appear. Maggie loved to watch from her window as they stepped off the *Jekyl Island* or their personal yachts onto the dock, the women, some wrapped in furs— which they quickly shed in the Georgia warmth and in Jekyl's relatively unpretentious atmosphere. It all seemed rather grand to Maggie, but she had been told that, compared to other fashionable resorts, Jekyl's guests made an effort toward what they considered simplicity. No excessive ostentation was tolerated without rebuke, and the guests strived to enjoy the natural setting.

Maggie was assigned five rooms to care for on the second floor of the clubhouse. They soon filled with guests from New York and Chicago. After her morning cleaning was done, she had several afternoon hours free before she had to return to fluff the pillows, put out more fresh towels, and turn down the beds for the evening. So, it seemed, did the waiters. From three until five each afternoon they rode bicycles, frolicked on the beach, and walked the wooded trails. Maggie felt invigorated by the exercise and the fresh air—free of the cinders and smoke that often clogged the atmosphere in New York.

She was delighted at the wild turkeys that nibbled around the edges of the wood and the occasional doe or fawn that peered at her from the underbrush. She loved to walk on the hard strand of beach where the waiters sometimes held bicycle races and where the millionaires drove their carriages. She would pause now and then to pick up a shiny shell to add to her growing collection. *Treasures from the sea,* she called them in her little notebook. *God's bounty ... and all for free.*

At night, after the last crumb was eaten and the tables cleared in the clubhouse dining room, usually by nine o'clock, the waiters were again at liberty to join the women employees. They sometimes built bonfires on the beach or, once in a while, one of the club members' wives would sponsor a dance for club workers in Frederic Baker's stables, with musicians brought in from Brunswick to play for the occasion. The little band of three could pick up the melody and play any tune a club worker could hum or sing for them, though they always began with their own standards and favorites.

The band's talent for playing extemporaneously and without written music was much appreciated by the immigrant workers who came from all parts of Europe. The group could play the Irish jigs that Maggie knew as a child or the Austrian polkas or Polish mazurkas that other workers requested. These same three musicians had played for years for this diverse population employed by the club, and they had learned little by little what the workers liked to hear.

One among them was a fiddler named Dan, who would on occasion let loose with a lively tune that reminded Maggie of the music she used to hear in the little pubs in Doolin. The workers danced as though their lives depended on it, each one teaching the others the dances from his homeland. Maggie would never forget the night that Hector tried to teach them all Greek dancing in a long line, with the leader—Hector himself—holding a handkerchief that joined him to the next person in the line. The music was unfamiliar to the musicians, who for the first time that evening had difficulty with the changing rhythms Hector so patiently tried to vocalize.

Maggie never laughed so much as she did at those efforts to learn the other dances. Some of the workers caught on quickly, but others, like George Harvey and Bert Stallman, were lead-footed and clumsy. Nonetheless, they all tried, and in the trying they bonded as a group. She began to feel at ease with the young waiters from England and France and Greece, as though they were her Irish brothers. Deep inside they all experienced the same longings, the same homesickness for their old lands, and the same hopes for the future. And they became her friends.

After one of those dances, as she was walking back to the clubhouse, Deirdre at her side, Hector caught up with them and fell into step beside Maggie.

"I've been watching you," he said, and Maggie heard Deirdre giggle as she dropped back to walk with Dolores.

"Really? Then you must have found my performance tonight quite a sight! I think I have two left feet." She laughed, trying to keep the conversation light, though her heart was pounding at his nearness.

"Not at all, you dance with grace and joy. That's what I like, the joy."

"Hector, I think you've kissed the Blarney Stone, you and your way with words."

"No, I really mean it," he said quietly. "Just being with you brings me joy."

Maggie didn't answer. She was breathless at the liquid warmth of pleasure that suddenly flowed through her body. She thought of how differently she had reacted with Stuart under that New York street lamp on Christmas Eve. Hector's words, for reasons she could not explain, fell welcome on her ears.

"I hope I am not taking too many liberties in saying these things," he said.

"Oh no, not at all," she replied quickly. "It's just that I don't know what to say in response." She knew that she didn't want to turn it into a joke, as Deirdre might have done, but she was fearful to let the conversation become too serious.

Finally, desperate for something to interrupt the silence, she said, "Tell me about Greece."

His face darkened. "I'd rather have you tell me about your home in Ireland."

"Ah, but there's so much to tell. Where could I possibly begin?"

"How about the day you were born? I want to hear it all."

She laughed. "Well, the first sound I heard on the day I was born was the dinner bell ringing to call my father home from the fields."

He echoed her laughter.

"Ah, you don't believe me, do you?" she asked, "But I'm quite serious. The bell was ringing just as I was being born. My mother's name was Abby, and she was from the neighboring village when she met my father at a market in Galway. It was love at first sight, she told me."

"What the French call a *coup de foudre*. The best kind of love. The kind that was meant to be from the day the earth began," he said earnestly.

"Why, Mr. Deliyannis, I do believe you're a romantic." She hoped her tone was light.

"That I am, Miss O'Brien. That I am. I confess. I know that for me there will never be but a single love in this life. That I know."

"How can you be so certain? Life is long, and none of us can see into the future."

"That I know, Miss Maggie O'Brien." He looked at her so intently that she felt herself flush. Drawn into the depths of his eyes, she felt as though she could see unspoken thoughts and words, yearnings and fears, the past and the future. His hand touched hers and she felt she was losing her bearings.

All too soon they were back to the clubhouse. "Well," she said reluctantly, "I guess I must say good night. It's nearly eleven, and we have to be up early tomorrow."

"Perhaps I'll see you at the beach in the afternoon."

"Perhaps. I don't know." She wavered. She had planned to spend the afternoon writing letters to her father in Ireland and to her cousin Kate, married now and living in Missouri. "Thank you for walking me back. Someday you must tell me all about Greece."

"And I want to hear about Ireland. And about what happened after the ringing of the dinner bell. What a dramatic beginning you had! I must hear more."

"And so you shall, in due time. For now," she said softly, "good night."

"Sleep well," he said, doffing his cap and smiling that devil-may-care smile that Deirdre said could break a girl's heart, though Maggie thought it belied the intensity deep within his eyes. Then he turned and walked into the night toward the male servants' dormitory.

Maggie entered the clubhouse to climb the three flights of stairs to her room. Hector's smile lingered in her mind, and she sensed its incongruity with the shadowy look he gave her when she asked about Greece. *A man of many moods,* she thought, *and all fascinating.*

She might have tarried below and talked with him for a few moments longer, as the other girls did with the waiters who walked them back, some holding hands, but she was apprehensive, concerned that the more she saw of him, the more difficult she would find it to break away. There was a magnetism about his eyes, his smile, his olive skin, and wavy hair, and something told her that, unless she avoided him, she would be drawn into a situation that she could not control—even more, that she would not want to control.

As Hector walked back to the servants' dormitory, he brooded over the evening. How could he tell her about Greece? He had, in fact, never set foot in Greece itself, but it would be hard to explain the situation to someone like Maggie, who was Irish to the core and who was imbued with her homeland, her heritage, and her history. How he could claim to be Greek but not know the country? The fact is, technically, he supposed, he wasn't Greek at all, but rather part of a Greek-speaking minority living under the control of the Ottoman Empire.

He had grown up in the ancient city of Smyrna in western Anatolia, which was protected by a jut of land that formed a bay on the waters of the Aegean. Seven miles from its shore lay the small island of Khios, claimed by both Ottomans and Greeks at various times, where his grandfather, like the ancient Ionian poet Homer, was born.

Where Hector's family lived, on a winding street overlooking the bay, most of the residents were Muslims. The neighbors were kind to them, even though Hector's family did not accept the laws of Islam, but rather the Greek Orthodox faith. But it was not always easy living under Ottoman rule. While the Muslim people were generally tolerant of Christians and Jews, their tolerance did not extend to Greeks who longed for political independence.

His own father had died on his way to do battle with Ottoman soldiers, when he set out from Smyrna in the stealth of night to fight alongside his brother in the Cretan rebellion against Ottoman control in 1897. Hector was only nine. Since then he had done all he could to help his mother feed his younger brothers and sisters. He had hired out on a fishing boat when he was twelve and brought home all that he could, usually more fish than money, at the end of his excursions, but at least they could eat the fish.

Life had been hard for his mother with five children to support. His mother made what money she could, embroidering silk shawls and doing finger work. But she could not afford a sewing machine, and all her work was crafted by hand, often at night in yellow lamplight. She refused the generosity of her Muslim neighbors out of pride, but Hector knew that her eyes were growing worse, and there was no money for spectacles.

Finally, in 1910, as soon as he was old enough, Hector decided that he could better help his mother by coming to America. It would be one less hungry mouth for her to feed, and he could send more money home than he could ever earn in Smyrna. In time, he hoped, he might find a way to bring his family, or at least his mother, here where he could care for her.

"Tell me about Greece," Maggie had asked. What could he tell her? It was certainly not something he wanted to begin on the steps of the clubhouse with a bevy of gaily laughing chambermaids streaming by. It was not something he could talk about lightly. But he did want to tell her about his life. He wanted to tell her everything. And someday he would, when, or rather if, the time was ever right.

Chapter Six

IN SPITE OF HECTOR'S INVITATION to meet him at the beach the next day, Maggie wanted to prove to herself that she could resist the temptation and hold firmly to her plan to write letters instead. After she recorded her feelings of the night before in her little notebook. She wrote to her father, begging him to write back, though she doubted he would.

In the three months she had been in the United States, he had written to her only once, a brief letter shortly after her mother's death, a letter that must have been difficult for him to write for he was a man who rarely expressed his feelings. "I am glad for you, Maggie," he wrote, "that you have found a good position for the winter months, though my heart is torn asunder by my grief and your absence. I wonder if I will ever see you again in this life. Your loving father, Daniel O'Brien."

It hurt to remember that letter and to think of her mother bearing so bravely her dark secret to let her daughter depart for her new country with lightness of spirit. Had Maggie known of her mother's illness, she would never have left, a fact of which Abby O'Brien was well aware. Now, what was done was done. It was her father who occupied her thoughts more and more. She wanted to go home to be with him, but there was not enough money. All she could do was to write him long, loving letters and hope he understood. She wanted to bring him to New York to be with her, but he made no reply to her entreaties.

Still she wrote, and perhaps with the aid of her brother, they could eventually afford his passage to the United States. If he refused, then she would have to go back to Ireland. She couldn't leave him alone forever on that windy, lonely cliff overlooking the sea. It had been wild and wonderful when she was a child, and she knew her parents had been happy there. But now her father was alone, with only the ghosts of the past to keep him company.

She remembered how the voices of the winds used to beckon her to the edges of the cliffs until her mother would snatch her back to safety. She tried to shake off the thoughts of that cliff's edge, but they would not leave her. Her father must come to America. She would persuade him. But she knew he would never want to leave Ireland.

She wished there were some way to convey to him the beauty of the little island where she now found herself. He had never seen a land like this, so filled with surprises at every turn. During her first walk on the paths through the forest, she had noticed dead ferns clinging to the live oak trees and told Sam Denegal, one of the groundskeepers, how sad they made her feel.

"Oh, them ferns ain't dead. No need to feel sad, missy. They gon' be resurrected in the nex' rain," he told her. "Hallelujah!"

He was right. A good soaking shower the following morning did the trick. As Sam had predicted, by afternoon the once brown, shriveled ferns stood erect, green, and lush again. She agreed with Sam. *Hallelujah!* she thought. Her father, too, might find his life restored in this country. Maggie had written him about the resurrection ferns in her letter and hoped that he might see their meaning and realize that renewal was possible, even for a broken heart.

She worried about him, because she knew that her brother was not there for their father as she would have been. She thought of Brendan at his new home in Lochrea. It was less than fifty miles from Doolin, but it might as well be a thousand. She knew he would come to see her father when he could, but he would not come often. They had all missed Brendan when he left home to marry. Maggie remembered their wonderful days as children when they had played together along the cliffs and he had taken up for her at the little village school where Paddy Muldoon had jerked her down by her pigtails and made her cry. Paddy had gone home with a black eye, and Maggie had gone home with a hero.

Brendan was tall and blond, blonder than she, and almost Nordic looking. Although he had been thin as a growing boy, he was strong and lithe, able to take on boys bigger than he and come out the victor, even against bullies like Paddy Muldoon. His even features and blue eyes, with only flecks of the gray that colored her own eyes, made him the darling of the village girls. But he was a quiet boy, not at all interested in girls until, at nineteen, he met Maureen, a red-haired beauty from Lochrea whose father raised horses that he took every year to Galway races. Maggie loved Maureen and knew that she was good for her brother, though she grieved at the loss of Brendan from her daily life. It was her moping about so after Brendan's marriage that had prompted her mother to suggest that she needed a change.

One day as Maggie was drying the dishes while her mother washed, Abby had suddenly turned to her daughter and, without preamble, as though she had been mulling it over for some time, said, "My cousin Eleanor is in America with her daughter, Kate. She lost her husband some time ago, poor dear, and ye could perhaps cheer her up with a visit."

She wiped her hands on her apron and reached into the very back of the kitchen cupboard by the sink, bringing out a little glass jar wrapped in paper. She poured out its contents on the table. Maggie had never seen so much money in her life.

"Count it out," her mother said. "I think there's almost sixty pounds there. I was saving it for my old age, mine and your dad's, but I think we can put it to better use now."

Maggie remembered that magic moment, as the late afternoon sun spilled over the kitchen table, making the coins glitter and shine. Suddenly she longed to go, even though the thought of leaving her family was painful. It was a lure she had chosen not to resist, even though she and her parents knew what a "visit" to America often meant. Whether they would ever see one another again, they could not know.

Hector was keenly aware of Maggie's absence on the beach that January afternoon. It was too cold to swim, and he and several of the other waiters had elected to walk the shore instead, tossing shells back into the sea, and examining the jellyfish, whelks, and horseshoe crabs the tide had washed onto the strand, but he never got too far from the entrance to Shell Road where he could see her if she should arrive.

His English friend, George, was more curious than most about the sea creatures, many of which he had never seen before. Hector, on the other hand, had grown up with the ocean and its bounties, though he didn't know the English names of some of the shellfish and crabs that littered the beach. The sandy shore was wide enough for a hundred-yard dash from the dunes to the sea, a magnificent wide beach.

The water was shallow and calm, and it was said that one could walk half a mile from shore and still touch bottom. None of them knew whether it was really true or not, for no one ever went out so far. Hector was a good swimmer, though he would have preferred somewhat deeper water, but it was perfect for George, who had never learned to swim, though he longed to learn.

"Hey, fellows, why don't we have a bonfire on the beach Sunday night and a kind of clam bake?" said Bert, who seemed to be their unofficial social director and who always had his Brownie camera with him.

"Sounds like a jolly good idea," George said.

The men began to discuss the possibilities, though, as always, there were difficulties. Dinner at the club sometimes dragged on until nine, and it was hard to get away before nine-thirty or even ten. On Sunday nights, however, club members often dined somewhat earlier, particularly when there was a concert or a lecture after dinner. Perhaps the waiters could conspire to make the service a bit faster in the dining room, although they were always at the mercy of the chef and pastry cooks.

Hector had drawn the plum assignment of waiter to J.P. Morgan's table for the season. He was intensely aware of his duties and opportunities in serving the richest couple in America. Not only could he hope for a handsome tip at the end of their stay, he felt it could do him a great deal of good back in New York, should he apply for a job somewhere like the well-known restaurant, Delmonico's, to note that he had been J.P. Morgan's waiter for a season at Jekyl Island. Perhaps Mr. Morgan would even give him a reference if he approved of his service. He certainly didn't want to do anything to jeopardize his relationship with the Morgans.

Still, he thought a beach outing on Sunday evening a wonderful idea. He knew that they did that sort of thing in the summer in New England—clambakes, they called them, and it sounded like a splendid affair, especially for this calm seashore. Near Smyrna the coast could be treacherous, and most people in fishing boats tried to be on shore and safely in their homes by dark.

Maggie and Deirdre heard about the beach party from Dolores, who was very excited. Although they had built bonfires on the beach before, the weather had been too chilly for them to stay in the night winds for very long. But the past few days had brought an unseasonable warm spell for Georgia in late January. Everyone looked forward to a night of roasting oysters from the club's oyster beds and enjoying the beach as though they themselves were millionaires.

Club members were tolerant of the workers' use of the beach, within certain restrictions, of course, and provided they went about their tasks with efficiency and appropriate decorum. They were not permitted to drink alcohol, even though the members themselves enjoyed the finest wines in the dining room and sipped cherry cordial or brandy in the men's drawing room after dinner.

Mr. Grob felt that, if the workers were happy, they were more likely to perform good service, earn substantial tips from club members, and return eagerly the following season, ready to do an even better job. He wanted the positions at Jekyl to be coveted among the best of those in service in New York—waiters, domestics of all types, bicycle men, even the taxidermist—all had to be of sterling quality. Thus, he encouraged them in their plans for the Sunday beach party, suggesting that he himself might join them briefly after dinner.

It was unusual for Ernest Grob to participate in the workers' activities. Members of the managerial staff were in a position somewhat apart. They had their own dining room in the superintendent's cottage, where those in the higher positions such as Mr. Grob, Mr. Falk, Captain and Mrs. Clark, and the island schoolteacher, Bertha Baker, took their meals. Mr. Grob, the highest-ranked member of the staff, was sometimes even invited to dine in the homes of club members. For the most part, however, there was a strict hierarchy on the island, not only among the millionaire guests, but also among the employees themselves. Thus, Mr. Grob's suggestion that he might briefly attend the beach party gave it a special aura of importance.

Sunday dawned bright and warm, and excitement permeated the atmosphere among club workers throughout the day. All the arrangements were made for the beach party, but the day seemed to drag on endlessly. In late afternoon they heard thunder in the distance, threatening to put an end to all their plans. However, by seven the threat of the storm had passed, leaving in its wake a spectacular sunset, as the evening settled into a warm golden twilight that illuminated the clubhouse facade.

A professor from Columbia University, Edward Lee Thorndike, guest of club member Helen Hartley Jenkins, was to speak in one of the drawing rooms about his new book on animal intelligence. Hector had heard one of the club members grumbling about it at the noon meal, but even that reluctant gentleman dutifully planned to attend. As expected, members came to dinner at seven and had already filed into the drawing room by eight-thirty when the lecture was to begin.

The waiters completed their duties quickly, shed their white jackets, and headed for the beach, where other workers had already begun to gather. A full moon reflected from the shells of the roadway lit their way. The bonfire was blazing by the time Hector reached the beach, and flames danced high into the air. The night air was brisk, but the wind was calm. It was a perfect evening for the beach party.

Maggie had arrived before him and was helping spread blankets on the ground and setting out food on the sawhorses and planks that stable hands had brought out to serve as tables. Hers was the first face he saw illuminated by the firelight when he arrived, smiling and rosy, filled with joy and anticipation.

They saw each other almost daily now and had established little ritual greetings.

"Miss O'Brien, I presume," he would say.

"Indeed," she would respond with a mock imperious nod, though her heart would leap each time she saw him.

"Mr. Deliyannis, at your service." He would bow low as she passed, smiling at his gesture. They both enjoyed the silly game, their little parody of the formality of their millionaire guests.

As the flames died down and the coals of the bonfire began to glow red, the party-goers put corn on to roast, and laid sweet potatoes, partially baked before the outing, among the ashes to complete their roasting. Clams baked quickly, as did the oysters, except for those fished up from buckets of salt water, shucked, and eaten raw. Ernest

Grob had asked the kitchen to send out several gallons of lemonade and tea, along with cakes and pies from the pastry chef. On another part of the beach, quail from the day's hunt were roasting on a spit. The quail were always abundant, an easy target for the hunters, who were required to turn over their game at the end of the day for use in the clubhouse kitchen.

Food had never tasted so good to Hector, and he ate with gusto. Perhaps it was the open sea air and the joy of being outside in the velvet winter night. Or perhaps it was being able to eat with Maggie at his side.

True to his word, Mr. Grob appeared just as they had finished eating and as Charles Brinkman, the gamekeeper, was beginning to strum on his ukulele some of the popular songs of the day, while a chorus of waiters wailed the lyrics. Hector thought it sounded like the mating call of a group of sea lions, but he only laughed, wishing that he, too, knew all the words.

Walbert, the taxidermist, the absolute picture of fashion with his handlebar mustache, had a fine tenor voice and seemed to wince at the sounds coming from the group of waiters. He sang in the Faith Chapel choir and in a barbershop quartet back in New York and, before the evening was over, would find other good voices to join him in splendid renditions of "Shine on, Harvest Moon" and "Bicycle Built for Two."

Hector himself had an excellent baritone voice, but he knew almost none of the songs and kept it to himself. He remembered well the evenings he and his younger brothers had chorused the popular Greek tunes, even at times serenading ladies of their choice in the city squares until the police came to chase them away for disturbing the peace. But even the peacekeepers complimented them on their singing and asked them to leave with reluctance. He longed to join in, perhaps even sing some of the songs from his homeland, but he was the only Greek at Jekyl for the season, and no one would even recognize his language, with the exception of Professor Thorndike, who was no doubt still back at the clubhouse regaling with his knowledge any millionaires who might linger in the parlors.

He turned to Maggie. "How about a walk until they learn to harmonize?" he suggested.

She laughed. "That might be a long walk."

"All the better," he said.

She drew her wool shawl about her shoulders and let him help her to her feet. Beyond the fire, which the workers had built up again for warmth, stars penetrated the dark sky with myriad pinpoints of light. The tide was out, and the beach was wide, sprinkled with other dark figures walking by the water's edge. Hector offered Maggie the crook of his arm. She took it readily.

They never had enough time to be together and to talk, even though they seized whatever moments they could to sit on the steps of Faith Chapel and spin out their dreams to each other. She had told him about growing up in Ireland, the cliffs where she had played as a child, the little school she attended in the village, their weekend trips into Ennis to sell spring lambs from their pastures or sugar beets and cabbages from their fields. After the shearing in the springtime, sometimes she had gone with her father as far as Galway to sell the wool. But what she told him most about was the breathtaking spectacle of the coast, with its craggy cliffs, the Aran Islands in the distance, so wild and different from the gentle sands and sea oats of Jekyl.

They had both grown up beside the sea, though Maggie, like George, had not learned to swim in the icy waters that surrounded her homeland. Hector's Aegean, on the other hand, was warm and welcoming, much like the waters surrounding Jekyl, only clearer and more inviting. Here in Georgia, the golden silt from the marshes gave the water a brownish, murky color, beneficial to the nurturing of the tiny sea creatures born in the marshes.

Maggie had not asked him again about Greece, sensing his earlier reluctance to talk about it, but the intimacy created by the darkness away from the bonfire made her bolder.

"Please tell me about your homeland," she said, as they strolled arm in arm down the beach.

It was a question he had thought about since that night after the dance in the Baker stables. He took a deep breath and looked up at the stars.

"The nights in my homeland are much like this one, though the beaches are not so wide," he began. "Men have fished in the waters of the Aegean, beside my family's home, for thousands of years."

She was silent, waiting for him to continue.

"I suppose they have here as well," he went on, "for there were people already here, I'm sure, when the Europeans arrived. But while the sea reminds me of my homeland, this island is nothing like Anatolia where I come from."

"But I thought you were from Greece," she said.

"I said Smyrna." He was determined now to tell her about his family and gauge her reaction. "It's really in the Ottoman Empire."

"But how can you call yourself a Greek?"

"Because I am Greek," he said quietly. "There have been many Greeks in Smyrna for thousands of years. My grandfather came from the island of Khios not far away. It's still under Greek control. He claimed his ancestors fought for the Greeks during the Trojan War, though I suspect his story is pure invention.

"When I was born my Anatolian grandmother suggested that I be named for Homer's Trojan hero. I was told my father laughed heartily at that suggestion. He said he didn't like the name Odysseus anyhow, and Hector was a hero admired even by his Greek foes."

Maggie listened intently. It was the longest speech she had ever heard Hector make. "Is that why your grandfather came to Smyrna—because of your grandmother?"

"Not why he came, but it's why he stayed. He came because there was a fishing fleet that needed workers, but then he met my grandmother, and he could never leave. You see, that's one reason I know that I will never have but a single love in my life. That's the way it has always been for the Deliyannis men.

We don't love easily, but we love completely."

He watched her face as she absorbed his words. He knew that to most of the world he portrayed a jovial exterior. He laughed easily and loved life in all its varieties and complexities. But this fire that smoldered inside was something he seldom showed to anyone.

"Did her family accept him?" she asked.

"Not at first. They liked him, but he was a Christian, after all, and they were Muslims. But in the end the determination of my grandmother won them over, and Papi married her in the church after she accepted his faith. They built a little house on one of the hills of the city. The city is laid out like this. Let me show you." He bent over to pick up a broken shell and trace a series of lines in the sand.

"The sea is here, and the roads run beside it, in little terraces up the slope. My family's house is here." He pointed to the second line near the sea at the upper tip of his crude map. "That is where my mother lives today with my two younger brothers and my little sisters."

"And what about your father?" she asked.

"Dead."

"Oh, Hector, I'm so sorry." She put her hand on his shoulder. He lifted it from his shoulder and brought it gently to his lips.

"It was a long time ago. He was still a young man, not yet forty. I was only nine, and one of my brothers was still a baby."

"What happened? Was he ill?" They were holding hands now, as he talked on.

"I never knew a stronger man, but he was also a stubborn man."

"What do you mean?"

"The people on the island of Crete were fighting for independence from the Ottomans, and my uncle Georgios lived there. He asked my father to come and help in the struggle. My mother begged him not to go, but he went anyway, sure that he would not die in the fighting."

"Were they successful in the struggle?"

"Not really. Crete is still controlled by the Ottomans, but no matter who won, my father is dead."

"But he died fighting for something he believed in," said Maggie. He squeezed her hand.

"He died in a storm when his boat sank while he was still on his way to Crete. He never held a gun or raised a sword against the soldiers. His death was a waste." Hector stared at the gentle waves lapping onto the shore. "It was a storm that came out of nowhere on a night like this one, they told me. Almost as if the gods had cursed him."

"Perhaps God was protecting him from taking the life of another," Maggie said gently. "We can never understand the ways of God."

Hector looked at her intensely. "I have never thought of it that way. All I knew was that I had to grow up without a father in a country where life was hard for my mother. I want to bring her here, to America, where life can begin again."

"Oh, Hector, it's the same for my father. I want him here for the same reason, so that he can see it is possible to start over." They had stopped walking and turned to face one another.

"Just your father?" he asked. "What about your mother?"

"She died not long after I came to New York. I thought I had told you. I didn't know she was ill when I left," she said. "My father is alone now and I think very lonely."

Hector's face brightened. "Perhaps we should introduce your father to my mother." Suddenly he laughed aloud, and the fullness of life flowed through him once more. Maggie laughed too. He was joking, of course, but it was a cheerful thought that their parents might find not only renewal, but love again. Somehow it didn't seem so impossible. It was hard for Maggie to think negative thoughts when Hector was about.

"We'll definitely have to give it some consideration," she said, smiling. "Have you seen the resurrection ferns that grow here on the island?" she asked suddenly. "They wither and seem to die, but they spring to life again in the next rain. I think love for people is like rain for the ferns."

"Maggie, you are a wonder," he said.

They had walked well beyond the range of the firelight and farther than the others strolling on the beach. Hector gently lifted her hand once more to his lips.

"Well, now, if you're going to kiss me, you might as well do it right," she said, tilting her face toward his. He didn't wait for a second invitation but drew her close.

"Maggie ... oh, Maggie, if only you knew how long I have wanted to do this."

His mouth touched her lips and he felt fire leap between them. He held her close and closer for a long moment as their bodies strained toward one another. Finally with all the will he could muster, he tore himself away, knowing that he had better take her back to the firelight, or else he could never let her go.

Maggie stood there, amazed at her own sauciness. *If you're going to kiss me, you might as well do it right.* Had she actually said such a thing? Where had it come from? It was something Deirdre might have said. But as she felt Hector's lips on hers, soft at first, then more urgent, she was not sorry she had said it.

She had been kissed before, several times back in Ireland by Bobby Callahan and once in New York by an Irish policeman under a streetlight. But she had never been kissed as Hector kissed her. She had never felt such urgency and longing. It was as though her will had vanished and her soul had merged with his in that single embrace. She never wanted it to end. She felt her body melting into his. She never wanted to let him go. But Hector drew back.

"I think we'd better go back to the bonfire," he said hoarsely.

Maggie was crestfallen. She wanted to hold him in her arms again, drink his kisses, and hear him whisper in her ear that he loved her. Instead he took her hand firmly and placed it again in the crook of his arm. Then he turned her around and began to walk her back toward the bonfire. Couldn't they at least go on walking and talking? Had he not liked her kiss? Had he been offended by her boldness? She felt humiliated and disappointed. She could not hear the wild racing of his heart.

Back in her bedroom on the fourth floor of the clubhouse Maggie wrapped herself in a blanket and let her tears flow. As she tried to collect herself, she remembered a poem she had learned by heart when she had first arrived in New York and had been so avidly reading American literature, a poem by a woman from Massachusetts named Emily Dickinson. It expressed her feelings better than anything she could have said herself, and she went to her desk to copy it into her journal.

> *Except the heaven had come so near,*
> *So seemed to choose my door,*
> *The distance would not haunt me so;*
> *I had not hoped before.*
>
> *But just to hear the grace depart*
> *I never thought to see,*
> *Afflicts me with a double loss;*
> *'Tis lost, and lost to me.*

She wished she could have said it so well. Underneath she wrote about the evening and how close to heaven she had felt when Hector kissed her, but how desolate she was at his taking her back so abruptly to the fireside.

When Deirdre had seen her dejection, she'd offered to walk with her back to the clubhouse and Maggie accepted gratefully, glad to leave behind the warmth and song that seemed so carefree. Deirdre had asked her no questions. She just held Maggie's hand as they walked back in silence.

Maggie wondered who or what the poet had lost. She knew Emily Dickinson had never married. In fact, she had died the year the Jekyl Island Club was founded, in 1886. Perhaps it was a sign. Perhaps that would be Maggie's fate as well. The words resounded within her as though she had indeed written them herself, but for Maggie all good poetry did that. She was trying, like Cousin Eleanor had told her she must do, to master her pain. As she thought of Miss Dickinson's poem she saw the beauty that could come from pain. If only she could write like that, she thought, she would almost welcome the pain. But she knew she couldn't. Still, she wrote in her journal every day. It seemed to help a little to confide her feelings even to the blank page before she cried herself to sleep for three nights straight.

Chapter Seven

MAGGIE DID NOT SPEAK to Hector again for several days.

"Maggie!" She heard his voice when he called out to her from a distance, but she pretended not to and turned away.

She had made herself much too vulnerable during that walk in the moonlight, and she had been so hurt by what she perceived as his rejection that she could not simply resume their lighthearted encounters. Instead, she went about her work with increased diligence and determination.

Deirdre cornered her in the corridor outside her room after their evening meal. "Hector wants to talk with you," she said. "He can't understand why you've been avoiding him."

"If he wants to talk with me, he can ask himself," Maggie said.

She was not trying to be coy, for she was not practiced in such tactics, and her mother had once told her that "a girl who is coy can lose the boy." She was merely afraid that, if she let him close to her again, he would reject her once more, and she didn't think she could endure it. It was not egotism on her part or a general fear of rejection, just a feeling that he could cause her more pain than she had ever before felt.

Early the following afternoon, as she was taking the dirty bed linens to the club laundry, she heard a voice behind her. "Please, may I carry that for you,

Maggie?" Her heart leapt as she recognized Hector's voice.

"I can manage quite well, thank you," she said, without looking at him.

"Please, Maggie, don't be angry with me. I can't bear it. I don't even know why you're angry."

"I'm not angry. And it's of no importance, really," she said, knowing that it was of the greatest importance in the world.

"Maggie, please, will you go walking with me tonight after my dinner shift? We can talk then. Now I'm already on duty, and Mrs. Morgan will be coming to the dining room any minute now. Say you will, please, or else I shall be fired for pleading with you so long that I neglect my duties and Mrs. Morgan altogether."

She looked at him for the first time. The wretchedness he felt was evident in his eyes. He, too, looked as though he had not slept for days. Suddenly she forgot herself and thought only of him and how she might ease his suffering.

"All right then. Tonight. I'll meet you at the *porte cochere* at nine-thirty. We can walk for half an hour."

His face brightened as though the sun had suddenly come out. "I'll be there. Thank you, Maggie."

He gently touched her hands, which were still holding the heavy basket of dirty sheets, and raced back toward the dining room. She noticed that he was already dressed in his white waiter's jacket. If Mr. Falk or Mr. Grob learned what he had done, slipping away from the dining room like that when he saw her through the window, he would certainly be reprimanded, but she was glad he had done it. Her basket felt lighter, and she knew that she was smiling foolishly at the wrinkled sheets, which gleamed white as Hector's jacket in the sunlight.

At nine-thirty that evening when Maggie arrived, Hector was already waiting for her and anxiously pacing the grass just outside the *porte cochere*. He smiled uncertainly and stepped forward.

"Thank you for coming," he said.

"Shall we walk?" she said, drawing her wool shawl tighter around her. The brief warm spell of late January had passed, and the nights were cooler now, dropping sometimes into the forties. But Maggie liked the brisk air. It reminded her of Ireland.

They walked in silence away from the clubhouse, passing between the Ferguson cottage and the club annex. It was not until they had nearly reached Shell Road, where the only light came from the moon and its reflection from the white shells that paved the road, that Hector broke the silence.

"Maggie, are you upset that I am not really from Greece?"

She began to laugh. "What? Of course not. Why should I be?"

"Then why? I know it sounds silly, but all I could think of was that you thought I had misled you about my homeland. Why are you so angry?"

"I'm not angry, Hector," she answered. "I guess I was hurt. I felt that you didn't care for me at all when you dismissed me so abruptly on the beach."

"Not care for you! Dismissed you!" He stopped in his tracks and turned to face her. "What do you mean?"

"You kissed me once, then pushed me away and took me back to the bonfire."

"Maggie, believe me, it was not because I rejected you, but because I care for you so much."

He grasped her upper arms. "I hope you don't think me presumptuous for saying that, but I have wanted to say it since the first moment I saw you. I couldn't trust myself that night. I love you. I wanted you so much."

She searched his eyes and saw their earnestness. Had she really been such a fool? So naïve as not to understand?

"You are stronger than I am. I could not have turned away so easily," she said.

"Do you really think it was easy?"

"I don't know. I don't ..." His eyes reflected the fire she felt within herself. "Oh, Hector. Can you forgive me? I have been so foolish."

"Maggie ..." He lifted her hands to kiss her fingertips.

"Never push me away again," she said, walking into his arms.

"Maggie ..." He brushed his lips against her hair.

"Never," she said firmly, wondering again where her boldness was coming from, but not really caring. She had so wanted to feel his arms around her.

He held her close, his hand behind her head, kissing her hair, her forehead, her nose. He drew back to look at her face.

This time he kissed her hungrily, like a man starving for her lips.

"Oh, Maggie," he said huskily. "I know it's sudden. But I also know that you are different from everyone I have ever known. I love you. I want to spend the rest of my life with you."

"Oh, Hector." She felt tears of joy stinging her eyes.

She took his face between her hands and, hardly breathing, returned his kisses slowly, sweetly at first, then with the same hunger she had sensed in him.

This time it was she who drew back. "We must move on."

His right arm around her waist and her left arm around his, they clung together against the chill night air, their steps in unison as they moved closer to the sea. To the left where the road opened out onto the shore, stood a tiny beach cottage, where club members stored beach chairs, blankets, pails and shovels for their children, and where they changed into bathing suits when they decided to brave the winter waters. It was never locked, for no one unconnected with the club was ever on the island.

Hector let Maggie go for a moment, leapt up to the little porch, and went in to fetch two blankets.

"We can sit among the dunes," he said.

This night there was no firelight. They found shelter behind one of the massive sand dunes angled to block the chilly wind blowing from the north. Hector spread one of the blankets on the sand, so they could sit down. Maggie nestled in his arms, where she felt safe. He took off his jacket and placed it behind them, like a pillow, wrapping the other blanket around them to keep them warm. It was their own private world in which they belonged to one another.

She snuggled against his chest, feeling the need to be even closer though there was no space left between them. Her body responded to his in ways she had never felt before. As he drew her close, his hand brushed against her breast, and she felt her own spontaneous reaction. She grasped his hand and guided it slowly back to her breast.

She briefly remembered her mother's words, "Maggie, you lead with your heart, not with your head." If that were true, then so be it. If it was wrong, she no longer had the will to care. She felt free. How did the poem put it? *Free from the weighing of fate and the sad discussion of sin.*

He kissed her hair, her shoulder, her lips, touching her breast with tentative fingers through the soft fabric of her blouse. It was she who undid the buttons and placed his fingers against her skin. As she felt the warmth of his hand, she arched her back, straining to be still closer to him.

"Oh, Hector," she moaned. "I think I will die without you. God has brought me to you. Please hold me. Help me." She was beyond wanting to separate her body from his, but he seemed to hold back, still unwilling to push the moment further, though she could feel the hardness of his body as he held her tightly in his arms. She was afraid he might draw back, and she held him even tighter.

"Oh, God," he murmured. "I love you, Maggie. I love you," he said over and over again.

She strained toward him and his body responded powerfully. Slowly, hesitantly, he moved his hand beneath her skirt. With a sharp intake of breath, she guided him by instinct to touch her wet softness. She shivered, and he wrapped the blanket tighter around her.

Hector felt an extraordinary combination of urgent desire and gentleness, as though it were, for him as for her, the first time he had ever abandoned his body to another. Her inexperience touched him deeply, and he wanted to be gentle, slow, understanding, to accept, as she did, that God was joining the two of them, as he so profoundly believed, in a preordained embrace. It was as though that moment had been foreseen from the beginning of time.

Maggie was, he knew beyond any doubt, the only woman he would ever love, and he was giving not only his body as she seemed to want, but also his heart, the heart he had always reserved for this moment, into her care. It was hers to nourish or to break, and he prayed fervently to God that she would nourish it and hold it close for as long as she lived.

He held back as long as he possibly could, until he could stand it no more, before entering her. She moaned her pleasure and pain, and he felt them both shudder as the membrane of resistance in her body gave way to welcome him and they joined as one body. A great wave of desire and fulfillment washed over them both.

When the thunder of their coming together subsided, they lay still for a long time. He held her in his arms, kissing her moist forehead, wrapping her in his embrace, as she tucked her head into the hollow of his shoulder and wept softly. He realized at that moment that his own cheeks were wet with tears as well.

If this be wrong, he thought, *then God forgive us both.* But it felt so right.

The sea oats waved above them, and the stars grew dimmer as the full moon rose over the horizon, peeking over the dune where they lay in one another's arms. Bathed in the golden moonlight that washed the sea, the sand, and their young bodies, they held each other, feeling at one with the universe and with each other.

"The moon is like the face of God, smiling down at us," Maggie said. Hector nodded.

They sat up now, leaning against the pillow of his jackets piled against the dune and looking at the ocean where the round moon had risen high, making a bright streak across the ocean.

He echoed her thoughts. "The reflection is like a pathway leading home, the golden road to God."

"Yes," she said, breathlessly, leaning her head back against his shoulder, as his arms tightened around her, as though he could not let her go.

"Shall we have our wedding back in New York?" he asked her suddenly.

"I feel that we are already married in the eyes of God," she said.

"But I want to marry you in the eyes of man as well. I want the whole world to know you as my wife. The anniversary of my birth will be the day of my new birth, if you are willing."

"And when is that?" she asked.

"May 8th."

"Then that will be our wedding day," she said. "Our second wedding day."

"Maggie, I can never love you more than I do at this moment."

She did not want the night to end, as she let the moonlit sea, the bright stars, and the shell-strewn beach burn their memory into her heart.

"It is my promise from this moment on," Hector said, "that I will love you like this always, that I will be faithful to you, until death do us part. You are my wife."

"And you are my husband," she whispered, tilting her head back for another of his kisses. "This is our real marriage vow. We can never be more married than we are now."

"My beloved." He kissed her again. "My heart. My soul. My only one—forever."

It was as though both of them were speaking in unison, feeling the same emotions, the same oneness, and neither could tell where one began and the other ended.

Maggie was unable to sleep that night. When Hector walked her back to the clubhouse and discreetly kissed her good night in case anyone was watching, she climbed the stairs, her mind too excited to even think of sleep, though her body was exhausted. She put on her nightgown and leaned against her pillow, leafing through her little volume of Emily Dickinson. Here and there she found lines that captured her feelings, her thoughts about the night, but the words she came back to again and again were:

Let me not mar that perfect dream
By an auroral stain,
But so adjust my daily night
That it will come again.

She dreaded the dawn that would bring this magic night to an end. She knew it had been no dream, however perfect, but a reality that would be her new life. She and Hector together had just created their future in this new country. It was a night that made her want to write her own poems or at least record her feelings. She got up to sit at her desk, hugging herself with the memories of the evening and writing in her journal.

Tonight, she wrote, *was the second beginning of my life. This time there was no dinner bell, but only the gentle lapping of the waves along the shore.*

How could she describe what had happened? It was truly as though she had been given a new life, with Hector at its core. She smiled inwardly and outwardly. On May 8th she would become in the eyes of the world what she felt she already was, Mrs. Hector Deliyannis. She wrote the date and her new name in her journal over and over. She would not tell anyone yet. It would be her precious secret, hers and Hector's. Their world—their Eden—had just begun.

Chapter Eight

◦ MAGGIE, HUMMING AS SHE WENT, carried the basket of dirty linens from the five rooms she had cleaned that morning to the clubhouse laundry. It was now the end of February. Although she and Hector had agreed not to repeat their love-making, however intense their desire, until they could be married in the eyes of the Church, she had never been happier than she was this past month with the assurance that she was so loved.

Her dreams of that Golden Door to America she had entered so recently had never been as vivid and wonderful as the reality. Thank God she had not been able to find employment in New York and that Kate had been so insistent that she apply for this job at the Jekyl Island Club. From the moment Maggie arrived at Jekyl, she was convinced that she had the luck of the Irish.

As she set down the basket, she felt a wave of nausea sweep over her and barely made it outside before she vomited onto the sand. The fresh air made her feel a little better, and she leaned back against the balustrade of the outside stairs.

"Are you all right, honey?" She heard a sympathetic voice behind her.

"I'm feeling a little better, thank you," she answered, looking up into the concerned dark eyes of an attractive, light-skinned Negro woman. It was Aleathia Parland, the wife of Page Parland, caretaker for the Edwin Gould family. She had been bringing the Gould linens to the laundry when she observed Maggie's hasty departure.

The Parlands were virtual fixtures at Jekyl Island. They lived in the little house the Gould family had built for them behind Cherokee Cottage, which belonged to Mrs. Gould's mother, Hester Shrady. Page and Aleathia had a reputation for efficiency and friendliness among club workers and were much respected by black and white workers alike. Minnie Clark often entrusted to Aleathia tasks that involved caring for apartments in the nearby Sans Souci and the club annex, as well as some of the cottages, both during and after the club season.

"Do you think you ought to have Doc Merrill take a look at you?" Aleathia asked. Each season the club's executive committee hired a doctor-in-residence during the months the club was open. They had once, fifteen years earlier, lost a club member to a heart attack because he had been unable to get medical attention in time, and club officers were unwilling to take any more chances with their members' health.

"I'll be all right. It always passes in a few minutes," Maggie answered.

Aleathia looked at her intently, at the pallor of her skin, into her eyes, and, when she had satisfied herself, she asked, "When did you have yo' last period, chile?"

Maggie was startled by the directness of the question, because she was already concerned about the fact that her monthly flow was two weeks overdue. And she was half certain that she knew the reason, though she had refused to let herself dwell on it. She wanted nothing to mar her happiness.

"I ... I don't remember," she stammered.

"Now don't you be fibbin' to Aleathia," the woman said. "I ain't gon' tell nobody. I just want to help."

Maggie believed her and, released from her inhibitions by the woman's gentle tone, which reminded her of her mother, she suddenly burst into tears. Aleathia put her arm around the girl.

"Why don' we get these sheets to the laundry and then walk over to my house, and I'll fix you a glass of iced tea. Yo' work's all done for the mornin', I 'speck, and you could stand to get off your feet for a while."

Once they had deposited their baskets in the club laundry, Maggie followed Aleathia across the road, past Faith Chapel, and down the lane toward the Parlands' house. It was a small cottage, little more than a living room, a bedroom, a kitchen, and a comfortable front porch with two rocking chairs where Maggie longed to sit. Instead Aleathia led her inside and gestured toward one of the ladder-back chairs at the kitchen table, while she set about chipping ice to put in glasses for tea.

Maggie felt strange being inside the Parland house, for the black and white servants had little interaction, and Maggie had never even known a black person before she came to the Jekyl Island Club. She found the black workers friendly and engaging, always ready to share their stories or songs with anyone interested. She had listened to John Cain's tall tales and heard his famous laugh that amused the island children as well as the adults, and she had learned that the person she should ask about the plants in the forest and on the grounds was Sam Denegal, who knew more about nature in the area than anyone else on the island. But she had not talked to any of the women before.

Aleathia handed her a glass of sweet tea and poured one for herself, but she did not sit down at the table with Maggie. Nonetheless, her voice was friendly. "Now, honey, you want to tell Aleathia about it?"

Maggie hesitated, for she knew that Aleathia often worked for Minnie Clark, and she felt that she should tell no one of her fears if she ever hoped to come back to Jekyl or get a job in service in New York.

"Yo' secret's safe with me, chile, but I reckon you need somebody to talk to," Aleathia said. "Those tears come from somewhere. Ain't that a fact? You gon' have yo'self a baby, I'm willin' to guess."

Maggie had not expected the bluntness of Aleathia's words. At first she said nothing, but the kindness in the black woman's face helped her to break through the wall of silence she had built for herself.

"I don't know for sure," she said hesitantly, but she was afraid that it was true. She had just not wanted to face it, to put it into words.

"But it's possible?" Aleathia asked. "I ain't gon' ask you who the daddy is, but you need to tell him. It ain't one of them club members, is it? You ain't been foolin' around with any of them, I hope."

"Oh, no, no. Nothing like that. Of course I'll tell him if ..." Maggie began. Then she remembered Aleathia's connection to the head housekeeper. "Please don't tell Mrs. Clark. She would fire me for sure, and I need the money to bring my father here from Ireland. Please don't tell anyone."

"I ain't studyin' tellin' nobody. I just want you to know you got a friend. It ain't right to be all alone at such a time. And, honey, let me tell you, a baby is always a blessin' so don't you be thinkin' about how you can get rid of it."

"Oh, no! I could never do such a thing." Maggie was horrified at the thought. She was brought up in a good Catholic family and taught to respect life. The idea of getting rid of her baby would never have crossed her mind. "If I'm expecting—" she began.

Aleathia laughed gently. "I don't think there's no 'if' about it, honey. You got the look, and you got the mornin' sickness. The only way to be sure is to see a doctor or a midwife."

"Oh, I couldn't go to the club doctor. Everyone would know." She hadn't even discussed the possibility with Hector yet.

"They's a lady lives on Red Row. Used to deliver babies over in Brunswick before she come to live out here. Maybe she could help," Aleathia said. Red Row was an area of small houses where black workers lived outside the club compound. Maggie had heard of it, though she had never been there. "I could fetch her here, if you like."

Again Maggie hesitated, but she did want to be sure, and she didn't want to talk to any of the white workers for fear she could not trust them to keep her secret. Aleathia's earnest, sympathetic face was reassuring, and Maggie knew instinctively she could trust her. She had thought of talking with Deirdre, but was concerned that Deirdre might unwittingly reveal her condition to someone else. She knew that she would not do it maliciously, but words seemed to bubble past her lips without much thought or reserve, and she worried that the secret would not remain long in confidence if Deirdre knew.

"What's her name?" Maggie asked. "Can I trust her?"

"She's called Tranny, Aunt Tranny. If Aleathia tells her to keep a secret, she'll keep it. I'm sure of that."

"If you're sure, I'd be grateful if you could send for her." She felt a sudden relief, knowing somehow that she could count on Aleathia to keep her word. There was a sense of dignity in the woman, a solidity, a trustworthiness, and she felt relaxed in her presence, in this warm kitchen that reminded her of her mother's kitchen.

Aleathia went to the back door and called in a loud voice, "Tommy?"

A little boy about eight years old who had been playing mumblety-peg under a nearby pine tree presented himself at the screen door. "Yes'm?"

"You run over to Red Row to see if you can find Aunt Tranny. I'll give you a nickel if you bring her back." The boy's face lit up, and he dashed off through the pine trees. Less than fifteen minutes later he returned, leading an elderly lady by the hand.

"You send for me, Aleathia?" the woman asked.

Aleathia held open the screen door for the woman to enter and handed a nickel to the shiny-faced boy who was smiling broadly. "Thank you for comin', Tranny. Come on in. How you been doin'? You want a glass of tea?"

The old woman ignored her questions.

"You send for Tranny?" she asked again, looking with curiosity at the young white woman seated at the kitchen table.

"This here's a friend of mine," Aleathia said in response to the unasked question and gesturing toward Maggie. Tranny looked at Maggie with unabashed curiosity but she did not ask her name.

"She needs to know whether she's expectin' or not. We thought you might could help out. Ol' Doc Merrill ain't got time to see her today."

"Uh huh," said the old woman thoughtfully, chewing on the side of her inner cheek and accepting the glass of iced tea that Aleathia held out to her.

She walked on into the living room and set her glass down on a low table in front of the sofa. Then she lowered herself with the difficulty of an arthritis sufferer into one of the armchairs.

"Well, let's have a look. Bring a stool, honey, and set right here in front of me," Tranny instructed Maggie. Aleathia gestured toward a footstool in the corner, and Maggie brought it to the feet of the old woman and sat down. Tranny squinted as she peered intently into the young woman's eyes, lifting the lids.

"You been feelin' sick in the mornin's?"

"Yes," answered Maggie, "and some afternoons as well."

"Uh huh, and when did you last have your monthly flow?"

"Six weeks ago, the second week of January," Maggie answered truthfully.

"Unbutton your blouse, honey," the woman told her, and Maggie obeyed.

The old woman looked at her swollen breasts and reached under Maggie's underclothes to touch them here and there.

"That feel tender?" she asked.

Again Maggie answered truthfully, "Yes."

"You noticed any changes in the color around the nipples?"

"I ... I think it may be a little darker."

"Any changes in bathroom visits?"

"I have to go more frequently than I used to."

"Well ..." Tranny said slowly, taking her time, examining the edges of Maggie's face and looking intently into the irises of her eyes. "They's more examinin' I could do, but t'aint nec'ssary. No doubt about it. I'd say along about November or December you gon' have yo'self a *fine* baby. You look like a good, healthy girl. Good hips," she said, appraising her body. "You shouldn't have no problem. Uh-uh, no problem a-tall."

"Well, that's mighty good news," Aleathia said. She reached in her pocket and gave some coins to Aunt Tranny. "For your trouble, and I thank you."

After the old woman had finished her tea and gone, Maggie said, "Thank you, Aleathia. I'll repay you."

"Nothing to repay. That's what God give us money and time for, to help people who needs us. And you looked like you needs some help. Now you go tell the daddy. I 'speck he'll do right by you."

"I will tell him," said Maggie. "I will." And she hugged Aleathia, whose arms surrounded her with warmth and comfort.

It took Maggie three days to find a way to broach the subject with Hector. She felt awkward about raising the matter, but, finally, on Sunday evening, during one of their long walks outside the club compound, she found the courage.

She had not expected his reaction. He searched her face with his eyes, almost disbelieving. Then a broad smile crept across his face, and he leaned his head back and laughed, a full, long, hearty laugh that bespoke only joy.

"Maggie, Maggie," he said. "You are a treasure! A baby! Our baby! How wonderful!" Maggie, wrapped in his arms, found herself laughing with his contagious joy and crying with relief all at the same. Then suddenly he drew back and looked at her intently, "You're sure, aren't you? This is not some cruel joke. You're not going to tell me tomorrow it's not true and you were just teasing me."

"Of course not, my love. It's absolutely true. Do you realize that our baby, if it's a boy, could grow up to be president? He'll be born in this country."

Hector looked wonderstruck, as though such an idea had never occurred to him before. Again he laughed, almost dancing on the crushed moonlit shells beneath their feet. His joy was unfeigned, and he could barely contain himself.

"There is one little problem," she said teasingly.

"What's that?" He was suddenly serious and anxious.

"You haven't said you loved me all evening." She smiled up at him with her eager open face, hungry to hear the words once more.

"Maggie, Maggie … I shall say it every day for the rest of my life. You'll tire of hearing it." Then he shouted at the top of his voice, "I love you, I love you, I love you," startling a whole family of raccoons crossing the road just ahead of them and sending them scurrying to the safety of the palmettos that lined the roadway.

Then he grew quiet, drew her toward him, and looked in her eyes. "I love you, Maggie O'Brien, forever and ever."

She put her arms around his waist and pulled him close. "And I love you too, Hector Deliyannis. Forever and ever."

He looked at her, now serious. "You know, of course, we should get married right away, not wait until May. Where can we find a Catholic priest? Do they ever come to the island?" There seemed to be a steady stream of Episcopal priests and an occasional Presbyterian who came to give sermons in Faith Chapel on Sundays, but so far, no Catholics at all.

"I'm not sure …" Maggie hesitated.

"I'm Greek Orthodox, you know," Hector reminded her. "Do you think there is any problem in a Roman Catholic marrying someone from the Greek Orthodox Church? Do you think a civil ceremony will suffice for the time being if we can't get permission from the Church? Can we marry in Faith Chapel?"

Maggie laughed at his endless list of questions. "Maybe Mr. Grob can help us work it all out."

"What a good idea! Let's go back now and find him."

"I think it can wait until tomorrow," she said. "One day won't make any difference. And I saw him on the porch of his cottage talking with Miss Baker when we left. The only free time he has is in the evening. Let's not disturb them."

"Oh, no. We won't disturb them. I hear he's sweet on Miss Baker. But tomorrow first thing. Now we must get you back to your room. You shouldn't be out in this night air. Are you warm enough?"

Maggie smiled at his solicitous manner. She had never been happier. No, not happy—joyous. She felt as though Hector's passion for life had melted into her, that she had become a part of him and could feel that same boundless energy. She was suddenly, like him, thirsty for all life offered.

They sat side by side in Mr. Grob's office the next morning, as soon as Hector's breakfast shift had ended, and Hector told him that they had decided to be married. Ernest Grob was delighted with the news and agreed to do all he could to help.

"You know that we don't necessarily encourage these staff romances, but occasionally they happen, and I'm always pleased when they work out like this."

"Do you think it's all right for a Catholic and someone who is Greek Orthodox to marry?" Hector asked.

"I would assume so. After all, they were once a single church," Mr. Grob reminded them. "But I suppose we should find out."

Hector nodded. He knew that finding a Greek Orthodox priest to consult in south Georgia would be next to impossible, but he had no problem himself with being married by a Catholic priest. He would prefer that the marriage be blessed by God rather than by a county magistrate, even if he had to proclaim himself a Roman Catholic.

"Good. Then I'll contact Bishop Keiley in Savannah and Father Cassagne in Brunswick to see what we can work out. Is there any particular date you'd like?" Mr. Grob asked.

"As soon as possible," said Hector, squeezing Maggie's hand.

It took Mr. Grob five days to get an answer. The bishop replied by mail to his telephone inquiry, informing him that he would arrange for a Catholic priest to be on the island on March 23. That would give them time to post the required banns to announce their intent and to make all the arrangements.

When Maggie told Deirdre the news and asked her to be her maid of honor, Deirdre squealed with delight. "Glory be! You're the lucky one, ye are!"

The community of club workers was ecstatic at the news, which Deirdre spread as rapidly as she could, with Maggie's approval, and everyone was eager to help Maggie and Hector plan the wedding. Since flowers were abundant on the island in March, the chambermaids set about making plans to decorate the church with Cherokee roses, orange blossoms, and gardenias, and Ray Etter, the wife of the club's bookkeeper, John Etter, asked if she could make the bridal bouquet. They decided among themselves that Maggie's cream-colored lawn dress would be fine for the occasion, and Minnie Clark agreed to lend Maggie a string of pearls that had belonged to her mother.

When Maggie told Aleathia Parland and asked her to come to the wedding, she said, approvingly, "You done gone and got yourself a fine man, Miss Maggie, a *fine* man. A han'some one too."

As the days slipped by and their wedding date grew closer, they continued to perform their duties with diligence. The waiters all teased Hector in a warm-hearted way. They no longer called him Hector the Greek, even in the good-natured manner they had before. In fact, none of them thought of themselves anymore as George the Englishman or Stéphane the Frenchman or Horst the German. They were all Americans now, working hard side by side, complaining together about the demanding diners, laughing together at the same jokes, and enjoying the same sunsets before dinner and the same starlit nights after dinner. Hector had learned the words to some of their songs and even taught them one from his own homeland, though their pronunciation was atrocious.

Like Maggie, he told no one about the baby, though he was bursting to do so. But they had agreed that it would be best to wait until after the wedding and their return to New York to tell their new friends. In the meantime, Maggie had written to her father to tell him that she was planning to be married. It was the one duty she knew must be performed at once. She debated whether or not she should tell him as well about the baby, but she decided that it might be best to wait. Although her father was a good Catholic and would be delighted that they were starting a family at once, she knew that he was also deeply conservative about such things. She thought he might have difficulty accepting the news of a baby conceived before the official marriage.

Once they were wed, though, he would accept the fact without question. She knew that, and he would not condemn her or Hector if the baby arrived a few months early. Right now she still felt rather vulnerable, but in less than a month she would be Maggie Deliyannis, and she knew that her father would embrace Hector, his loyalty to his family, and his love of life. At least she hoped so.

In so many ways they were alike—Daniel O'Brien and Hector Deliyannis. The fact that they grew up in different countries speaking different languages was irrelevant. They shared so many things of the heart—most of all a love for Maggie. They could not help but like one another. Maggie felt as though she were the luckiest woman on earth.

The days passed in a haze of happiness for Maggie. Everyone seemed pleased about the upcoming marriage, no one more so than the lovers themselves. They had agreed, despite their desire for one another, to stay within the confines of the club compound after dark. Neither of them wanted anything to mar the perfection of their wedding day, when they wanted to join together in the eyes of the world as they felt they were already joined forever in the sight of God.

Maggie had no regrets about their night together on the beach, or about their decision to wait until marriage to fulfill their future desire. But now that it was only a matter of weeks, their restraint merely served to heighten their desire for one another. It was difficult for them to keep from touching one another, and they often stole deep, hungry kisses in the shadow of Faith Chapel after dark on a moonlit night. They could hardly wait for the moment when they could be together always to lie in one another's arms and spin out the bright yarn of their future dreams.

Chapter Nine

⁂ HECTOR MOVED LIGHTLY throughout his dinner work hours, as he gathered delicacies from the kitchen to serve at the Morgans' table. He grinned with appreciation as he accepted the congratulations of Mrs. Morgan, who had heard about his forthcoming marriage from Mr. Grob. On the early March evening when she congratulated him, she slipped a ten-dollar gold piece under the saucer of her coffee cup, where he would find it when he cleared the table.

When he tried to thank her the next morning, she said, her eyes twinkling with merriment, "Why, Hector, how can you imagine that I would do such a thing? You know that Mr. Morgan would never permit me to be so frivolous with his money." They laughed together, sharing a secret, and he brought her an extra-large serving of fruit for breakfast.

Finally, all plans were in place. By a stroke of good fortune, a priest by the name of P. J. Luckie had notified Bishop Keiley that he would be in the Savannah area in mid-March and for several weeks thereafter. It was a fortuitous arrival, because Father Cassagne, the priest from Saint Francis Xavier in Brunswick, planned to be out of the city on March 23, the date that Maggie and Hector had selected for their wedding. Thus, Father Luckie had agreed to perform the ceremony. It would not be his first trip to Jekyl Island.

Many years earlier, while the priest served in a Catholic mission in Brunswick, Charlotte Maurice had invited him as her guest to the island where he had conducted a service in non-denominational Faith Chapel. He had become a fast friend of the Maurice family and had been distressed to hear of Mrs. Maurice's death in 1907 while he was in California. He welcomed this opportunity to express his condolences in person to her husband, Stewart, who, learning of his impending trip to Jekyl, immediately offered him hospitality during his stay.

"I think it's a good omen," said Maggie, when she learned the news, "to be married by a priest named Father Luckie."

"It seems to me entirely appropriate." Hector squeezed her hand and grinned. "After all, I have felt lucky from the moment I first saw you on the ship from New York."

Maggie only smiled, but she, too, felt amazingly fortunate in all that had happened, that they should have met at all among the millions of people in America, that they had come to this beautiful spot, like a piece of heaven on earth. When she thought of how she had resisted accepting the job, she could only thank God for leading her here.

On Wednesday evening, three days before the wedding, Bert approached Hector in the kitchen as he was waiting for the chef to douse Mrs. Morgan's cherries jubilee with brandy. "Want to go for a swim tomorrow afternoon? George, Stéphane, and a whole group of us are going to the beach. It may be your last swim as a free man," he teased.

The group was planning a little surprise party for Hector after the dinner shift the next evening, and they wanted to keep him occupied and away from the clubhouse while the kitchen staff set up the arrangements. They always had a few hours off between lunch and dinner, and it should be enough.

"Sure," Hector answered. "What time?"

"We'll walk over together about three o'clock. Okay?"

"Wonderful! Now I'd better get Mrs. Morgan's dessert out to her."

Thursday dawned sunny and warmer than usual, and the waiters looked forward to their afternoon of freedom on the beach. Hector had not seen the ocean for nearly a week. He had spent afternoons writing letters to his mother and learning to ride a bicycle. Mr. Evans, the club's bicycle man, hired to maintain the two-wheeled vehicles in peak condition and to teach members to ride them, was also teaching Hector. The bicycle was a craze in New York, and waiters who had been to Jekyl in previous years already knew how to ride. Hector had watched them with envy as they sailed down the hard beach, their wheels spinning in the sunlight. He was determined he would learn as well, and so he had, quite easily, thanks to his well-toned body and athletic prowess that made all such tasks simple.

He had written to his mother about the experience. Writing in Greek, he tried to capture the feel of it. "It seems so simple now. I don't know why it was so difficult at first, but there is an incredible feeling of freedom, as the wind rushes by. I wish I could share this wonderful place with you." He wrote her also about Maggie, as he had in every letter since he had met her, telling his mother about the winter-wheat blond of her hair and the blue-gray of her eyes, changeable like the colors of the sea, how when she laughed a little dimple formed in her right cheek.

"You will love her, as I do. How I wish you could be here for our wedding in the most beautiful little church on earth." He had heard nothing back from his mother. It was much too soon, but he knew that she would not seriously object to his marrying outside the Orthodox faith. There was already enough precedent for that within the family, and they had all been taught tolerance for others' faiths.

That afternoon Hector hung his white waiter's jacket on the hook behind his door and grabbed his bathing costume and a towel. He planned to change in the little bathhouse on the beach. Stopping by George's room across the hall, he tapped on the door. "George, are you ready?" It was nearly three o'clock, and he could hear the voices of the others beginning to gather on the porch of the dormitory.

A muffled voice inside called out, "One moment!"

Hector waited in the hall until George, already attired in what passed for a swimsuit, with a large towel around his shoulders, opened the door. Because George didn't know how to swim and had in fact never been to a beach before he arrived at Jekyl, he did not have a proper bathing costume. Hector had given him an extra pair of trunks, and George had managed to find a shirt to match, but it was ill-fitting and not like the bathing suits of the other waiters. The jersey had little sleeves, which suited George just fine, for his skin was fair and freckled, and he sunburned easily.

"Why don't you teach me how to swim today?" George asked, peering out at him hopefully.

Hector laughed. He had asked George to be his best man, although the two could not have been more different from one another. George shared none of Hector's physical prowess, but he was a good friend.

"I don't know, George, I think you're a hopeless case." Hector laughed at George's mocking scowl. In fact, he had tried to teach him before, but George panicked every time his face was under water. "If you can't put your head under water, you'll never learn to swim," he told him.

Hector himself had been a good swimmer since childhood. Born on the Gulf of Smyrna, he had no choice but to learn to swim, since that was the major summer pastime of most of his boyhood friends. They could not afford bicycles, but the waters of the Aegean were free and available. George admired Hector's natant skills, just as Hector admired the other waiters who sped along the sand on whirring wheels.

"Come on, old chum, don't give up on me," pleaded George playfully, slapping Hector with his towel.

"Ah, George," he replied, trying to dodge the towel, "you know I'll never give up on you."

Once in the ocean, however, it did seem a useless effort. George was a non-swimmer and it looked as though he would be all his life, despite Hector's best efforts to show him the simple mechanics of the crawl. So far, all George had learned to do was float on his back, once Hector helped him into position. The salty Atlantic waters made him buoyant, and his face was out of the water. But anything else seemed beyond his psychological capabilities. He felt as though he were going to suffocate whenever he was face down in the water, and he simply couldn't do it.

"That's okay, old man," said Hector. "You sunburn too easily anyhow. You better stay on dry land where you can find some shade."

They joined the other waiters back on the beach to dry off and swap stories of their lives back in New York. Only a few of them had known one another before they came to Jekyl, but those had delighted in telling outlandish tales about each other, mostly invented. The group was rarely in a serious mood, and there was much scuffling, towel slapping, and splashing in the tidal pools that had formed along the shoreline when the tide went out.

His ubiquitous Brownie camera in hand, Bert lined the waiters up in front of a driftwood tree trunk, perhaps the mast from an old sailing ship that had washed up on shore, to snap a picture.

"Take one more, Bert. I'll get these boys organized," George announced.

He lined them up again, leaning against the driftwood trunk, their arms folded across their abdomens. Two of them were lying on the sand in front of the group, and a couple of the dishwashers, not in bathing costumes, peered from behind. "Okay, we're ready," George announced, and Bert once again snapped the lens.

"We have," he announced with mock seriousness, "immortalized the moment."

Stéphane had brought a soccer ball, which he began to kick about. Most of the young men had played as children in their respective countries. The current rage in America was football, played with an odd-shaped ball pointed at both ends, unlike anything Hector had ever seen in his own country. They had noticed some of the college-age sons of club members tossing such balls about, but the immigrant workers all felt more comfortable with the familiar round soccer ball. The best player among them was an Italian named Paulo, but Hector was a close second.

They raced up and down the beach, kicking the ball, sometimes passing it with a blow to their forehead, and trying to keep it away from the water. As they played, dark clouds were beginning to gather, and the water was getting a bit choppy. With a high kick by Paulo, whose bare foot was powerful, the wind caught the ball and sailed it into the water, where the tide was coming in again.

"I'll get it," yelled George, who was closest to the spot where it landed, and he waded out into the water. When he was waist deep, he seemed within an arm's length of the ball. He reached out for it, but a wave snatched it from him just out of range. He moved toward the ball, confident that he could retrieve it before it drifted away again, but the sand shifted beneath him, and he found himself shoulder deep in the water.

"Damn," he muttered, reaching out once more for the ball. A wave washed over him, and he went under. He came up sputtering and gasping for air. Suddenly there was no sand beneath his feet, and the ball had drifted ever farther from his grasp.

George was struggling to keep his head above water. The others began to laugh, not seeming to realize that he was earnestly in trouble, but Hector sensed his panic. He knew the sands could be uneven at that depth. There were submerged sandbars, and with a bit of splashing about George could no doubt have found his footing again, but he was seized with fear.

Hector raced toward his friend, diving head first into the surf once he was knee deep into the surging waters. The usually gentle surf was becoming rough and unpredictable with the incoming tide. Distant lightning split the heavens. The sky was growing darker, and the wind had begun to blow as though it might rain at any moment.

Down the beach people were scurrying for shelter, but the waiters all stood riveted to the spot watching Hector's powerful swim toward the struggling

George. Several of them moved closer to the water, unsure of what they could do to help. If Hector could reach George before he disappeared again beneath the murky surface, they thought it should be all right. He was strong and confident and could pull his friend into safer waters.

But George slipped once more out of sight. Hector swam toward the spot where he disappeared and dived below the surface to find him. George, struggling and frantic, found Hector before Hector found him.

He seized his rescuer around the head and shoulders, trying to scramble out of the grip of the suffocating sea. Hector fought to free himself, but George held tight, making it only once above the water line, where he gasped for air, but breathed in mostly sea water, as a wave slapped him in the face. Hector held his breath as long as he could, fighting for the surface, but feeling the tide's undertow dragging them into the deeper waters.

He, too, was beginning to panic. He tried desperately to pry George's arms from around his neck, but George was holding on, showing more strength than Hector had ever thought possible. He was clawing at George's arms now, at his body, in a frantic attempt to escape his death-clutch, but George was like an octopus, holding him in the depths of a salty world where there was no air.

Hector, losing consciousness, tried desperately to hold on. Suddenly he saw Maggie in her white lawn dress, wreathed in orange blossoms and Cherokee roses that floated around her, her long hair loose and waving gently like the folds of her gown in the movement of the sea. She smiled at him, reaching out her pale arms as though to lead him to safety. As he stretched toward her beckoning image, he felt the salt water enter his lungs, and he closed his eyes, abandoning himself to his vision beneath the sea.

The storm passed without rain. By the time Stéphane had reached the clubhouse, running as fast as he could, the sun was once more spilling from behind the scudding clouds. As he screamed for Maggie, people looked out the windows of the upper floors, trying to figure out what the hubbub was all about. Stéphane called her name again and again, almost sobbing from the effort, until finally, she appeared at the service entrance.

"What is it, Stéphane? What's wrong?" Fear gripped her, for she saw tears streaming down his face, flushed from the effort of his race.

"Oh, Maggie, Maggie, it's Hector. Please, you must come—now!"

"Come where? Where is Hector? What's happened?"

Stéphane couldn't bring himself to say the words. He only gave her an agonized look that spoke eloquently to her heart. He turned away and flagged down the Maurice coachman, Charlie Hill, who was on his way to the blacksmith shop with his brace of horses, one of which had thrown a shoe during Mr. Maurice's afternoon drive on Palmetto Road.

"Charlie, can you give us a ride down Shell Road to the beach? It's an emergency."

Charlie took one look at the anguished face of the young man and the fear in Maggie's eyes, and, without asking questions, replied, "Get in."

He applied the whip to the two horses, something he rarely did, and they broke into a gallop.

"Stéphane, what's happened? Hector's all right, isn't he?" Maggie implored, trying to control the racing of her heart.

"I don't think so," he answered, trying to stifle the sobs rising up in him once again. "He swam out to save George, but George grabbed hold, and ... well, we can't find either one of them. We tried to help them, Maggie. We tried. But we couldn't find them." A sob escaped despite his obvious efforts to hold it back.

Charlie drove the carriage out onto the hard strand and headed for the tight clump of people gathered south of the entrance.

Maggie did not wait for him to stop completely before she jumped out of the carriage. She felt a momentary relief to see Hector lying face down on the beach, with George stretched out a few feet away. They had found them, and her heart leaped in hope.

Bert was astride Hector's back, pressing down and trying to force the water out of his lungs to let the air in once more. Paulo was doing the same over George. Maggie had seen a boy almost drown once in the Atlantic on the Dingle coast, and she dropped to her knees beside Hector, holding her breath, her face ashen, waiting for the cough and sputter that would tell her that Hector would be all right. But it did not come. Bert kept trying again and again, refusing to give up.

"Hector," she whispered his name over and over. "Hector. Hector."

Someone had gone for Dr. Merrill, and he drove up now in his T-model Ford, parking about ten yards away. He watched the resuscitation efforts for only a few seconds before he asked Bert to move aside. With the help of one of the waiters, they turned Hector over on his back, and Dr. Merrill leaned over him, pulling up his eyelids and pointing a little flashlight into his eyes. He pulled out his stethoscope and listened at his chest for a heartbeat.

Maggie watched hopefully. He shook his head.

She was dimly aware of a mournful keening sound rising up from some place inside where she had no sense of creating it. Without any conscious effort on her part, she crawled toward Hector, pushing everyone out of the way, and gathered him in her arms, oblivious to the wet black bathing suit that was staining her dress. She held his head and shoulders in her lap, her cheek against his dripping hair, rocking him back and forth, kissing him, leaning over him, and making wordless sounds.

Tears flowed, unstoppable, down her cheeks, and onto Hector's upturned face, where they ran like rivulets through the drying sand that still clung to his cheeks, as she tried tenderly to brush them away. She had no sense of doing any of these things, but of watching them from a distance, from cliffs overlooking the sea, from a great height. A part of her was not there, but was somewhere else, where Hector, the rest of Hector, was, for here, on the beach, there was no life, no spirit.

She had no idea how long she sat there, holding and rocking Hector's body, until her bodice was soaked through with seawater and tears. She resisted any effort to pry him loose from her arms. Finally someone fetched Deirdre to come and bring Maggie back to the clubhouse. She knelt beside her friend.

"Ye can't stay here, Maggie. Ye have to let him go." She heard Deirdre's voice at her elbow, like a distant wind. Little by little, Deirdre gently loosened the grip of her arms. Maggie moaned as she felt Hector being taken from her. John Cain was there with his wagon, pulled by his mules, Pete and Julia. She watched, uncomprehending, as the men wrapped Hector's body in a sheet and loaded it onto the wagon, where George already lay. The *Jekyl Island* would be waiting at the dock to take the bodies into Brunswick.

Deirdre helped her stand, and then turned her slowly back toward the clubhouse in the direction the wagon had gone, her arm tight around Maggie's shoulder. Charlie Hill waited, this time at Mr. Maurice's instructions, to bring her back in his carriage. But she would not get in, instead putting one foot before the other as though in a daze. Dusk was falling around them, absorbing the colors of the day into a misty gray.

Deirdre held her as they walked, speaking in her ear from time to time, occasionally stopping to turn face her toward Maggie and take her in both her arms. The coachman, following slowly behind, halted the carriage to wait, powerless, his head bowed, while Maggie put her face on the shoulder of her friend and wept out all she could of grief.

The next day passed without her conscious participation. She remembered once more her Cousin Eleanor's words about controlling grief. She must have carried out her duties, though she had no recollection of doing so. Perhaps someone else had done the rooms for her. In the days that would come, she could not remember.

Only a few moments made any distinct impression on her waking mind. Mr. Grob had asked her in the morning about Hector's family, about whom he should notify, but Maggie was unable to help. "His family lives in Anatolia," she said, "in Smyrna. His mother is a widow," but she could go no further. She remembered only that he had drawn her a map in the sand and said, "My family's house is here." But she had no address.

She did not even know his mother's first name. There was time for that in the future, always time. Hector had always said, "My mother," and that was enough. She never asked, though she realized now, too late, that such details were important.

Mr. Grob nodded sadly. "I will take it up with the club's executive committee to see what they think it best to do with the body. It's at Miller Funeral Home in Brunswick now."

No one had information about George Harvey's family either. All they knew is that he was from Liverpool. His employment application gave only his New York address, where all his references lived. They would have to think of requiring more information in the future for such cases of emergency.

A meeting of the executive committee was called in the early afternoon, and the club president, Charles Lanier, a distant relative of the famous poet, laid out the committee's options. They could ship the bodies back to Smyrna and Liverpool, if the families could be located and could afford to pay the charges. They could purchase a burial plot at Evergreen Cemetery in Brunswick.

"Or," Lanier suggested, "we could bury them here on the island in the old du Bignon cemetery."

The vote was unanimous for the latter option. They would try to contact relatives, of course, but they had little hope the families would be able to pay for shipment of the bodies. The club season was nearly over, and it would take weeks to make contacts and arrangements, if it were even possible. The committee decided to hold a brief funeral service in Faith Chapel the next day with interment to be in the old cemetery at the north end of the island. Father Luckie's trip to the island to perform a marriage had already been canceled.

At noon the following day the bodies were brought back to the island by boat in identical simple caskets. Workers loaded them on the back of John Cain's wagon to be transported to Faith Chapel for a brief service.

Maggie had come to the chapel early, while it was still empty, to pray, but she found herself too numb to do anything more than sit in the dark wood pew and stare at the sunlight filtering in colored patterns through the stained glass windows. The window over the altar depicted the birth of the Christ Child. Maggie gazed at the tiny infant and his mother, the three men bearing gifts kneeling before them, the mottled blues and deep rich burgundies making colored designs on the floor of the tiny chapel. The child had no father depicted in the image—like her own baby—no father. No earthly father.

"Oh, Hector, where are you? Why did you go away?" But there were no answers to her question—only silence.

This was to have been their wedding day. Hector had been so happy, as she had been. Now the flowers that were to decorate the wedding chapel had been gathered into funeral wreaths for his grave.

As the chapel began to fill with people, club members and servants alike streamed into the pews. The waiters and kitchen staff served as pallbearers, and some did double duty in the choir. Reverend Boykin, summoned from St. Mark's Episcopal Church in Brunswick, preached a brief sermon about the glory of heaven and the sorrows of earth where loved ones would miss the two young men, "taken untimely in their youth, one ..." He paused and gazed sympathetically toward Maggie. "...almost on the eve of his wedding."

Mrs. Morgan, seated in the pew behind Maggie, leaned forward and squeezed her shoulder. Maggie felt the tears she had tried to hold back begin to flow.

When the service ended, club members paid her their respects, for she was as close to kin as either of the young men had at the service. However, rather than follow on foot behind the coffin-laden wagon, as it made its way for three miles down Riverview Road to the du Bignon cemetery, most members filed back quietly to the clubhouse for an afternoon scotch on the club veranda.

Maggie knew that many of them would refuse to make the long walk, but she had wanted it that way, as it was done in both her and Hector's homelands, where the mourners walked behind the coffins to the burial site. Only those who truly cared about Hector and George had the right to follow their funeral wagon, she thought.

Mr. Grob, though he too knew that few mourners would continue to the graveside, acquiesced to her request, despite the grumbling of some who would have attended the final rites, provided they could come in their carriages. A few of them *did* come by carriage despite her request—Mr. Maurice, Mrs. Morgan, and the four members of the executive committee who were on the island—to stand soberly beside the grave as the minister spoke the final words over the coffins. Only the servants and managerial staff walked slowly behind the bodies in a long, solemn, and silent march that wound its way along the edge of the marshes that lay west of River Road.

The little cemetery enclosed in tabby walls already contained graves of members of the French du Bignon family, who had taken possession of the island in 1792. Three elaborately carved tombstones bore the names of Félicité Riffault, Joseph du Bignon, and Ann Amelia du Bignon, and lay horizontal to the earth, cold gray marble beneath the oaks and cedars hung with Spanish moss.

Maggie stood quietly watching the men lower Hector's coffin into the sandy soil in the rear of the graveyard. From the site she could see the marshes sparkling in the sunlight, remembering the bright promise of the day they had arrived and the foolish innocence and hope she had brought with her. An unbidden tear of bleak uncertainty rushed down her cheek.

For everyone else, the "drowning incident," as it was called in the Brunswick newspaper, ended with the burial. It was time now to get back to the routine of their lives, but for Maggie there was no life—only emptiness.

"You're young," Minnie Clark had assured her at the graveside in a voice that was intended to sound comforting. "There will be time to heal, and you will doubtless meet another young man."

Maggie was horrified. How could anyone even think such a thing? She knew that Minnie only meant to be kind, but such a suggestion seemed absurd, even cruel, to Maggie. She didn't want to meet another young man. She wanted Hector—no one else. She felt a sense of rage rise within her, but Deirdre, sensing her reaction, reached out to her once more, put her arm around Maggie's shoulder and turned her away from Minnie.

"She doesn't mean anything, Maggie. It's just something to say when one can't think of anything else. Let it go."

She knew that Deirdre was right. She only wanted to lash out at Minnie because she could do nothing else.

She did not want to leave the graveside and abandon Hector there alone. She had placed the flowers that were to form her small bridal bouquet on his coffin, though the club had purchased an even larger bouquet to place on the mound of earth that would be left when the coffins were lowered into the earth. When the undertaker tried to remove the bouquet, in order to place it with the other flowers on the mound of earth, Maggie protested.

"Please, leave it where it is. I want *him* to have it." As the casket was lowered into the damp earth, the bouquet of Cherokee roses and orange blossoms remained in its place, to be buried beneath the sandy soil.

One by one the mourners turned back toward the club compound. Among the last to leave were Page and Aleathia Parland, who, with the other workers, had followed the funeral wagon at a solemn and respectful distance.

As they left, Aleathia approached Maggie and touched her arm. "I'm so sorry, Miss Maggie." Maggie managed a nod and a weak smile of thanks.

Finally the only ones remaining were Deirdre and Maggie, who knelt on the soft sand around the grave. The sun was sinking over the marshes, and the golden streaks in the sky were beginning to fade to a soft pink. Deirdre knew they had to start back to the clubhouse, for it was a long walk. She put her hand on her friend's shoulder.

"Come on, Maggie, let's go. You must let him be now. He belongs to God."

Maggie made no resistance as her friend took her arm, helped her rise, and turned her south on River Road. The two women, one with her arm around the other, were small against the vastness of the marshes stretching toward the sunset.

Chapter Ten

MAGGIE HAD ACCEPTED with as much grace as she could muster the condolences of her friends and the few club members and guests who knew of her relationship with Hector. But by dusk, when she and Deirdre arrived back at the clubhouse, she felt a desperate need to be alone, to escape even Deirdre, and let loose all the feelings she had dammed up inside her throughout the day. Her only thought was to find someplace that she could cry, scream if she wanted to, and disturb no one else. There was only one such place on the island—the beach, where the sounds of the sea and wind would absorb her grief.

The crushed shell of the roadway crunched beneath her feet. Its whiteness barely penetrated the gathering darkness, but it was bright enough to keep her from straying toward the woods that lined the path. She stumbled blindly toward the beach, tears stinging her eyes.

Suddenly she sensed a movement among the palmettos to her right. A doe and its fawn raised their heads anxiously and stared in her direction for a long moment before bolting for the safety of the deeper wood. It was their time, and she knew it, for always at dusk deer, wild turkeys, and raccoons emerged boldly from the thick foliage and began to roam the more easily traveled roads and bicycle paths that club laborers had cut through the dense undergrowth and the tangle of palmetto fronds. Night hunting was forbidden, and the woodland creatures were safe from their human predators in these hours of darkness.

The night air was chilly, and she drew her shawl tighter around her and bent her head forward against the blustery winds blowing in from the sea. She had never felt more alone in her life, and she wished she could have reached out to stroke the soft nose of the fleeing doe and put her arm around its tense neck to calm it and to let it know that she meant no harm. She had heard stories about the taming of a deer raised from a tawny fawn, but she had never touched one—not a live one at least. Nonetheless, she knew that the fur around its muzzle was soft, for she had bent to stroke the head of a dead doe that Archibald Maurice had shot only the week before and hung head down, suspended by its hocks, near the taxidermist's shop to have his picture snapped with the animal before Mr. Walbert began his work.

Like Hector, the doe had died unexpectedly, in the prime of its life, in this case for a huntsman's whim and sport. It was so pointless, she thought. The Maurices would not likely eat the venison, which most club members considered wild tasting, despite the chef's best efforts to soak it in vinegar water and parboil it before he roasted it. More often it wound up on the table in the help's dining room, if it was not fed to the hunting dogs. Hector's death at least had been heroic, as he had dived into the surf to rescue his friend George, who would become, in his panic, an agent of death.

A family of raccoons, five in all, scurried across the road in front of Maggie, reminding her of the raccoons, perhaps the same ones, that Hector had frightened with his whoops of joy and shouts of love the evening she had told him about the baby.

When she reached the end of Shell Road, the beach was dark, though the stars were brilliant above and the chilly night was crystal clear. She stumbled through the dimness across the dunes to the spot where she and Hector had once taken refuge from the cold night winds that blew over the sea. The spot where he had wrapped her in his arms and she had leaned back against his shoulder, as they both gazed eastward toward the old world they had left behind forever for the new. Where they had told each other their stories, their hopes, their griefs, their dreams.

She liked to imagine that the winds blew all the way from Ireland, from the lighthouse on Fastnet Rock, from the cliffs of Mohr, even from her father's pastures where as a child she used to breathe the damp salt air while she played around the standing stones, remnants of some ancient Celtic ritual. The sea had always been a comfort, making her feel closer to home, until the day it had swallowed up Hector, leaving her bereft in a world she no longer knew.

She nestled in the shelter of the dune, half-hidden by the waving sea oats, making herself as small as possible, her legs drawn up and her forehead resting on her knees. Her dress of white lawn stood out against the darkness of night. This was to have been their wedding day and this dress her wedding dress. Instead she had worn it to Hector's funeral, covered by a borrowed black shawl. Grateful for the restless sea that muffled the sounds of her ire and mourning, she clutched the shawl tightly about her shoulders.

She didn't know how long she had raged unseen and unheard at the sea that had taken Hector's life. By now the quarter moon had risen midway in the sky, pouring its sliver of molten silver over the water and beckoning her forward. How easy it would be just to walk across the sand, into the sea, to follow that thin pathway of light into oblivion. The tide was coming in, and the narrow strip of bleak light led to the far horizon.

She thought of the night of the full, golden moon when she and Hector had wrapped themselves together for warmth, when they had become as one flesh. The wide path the moon cast on the sea that night was a highway they could have followed side by side to their homelands to the east. Now the sea looked dark and threatening, except for the narrow, almost sinister, argentine pathway that ran restlessly across the water. How long ago it now seemed—

that splendid night. Now she shivered with cold and desperate loneliness. There were not enough tears to empty out her grief.

"Maggie, is that you?" a voice behind her said.

"Maggie?" It spoke again. It was a young man's voice.

She lifted her head and peered from beneath swollen eyelids. "Yes, sir." He was carrying a lantern, which he raised to see her face. "May I help you, sir?" Hers was an automatic response, for when she heard that aristocratic New York accent, she knew that it belonged to someone she had come to serve.

"May I sit down?" he asked gently, lowering himself to the sand beside her without waiting for a response.

"Yes, sir. Of course, sir."

She felt embarrassed to have been found like this, dissolved in personal emotions, by her betters. Her training from Mr. Falk and Mrs. Clark had been very clear on that point. No matter what she felt, she was never to show it. Whatever her reactions to situations, she was never to have a personal response. But suddenly she no longer cared what anyone thought. She was a woman with pain in her heart, and the world could think whatever it wanted. She needed to weep, though she had tried to keep her grief private.

She recognized the young man. It was David Barrett, who had registered at the club as a guest of Frederic Baker. He was staying in the clubhouse, because the Bakers were not on the island, and their house, Solterra, was closed for the rest of the season. She had cleaned his room during his two weeks on the island, and she knew him to be a tidy young man who, like her, enjoyed reading poetry. She had noticed books of Wordsworth and Keats lying on the nightstand in his room.

He always seemed a bit sad to her and he tended to keep to himself, except for his friendship with a willowy blond man whose name she did not know. She had seen them walking together beneath the live oak trees, playing tennis, and bicycling occasionally beyond the limits of the club compound. And once, after tapping lightly on the door as she had been instructed to do and hearing no response, she had quietly let herself into the room. There she had seen the two still sleeping, sprawled out like little boys, the bedclothes rumpled as though they had had a restless night. She had quietly let herself out again and waited until she saw them leave, tennis racquets in their hands, before she went in again to clean Mr. Barrett's room.

"Maggie," the young man said quietly, "I was so sorry about Hector and George. I know what Hector must have meant to you."

Tears welled up in her eyes and spilled over the rims. She knew that she did not cry prettily like the young ladies of his class, the delicate beauties he saw every night in the club dining room and at the cotillions he no doubt attended in New York. She knew that her face was blotchy and her eyes puffy. And she could hardly breathe.

"Oh, sir ... Hector ... I ... we—" It was all that she could say before the tears overwhelmed her.

"Now, now, dear girl," he said, patting her awkwardly on the shoulder. "Try to be strong."

"I'm sorry, sir." She tried to catch her breath. "I can't help—" she sobbed, feeling herself lose control once again.

He put his arm around her shoulder and held her gently. "Oh, Maggie, I'm so sorry for you. I saw you leave the clubhouse a while back, and when you didn't come back, I came looking for you. I was a bit worried. I know that you were very fond of him. I've seen the two of you together. Your affections for each other were so obvious. I heard you were going to be married."

His strong arm around her shoulder and the warmth of his hand on her back somehow made her feel better, calmer, as though the world might not end after all. She did not draw away from his embrace, as she knew she should have, for she found comfort there. His lantern made a golden circle that encompassed the two of them and for a time shut out the darkness and the lure of the silver moon. It made her think of the way her brother Brendan used to comfort her when she fell and scraped her knee.

They sat together for a long time, and finally she rested her head on his shoulder.

"I know what it's like to lose someone you love, Maggie. There was someone once …" His voice trailed off. "But life reasserts itself again. It always does, I suppose, one way or another." He seemed to speak from a depth and distance that belied his years. She listened to his words as though they came from far away, and she would one day recollect them as though they were from a dream.

"Grief is the price we pay for love," he said. "It always ends in grief and loss. There seems to be no other way."

She heard a painful wisdom but also bitterness in his words and wondered where it came from, what sorrow he might have known, this handsome young man who seemed to have everything.

"You were not here in past seasons, were you?" he asked. She shook her head.

"And you never met Mr. and Mrs. Struthers, did you? But they prove my point. They had loved each other since they were children together in Philadelphia—a handsome couple—and God granted them many years of happiness. But when she died last winter, he grieved himself to death and died less than a month later. It said so, right in his obituary: 'He died of grief.' It is always grief that wins out in the end—not love. But it never stops the best of us from loving, because it's always worth the pain," he said wistfully. After a long pause, he said gently, "I don't suppose any of that is much consolation to you."

"Oh, yes, sir," she replied automatically. "It is consolation." She groped for words to interpret what he had said. "It means that we are all in this life together, and that we're not all alone in our sorrow, and that in itself is some comfort."

He looked at her suddenly and drew back. She felt instantly that she had overstepped her bounds. His kindness was, after all, merely the *noblesse oblige* of his class, and she had no right to share her own feelings with him.

"Will you be all right, Maggie?" he asked earnestly, searching her eyes for his answer. "You won't do anything foolish, will you?"

She shook her head in an effort to reassure him, but she knew that she would not be all right. That her predicament went beyond the death of Hector to her own situation. What would she do? Where would she go? It all seemed so hopeless now. Perhaps if he had not come to her just at that moment, she might have been tempted to walk into the sea. But he was here, and he had stopped her. He seemed to be peering into her soul as he asked those questions, knowing what was in her heart. She covered her face with her hands.

"What is it, dear girl? Can I help in some way?"

"Oh, Mr. Barrett, how can I ... What can I ...?" Her voice hesitated. Then the words came in an unforeseen rush. "I'm with child." She blurted them out, wishing instantly that she could recall them.

What must he think of her? That she was a foolish, easy girl who had no self control. But it was not like that at all. She had loved Hector so, and she knew that he loved her. She was not sorry. She would never be sorry that she had given herself to him wholly or that she had some part of him growing within her. How could she have even thought of drowning herself and their child? The memory of their night together, on this very spot, still made her tremble. It had been her most complete and perfect moment, when she felt for the first and perhaps only time in her life that she had become one with another and the universe made sense.

"Well, that *is* a problem, isn't it?" he said, with a tinge of embarrassment in his voice. He hesitated a moment and then said, "Poor thing, but you mustn't despair. There are places that will look after you until after your confinement. I know of such a place in New York, if you'll be going back?" His words held the question, and she nodded wearily. "It was one of my mother's favorite charities," he said, "and my father has continued to support it since her death. Here, I'll give you the address."

Charities. She flinched at the word. She had come from a long line of proud Irish people, determined, even in the face of poverty and famine in the years when the potato crop had failed, to earn their own way, never to live off the charity of others. But what choice did she have? She had no family here to humiliate by her actions. Even Eleanor and Kate had by now left New York.

"And when you're ready, come to see me, and I'll help you find work and a place to live."

The sound of the sea was more gentle now, almost calming with its regular rhythms. He took a calling card and a pen from his pocket and scribbled on its back.

"There," he said firmly, "here's my card with my address on the front, and I've written the address of the place that can care for you in your confinement on the back. I'll help you all I can. I'll even make a place for you in my family's household, if necessary." She smiled at him weakly but gratefully.

"As for me, I'm leaving in the morning for New York. But I'll only be there a few days. I have to make a quick trip after that for my father to settle a financial matter—but I'll be back in a few weeks, by the end of April at the latest. If you need anything before your baby comes, you can find me at this address.

"In any case, once the child is born, I want you to come and see me. Let me know you're all right. You'll need a job, and there'll be a place for you in the Barrett household. And for the baby too. That I promise." She heard strength and truth and kindness in his voice.

He stood up and held out his hand. "Now let's get you back to the clubhouse. This night air is really chilly, and if there's one thing I can't bear in the spring, it's cold and damp sea air."

He smiled at her and took her hand in his. He pulled her to her feet, and gave her his arm. She felt like a lady, as they walked down Shell Road back toward the clubhouse, and some of the darkness had lifted from her heart. There was no chance of meeting anyone at this hour on the dark road, but she watched the approaching shadows carefully, ready to withdraw her hand from his sleeve, should there be an unexpected encounter with a club member or servant. Had anyone seen them together like this, she was sure she would be fired on the spot. Neither Mr. Falk nor Mrs. Clark would have stood for it. At the moment, however, she was too exhausted to care.

True to his word, young Mr. Barrett left on the early morning launch for Brunswick. Maggie watched from the window of her room, as the *Jekyl Island* pulled away from the dock. Strange, she thought, how she had confided her situation to no one among her own friends, only to David Barrett and Aleathia Parland, both of whom lived in different worlds but who had shown her only kindness. She had once thought of confiding in Minnie Clark, who seemed able to handle any situation, but she was afraid. She would need references in the future. As friendly as Minnie had been, she wasn't sure the head housekeeper would understand, particularly remembering her comments at the graveside. No, she must tell no one else.

When she went to clean Mr. Barrett's room, Maggie found an envelope with her name on it perched on his dresser, where she could not miss it. Inside was thirty dollars, a tiny gold ring on a thin gold chain, and a note.

Dear Maggie,

This ring is for the baby. It was given to me by my grandmother when I was a tot. I was saving it for my son, but I know now that I will never have a son of my own. I have worn it around my neck for years for luck. I want you to have it. Perhaps it will bring your baby luck as well. I look forward to seeing you again in New York. Take care of yourself, and God be with you.

Yours sincerely,
David Barrett

Maggie held the little ring in her hand, then slipped the chain around her own neck to keep for her child. She would treasure it always. She put the thirty dollars, which she knew she would need, in her pocket, to be packed away later in her duffel bag. She knew she would never forget David Barrett and his generosity.

The few remaining days of the club season passed quickly. Maggie's nausea, which she had begun to feel only sporadically, had disappeared altogether. The fresh air of the beach, where she took long, solitary walks during her afternoon hours of free time, made her feel much better. The weather had turned warm again, and the sunlight felt good on her back. She had never known how physical grief could be, but there was an ache between her ribs she had never felt before and hoped she would never feel again. She tried to control her pain for the sake of her unborn child.

There were still times when the lure of the siren sea was great. It seemed an easy solution and its call was compelling. But the thought of the child in her womb—Hector's child—held her back, calmed her, gave her a reason to go on. Having no one to talk to most of the time was the hardest part of all. But she told the seagulls and the raccoons, shouted her story to the winds, wrote copiously in her journal, and kept the secret in her heart from human ears.

Once Aleathia Parland had waited for her again outside the club laundry.

"Are you all right, chile?" she asked sympathetically. "You lookin' a little peaked."

"I'm fine, thank you, Aleathia. I just miss Hector."

Aleathia nodded. "I know, honey. I been thinkin' 'bout you. You got a place to go when you go back to New York?"

"I have an address where the baby can be born. After that I'm not sure, but I think there is someone who will give me a position, someone who knows the situation."

"That's a blessing." Aleathia smiled. "You let me know if Page and me ... if we can help in any way, y'hear?"

Maggie nodded and squeezed her hand. She was a good woman, kind and discreet. Maggie would always regard her as a friend.

Maggie threw herself into her duties to the extent that she was coming to be known as the most reliable and diligent chambermaid at the club. Work was a refuge, a haven, for when she was changing bed linens and dusting tables, it was easy to forget herself. She could always find enough work to do, for the clubhouse was filled to capacity from mid-March until just before Easter, by which time most New Yorkers liked to be back in New York for the spring social season.

Only Mrs. Morgan, professing to be stunned by the suddenness of her waiter's death, had left the day after Hector's burial. She had announced her intentions following an incident in the dining room the morning after Hector's burial. Paulo, who had been assigned to take over Hector's tables in the dining room, served Mrs. Morgan her breakfast omelet.

She looked at it with disgust. "Young man, this is not the way I like it cooked. It's much too brown," she announced. "Hector would have known."

"Yes, madam," Paulo said, picking up the omelet and taking it back to the kitchen. He knew that it was simply Mrs. Morgan's way of saying, "I miss Hector." He missed him too and was having to do extra work in his absence, but she wasn't making it any easier.

That afternoon Mrs. Morgan expressed her regrets to Mr. Grob, who was to make her arrangements to return to New York. Jekyl had become too depressing for her, she told him, and she simply couldn't tolerate the abominable service in the dining room. "It's all *sooo* terrible," she said. "Hector was so young and handsome. And his service was impeccable."

Mr. Grob nodded obligingly and made arrangements to have her private train car ready to depart on the afternoon train out of Brunswick.

Minnie Clark assigned the cleaning of the Morgan apartment to Maggie, who accepted the extra work with gratitude. Climbing the stairs to the top floor of the large gray building known as the Sans Souci, which stood next to the clubhouse, Maggie set to work with her usual determination. Only once, when she went out on the balcony to shake out an eiderdown, did she almost succumb to tears. The shock of the beauty and scope of the marshes flooded her with memories of the day she had arrived, the day she had first spoken with Hector. The sight was too much for her laden heart. She turned her back to the view and resumed her work, shaking off her memories with the dust as best she could.

Finally, just before Easter, the clubhouse, the Sans Souci, and the cottages that dotted the club compound emptied out, as preparations began for the club's closing. Like the other chambermaids, in a final flurry of activity, Maggie cleaned and dusted the rooms in her charge one last time, plumping the feather pillows and covering all the furniture with white sheets.

The season was over. Club members had already returned to New York, and the seasonal employees, their duties done, boarded the *Jekyl Island* launch one last time, to be transported to Brunswick, where the Mallory steamer waited to take them north again.

Somehow, on the island her pregnancy had seemed almost a dream, not quite real. In the cold of New York, however, she would have to confront its reality. She would have to confess her dilemma to someone, though perhaps it would be easier with strangers. Her one comfort was the check that Mr. Grob had issued to her, as to all the other chambermaids, early this morning for her season's services. It was safely tucked inside her notebook, carefully placed in the bottom of her duffel bag, along with the gold ring and the thirty dollars David Barrett had left her.

She had no intention of letting the bag out of her sight during the entire voyage. The money she had earned, the tips that munificent club members had left for her on the dressers of their rooms when they departed, and even the ten-dollar gold piece that Mrs. Morgan had given to Hector and which

Mr. Grob had pressed into her hand that morning, would have to tide her over until after her baby came.

Although her pregnancy had not begun to show, she knew that she would be unable to accept another domestic position in the short time she had left before the world would be able to discern her condition. She had always planned to be frugal and try to put some of her earnings away toward her father's passage, if not this year, then perhaps next. But the baby changed everything. It would need so many things.

Tucked inside her notebook were the addresses that David Barrett had given her that night on the beach, both his own and that of the charitable institution that he said would house her during her confinement. She must go there as soon as possible when she reached New York to see what arrangements could be made. It was a task she dreaded. Asking for charity, for assistance, for protection during this time was difficult, and she knew it would humiliate her father to know that it was necessary, perhaps even more than her pregnancy would shame him.

Nevertheless, she felt fiercely protective of her unborn child, and the better part of her was happy to have this life within her as an extension of her love for Hector. The baby would never suffer for her sins, if that's what they were. Somehow she would make certain that the child had a good home and advantages, even if she had to slave for the rest of her life in a rich man's house.

Her baby, hers and Hector's, would be an American. He or she would have the opportunities that all Americans enjoyed, and, in the end, Maggie knew that her child would make her father, Daniel O'Brien, proud. Since the child would be born in America, as she had once reminded Hector, if it was a boy, he would even have the right to be president some day. Although she tried in her heart to think of the baby as "he" or "she," somehow she knew in her heart already that it would be a boy. Perhaps he would have Hector's dark compelling eyes and irresistible smile.

The trip north was on the whole uneventful, though the steamer rocked mightily in a spring storm off the Carolina coast during their first night at sea. Maggie felt her old nausea return and spent much of the first leg of the trip in her bunk, trying not to be sick. Even when the weather grew calm again, she still had to confront the worst part of all—the uncertainty that awaited her in New York.

Chapter Eleven

19 APRIL 1912 NEW YORK CITY

THE STEAMER REACHED NEW YORK harbor none too soon for Maggie. She was glad to be off the ocean, for, in addition to the storm, when they had docked in Wilmington two days earlier they heard the awful news about the sinking of the *Titanic*. Not only had the sea taken Hector, it had swallowed up all those other men, women, and even children as well. It made everyone on the steamer apprehensive and gloomy for the rest of the voyage. She was glad to be back on dry land.

Maggie clung to Deirdre at the dock, reluctant to say goodbye even though Deirdre's cousin Michael was waiting for her.

"You will keep in touch, won't you, Maggie? And let me know how you're doing?"

"I will, Deirdre. That I will," Maggie assured her, with a final hug and a wave as her friend rushed to meet her cousin.

She envied Deirdre's having someone to take her home. She herself would have to find a hotel until she could make other arrangements. *How I dread the next few days,* she thought, shifting her bag to her right hand. She walked toward Whitehall Street at the end of the pier, distracted by her thoughts and hardly noticing her surroundings. What, she wondered, would be the best possibility within her budget and her limited knowledge of New York hotels?

Suddenly she sensed a movement at the end of the wharf and, looking up, she saw the waving hand and the familiar face of Stuart O'Neil. He rushed forward to take her bag.

"Stuart, what are you doing here?" she asked.

"I told you I'd be here when you got back," he said simply. Although she was immensely glad to see him and even relieved to have someone waiting for her, she was also a bit annoyed at his presumptuousness in meeting her steamer.

"You look a little pale," he said, peering at her closely.

"We had rough weather. And I was seasick during the trip."

"I'm glad you're here safely." He squeezed her arm. "You heard about the *Titanic*, I guess?"

She nodded, sick at heart and wishing he hadn't reminded her about the terrible tragedy that she had tried not to think about while they were still at sea.

"Where do you plan to stay now that your cousins have left New York?" he asked.

"Right now I just hope to find an inexpensive hotel and have a good hot bath."

"I thought you might be needing a room, so I took the liberty of booking one for you at a boarding house not too far from where you lived on Barrow Street. I thought you might prefer that area since you already know it."

A part of her was glad to know that she had a place to go, but another part was annoyed that he had presumed to make her arrangements. She saw it as a form of possessiveness that she had no intention of accepting. "You shouldn't have done that, Stuart. How did you know that I hadn't already booked something?"

"We could always cancel one of them," he said practically.

"I suppose so," she said, though she was uncomfortable with his use of the plural "we."

He had a carriage waiting for them on Whitehall Street. Finally, settling beside him in the vehicle, Maggie relaxed a bit and asked, "How was Kate and Patrick's wedding? Did you go? Tell me all about it." She knew it was a question she had to ask, though it was painful to think of any wedding at all just now.

"Yes, I went. It was simple and very beautiful. Kate never looked better, and Patrick was one happy fellow. I saw them all off at the railroad station when they caught the train to St. Louis. Your cousin Eleanor asked me to say goodbye for her."

"How did you know, by the way, which steamer I'd be on?" Maggie asked, for it had suddenly occurred to her that she had not notified him of her arrival.

He looked at her a bit sheepishly. "Maggie, I've met every steamer from Brunswick for the past two days. I knew you'd be home about a week or so after Easter."

"You shouldn't have done that," she said, with some exasperation. "Please don't expect anything from me. I can't love you the way you want."

"I don't expect anything. I just wanted to be here for you." He looked crestfallen, and she felt guilty for scolding him.

The boarding house he had selected was a rare find. The rate, including breakfast and dinner, was only a dollar and a half a day, inexpensive for New York, and the room was spacious and clean, tastefully, though not lavishly furnished. Mrs. Cavanaugh, who ran, it was a pleasant elderly lady, in her late sixties perhaps, and she seemed genuinely glad to have Maggie there.

"How long will you be staying with us, Miss O'Brien?" she asked.

"I'm not sure just now. A lot of things are uncertain. May I just say a minimum of a week or two for now? I should know more in a day or so." She knew that she could not afford much longer than that without having a job, even at these prices, and at this point she did not know what lay ahead.

The very next day she took out the card that David Barrett had given her. He had scribbled the name and address of Messiah House, as it was called, and the address was on the other side of Manhattan. She thought it best to deal with the matter as soon as possible and get it behind her. Otherwise she would live much of her life for the coming months in a state of uncertainty.

She longed for her mother just now, but feared she might have been deeply disappointed in her daughter. Still, somehow, she thought her mother might understand under the circumstances. Her mother had always prayed for young girls who got into trouble in Doolin and who sometimes came to her for help or advice. She would have understood how much Maggie loved Hector and she would have mourned the dreadful accident that took him from her forever.

Maggie dressed carefully, wanting to appear neat and properly attired when she went to Messiah House. How does one go to a perfect stranger and tell the person what she knew she must? At least she wanted to know that she looked like a good, Christian girl.

The carriage that took her across town stopped in front of a three-storied structure with a gothic-looking facade. Nothing seemed inviting about the place. But Maggie steeled herself for what lay ahead and, chin high, walked for the first time into the place that might become her home for many months.

A matronly-looking woman sat behind a small desk in the main foyer of the building. "Yes, miss?" she asked.

"I need to talk with someone."

"May I know the nature of your business so that I can point you to the right office?"

Maggie could feel her face flushing, though the woman had a kindly face.

"I … need to talk about the possibility of coming here for my confinement," she said, finding the words she was so desperately praying for.

"I see," said the woman in a neutral tone. "That would be Mrs. Davenport, our supervisor." She picked up a telephone receiver from the instrument on her desk.

"Mrs. Davenport," she asked, "Can you see a young lady who is here in need of assistance?" There was a brief silence. "Oh, I'd say three or four months at most ... thank you. Right away."

Maggie listened intently, wishing that she could hear both sides of the conversation.

"Her office is the third door on the left. She asked me to send you right down."

Maggie thanked her and headed down the ill-lit corridor. The third door on the left, however, opened into a sunny, cheerful office, where an attractive, middle-aged woman sat behind a large oak desk. Maggie paused for a minute, taking it all in, for she had never seen a female executive before. Papers were spread out before her, and stacks of manila folders were on the sideboard behind her desk. She was clearly a woman with much work to do, but looked efficient enough to do it all.

She stood up, walked around the desk and held out her hand. "I'm Susan Davenport. And you?"

"My name's Maggie O'Brien."

"And how did you find out about Messiah House, may I ask?"

"A young gentleman told me. He said it was one of his mother's favorite charities."

"We have many people, many women among them, who are very generous toward Messiah House. Do you know her name?"

"A Mrs. Barrett."

"Oh, yes, Lydia Barrett. We lost her a few years ago, unfortunately. She died of a sudden stroke. God rest her soul. Her husband has continued some of her benefactions in her memory, I'm happy to say. She was a kind and generous lady, and I'm sure she is missed by many." She paused briefly, then looked intently at Maggie. "I understand that you're in need of assistance. For a confinement, I take it?"

"Yes, ma'am." Maggie could feel the blood rising to her face.

"Was the young Mr. Barrett the father, may I ask?"

"Oh, no. He was just someone who offered to help. The father ... we were about to be married, and he was drowned ... We were about to be married," she repeated.

"Yes, of course," said Mrs. Davenport, as though she had heard such stories many times before. "But the past is past, and now we must decide what is best for you and your baby. Do you plan to keep it?"

Maggie was startled by the question. "Certainly!"

"There's no possibility you might change your mind?"

"No, no possibility."

"I only ask because we have many young childless couples who come to us looking for babies to adopt. Sometimes they are willing to help with the support of the mother, if they know the baby is to be theirs."

"No, I could never give up my baby. If that is what I must do to find help here, then I have come to the wrong place." Maggie was already starting to rise.

"Please, Miss O'Brien, that is not a condition of our assistance. It's merely a question I put to all the young mothers-to-be. Many are grateful to know that their babies will go to a good home, for it is difficult in New York for a young unmarried woman to support herself and a baby."

"I'll find a way," Maggie said with determination.

"Let me offer you an option for the immediate future. We are a bit shorthanded in the kitchen at the moment. Do you think you might find it possible to come here now, while you are still able to work? The wages would be very small, I'm afraid, a pittance really, but it would provide you lodging and board—a place to live during these next few months. Only as long as you are able, of course," she added hastily.

"You may stay here under the same conditions for up to three months after the baby comes. After that, you will need to make other arrangements."

"Yes, that would work out very well for me. I think that after the baby comes I will have a position waiting for me. But it might be good to stay here a few months, at least until the baby is sleeping through the night. I wouldn't want to disturb the household."

"We're accustomed to all that here, and we have a nursery where you can leave the child during the day while you work. Are we agreed then?"

Maggie nodded eagerly.

"When would you like to move in?" Susan Davenport seemed to be encouraging her to come as soon as possible.

"I've just taken a room in a boarding house, and I've told the lady who runs it that I will be there a minimum of a week or two. Would it be possible for me to move in a week from Saturday?" That would allow her to honor her commitment to Mrs. Cavanaugh.

"That will be fine, though the sooner the better. We are really short-handed just now. One more thing. We are a religious house, and we expect the women who come here to attend the Sunday service. Will that be your practice?"

"Yes, of course," said Maggie, though she wondered what would happen to a Jewish girl who presented herself at Messiah House. Did they only accept Christians? But for her it was a wonderful arrangement, one that she accepted gratefully.

When she went back to Mrs. Cavanaugh's boarding house, she spoke immediately to the proprietor about her plans to leave in eight days. Mrs. Cavanaugh appeared to be disappointed that she would not stay longer, though she reluctantly agreed to the arrangement, requesting that she pay the twelve dollars in advance for the days she would be in the house.

Although Maggie felt guilty about doing so, as kind as he had been to her, she would not tell Stuart O'Neil where she was going. She decided, in fact, not to tell him at all that she planned to leave Mrs. Cavanaugh's boarding house. It would require too many explanations. She could write him a letter afterwards, without a return address, thanking him for all he had done to help her.

He came by to see her only twice while she was there, as though fearful that she would be annoyed at his coming more often. Each time he brought her the latest news, which he always heard from the people he met on his beat.

They always seemed to know more than the newspapers, and they loved to talk about what was happening in New York and the world beyond.

Stuart hoped to interest her in something they might do together. Each time she made some excuse and refused even to go walking with him. Once he invited her to go to a picture show, where a new film called *Far From Erin's Isle*, which he was eager to see, was playing. She had never been to a picture show in her life, but, despite her sincere desire to see a film, she resisted the temptation. She did not want to encourage Stuart, for she feared he would only be hurt in the end.

On May 3, Maggie packed her duffel bag once more, said farewell to Mrs. Cavanaugh, and hailed a carriage to take her to Messiah House, dropping out of the life of Stuart O'Neil with no explanation.

"Should I forward any mail?" Mrs. Cavanaugh had asked, fishing for an address.

"I don't expect any mail," Maggie said simply, nodding her goodbye as she closed the door behind her. She had written to her father and sent the new address at the same time she had told him about Hector's death. She did not mention her pregnancy.

She knew that Stuart would be disappointed and that, despite what he said, he hoped that someday, because of his devotion, she would come to love him as he loved her. She wrote to him as well a letter designed to leave him with no illusions.

Dear Stuart,

I have deliberately departed Mrs. Cavanaugh's without leaving an address, and although I thank you for all you have done for me and for caring about me when I most needed it, I do not deserve your kindness. Someday, perhaps, our paths may cross again. For now please do not try to find me.

I remain, yours sincerely,

Maggie O'Brien

She had tried to make the letter friendly but distant as well, in order not to encourage his romantic fantasies. She knew he would wonder about her motives, but she hoped he would just think she wanted to stand on her own.

Although she missed the news that Stuart often brought to her from his encounters in the streets, she was not totally cut off from the news of the world. Messiah House had a reading room on the second floor, and Susan Davenport saw to it that it was well supplied with uplifting texts, copies of the Bible, religious tracts, and even the latest newspapers.

It was there that Maggie learned of the women's march down Fifth Avenue on May 10 as part of the growing suffrage movement. She thought that in one of the photographs she recognized the face of Deirdre, but the photograph was so grainy that she was not sure. She would like to have joined the march herself, for she had never understood why women, especially those with keen minds, were not allowed to vote, when any male dullard could do so. She knew that she could not vote in any case because she was not yet a citizen. But someday she would be.

For the moment, however, she had no inclination to display herself to the world. Her condition was still not really evident to anyone who did not know her, but she was beginning to notice that her clothes were too tight and she had already let out the seams as far as she could.

The drab-looking uniform they gave her to wear in the Messiah House kitchen was loose-fitting and shapeless to accommodate workers in various stages of pregnancy. Despite its lack of fashion, it was the most comfortable outfit she had, and she found herself spending more and more of her time wearing it.

Most of the women Maggie met at Messiah House were young, unmarried, and desperate. All of them were grateful for the respite and acceptance they found there, though some were bitter to have been abandoned by their baby's father. One of the kitchen workers, a girl named Lucy, who was only fifteen, had decided to give up her baby for adoption. Tears ran unchecked down her cheeks as she told Maggie about her decision.

"What choice do I have?" Lucy asked. "You're so lucky to have a job waiting where they will let you bring the baby. But nobody would hire me."

Maggie learned that Lucy had been raped by a business acquaintance of her father, an older man who accepted no responsibility for his actions and who made it seem all her fault.

"Papa blamed me for what happened and threw me out on the streets," Lucy told her with shame in her eyes. "I was a good girl, and I couldn't make him stop when ... you know ... when it happened." By now Lucy was crying quietly. "I miss my family," she said, as Maggie took her into her arms.

Although Lucy's mother came to see her every Thursday afternoon, she refused to take the girl home for fear of her husband's wrath. But she never left without telling Lucy that, with God's help, everything would be all right. It was hard to see how, but Maggie envied Lucy her mother's arms around her, comforting her, loving her.

For a few weeks a woman named Claire had the bunk next to Maggie's in the women's dormitory. Claire was married, but her husband had beaten her so often that she was afraid her baby would be born deformed in some hideous way, for the blows had not diminished with her pregnancy. Her face bore the evidence of his repeated thrashings in the form of scars and discolored flesh.

When Claire lost her baby after only two weeks at Messiah House, she begged to be allowed to remain. She had gone to the police before she came there, but they only shrugged it off as a domestic dispute, telling her there was nothing they could do. She had nowhere else to go, she said. Because Messiah House's mission was to care only for pregnant women and their children, Susan Davenport had no choice but to send her away. But she slipped money in the woman's pocket, enough to pay for her train fare to the city where her sister lived.

Maggie hugged Claire, who left, weeping, on a rainy afternoon. And

Maggie noticed a definite slump in Mrs. Davenport's shoulders for several hours after Claire had departed.

So many tragic stories unfolded at Messiah House, stories of indignities that women experienced at the hands of men who wielded power over them—supervisors, bosses, even fathers, husbands, and brothers. Maggie felt very blessed in her life not to have suffered what so many of them had endured. She heard of the beatings, of days when her new friends had been abused, locked in closets, and mauled at the hands of stronger men. Maggie's seemed a happy tale by comparison. At least she had a caring family and had experienced joy with a man who had loved her. No one had ever beaten her in her life or been cruel to her in any way.

Watching the other women come and go, Maggie realized that her situation could have been infinitely worse than it was. The gentleness of Hector and the kindness of such people as Aleathia Parland and David Barrett made her want to believe in the essential goodness of humanity. But the stories she heard from her new friends at Messiah House gave her reason to wonder about the fundamental cruelty of the world.

She found in the women here a renewal of her own strength and courage. Despite their hardships, few of them seemed ready to give up. Those whose spirits had not been crushed along with their bodies seemed to emerge from their experiences stronger and more determined to survive. Maggie had no doubt that some day these very women would be able to vote. Then perhaps things would change. The suffrage movement grew stronger with every day, and she knew that eventually she would become a citizen and join their numbers. She only prayed that, when given the right that men took for granted, women would help to change the laws to protect others like themselves.

The months at Messiah House went by more quickly than Maggie had anticipated, and she was surprised to realize that she was actually enjoying them. Her belly grew, but still she continued to work in the kitchen. Finally, in the first week of her eighth month, Susan Davenport called her into the office.

"Maggie, you have done a fine job for us. However, it's time we got you off your feet. I'm relieving you of kitchen duty as of today. Would you be willing to help out for a few weeks in the nursery? No heavy duties, of course, and only with the smaller infants. About all I'll ask of you is to rock the babies who cry and to perhaps change a diaper or two. It will be good experience for you." She smiled at Maggie.

Maggie was thrilled to be put in the nursery. There were older children at Messiah House as well, for oftentimes babies were brought back by mothers who could no longer care for them. Young couples only seemed to want to adopt newborns, but the house kept children up to three years old. At the age of three, if no one had adopted them, they were placed in the state's care, for Messiah House had no facilities to provide for older children. But someone usually wanted the smallest ones, at least for a while.

Maggie was amazed at the differences in the personalities of the babies, only a few weeks old. Some were colicky and demanding. Others were placid and somnolent. A few of the older babies, not yet placed, or whose mothers had elected to remain the full three months past confinement to which they could lay claim if necessary, were smiling and cuddly. It made Maggie eager for her own baby, though it seemed it would never come.

The final weeks dragged by. Finally, on November 20, Maggie awakened early with unaccustomed cramps in her abdomen. She got up to get ready for breakfast, and, as she was walking down the hallway to the bathroom, her water broke. She felt a rush of excitement as her contractions began in earnest.

She was one of the lucky ones. Her labor and delivery only took six hours from beginning to end, and at two p.m., the nurse placed her little boy in her arms. Like all new mothers, she unwrapped him from head to toe—Daniel Hector O'Brien—to count his fingers and toes. She had named him for her father and Hector. He was the most beautiful thing she had ever seen. And she had never been so happy in her life, except for that star-strewn night he was conceived.

She took to motherhood as though she had been born to the role. From the first moment she held Danny in her arms, she knew that her life would never be the same. She memorized every golden hair, every eyelash, every detail of his tiny body. He became from the moment of his birth her reason for living, and she knew that her purpose in life had been to bring this perfect child into the world.

He seemed to respond by recognizing her instantly as his mother, nestling contentedly in her arms while she sang to him the Irish lullabies her own mother had sung to her as a child. He watched her intently as she read to him the works of the American poets she had come to love, Emily Dickinson and Walt Whitman, even the beautiful poem of Sidney Lanier that had so moved her when she saw the Marshes of Glynn. Even though she knew he could not understand her words, Danny's little eyes seemed to sparkle at every line, following her voice and her expression.

Soon he began to smile in response. His smiles were her daily reward, and when he began to gurgle and coo at the sound of her words, she felt as though she were listening to the most amazing poetry the world had ever created— the contented sounds of her son, her only joy.

But she knew that her time at Messiah House would soon be over and that her world would change in ways she could not foresee.

Chapter Twelve

ON A COLD MID-FEBRUARY MORNING, Maggie stood in front of the imposing house on Fifth Avenue gazing up in awe. She was not sure whether she should go around to the service entrance or directly to the front door since she wanted to see the young master. She kissed her son on the cheek and shifted him to her hip for support, while she fumbled in her pocket for David Barrett's card to verify once more the address.

Yes, she thought, *this is it.* It looked very formidable with its Italian Renaissance facade, its heavy dark green door, almost black, and its brass lion's head knocker. Since it was Mr. Barrett she had come to see and not one of the servants, she thought it best to try first at the front entrance. If they would not let her in here, she would go to the service entrance.

Mustering up all her courage, she climbed the stone steps and raised the heavy knocker, tapping it twice. Within seconds the door swung open, and a tall dignified-looking man about fifty stood looking down at her. "Yes, madam?" He sounded unsure of her status. "May I help you?"

"I'm here to see Mr. Barrett," she said.

"Is Mr. Barrett expecting you, madam?" he asked, looking puzzled.

"Well, no, I mean, yes, but not at any particular time. You see, he told me to come and see him. He gave me this card." She held out the card to the man, who peered at it closely and gave her a strange look.

"Mr. *David* Barrett, madam?"

"Yes, that's it, Mr. David Barrett," she nodded hopefully. "Please tell him that Maggie from Jekyl Island is waiting to see him."

"Maggie from Jekyl Island," he repeated dutifully, nodding slowly. "Please wait here for a moment, madam." He did not invite her in but instead closed the door again. Maggie bounced Danny in her arms to keep them both warm. The sight of his face warmed the wintry chill of the wind.

"Well, Danny, here we are. This may be your new home," she told him. He was gazing earnestly at her, with the innocent sobriety of which only babies are capable, but at the sound of her voice, he broke into a responsive smile. His cheeks were aflame with the cold, though the rest of him was snugly wrapped in a warm blanket and his head covered with a knitted cap that the Messiah Home had given her. She would never forget the kindness they had shown her, with the matron giving her a five-dollar bill on her departure.

After a two-minute wait in the icy wind, the door swung open again. "Beg pardon to keep you waiting, madam. Mr. Barrett will see you in the library."

"Thank you very much," said Maggie, stepping through the doorway onto a dark crimson oriental rug and into a corridor of mahogany wood and maroon damask wallpaper. "The library is here, madam." The butler gestured to his left. "Please have a seat. Mr. Barrett will be down in a moment." He waited until she had entered the room and closed the heavy pocket door behind her.

She sat gingerly on the edge of a Queen Anne sofa near the fireplace. The cheery blaze in the grate warmed her and made her feel more at home in this alien world. She thought longingly of the peat fires in her parents' home in Ireland and how cozy they made her feel following an afternoon of playing in the pastures or helping her father and Brendan in the fields. Of course, she had not come home to such luxury or grandeur, but the house had always been welcoming, and her mother had always had a pot of stew or a teapot simmering on the stove.

Danny was beginning to fidget in her arms, and she wondered if he needed his nappy changed, but there was nothing she could do about it just now, until Mr. Barrett instructed her in her duties and showed her to her room. She hoped desperately that he would remember his promise on the beach. It seemed so long ago now, and Jekyl Island so far away from this cold, wind-swept city. She had brought not only his card, but also the little gold ring that he had left for her on the dresser, to remind him of his promise. She knew, of course, that if he did not wish to keep it, nothing compelled him to do so, but she counted on him to honor his word.

Suddenly, the door rumbled open, and Maggie stood up in anticipation, expecting to see the friendly face of David Barrett. Instead, an austere-looking gray-haired man of medium height, with a clipped mustache, strode in and gave her a dark, piercing look. "So you are here to see my son?" he asked sternly, a muscle quivering around his mouth.

"Yes, sir, if you are the father of Mr. David Barrett. He asked me to come," she said, holding out the card as evidence. She was beginning to wonder if her decision to do so had been a wise one, but she knew that she must think of Danny, not of herself. She must stand her ground and insist on seeing her potential benefactor, indeed already her benefactor, for it was he who had sent her to the Messiah House.

"May I ask what your business with him might be?" He looked her and the baby over with a critical and appraising eye. It was clear that he could not imagine any business a woman like Maggie might have in his household.

"Well, sir, he was very kind to me at Jekyl Island. When he learned of my predicament last March ..." She hesitated, unsure of what she should tell him.

"And what predicament was that?" His voice was not sympathetic, and Maggie was reluctant to go on.

"Please, sir," she said, "if I might just see Mr. David Barrett ... the business I have is with him."

"My son ..." He hesitated, a muscle in his cheek beginning to tremble. "My son died on April 15."

"Oh, no, no ... Oh, God, no." Maggie felt the world beginning to collapse around her once more. She had counted so long on his help. He had been the only hope she had for a position where she might be able to keep Danny with her.

Her fatigue, the heat of the room after the cold outside, the tension she had felt from the old man's scrutiny, one more death in a seemingly endless chain, all crashed in upon her, and she felt her knees beginning to buckle. She tried not to fall, for she had Danny in her arms. Suddenly she realized that the old man was supporting her, leading her back to the sofa beside the fireplace.

When she was in control of herself once more and felt steady enough to speak, she asked, "How ... how did he die?"

"He was ... a passenger ..." The old man seemed to have trouble getting the words out, pausing for a long moment before he said, "On the *Titanic*." Then his face crumpled, and Maggie heard him catch something in his throat.

"Oh, no ... not that ... oh God, how awful. He told me how he hated the cold sea air in the springtime." Maggie remembered that it had been his excuse to walk her back to the clubhouse where it was warm and where she would be safe.

The old man seemed surprised by her comment. "Did you know my son well?" He seemed to be trying to keep his own emotions under control.

"Not really, sir, but he was a kind man. He promised to help me after my baby came."

"And was that your predicament?" he asked. "The baby?"

"Well, I don't think of him as a predicament now, sir, but at the time, since I had no husband, it did seem a bit of a problem. Mr. Barrett said there would be a place for me here, and for the baby. And he gave me this ..." She pulled the little ring, still wrapped in a white handkerchief, out of her pocket to show to the old man.

He looked at the ring in disbelief. "His grandmother gave him that ring! And he gave it to you?" There was a curious light in his eyes that Maggie did not understand.

"I didn't take it, sir," she said defensively. "He left it for me, with a note. He said it was for the baby, for good luck."

"He always told me that he was saving that for his son." He was looking at her with a new expression in his eyes. "What is your name, child?"

"Maggie, sir, Maggie O'Brien. I hope that it wasn't giving up the ring that brought him bad luck."

"No," the old man said bitterly. "It was not giving up the ring. It was having me for a father."

"What do you mean, sir?" His statement bewildered her, and she was not sure it was something she should have heard. She could have bit her tongue for asking him to elaborate.

"Have you any idea why he was on that ship, Miss O'Brien?"

"No, sir," she answered softly.

"Because of me." His eyes clouded, and she could see that he was having a difficult time controlling himself, for his hands were trembling. "I had sent him to London to handle a business matter for me. He was a very dutiful son, and he went without question, cut his vacation short at Jekyl Island to go to London. He wanted to stay for a month to visit an old friend, a boy he had known in college—" His voice broke.

"It's all right, sir. You don't have to tell me."

"No, I want to tell you. I need to tell you. Please, let me continue. He had already booked his passage back on May 2 on the *Olympic*. But I—" Tears were rolling down his cheeks now, unchecked. He took out his handkerchief and blew his nose. "I, his *loving father*," he said with bitter irony in his voice, "I forbade him to stay because I didn't want him to see his friend.

"I canceled his reservation without even asking him and booked him a cabin two weeks earlier on the *Titanic*—a second-class cabin, because all first-class tickets were booked at the time … not even on first class—a *second-class* ticket …" His shoulders were shaking. He could not go on.

Maggie touched his arm, feeling sympathetic tears welling up in her own eyes. "I'm so sorry, sir. I know what it's like to lose someone you love."

He looked at her as though he were seeing her clearly for the first time.

"Yes, perhaps you do." He seemed more collected now. "What is the baby's name?" he asked.

"Daniel Hector O'Brien, for his father and my father," she smiled. "Would you like to hold him? Babies always make people feel better."

"For his father ... Oh, I see, D.H., Daniel Hector ... May I?" he asked, taking the baby in his arms. "The initials are the same. David Henry. Very discreet of you. And which is your father's name?

"Daniel," she answered, genuinely puzzled. "I'm sorry, sir, but I don't understand. What do you mean by 'discreet' of me?"

"I see through your little subterfuge, Maggie O'Brien. And I see why David gave you that ring. But there are things I don't understand. What were you doing at Jekyl Island?"

"I was a chambermaid, sir. I cleaned Mr. Barrett's room ... and lots of others as well."

"Oh, I see. And you're Irish. I suppose he thought I wouldn't approve."

"Approve what, sir?" She was not sure, but she thought she was beginning to understand.

"My son's relationship with you. And I suppose there are many fathers who would not. But, Maggie, I am, in fact, very happy you came to me. It puts to rest fears I had, rumors I had heard ... And your son here, D.H. like my David, is living proof that they were not true!" He was beaming now, looking at the baby avidly. "I see that he is blond like David."

"He is blond like my brother Brendan," she corrected him.

"And he has the Barretts' blue eyes."

"My mother's blue eyes!" She did not like the turn this conversation was taking. "Sir. I am very sorry for your loss and sorry that I bothered you. Mr. Barrett had promised me a post in the household and a room where I could keep my baby with me. That is all. Otherwise I would not have come here."

She reached for the baby, but Mr. Barrett stood up and began to walk him around the room. "Yes, indeed, a baby is exactly what we need in this house."

"I think we had better go, Mr. Barrett."

"Go?" He looked startled. "Go where? No! You mustn't leave. I'll have Benton show you to your room. I'll have a crib sent up. You'll dine with me this evening. Where are your bags?"

"I left them in a locker at Union Station, because I was not sure that Mr. Barrett would remember me."

"Not remember you? How could anyone forget such a thing? Give me your locker key, and I'll send my chauffeur Friedrich in the car to fetch them."

"No, sir, please, you have no obligation to give me a post, and I don't want to be a bother. I'm sure that I'll find something else."

"That's very commendable, but it's nonsense, my child. You're staying here, and that's final. Now give me the key, and *I'll* show you to your room."

"Mr. Barrett, I think you may have the wrong idea about the baby."

"Wrong idea? I don't think so. It all seems very obvious," he said with finality.

"You think your son is his father, don't you?" She went on without waiting for him to reply. "But he isn't—wasn't. Danny's father was a waiter at the Jekyl Island Club. He drowned two days before we were to be married. Mr. Barrett took pity on me and promised to help. He was a good man, your son."

"And you're a good woman, Maggie, still trying to protect him. Please understand. I am not judging you for what happened. I'm glad it happened, in a curious way, for here is a child of my own flesh and blood, and his very existence proves that David was … normal."

"Normal, sir?"

"You don't understand, do you? How could you? Obviously you had no reason to think he was anything but a warm-blooded man."

"He was kind to me, is all." She reached for Danny, but Mr. Barrett refused to give him up.

"We'll talk more about this later, Maggie. For now, come with me." He strode from the library and up the stairs, Danny still in his arms, leaving Maggie no choice but to follow.

He led her to a large bedroom on the second floor. A mahogany four-poster bed stood between two airy windows. A tapestry-upholstered chaise longue with a floor lamp beside it sat in one corner of the room. Beside the bay window that opened onto Fifth Avenue was a small inlaid mahogany writing desk and chair. A large armoire with carved doors stood on the wall opposite the bed, and a dressing table with a three-paneled mirror sat against the wall beside a door that Maggie imagined must be a closet or a bath.

"This will be your room for the time being. It was my wife's room—you know, David's mother."

"Oh, no, sir. Please, Mr. Barrett, I can't stay here. I came looking for a position on the domestic staff. This is not suitable." She had never stayed in such a room, so large that she felt overwhelmed by the space.

"I will hear no more of that silly talk. I shall have a crib sent over from one of the department stores as soon as possible. I hope you will be comfortable, my dear. There is a bath through that door. I will send up Mrs. Fowler to see to your needs. Dinner is at seven."

He held Danny out to her and, smiling, touched his little cheek gently with the back of his hand as she took him from the old man's arms. Danny gazed at him and gave him a sleepy smile. The old man beamed, nodded to Maggie, turned on his heel, and left brusquely, closing the door behind him.

Maggie sat gingerly on the bed, trying to think what she should do. She was furious at his imperious nature and at his obstinate assumption of the role of grandfather. It was obvious that he was not going to permit her to leave, if he could help it, and that he was determined not to believe her. Perhaps she could stay for just one night and straighten it all out in the morning. Or perhaps she would just have to slip away when he was not in the house. The fact was, she had nowhere else to go, and at least they would have a place to sleep for tonight.

She unwrapped the blanket from around Danny. He was obviously nodding, and she knew that she would need to change him before he fell asleep. She had brought extra nappies, wrapped in the blanket. As she was changing him, there was a soft tap on the door.

"Yes?" she called.

"May I come in? It's Mrs. Fowler," said a woman's voice from the other side of the door.

"Yes, of course," she replied.

Mrs. Fowler was a full-bodied, still attractive woman in her mid-fifties, not very tall, and she had a friendly face and graying hair that had once been dark blond, like Maggie's.

"You'll need a diaper pail, won't you? We'll get a nursery set up soon, and hire a nurse, I'm sure. In the meantime, I can surely help with the little fellow."

"I can manage quite well, thank you. None of that will be necessary, for I won't be here for long. Only a day or so at the most," Maggie assured her.

"Mr. Barrett seems very excited about your arrival. I haven't seen him looking so happy since Mr. David ... since they found him, and Mr. Barrett had to go and identify the body. It was his only son, you know." Maggie thought she saw a tear gleaming in Mrs. Fowler's eye, but it may have only been a trick of the light.

"He sent me up for the locker key. He said he forgot to get it from you. Friedrich is bringing the car around."

"Well, I suppose I *will* need Danny's things." She fished inside her pocket. "Here it is," she said, holding out the key to Mrs. Fowler, who took it with a smile and disappeared from the room.

Within less than an hour she was back, bringing all Maggie's worldly belongings with her. When she tiptoed into the room, after tapping softly on the door and receiving no response, she found both Maggie and Danny sound asleep on the big four-poster bed. Maggie had placed a pillow beside Danny to keep him from rolling off, and he was sleeping, nestled against his mother, his tiny fist curled around her index finger. Mrs. Fowler smiled down at the sleeping pair, as she spread a light coverlet over them to keep the winter chill away.

It was dark outside when Maggie woke up. Danny was whimpering beside her, and she reached out to pull him close to her and nurse him. She knew he must be hungry.

She wondered what time it was. Mr. Barrett had mentioned something about dinner at seven, but she had no watch, nor was there a clock in the room. Danny nursed avidly at his mother's breast. She began to realize that she, too, was hungry. She had not eaten since her final breakfast this morning at Messiah House. Somewhere from the hallway she heard a clock strike the half-hour, though she had no idea which half-hour it was. Had she missed dinner entirely?

Fifteen minutes later, after Danny had finished nursing and Maggie was rebuttoning her blouse, Mrs. Fowler tapped on the door again.

"Come in," said Maggie.

Mrs. Fowler opened the door a short distance and peeked in, "Ah, all awake, I see. I hope you had a nice nap. Please forgive me, but while you were asleep I took the liberty of unpacking your things. I have put your bags in the storage room in the attic. You will find your clothes in the armoire," she said, opening both the doors to reveal her clothes draped over the hangers, as though they belonged there, and, on the left, a chest of drawers where Mrs. Fowler had stored her underclothes and nightgown.

"Your personal items are on the dressing table." She gestured toward Maggie's hairbrush and writing paper, neatly stacked on top of the little notebook she used as a journal. "I kept them all together there so you could find them more easily."

"Thank you," said Maggie, "but there was really no need. I will be leaving in the morning." But she was already beginning to realize that things were getting more complicated.

Mrs. Fowler frowned worriedly. "Must you leave so soon, my dear? Mr. Barrett is so delighted to have his grandson here."

"He is not my son's grandfather, Mrs. Fowler."

The older woman nodded gently. "I know, Maggie. Mr. David had no interest in women. We all knew that, but don't you see, you are for Mr. Barrett his way of proving to the world that we are all wrong." She smiled at Maggie, a compassionate smile that understood but wanted to make Maggie understand as well.

"You don't know what he was like before you came. He was morose, depressed, feeling guilty for having booked his son on that dreadful ship without his permission, believing that it was he who condemned the young master to death."

"I'm very sorry for him, but—"

Mrs. Fowler interrupted her. "They quarreled before Mr. David left, when he told his father that he planned to spend a few weeks with a young man his father had always despised, a young man he blamed for his son's … problems." She sighed deeply, thoughtfully, resigning herself to talking about an unpleasant topic.

"Let me tell you the whole story, Maggie. And please understand, I would not tell this to another soul in the world, but you deserve to know everything before you make up your mind." Mrs. Fowler sat down in the straight chair before the writing desk.

"Before he went off to college, Master David seemed to enjoy… an ordinary social life. He went to all the cotillions, and was all but promised to one of the Lorillard girls. Then, when he went to Yale, he seemed to change. Oh, for a time, it was fine. His little sweetheart went to New Haven for a dance or two, but then he stopped inviting her. It broke her heart. As you know, he was a handsome lad with great prospects."

"Yes, I remember," said Maggie.

"When he came home from college he always brought the young man in question, his roommate, Elliott Kingston. They rarely attended the parties in New York, though they did go to the theater and concerts. The summer of 1908, between their junior and senior years at Yale, they went to Paris together, and things never seemed the same after that.

"Mr. Barrett was convinced that there was something unnatural in their relationship. Anyhow, the next time the Kingston boy came to the house, Mr. Barrett made a huge scene—ordered him out and demanded that Yale assign his son another roommate."

"Oh, my," Maggie said.

"Mr. David was mortified, of course. But his father had his way, and after their graduation, I don't think Mr. David saw the Kingston boy again until he went to London. Elliott Kingston is with a banking firm in England now, one in which his father owns a great deal of stock. When Mr. David got to England at the beginning of April, he wired his father, in a rather uncharacteristic moment of defiance, that he would not be starting home until the first of May because Elliott had invited him to spend a few weeks at his country house in Yorkshire."

Maggie nodded, frowning slightly.

"Well, you know the rest," said Mrs. Fowler. "And as always, Mr. David obeyed his father and started home on April 10 as Mr. Barrett had instructed." She hesitated for a long moment. "They found him in the water two weeks later, floating in his life jacket and frozen to a buoy taken from the ship before it went down. Since then Mr. Barrett has seemed a broken man ... until you arrived this afternoon. David was his only child."

Maggie started to speak, but Mrs. Fowler held up her hand. She seemed determined to get everything said before Maggie could react.

"I have never seen such a change come over anyone in my life. He actually smiled at cook when he told her there would be an extra person for dinner. He has already sent Friedrich to Macy's to buy a crib and a high chair, as well as some clothes for you and the baby. So you see, Maggie, it would be a cruel blow for you to go away again so soon."

Maggie had listened carefully and patiently to Mrs. Fowler's story. She remembered the morning at Jekyl when she had entered young Mr. Barrett's room when he did not answer her knock and found him and his blond companion still sleeping and tousled, like two little boys. She had thought nothing of it, for she had so often seen her brother and his friends sleeping over together and rumpled in the bedclothes.

But she wondered if perhaps Mr. Kingston had also been a guest at Jekyl at the time. Perhaps the two had seen one another again before he went to England. Or perhaps it was someone else, a part of Mr. David's effort to forget his friend in England. Or perhaps it was nothing. She would never know.

In any case, she recalled the young man's kindness to her, and she didn't want to hurt his father, whom he had obviously loved and wanted to please, despite his domineering nature. But she could not allow him to think that Danny was his grandson.

"Mrs. Fowler, I would like to help, but I really don't think it's such a good idea. Danny and I need to find a permanent situation, and this can obviously be only temporary. I can't lie to Mr. Barrett, not even for his own good."

"Of course you can't, my dear. In fact, he told me that you had already 'invented' what he called a 'poppycock story' about some waiter at Jekyl Island to protect his son. You can tell him the truth all you want. I don't think he is in any frame of mind to hear it—at least not just yet. But why don't we allow him his euphoria for a time? It may be all he needs to snap out of his depression. Then, when the time is right, I'll help you make him understand the truth. He is really a good man, despite that gruff exterior."

"I don't know …" Maggie hesitated.

"Stick to your story, if it makes you feel better. That way you won't be lying. He won't believe you anyhow. But just don't go away. Not for a week or so, at least. That way you can have a place to stay while you look for a suitable position. Someone will be here to look after the baby for you, and when you find something, maybe then he will be ready to listen and you can leave. Please, Maggie. Just for a little while."

It made a sort of crazy sense to Maggie. It would be nice to stay in this lovely room for a short time and to have someone care for Danny while she looked for a job, but she would never pretend that David Barrett was Danny's father.

"Well ..." She hesitated. "Perhaps just for a little while."

Mrs. Fowler got to her feet and gave her a quick hug. "Thank you, my dear, thank you. Now dinner will be served in ten minutes. Just come down to the dining room when you hear the gong."

The woman picked up Danny, who squirmed in her arms and obviously needed to be changed again. "Oh, here," Maggie said, "let me change him if you would like to hold him."

"No need, dear, I'll just take him to the nursery which we've set up temporarily in the guest room next door. Suzanne, cook's daughter, has agreed to take care of him during dinner. She has two children of her own, so she will be able to look after him with no trouble at all."

Maggie felt uneasy as she watched Mrs. Fowler take Danny out of the room, and he began to cry at the unfamiliar smells and sights without his mother close by. "Now don't you worry," Mrs. Fowler said, sensing Maggie's anxiety. "He'll be fine."

His cries quieted quickly, and she heard a woman's voice, singing to him in the next room. Maggie felt reassured by the sound of Suzanne's clear, sweet voice. *Perhaps,* she thought, *it will be all right after all.*

Chapter Thirteen

Dinner was a strained affair. Maggie had expected Mrs. Fowler to dine with them, but only Mr. Barrett and she were seated at a table large enough to accommodate twelve people with ease. The table setting was formal, lit by two large candelabra. Maggie had never been confronted by so many forks and spoons at a single meal.

A woman she had not seen before served them one course at a time, and Maggie found it difficult to make conversation with Mr. Barrett, though both of them certainly tried.

"Where do you come from, Maggie? I can hear by your accent that you're Irish," he observed.

"Doolin," she said. He nodded, but it was obvious that he had never heard of it.

"And do you have family there?"

"My father. And my brother Brendan and his wife and child. But my brother's family lives in Lochrea."

"Your mother is not living?"

"She died more than a year ago, and my father ... my father is all alone now." Maggie blinked back tears that threatened to spring to her eyes.

"I'm sorry to hear about that, Maggie. My wife died several years ago as well. A stroke. David had no mother either, I'm sorry to say."

"Yes, I'm sorry too, sir."

"Perhaps that is why he felt drawn to you," he suggested.

"He did not know about my mother's death," she replied.

They sat silently, focusing on their food. Maggie stared at the forks to the left of her plate. She had had no difficulty with the soup spoon, but she watched Mr. Barrett through every course, waiting until he had picked up the correct utensil and trying to follow his lead throughout the meal. He did nothing to make it easier for her and seemed unaware of her discomfort.

Finally, toward the end of the meal, as they were waiting for dessert, he asked her, "Now, tell me, Maggie, what do you like to do?"

"*Do*, sir?" She wasn't sure just what he meant. She did whatever was needed. She worked. She took care of Danny. "What do I like to do? I like to take care of my little boy. I like to go to mass. I like to do what others need to have done for them." To her it seemed the perfect response, balancing her motherhood, her service to God and to her employer.

"I mean in your spare time."

It was an alien concept to Maggie. She had never really had what might be called spare time. There was always something that needed doing. Sometimes at night when she was alone and after Danny went to sleep, she wrote in her journal and she read the American poets. Perhaps that was what he meant.

"I write a bit and read poetry sometimes," she answered.

"Ah, you read poetry. David liked poetry as well."

"And what do you like to do, Mr. Barrett?" It was the first time she had addressed him by name.

"Oh, I go to art exhibits, ride in the park, spend time at my club, that sort of thing. But I have little free time. I'm a lawyer, you know."

"I see," she said, to ward off an uncomfortable silence.

Finally dessert came, a delicious chocolate mousse, which Maggie ate with relish before she made her excuses and took refuge in her room for the night. She stopped at the nursery door to get Danny, but found that Suzanne had already put him to bed for the night in the little crib. It would be the first night since he was born that he had not slept nestled beside his mother. But he had not resisted the crib, according to Suzanne, and he was indeed sleeping soundly, despite his late nap, so Maggie decided not to disturb him. She would come to regret that decision.

In the days that followed, Suzanne continued to put Danny to bed before dinner ended, and Maggie found herself sleeping alone, though she always tiptoed in to kiss him goodnight. Each morning she rose early to nurse him and play with him before breakfast when they were both fresh and cheerful. They had always cuddled upon awaking in the morning.

Perhaps it was time he had his own crib, but she missed snuggling him in her bed. His sweet face and eager eyes always lit up when she walked into his room and picked him up from his crib. She loved his baby smell and the softness of his skin. He made her every day worthwhile, and she spent every moment she possibly could with him.

She was eager to find a place of their own, for she felt constrained in the Barrett household. She scoured the newspapers daily for positions advertised, and, in the afternoon, when she returned from an occasional interview, she found her way to the kitchen where the cook, Suzanne's mother, Pauline Dumont, would make her a cup of tea.

It was relaxing to sit in the kitchen, where the smells were homey, and the conversation something she could relate to. Although Pauline spoke with a French accent, she reminded Maggie of her mother in some ways. She was about the same age, a bit frail, but always smiling and ready to serve something tasty. Friedrich, the chauffeur, was there almost every day, and once in a while Mrs. Fowler would pop in to give instructions to someone. Maggie loved their down-to-earth qualities, their simple ways, their homespun philosophies. And they seemed to enjoy her presence as well.

Even so, she was growing increasingly uncomfortable with the arrangement. She had twice suggested to Mrs. Fowler that she felt it was past time for her to leave, but on each occasion Mrs. Fowler said, "Just a few more days."

Maggie had been two weeks in the Barrett household when she rushed in on Monday afternoon from her most promising interview. Her first thought was of Danny, but he was still napping, so she hurried back downstairs to share the details with Pauline and Friedrich. As she reached the bottom of the stairs, Mr. Barrett was just coming out of the library.

"Oh, there you are, Maggie. Why don't you take tea with me this afternoon. I just rang for Mrs. Dumont to send it up."

"All right, sir, I'll be right in," she agreed reluctantly, resigning herself to sharing her good news with the servants later.

She wasn't surprised to find Mr. Barrett already home from his office. Friedrich had confided to her that he was these days little more than a figurehead at the legal firm where he was senior partner. His name still brought in a great deal of business, though most of the actual work was done by the younger members of the firm, particularly since the death of Mr. Barrett's son. Friedrich suggested that he seemed distracted most of the time and that he even spent many afternoons at the Union Club, rather than at the office.

Still he kept up the pretense of his busy life, and Maggie saw little of him during the day, except for breakfast and dinner, which he always insisted they take together. They had not shared teatime before.

Maggie sat down on the sofa opposite the wingback chair where Henry Barrett had settled and was looking through a stack of papers.

"I hope you had a good day, sir," she ventured.

"Fine, fine," he said, without looking up. Finally he set the papers aside and focused his attention on her. "Now tell me about your day."

"Well, I went to an interview this afternoon for a position that looks very promising," she began. She could hold in the news no longer.

"Position? What kind of position?"

"As a maid for the Frederic Bakers. They're members of the Jekyl Island Club, and I was able to list the head housekeeper and the superintendent there as references. That should help, I hope. They seemed to like me well enough, though nothing is definite."

It was in Frederic Baker's office that Mr. Falk had first interviewed her for the position at the Jekyl Island Club. She felt that it was a good omen. The Bakers hadn't gone to Jekyl this season because of Mr. Baker's health, but they hoped he'd be better by spring. They were looking for a replacement for a maid who was getting married in early June, though Maggie hoped she would know something certain before then. They had seemed impressed by her references.

"A maid, you say?" He sounded disbelieving. "How could you even consider such a position?"

"I beg your pardon, sir, but it's the only type of experience I have."

"Surely you can find something more suitable if you insist upon seeking employment. But that isn't really necessary, you know."

"Yes, sir, it is. Danny and I can't stay here forever, and I need to find a way to support him."

"How absurd!" he said disdainfully. "David's son will have every advantage. He certainly won't have to live on a maid's salary!"

At that moment, before Maggie could protest his use of the words "David's son," Pauline entered the room, carrying a large silver tray, loaded with a teapot, cups, and several plates of small sandwiches and sweet biscuits, much too large and burdensome for her tiny frame. Ordinarily Suzanne would have brought the tray, but she was spending most of her time now in the nursery. Maggie, who could see Pauline struggling to set the tray down, rose instinctively to help her.

"Let me take that, Pauline. It's too heavy for you."

Pauline looked nervously at Henry Barrett, whose face was growing redder by the second.

"Thank you, Mrs. Dumont, that will be all," he said brusquely, and Pauline nodded, almost curtseyed, turned, and fled from the room, closing the pocket door behind her.

Henry Barrett turned to Maggie, who was pouring him a cup of tea. "Don't you ever do such a thing again."

"Do what, sir?"

"I pay these people well to do these tasks. When they can no longer perform them, I will find someone to replace them, as they well know."

"But she's getting on in years, sir. The tray was heavy. I was afraid she might drop it."

"She was not pleased that you made her seem old and incapable, Maggie. She needs this job, and she wants to do it. Otherwise she would leave my service."

"How long has she been here, Mr. Barrett?"

"Twenty-two years," he answered curtly.

"And you would turn her out for not being able to carry a heavy tray, with all that wonderful food that she prepares for you every day?"

"She would have a suitable pension, of course."

"And what might that be? Fifteen dollars a month? How would she live?"

"She has a daughter who will look after her."

"And suppose she didn't?" It was the most she had talked with Henry Barrett since her arrival. She had not intended to let her feelings show so openly, but she had watched him interact with the servants and knew that he had no idea what their lives were like.

"But she does," he said with finality. "These are my employees, and I'll thank you to keep your radical ideas to yourself in my household."

"This is a free country, Mr. Barrett, in case you hadn't heard, and freedom to think and speak as one chooses is one of the things that makes it a great land." She knew from that moment she could no longer stay in his household, that she should have left long ago and would have done so, had Mrs. Fowler not begged her to stay.

Henry Barrett sensed her change of mood and sought to mollify her. "Sit down, Maggie, and pour yourself a cup of tea."

"Mr. Barrett, we need to talk, so I will sit, and I will pour myself a cup of tea. But this will be the last time I do so in this house. I am taking Danny tomorrow morning and moving to a boarding house where we can have a bit more freedom and privacy than we have here."

"How absurd!" said Henry Barrett. "Who will take care of Danny while you are away? As you are each day," he reminded her.

"I will work something out. But we can't stay here any longer. I don't want Danny growing accustomed to the luxuries of this household. And you must face the fact that your son was not his father."

"That I will never accept, because it isn't true. The ring he gave you proves that. It was his acknowledgment of the child. Of that I have absolutely no doubt."

"It was only his way of being kind. You must stop being such a stubborn old man and insisting on something that never happened," she said impetuously, feeling her Irish temper rise.

Henry Barrett gasped. "How dare you speak to me in such a manner!"

Maggie was sure now that he would send her away, even if she hadn't already decided to leave of her own accord. No doubt it would be best for them both. And for Danny. Mr. Barrett would simply have to come to terms with the fact that his son was not her baby's father. She felt sorry for him, but she could never sacrifice Danny's life, or her own for that matter, to satisfy his fantasies. She would have a few more hours to think through her limited options, but one thing she knew for sure, this was her last night in Henry Barrett's home.

The next morning when Maggie went into the nursery to get Danny, her breasts full of milk, the room was empty. No crib stood against the wall away from the drafty window. The rocking chair was absent. Even the chest that held Danny's clothes had been surreptitiously removed during the night. The child and Suzanne were both gone as well.

Maggie was frantic. She raced down the stairs and found Henry Barrett in the dining room, quietly sipping his coffee and reading the stock market reports.

"Where is he?" cried Maggie, feeling tears of frustration and fear well up in her eyes. "Where is he?"

"Now calm down, my dear. He's perfectly safe. He's with Suzanne."

"Where is he?" she repeated, uncomprehending. "Answer me!"

"Sit down, Maggie. You and I need to have a little talk about Danny. About his future."

"You have nothing to do with his future," she said, standing.

"On the contrary, my dear, I have everything to do with his future. That's what I must make you understand. Danny is my grandson, and I only want what's best for him."

"Danny is *not* your grandson, Mr. Barrett," she said between clenched teeth. "Why can I not make you understand that? Danny is the son of Hector Deliyannis, a waiter at the Jekyl Island Club who died on March 21 trying to save someone else from drowning. Danny is my son. I have told you again and again. *HE IS NOT YOUR GRANDSON.*" She said the last sentence very slowly and loudly as though she were trying to explain it to a retarded child.

"Maggie, I know that is your story, but I also know that David gave you a ring for the child that he said all his life would belong to his own son some day. I had almost given up ever having a grandson."

"Mr. Barrett," she said, close to tears. "I never wanted to hurt you in any way. I stayed because Mrs. Fowler begged me to. She told me that when you felt better, when you had recovered from your son's death, that she would help me convince you of the truth."

"Is that so? Well, we'll see about that." He rang the bell beside his plate. Benton, who always served Mr. Barrett's breakfast, appeared at the door that led to the butler's pantry.

"Yes, sir?"

"Benton, please ask Mrs. Fowler to come into the dining room."

"Right away, sir." Benton vanished through the archway into the foyer, and Maggie could hear his footsteps on the stairs.

"I have a note from David, Mr. Barrett, one that will prove that I am telling the truth. I'll get it!"

"In due time. Let's hear what Mrs. Fowler has to say about it all first." Henry Barrett took a sip of his coffee. "Would you care for your breakfast now?" he asked in an annoyingly unperturbed voice.

She shook her head tensely, too angry to think of eating. How could he doubt her word? *Thank heaven for Mrs. Fowler,* thought Maggie. *She can help get all this straightened out.*

The grandfather clock in the foyer was chiming nine o'clock when Eloise Fowler stepped into the dining room. "Oh, there you are," said Henry Barrett. "Now what's all this about your helping Maggie to—how did she put it, 'convince me of the truth' on the matter of Danny's father? Is that a fact?"

The color drained from Mrs. Fowler's face at his words, and her eyes bore into Maggie's. For a long moment she said nothing. Then she turned to Henry Barrett and said, "I'm sure I don't know what she's talking about."

"Maggie here said you would help her straighten all this out, that you asked her to stay here against her will to make me feel better about David's death or some such nonsense as that."

"I presumed that Maggie stayed of her own free will because she had nowhere else to go. We all agreed that Danny would be better off here under his grandfather's roof than in the streets of New York." Mrs. Fowler did not look at Maggie.

"What?" cried Maggie. "You begged me to stay. You told me that Mr. Barrett was a broken man, and you needed my help to bring him out of his depression. You can't have forgotten such a thing."

"I'm sorry, Maggie," Mrs. Fowler looked at her sympathetically. "I would never say such a thing about Mr. Barrett. I'd like to back you up, and I know that you love Danny. But I just can't say what isn't so. And you know, as well as I do, that he is better off here, where he will have every advantage."

"He's my son!" Maggie cried again. "My son! Mine and Hector's. Where have you taken him?" She felt as though she were swimming against an impossible tide that was dragging her down beneath her depths.

"Please help me." Tears were streaming down her cheeks now. Tears of rage. Tears of helplessness. And she felt her breast milk beginning to leak onto her bodice.

"Maggie," Mr. Barrett said softly. "I don't think you can continue to stay here under the circumstances. Danny is safe. And you can see him from time to time, but he will stay within my custody. He is my grandson."

"No, he isn't! I have the letter to prove it. I'll show you." She ran for the stairwell and raced up to the room she had used for the past two weeks, Lydia Barrett's room. There she found the letter in the drawer of her desk, tucked between the pages of her journal. She held it tightly in her fist as she descended the grand mahogany staircase once more.

"Here it is. See for yourself!"

She held the letter out to Henry Barrett who took it from her, carefully unfolded the seams, adjusted his glasses and read slowly and deliberately the words his son had written: *"This is for the baby. It was given to me by my grandmother when I was a tot. I was saving it for my son, but I know now that I will never have a son of my own."* His voice wavered slightly. *"I have worn it around my neck for years for luck. I want you to have it. Perhaps it will bring your baby luck as well."*

He looked up from his reading. "So?" he asked. "And what do you think this proves?"

"He says right there, 'I will never have a son of my own.' Danny can't be his child, by his own admission," Maggie said triumphantly, but she had not reckoned with the ways of a New York lawyer.

"What he meant, of course, was that he could not acknowledge this baby openly as his own because he had a stubborn old man for a father, as you yourself have pointed out, Maggie. He thought he could never admit his mistakes and hope for forgiveness. He knew I wanted him to marry the

Lorillard girl. Don't you see, Maggie? This letter means nothing."

Slowly and deliberately he tore the letter in half once, then again, and stuffed the pieces into the pocket of his jacket. "It means nothing at all," he said with finality. Maggie stared at him, numb, realizing that he had just destroyed her only proof.

"How could you do such a thing?" she cried. "That letter was mine!"

"What letter, my dear?" he asked, as he took the square pieces of the note from his pocket and tossed them into the dining room fireplace.

Maggie fell to her knees in front of the fire, but before she could retrieve the paper fragments, they burst into flame.

She was speechless with disbelief. Her hands, reddened from the heat, formed into tight fists of aching, impotent rage, as she stood up and took a step toward the old man. Eloise Fowler stepped between them and grabbed Maggie's arm, holding her back from whatever she feared the young woman might do.

Then the housekeeper asked calmly, "Will that be all, sir?"

"Yes, thank you, Mrs. Fowler. That will be all. Perhaps you can help Maggie to see to her packing."

"You can't do this." Maggie struggled against the woman's tight grip, but her resistance was useless. Her voice was lost somewhere inside her, and her breath would not come. "You … can't … do … this."

Mr. Barrett rang for the butler, and together he and Eloise Fowler forced a struggling Maggie toward the archway that led from the dining room into the foyer.

"Let's go upstairs, Maggie, and see what must be done," said Mrs. Fowler.

Suddenly Maggie had no more will to resist. Her son was gone, and her anger gave way to powerless grief, as the two servants, one on each side, urged her up the stairs and into the bedroom. The desk drawer stood open, and Maggie's bed was still unmade.

She turned toward the older woman with an imploring gesture, tears pouring down her cheeks. "Why?" she asked in a voice that was almost inaudible. "Why are you doing this?"

"There are always things better left unexplained. I meant what I said, and you know I'm right. Danny is better off here. He will go to the best schools. He will have all the advantages a boy growing up in a wealthy New York family can have. All the things that people like you and I can only imagine, he will have for the asking. Don't you see, Maggie? It's for the best. Think of him, not just of yourself." Eloise Fowler had all her life longed to live that dream herself, a dream she had built around Henry Barrett, and she was convinced of the truth of her words.

"He *needs* me," Maggie whispered. "I'm his mother. Can't you understand? Where is he? Where have you taken him?"

"He's with Suzanne in the country. He has everything he needs. Everything."

"No!" Maggie cried. "Not everything. He doesn't have his mother!"

"Maggie, you're young. You can have other children. But Danny represents to Mr. Barrett his only future. He is so proud to think that David fathered a child. He needs that boy. It's his proof that all the whispers around the New York salons about his son were untrue. He *needs* the child."

"Danny's not evidence in a courtroom. I need him too. He's *my child.*" Maggie's whole body was wracked and trembling with helpless anger and frustration.

"No, Maggie," said Eloise Fowler. "Not any more. He belongs to us now."

Chapter Fourteen

FRIEDRICH COULD ONLY WATCH through the windshield of the black Packard as Maggie trudged the twenty-seven blocks to Mrs. Cavanaugh's boarding house. Henry Barrett had instructed Friedrich to *drive* her wherever she wanted to go, but she had refused to get into the car.

Mrs. Fowler had tried to give her a check for a large sum of money that Henry Barrett had made out in her name. But Maggie only snatched it from her and ripped it to shreds, leaving it on the dresser of the bedroom she had occupied at the Barrett mansion on Park Avenue.

Friedrich followed her discreetly in the Packard, pausing at the curb every few blocks to avoid overtaking her. His heart was heavy as he watched her, lugging her suitcase, shifting it from hand to hand as she wiped her eyes, but never putting it down once for all the twenty-seven blocks. He wanted to help her, but he knew that she would accept no assistance from him, for he, like Eloise Fowler, was contaminated in Maggie's eyes by his association with Henry Barrett.

Friedrich despised what Mr. Barrett had made him do, whisking the baby away in the middle of the night, and driving Suzanne and Danny to an inn near Southampton, Long Island. But he desperately needed his job as the Barrett chauffeur, and he felt he had little choice. He was even more shamed by the knowledge that at least Eloise had committed her treachery out of a long-standing and desperate love for Henry Barrett, but that his own had been done for material gain and because he had hungry mouths to feed, including his own. Although he knew why he had to do what he did, he was not proud of his complicity in taking Maggie's child from her. He knew that he would someday answer to God for his actions.

By the time Maggie reached the stoop of the brownstone boarding house, she was ready to collapse with exhaustion. She longed for the safety and comfort of her mother's or father's arms wrapped around her, but she knew that was impossible. She missed them more at that moment than at any time since she had left Ireland. Her eyes were swollen with tears of rage and grief as she stumbled toward her destination. She rang the bell, and when Mrs. Cavanaugh opened the door Maggie almost fell into her arms.

"Good heavens, child, you look awful! What's happened to you?"

"I need a place to live," Maggie said. "Do you have a free room?"

"How long do you need it, child?"

"I don't know."

"I have one free room at the moment, but it's promised to a gentleman from Omaha a week or so after Easter. Do you think you could find something else by then?"

Easter was only a month away, but for now it seemed an eternity. Perhaps she would have Danny back by then. Perhaps the job she had interviewed for that morning might work out. *If not*, she thought, *I'll think of something.*

"I'd be grateful for even a few weeks." She could not think beyond that. She still had more than seventy dollars of the money she had earned at Jekyl Island. If nothing else, perhaps Deirdre would have returned from the club's winter season by then and could take her in. All she wanted right now was a place to lie down for a while and think of how she was going to get Danny back.

"Then it's settled," said Mrs. Cavanaugh. "You'll stay here until my Omaha roomer arrives. And I'm happy to have you. Now come into the dining room, and I'll fix you a nice, hot cup of tea."

Never had a cup of tea looked so good. Maggie was tired and chilled from her long walk carrying her heavy bags, and her feet hurt. But none of that compared to the ache within. Mrs. Fowler had packed all the clothes that Mr. Barrett had bought for her, though Maggie had protested that she wanted none of them.

"Now, Maggie, don't act like a silly child. You will need them if you're going to work for someone in the New York social set. If you don't take them, Mr. Barrett will just give them to charity."

"Let him. I don't want them."

But Mrs. Fowler had already closed the suitcase with a final snap. Eager to be out of the house, Maggie took it as it was. She thought of leaving it behind, but too many of the things she cared about were inside— her only snapshot of her holding Danny, the photograph of her parents, letters from her father and brother, and her journals, with a lock of Danny's blond hair tucked inside.

Mrs. Cavanaugh's dining room was warm, and Maggie sipped her tea mindlessly, listening to the older woman's sympathetic chatter. Perhaps it was the tea or merely the normality of the moment, but it made Maggie feel stronger. Surely there was something she could do to get her son back. He was alive, unlike his father, and healthy. It wasn't hopeless. She would find a way, a lawyer who would help her. This was America, after all. The wealthy simply couldn't trample on people in this country. There was equality under the law.

Determination and anger began to replace her feeling of despair. First, she would find a place to live. Then she would go to the Hibernians and seek help from the members. If there was a way, and there must be, she would find it. She would never give up—never—not for as long as she lived. She felt hope rise in her heart.

Deirdre answered her knock and squealed excitedly when she saw Maggie at the door. "Maggie! Maggie! Where on earth have you been? I've tried everything to find you," she cried, throwing her arms tightly around Maggie's neck.

"It's a long story, Deirdre, and I want to tell it all to you, but right now I need a place to stay. I have a lead on possible positions, but nothing certain. Do you think that your mother would be willing to put up with one more person for a little while?"

"Yes, yes, yes," said Deirdre excitedly. "But where are you staying now?"

"At a boarding house. But I have to give up my room there on Monday. A man from Omaha was supposed to have come the week after Easter, but his trip was delayed because of those dreadful tornadoes on Easter Sunday. In any case, he's arriving this Monday, and I must give up the room."

"Then here you shall stay! Ah, Maggie. 'Tis so good to see you!" She squealed in delight.

Deirdre's mother, Mollie Callaghan, rushed into the parlor, still drying her hands, to see what all the excitement was about. "Mam, this is Maggie! I've told you all about her. Maggie, from the Jekyl Island Club."

"Oh, yes, of course. Deirdre has told me everything. What a sad story about your young man's death! I'm so very sorry, my dear. Deirdre is so fond of you. She really missed you at Jekyl this year."

Maggie smiled sadly. "I wish I could have been there. How did you find everything?"

"Well, it wasn't the same without you there. I just got back, a week ago."

"Did you go to Hector's grave?" Maggie asked.

"I did, Maggie, and I put wildflowers on it—and on George's too." She hugged Maggie and whispered in her ear, "I told Hector they were from you."

How Maggie longed to go there again! She knew that she would feel closer there to Hector than anywhere else on earth. She wanted to tell him about Danny, about all that had happened. About how she had wanted to give up, but her mother had always told her, "Faith is what keeps you going when there is no reason to go on." She believed that. It would all work out somehow.

"We all missed you, Maggie. None more so than me. Minnie Clark asked about you, and so did Mr. Grob and all the waiters who were back—Stéphane and Bert and many others. But I couldn't tell them a thing. You just disappeared when we got back to New York. Oh, and one other person in particular asked about you and wanted me to give you her best. Do you remember Aleathia Parland?"

"Of course, how is she?"

"Doing well, I think. Working too hard as always. But she seemed very concerned about you. I could only tell her I hadn't seen you since we got back to New York last year. She just said to tell you if I ever saw you again that she prayed for you."

Suddenly Maggie felt ashamed of herself for not confiding earlier in her friend, who obviously cared about her well-being. Tears stood in her eyes.

"Maggie," Deirdre asked, concern in her voice, "are you all right?"

Maggie nodded. "I need to tell you my story now. I think it's important that you know the truth, the whole truth."

"I'd better check on my pie in the oven, if you'll excuse me," said Mrs. Callaghan.

"Oh, Mrs. Callaghan, it's nothing that you can't know as well, and you will, but perhaps it *would* be best for me to talk with Deirdre first. I thank you for your discretion." Mollie Callaghan smiled at the two young women and quietly slipped back into the kitchen to leave them alone.

Maggie told Deirdre everything that she had held back from her at Jekyl Island, about the night on the dunes with Hector, the birth of Danny, the abduction of her son, and the treachery of Eloise Fowler. Everything. It came pouring out in a long, breathless narrative that left them both weeping at the end.

"I need help, Deirdre, not only a place to stay for a little while, but help in getting Danny back."

"Oh, Maggie, I don't know what I can do, but you surely have a place here as long as you need it. And we'll think about what can be done to find your Danny again."

Maggie hugged Deirdre once more and dried her tears with her handkerchief. It felt good to be with her friend again. Surely things would work out somehow. She did not understand yet that the working out is often not what we might envision.

The days that followed opened Maggie's eyes to the ways of the world and to the power of money and connections. Although the Hibernians found her a lawyer willing to help her fight Henry Barrett on a *pro bono* basis, for she had no money to pay him, he could never match the prowess of Henry Barrett's vast network of legal contacts. The man who was publicly proclaiming himself to be Danny's grandfather knew every judge in New York, and his firm was one of the most successful and respected in the country. It took relatively little time and effort for him to make a convincing case that Danny was his grandson and that his mother was immoral, incompetent, and without adequate resources to take care of the child.

Following the lawyer's rule of thumb that he who represents himself is a fool, Barrett had put together a legal team made up of members from his firm who uncovered and distorted every aspect of Maggie's life—everything, that is, except the true paternity of her child. The father of Danny, they contended firmly, was David Barrett, a fine young man who had died on the *Titanic*. But they painted Maggie as a loose woman who had given birth to the child out of wedlock.

Young David had been prevented from doing his duty toward her only by his untimely death, as his gift of the ring to the boy clearly indicated. He was a saint, but she was a slut, they proclaimed, unfit to raise a child. Moreover, she had no job, but had to live on the charity of others. She came from poor Irish stock, with virtually no family to turn to in her time of trouble. Mr. Barrett's lawyers said the word "Irish" as though it were a dirty word.

Maggie's young and relatively inexperienced lawyer tried valiantly to show that she was indeed a worthy mother of a good Catholic background. He wanted to show that she had been seduced as a virgin by an unscrupulous and swarthy Greek, but Maggie forbade that line of defense.

"If I was seduced," she said, "so was Hector. It was he who tried to resist, not I. I will not have you sully his name in the court."

"But, Miss O'Brien," argued her pale, thin lawyer, peering from behind his spectacles, "if we can't show you as a basic innocent in all this, we'll have no hope of getting your child back. We're dealing here with Henry Barrett, of Barrett, Bingham, and Swarthmore—not just with yokel lawyers. They play rough here."

"You will not paint Hector as a villain. He was my husband in the eyes of God. And I loved him. You'll just have to find another way."

The young lawyer shrugged, quickly losing interest in the case. Though he made a perfunctory effort to show her potential as a good mother, it was obvious even to Maggie that he scarcely believed it himself. He told the courts that Danny's real father was a Greek waiter at the Jekyl Island Club and that the couple was to be married. He brought in as witnesses Deirdre and any other Jekyl waiters or chambermaids he could track down to back up her story.

Henry Barrett's lawyers only scoffed at such a "fiction," arguing that it was a story concocted by Maggie O'Brien and her "chums" to keep her son away from his true family. They made an impassioned and brilliant case on behalf of the broken-hearted patrician grandfather who had lost his only son in the greatest tragedy of the century. He could give his grandson all the benefits that his fortune could provide—a good education, a safe home, and a sure future, while Maggie could give him nothing. The child's welfare must come first, they argued.

The judge, who had often dined with Henry Barrett at the Union Club and occasionally at Delmonico's, took only a ten-minute recess before coming back with his decision. He awarded full custody of the child, "hereafter to be known as Daniel Barrett, as requested by the legal petition, to his grandfather, Henry Barrett." He gave Maggie visitation rights one Saturday a month, "provided she bring no harm or disruption into the child's life," at which point he would be "compelled to reconsider her visitation rights."

Henry Barrett grumbled about even that small privilege to Maggie, but it was obvious to all concerned that the popular press would crucify the judge if he did not allow some small crumb to the mother.

Maggie was agape with horror and dismay as the hawk-nosed judge read his decision. When he leaned forward on his elevated desk and banged his gavel, she sat in stunned silence. Henry Barrett on the other side of the courtroom beamed his approval and shook hands with his lawyers. Her own lawyer gathered up his papers and stuffed them wordlessly into a cheap leather briefcase, but she did not move. She stared straight ahead, as the dull city light filtered through the dirty windows of the courtroom and the musty smell of despair permeated the walls and furniture.

How can this be happening? Her whole life had revolved around Danny since his birth. Through the painful weeks since she had seen him, her milk had dried up. Now she felt that her entire spirit was drying up. She longed with her whole being to see her son, to hold him in her arms. How could she live with only four hours a month and visits supervised by Eloise Fowler, whom she could not bear to look at sitting behind her employer in the courtroom? How could any mother live with so little? Where was the justice for all, for which America was so famous?

Maggie could hardly stand, much less walk, as her lawyer helped her outside to a waiting cab. The motionless driver waited as she climbed in, and his black horse, breath steaming in a white cloud from its nostrils in the late afternoon chill, stamped its foot in anticipation of their next fare and an evening meal.

The lawyer gave the address to the driver, who flicked his reins twice. The weary horse began to move forward at the first touch of leather on his back. Maggie rode through the streets of New York toward Deirdre's apartment seeing only darkness before her.

Deirdre was waiting for her in the parlor. She had wanted to accompany Maggie to the courthouse this day of all days, but her mother was ill, and Maggie had insisted that she stay there to attend her. She knew there was nothing that Deirdre could do to help that she had not already done with her testimony. She had counted on the good sense of the judge and the skill of her lawyer. Now she understood that she had been foolish not to recognize the influence of Henry Barrett. Now she understood the power of money.

The moment Deirdre saw her face, she knew immediately what had happened. She reached out to Maggie and held her once more in her strong arms.

At exactly two p.m. on June 7, Maggie rang the doorbell for her first visit with Danny at the Barrett home. Though the setting seemed sinister, her excitement at seeing her son for the first time in a month overwhelmed all the other feelings rushing through her.

Danny, almost seven months old now, stretched out his arms at once at the sight of his mother and laughed with the unbounded joy that had been so typical of his father. He clung to her throughout the visit, refusing to take a nap though he was clearly exhausted by late afternoon. When six o'clock approached, Eloise Fowler announced it was time for her to leave. As she ushered Maggie down the stairs toward the front door, Danny, in Suzanne's arms on the landing, grew hysterical, screaming and straining toward his mother.

Maggie could not bear it. Suddenly she turned and raced back up the stairs to take the child in her arms once more and plant a thousand kisses on his tear-stained face.

"I can't leave him, Eloise—I can't. Please, let me stay just a few moments more, at least until he falls asleep." But Mrs. Fowler had already rung for the butler and the chauffeur to pry Danny from her arms and escort her forcibly outside.

"I'm sorry, Maggie," Friedrich whispered in her ear as they reached the front door, but she scarcely heard him through her sobs. He closed the door behind her.

Though Maggie failed to notice, Suzanne, tears in her eyes, stood at the second story window of Lydia Barrett's old room, watching Maggie's unwilling departure and listening to little Danny's screams.

The next morning a bailiff appeared at the front door of the Callaghan apartment, the address Maggie had been compelled to provide to the courts, to serve her with a restraining order. She was never to visit the Barrett household again, it said, never to see her son, if Henry Barrett and the courts of New York could prevent it. Her presence had been "disruptive" and "traumatic" for the child, and could not be tolerated. Any violation of the order could result in her arrest.

How can he do such a thing? Is there no end to his cruelty? Maggie wondered as she read and reread the court order. Never to see Danny again? How could she live? He was all she had. He was her life.

In her earlier refusal to confide in Deirdre, Maggie knew she had completely misjudged her friend, for Deirdre stood beside her through her darkest hour, comforting her, consistently trying to understand and bring her whatever consolation she could. Deirdre baked her cookies and made her tea, and tried to soothe her in ways women show their affection and seek to bring some small solace to an unbearable situation.

She found photographs from Jekyl, photographs from the year before that Bert Stallman had given her this past winter, and gave them to Maggie. Two of them included Hector. But Maggie was inconsolable, and, although she was glad to have them, the photographs only made her cry all the more. One of them was the snapshot Bert had made on the beach the day Hector died.

"I think I must go back to Ireland," she would say to Deirdre at one moment. "At least there I can be of use to my father." Then a moment later she would say, "How could I even think of returning to Ireland and leaving Danny here in New York? What a foolish thought!" Her mind would not focus, and she seemed incapable of making any decision about her future.

Three days later a letter arrived for Maggie, forwarded on from the Barrett household. It was from Frances Baker about the position for which she had applied more than a month ago. She had forgotten all about it in her anguish over Danny. It offered Maggie a position in the Baker home, beginning on July 1, and provided the first bright moment in Maggie's life since Henry Barrett had taken her son.

She quickly found a pen and paper to write her letter of acceptance. At least it would give her something to occupy her time. And it would keep her on Fifth Avenue close to Danny. She could feel her heart lifting. She would find a way to get him back. There must be a way. This was America after all.

Chapter Fifteen

MAGGIE REPORTED ON JULY 1 to the Baker household at 815 Fifth Avenue, and she was surprised to see a black-ribboned wreath on the front door. When she knocked at the service entrance around back, it was the housekeeper, Isabel Flowers, who opened the door to greet her.

As they moved through the rear hallway, Maggie glimpsed through the open doors a parlor with the same kind of dark woodwork, oriental carpets, and heavy draperies that had adorned the Barrett household. They were closed, giving the room a somber cast. It all seemed a bit forbidding, particularly when Maggie considered the wreath of mourning on the front door. It was comforting to know that Deirdre and her mother were not far away and that she could see them on her days off.

In contrast to the apparent coldness of the dark house, Isabel Flowers greeted Maggie warmly, insisting at once that Maggie call her Isabel. Most housekeepers and butlers, who were at the top of the household hierarchy as far as other servants were concerned, preferred to be addressed by their surnames as a sign of respect and distance from those who merely served but did not supervise. Isabel, whom Maggie was delighted to know would be her supervisor, led her up the stairs to a small, whitewashed room on the third floor.

A little bowl of fresh flowers sat on a white doily on the bedside table, the one bow to grace and ornamentation in the stark room. A table and chair were by the window, and a clothes rack stood against the back wall. Plain white cotton curtains and a pull-down shade hung at the room's single dormer window, which overlooked a little garden at the rear of the house. Maggie could see a primrose bush in bloom and the branches of a poplar tree outside. Her room seemed to her more cheerful than the rest of the house.

"Before you present yourself to Mrs. Baker," Isabel said quietly, "I need to let you know that Mr. Baker passed away quite suddenly only two weeks ago, on June 15. It was quite a shock for Mrs. Baker. She's been very brave about it all, but she's not quite herself these days."

"I can imagine," Maggie sympathized. "I'm so very sorry. He seemed like such a nice man." She remembered Frederic Baker as a small, balding gentleman in his eighties, who sported a white handlebar moustache. Although he had been an invalid when she met him during the interview a few weeks ago, and he had looked rather frail, she had been struck by his positive spirit and sense of humor.

"He *was* a nice man. A good man. We shall all miss him very much," Isabel said.

Maggie felt an immediate kinship with Frances Baker, who was now well over seventy. She was a tall woman with an imposing torso, and a plain, sweet face. Dressed all in black as she had ever since her husband's death, her gray hair gathered in a simple knot on top of her head, she welcomed Maggie kindly. Although her eyes looked sad, she smiled and spoke gently to Maggie, who liked her at once and sensed in her the same life-affirming spirit she had noticed in her husband.

By the end of the month, Mrs. Baker had the heavy drapes opened once again to let in the summer sun. The house seemed to cast off its pall and embrace life once more. The Baker grandchildren bounded into the parlor on Saturday afternoons, not quietly or stiffly like most society children Maggie had seen, but chasing each other and laughing like her own Irish playmates in Doolin. They were, as Maggie learned, the children of Mrs. Baker's son and daughter by her first marriage to a Mr. Lake.

Her son, Henry Lake, and her daughter, Frances Thacher, brought them over as often as possible to help cheer their grandmother. Mrs. Baker indulged them absurdly. Maggie felt a vicarious joy as she watched grandmother and grandchildren together, while at the same time her own heart was breaking anew as she thought of Danny. She often found a reason to come into the room while they were there to polish a table or dust a lampshade or bring tea, when she could coax the cook into letting her perform the task.

"Who is this little girl, ma'am?" Maggie asked Mrs. Baker one quiet morning as she was dusting the furniture in the parlor. She pointed to a photograph of a toddler in a small gold frame on the mantle. The child did not resemble the Lake or Thacher grandchildren.

"That's Abigail," Mrs. Baker said softly. The photograph showed a beautiful child, fragile, angelic, with blond curls and a wistful smile.

"Another grandchild?" asked Maggie.

"Our own little daughter, mine and Mr. Baker's. The only child we had together," she said sadly. "She died of scarlet fever not long after the picture was taken, more than thirty years ago."

"Oh, I'm so sorry, ma'am."

Seeing the photograph of the child, Maggie felt an even stronger connection to Frances Baker and an empathy with her darker moments, for she had experienced the same losses that Maggie had, even though she had lost her child several decades ago. Maggie knew in her heart that her own despondence over Hector and Danny would never go away, and she understood the cloud of sorrow that came across Mrs. Baker's face when she thought no one was watching her. Nevertheless, she would never allow her gloom to persist, always casting it off with a cheerful remark.

Maggie wanted to emulate her mistress and tried to keep her pain under control, but it was no use. She was desperate to see her son again. As the days passed, she tried everything she could think of. Three times she knocked on the Barrett door and begged Benton to let her in. Each time he turned her away, reminding her that there was a restraining order against her and that, if she came again, he would be forced to call the police even though he didn't want to.

The next time she tried the back door, and Pauline answered her knock.

"Maggie," she said, "we all hate what happened, but you mustn't come here again. Mr. Barrett will fire us all and have you arrested. You can't afford to have an arrest on your record. No one will ever hire you again."

"I must see my son," Maggie pleaded. "Please, Pauline. Let me in. Have Suzanne bring him to the kitchen. Just so I can hold him for a few minutes. Please." Maggie was crying now.

"You know I can't. Suzanne is taking good care of him. Sometimes she takes him to Central Park," she confided. "Now please go away, and don't come back. For your good and for ours."

Maggie haunted Central Park when she had time off, but Suzanne and Danny never came when she was there. In desperation she took to spending her free hours, rain or shine, standing across the street from the Barrett mansion in hope of catching a glimpse of Danny and Suzanne on an outing.

Then one day, as she stood dripping wet in the rain, a policeman came.

"I'm going to have to take you in, ma'am," said the officer. "Mr. Barrett saw you standing over here and called us. You know there's a restraining order that prevents you from being anywhere near his house."

"Please, officer. My son is there. They have my son."

"I'm sorry, ma'am. I have my orders." He was pounding his hand nervously with his billy club.

"Can't you help me?"

"I wish I could, but there's nothing I can do, ma'am. Judge's orders. You can't come here anymore." He took her by the elbow and made a show of guiding her around the corner.

Once they were out of sight of the house, he turned to her. "Ma'am, Mr. Barrett wants you arrested. I'll let you go if you leave right now and promise not to come back, but if I ever catch you here again, there won't be a second chance. I'm sorry. I'm really sorry." His eyes seemed sincere, but they were little consolation.

As she walked slowly back to the Baker house, raindrops poured down her cheeks faster than she could brush them away.

Though she could not see him, she thought of Danny constantly, trying to visualize him as he grew. As Christmas approached she thought, *He will be walking now.* In her mind she saw him toddling into the parlor of the Barrett home to find his little gifts from Saint Nicholas. She had sent a package for him, a cuddly brown Teddy bear she had seen in Macy's window, held by a tiny boy mannequin that reminded her of Danny. She had no idea whether Henry Barrett would let him have it or not, but she knew that she would always send him birthday and Christmas presents, even if he didn't know where they came from, even if he never got them.

Mrs. Baker's family tried to make it a happy Christmas. Her daughter, Frances Thacher, arrived for breakfast with her husband, John, and their son, John Jr. Mrs. Baker's niece, Abby Steers, joined them in time to take coffee with the family at the breakfast table. Henry Lake, Mrs. Baker's son, arrived last, just before noon on Christmas morning, with his wife, Marie, and their two little boys, Henry and Freddy.

The family exchanged gifts and shared a festive Christmas dinner. They fussed over Mrs. Baker until she finally announced that she was exhausted. When they had all left, except for her daughter, who planned to stay until evening, Mrs. Baker announced that she was going up to her room to rest for a while.

At four o'clock she came downstairs again, looking refreshed. Her daughter was stretched out on the sofa in front of the fire reading. The young woman looked up from her book and smiled as her mother came into the room.

"I hope you had a good rest."

"Very good, thank you. I feel ready to take on the world."

Just then Maggie entered with the tea tray, which she laid on the table beside the sofa.

"Your tea, ma'am," she said. "Let me know if there's anything you need."

As she was turning to leave, Mrs. Baker said suddenly, "Maggie, why don't you take the rest of the day off? Perhaps you could persuade that old goat Henry Barrett to let you see your son. It *is* Christmas, after all."

Maggie was startled. "How did you know about my son, ma'am?" she asked.

"We read the newspapers, my dear. And we all think it's perfectly dreadful, though we're such proper cowards that no one will speak up to his face, particularly since he has the law on his side."

"You hired me, knowing—"

"I hired you because Minnie Clark and Ernest Grob gave you a first-rate recommendation. Oh … don't worry," she said, watching Maggie's face. "They know nothing of the situation, and after a flurry of talk, we New Yorkers won't mention it again, will we, Franny." Her daughter nodded in agreement, as her mother continued.

"But do know, child, that there was much sympathy for you, even on Fifth Avenue. We all watched how Henry treated his son David, a really fine young man. We don't know whether all those awful rumors were true or not. But whatever the case, he didn't deserve the harshness of his father."

"Mother—" her daughter interrupted.

"I don't care, Franny. She has a right to know. Now you go over there, Maggie, and don't leave until they let you in. Tell them I sent you. And if they give you any trouble, call me."

"Thank you, Mrs. Baker." Maggie beamed, emboldened by her employer's sudden revelation and encouragement, and by the thought that she might have a few supporters among their friends.

She dashed to the kitchen and took off her apron, quickly donned her coat and left by the servants' entrance.

When she reached the Barrett residence, it was already dark. She climbed the stairs to the front entrance and hesitated only a moment before lifting the heavy knocker and letting it fall with a loud clack against the brass plate. She felt the same apprehension before that door that she had felt the day she had first arrived with Danny in her arms. But the massive door remained staunchly shut. She knocked again. This time she was determined to see her son.

Finally, it opened a crack, and an elderly man whom she had never seen before peered out.

"Please, I'd like to speak with Henry Barrett," she said.

"I'm sorry, ma'am, they've all gone to Connecticut for the holidays, and then I think they may be planning a trip to Florida. I have no idea when they'll be back. I'm the caretaker."

Maggie felt no surprise, only emptiness around her heart, which seemed to have become a black ball of hatred at the thought of Henry Barrett. The façade of the house was cold and unyielding, and she heard its eloquent silence, so different from her last visit. "Thank you," she said, turning away as hot tears sprung to her eyes.

"Merry Christmas, ma'am," he said, as he closed the door.

The Baker home was quiet now that the holidays were over and the flurry of guests had departed. Then one morning in mid-January, Isabel assembled the staff in the help's dining room.

"Mrs. Baker has ordered a thorough cleaning and redecorating of the house from top to bottom," she announced. "We are to clean out the attic, scrub the floors, polish the silver, beat the carpets—in other words, a complete cleaning. The drapes in the parlor and dining room are to come down, as new ones will be delivered next week. Painters will be here tomorrow to begin repainting the foyer and stairwell. We're even taking on a few extra girls to come in each day and help with the work. If you know anyone who might be interested and has good references, let me know."

Maggie raised her hand timidly. "There is a young woman I've worked with at the Jekyl Island Club. She didn't go this year because her mother is sick and needed her nearby. I think she might be available."

"Have her come to see me tomorrow if you can contact her today," Isabel said.

Deirdre was at the servants' entrance to the Baker house at eight o'clock the next morning. "You just caught me, Maggie. Mam's all better now, and I leave for Jekyl on Monday next."

Isabel was delighted with her strong back and her willingness to work. And Maggie was overjoyed to have her friend at her side as they undertook their share of the labor to transform the Baker household. Side by side they cleaned and scrubbed, carried what Mrs. Baker considered trash from the attic to the back stoop where Philip Malloy, the chauffeur, and his helper, Rudy Mews, disposed of it.

Maggie found herself laughing at Deirdre's foolish ways and funny faces as they worked their way through the days. It was the first time she had laughed in six months, and it felt good.

In her typical feisty way, Deirdre found Rudy "dashing." They were both part of the temporary staff. Rudy was the son of the butler, and he had spent his childhood following Philip about the Baker garage, learning about Mr. Baker's automobiles, especially his Locomobile, and conceiving great dreams for himself. Although he now worked as a garage mechanic, he still spent as much time as he could tinkering with the Locomobile and studying its engine, which he could have taken apart and put together again in his sleep. Rudy planned someday to open his own garage and train other mechanics to work for him.

Never in the history of the world had taking out the trash been such an adventure. Deirdre exclaimed over every ancient lampshade they discarded. Her enthusiasm caught Rudy's eye, and each afternoon he borrowed the Locomobile, with Mrs. Baker's permission, and drove her home. As Maggie watched them leave, she smiled at her friend's newfound happiness that she could not help but envy.

The result of Mrs. Baker's brave efforts to remake her world was dazzling. The foyer gleamed with cheerful persimmon-colored paint, with a *faux* texture that made it look like expensive wallpaper. She had purchased a new Persian carpet for the area that reflected the colors and added drama with its intricate patters of persimmon, blues and tans. The house was so clean that, as Isabel Flowers boasted, they "could eat off the floor."

Maggie understood the grief and frustration that had caused Mrs. Baker's burst of energy. It was as though she was trying to say to life, "I am still here." Although the staff was greatly pleased with the change, it only seemed to depress Mrs. Baker more, for, once it was done, there was nothing left to do. She threw herself into her civic activities, church bazaars, and her clubs. In the afternoons, she read quietly in the sunniest spot she could find in the house— usually a southern corner of the parlor.

One Tuesday afternoon in late January, Frances Baker called Isabel Flowers into the parlor and announced suddenly, "We shall depart in one week for Jekyl Island—for Solterra. Please take care of the arrangements, and I'll notify my children."

When Isabel informed the staff that evening at dinner, Maggie caught her breath amidst the flurry of excitement the announcement created.

"Can we manage on such short notice?" asked Alexander.

"I think we have no choice but to manage. Three of us will go ahead to get everything ready there. We'll plan to leave on Thursday, and the rest of you will remain here to help Mrs. Baker get ready and to close up the house. Can we do it?"

There was a chorus of ayes and yeses, as the servants began to look forward to an early departure for a winter in paradise.

Isabel notified Maggie before she went to bed for the night that she would be one of those in the advance party to make the house at Jekyl ready. She had been impressed with the young woman's willingness to work and her intelligence. Best of all, since she had worked for the club, she would know the best workers to help open up the house. In fact, Maggie would be in charge of supervising the cleaning staff. Those left to come later, Isabel informed her, would be Annette, the upstairs housemaid, who doubled as Mrs. Baker's personal maid, the cook, the chauffeur, and a brand new nurse-companion, Miss Beatty, hired by Mrs. Baker's children to join the household staff and look after their mother.

"Best get your packing done right away, Maggie. We'll be leaving early on Thursday morning, and we have a big job to do. I hope your friend Deirdre will be willing to help as well."

Opening Solterra, the largest cottage on the island, would be a daunting task. It had not been used for more than a year and would no doubt need a thorough cleaning and airing. Maggie was grateful that it would keep her hands busy and at least some of her thoughts occupied.

Back in her room, she began to lay out her clothes, folding the garments one by one neatly into her duffel bag. She packed all her pictures—the photos of Hector Deirdre had given her, her picture of Danny, and the framed photograph of her parents, as well as her poetry books and Bible. Then she picked up her journal, the story of her life, and sat down at her little desk to write.

What will it be like to return to Jekyl—the place of my greatest happiness and greatest sorrow—the place where Danny was conceived and where I lost Hector? I want to go back, and yet I dread it. Thank God Deirdre will be there. And dear

Aleathia. It will be just as hard for Mrs. Baker as for me, I suspect. She and her husband spent many happy winters there. But if she can do it, so can I. God give me strength.

Chapter Sixteen

24 JANUARY 1914 BRUNSWICK, GEORGIA

THE TRAIN STOPPED AT THE BRUNSWICK station on Bay Street, which paralleled the dock. Maggie peered out the compartment window. They had left New York's Grand Central terminal buried in snow the previous morning to arrive now in a world of palm trees and camellias. She had already inhaled the soft Georgia air when they stopped to change trains at Thalmann Junction.

The trip had been so much easier by train, and she was grateful they had not taken the Mallory Steamer this time. It would have been too full of memories of her first meeting with Hector.

The *Jekyl Island* launch was already docked and waiting for them at the wharf just beyond the railroad tracks. Captain Clark, with his welcoming smile, was there to greet them. He told the new arrivals, "You can go ahead and board if you like, but I have several errands to take care of here in Brunswick. It'll be about forty-five minutes to an hour before we depart, so if you'd like to stretch your legs and look about a bit, you'll have plenty of time. Just listen for the boat whistle's fifteen-minute warning."

Maggie welcomed the news. "If you haven't done so before," she told Isabel and Alexander, "you might enjoy a stroll along Union Street. The houses are charming, and the street is divided like a boulevard, with lots of wonderful trees."

"I'd love to see them," said Isabel.

"So would I," Alexander agreed.

"Won't you come with us, Maggie?" Isabel invited her.

"I think I'll just stay closer to the dock," she said. "You go along, and enjoy your walk."

The small seacoast town had changed very little in the two years since Maggie had seen it. Shops and offices still lined Gloucester Street, and relatively little traffic, at least compared to New York, cluttered the roadway. There were a few more automobiles perhaps, but most of the vehicles were still pulled by horses or mules.

This time Maggie turned left onto Newcastle Street and strolled by the Oglethorpe Hotel, with its splendid Queen Anne architecture that boasted turrets much like those on the Jekyl Island clubhouse. She had never stayed there overnight, but she knew that many of the club members did so, particularly if they arrived by train in the late afternoon, rather than take the trip on the darkening waters to the island.

She looked forward to seeing Deirdre, who had arrived at Jekyl weeks earlier. Her spontaneous bursts of enthusiasm and witty comments always made everything seem more positive and adventurous. But in spite of her desire to see her friend, she dreaded setting foot the island as much as she looked forward to it. She believed she could never move on with her life until she had an opportunity to sit beside Hector's grave, pour out her heart to him one last time, and tell him about their son. Yet she had tried so hard to set aside her grief and could not be sure what feelings a return to the island might bring back.

It will be a good thing to be there, she told herself. *I need to do this.* And she could not deny that she still loved the island and anticipated with pleasure the warm weather after the awful chill of New York. Already she felt the sun on her back pouring its healing warmth into her body.

This time, however, it would be different. She would not be living in the clubhouse, but rather in the servants' quarters on the top floor of Solterra. Maggie remembered the splendid structure, but she had never been inside. She had heard that it once housed the president of the United States, William McKinley, and his wife when he came to Jekyl to heal some political wounds with an old Republican rival who had been on the island at the same time. Both men claimed they just happened to be here for a vacation, but Jekyl Islanders knew better, and Maggie had heard Mrs. Baker tell the tale several times.

"It may have decided the 1900 election," she had said, laughing softly.

Newcastle Street, like Gloucester, lay spread out before her like a picture postcard, with its little shops on either side. Maggie noticed the noisy T-model Fords chugging down the street, but they were compelled to weave their way slowly among the carriages, farm wagons, and bicycles, all moving with the same slow rhythms that Maggie had come to love the last time she was here.

It was different from Doolin, where time seemed to stand completely still, and yet it was even more unlike New York, where everyone rushed about in the ever-growing numbers of motorized vehicles that seemed to choke the city streets. Here people waited for one another, stopped to let children cross the street, and waved from their vehicles as they passed each other.

There were, of course, things Maggie didn't like about the South. The deference blacks were expected to show to whites, whether they deserved it or not, irritated her the most. She had read what she could about the old South before the Civil War, or the War of the Rebellion, as New Yorkers called it. And she hated the idea of slavery. It rankled her independent Irish spirit that one group could ever be arrogant enough to enslave another. But this was supposed to be the new South, where there was no slavery anymore, yet this foolish expectation of deference was to some extent still there, and, from what she had heard, it could be dangerous not to observe the regional customs. How could anyone have thought of enslaving intelligent, hard-working, and good-hearted women like Aleathia Parland or her ancestors? It was sickening even to think of it.

Looking in the shop windows and lost in her thoughts about the town and the region, Maggie suddenly heard the boat whistle's warning blast. She turned her steps toward the wharf and hurried back. She could already see people boarding the *Jekyl Island* and Captain Clark tipping his hat to everyone as they entered the vessel. Quickening her footsteps, she hoped to be able to talk with him for a moment or two before stepping onto the gently rocking vessel.

"Welcome back, Maggie O'Brien," he called out to her as she approached. "I heard that you would be coming down with the Baker entourage. It's good to have you here."

"And 'tis good to be back," she replied. "How is Mrs. Clark?"

"Fit as a fiddle, and looking forward to seeing you. We both hope you'll be coming back every season."

"I hope so too, Captain. It will be a bit sad, I expect, but I will be glad to see my old friends again."

"Some of the sadness will pass in time, Maggie, but I can surely understand," he said. He held out his hand to help her across the gangway. "Now welcome aboard."

During the crossing to the island she stood with Isabel Flowers on the deck, looking out over the spectacular view. The brisk wind took their breath away, but the marshes were so beautiful that they hardly noticed. As many times as Isabel must have made the crossing in the years she had worked for the Bakers, she seemed still dazzled by the sight. She pointed out to Maggie the gulls that followed the launch and the two porpoises that played in their wake, surfacing frequently for a breath of air. A crane at the water's edge stood poised, one foot held high, as though waiting for someone to paint his portrait or take his picture. Alexander Mews was inside the cabin, huddled behind the glass windows of the club launch and away from the cooler air.

Although it was warm by comparison with New York, it was chillier than Maggie remembered, especially on the water. The 1912 season, everyone said, had been unseasonably warm. Now the wind against her face reminded her of the brisk breezes of the Irish cliffs where she had grown up. She wanted to let it wash over her and cleanse her spirit. The cord grass in the marshes swayed with the passing of their vessel, as though bowing before it. The marshes, which nurtured so many creatures, seemed eternal, yet constantly shifting with every movement of the wake and tide. She never tired of them.

Maggie waited breathlessly for the turret of the Jekyl Island clubhouse to appear as they moved slowly up Jekyl Creek. A family of deer grazing along the riverbank suddenly raised their heads and watched in cautious immobility as the launch passed by. A covey of quail, startled by their passing, flew from a nesting place near the water's edge farther into the brush.

Then, as though conjured by magic, there it was, rising majestically upward, the little flag waving in the stiff breeze. The clubhouse. Maggie's heart began to race, and she felt a sense of panic rising within her. Could she step onto the island? This was where she had last seen Hector, where she had left him, where he lay beneath the soil. How could she come back, knowing he would not be there, that he would never be there again? *And yet,* she told herself, *he is here.* It was the only place she would ever find him.

The first footstep was the hardest. She stood at the gangplank for a moment, unable to move, to step off the rocking vessel onto the island they had both loved with such intensity. Then, suddenly, there was a gentle hand on her waist, as Isabel Flowers urged her forward, reassuring her. And once again Captain Clark stood waiting, his hand outstretched to help her ashore. "You can do it, Maggie," Isabel whispered in her ear. "I'm here beside you." She had told Isabel about Hector and Danny as soon as she felt she could trust her, and Isabel had taken her under her wing almost like a mother.

Maggie gave her a tearful smile, squeezing her arm in gratitude, and took a step forward. Captain Clark reached out for her hand and helped her take the other steps, until she was firmly on the wharf. Deirdre was there, waving with excitement, then holding out her arms in welcome. With a sense of relief, Maggie rushed into them, feeling that she had come home.

The gentle welcome and support that met her upon arrival strengthened her for the days ahead. She looked forward to a quiet afternoon when she could walk alone to the north end of the island and the little du Bignon cemetery. She wanted to go alone, for she needed to sit by Hector's grave for a time and tell him about their son.

For the moment, however, there were duties at Solterra that needed to be performed to get the house ready for Mrs. Baker's arrival the following week. Welcome, distracting duties. In some ways, it was better to be housed in the cottage than the clubhouse, for she had no real associations from the past at Solterra. But she missed having Deirdre just down the hall.

Maggie's room was on the third floor where, once again, she could look out over the marshes and the river or watch the club groundskeepers go about their tasks. She was sure her room must have the best view on the island. Her small bedchamber, simply furnished much like the one she had back in New York, was warm and cozy, and in one corner sat a brown wicker armchair, with chintz-covered pillows. There, after all her tasks were finished for the day—the rugs beaten, the duvets all shaken and aired, and the woodwork in the rooms Isabel had assigned to her thoroughly scrubbed and polished—she sat in that chair, wrote in her little notebook of her tangled feelings during her first days back at Jekyl, and gazed longingly at the sunset that burnished the waters of the marsh.

It was Sunday afternoon before Maggie had free time to go to the cemetery. As she walked along the river road, she gathered winter wildflowers along the way, even plucking a few camellia branches from the club compound's abundant bushes already rife with color. She was careful to break branches only in the most inconspicuous spots—down low—so as not to mar the beauty of the plant.

As she made her way toward the north end of the island, she strayed occasionally from the road to add to her bouquet some of the trumpet-shaped blooms of yellow jasmine, sweet-smelling winter honeysuckle, and even a few white diamond flowers and ladies' tresses, so like tiny orchids. She knew, the island would soon be rampant with flowers, but now they were relatively scarce and held only the promise of spring.

It took her nearly an hour to walk to the little cemetery on the edge of the marsh creek. The small tabby enclosure was peaceful, as the afternoon sun filtered through the live oaks and ancient cedar trees. She spread her woolen shawl on the ground beside Hector's grave, now marked by a little stone that bore his name, his place of birth, and the date of his death. Laying her flowers against the stone, she placed a few as well on George's grave.

Then she sat down on her shawl to talk to the man she still loved and tell him about their beautiful little boy and her life without them both. She completely lost track of time, and it was almost dusk before she realized that she must start back.

The one other thing Maggie wanted to do before Mrs. Baker arrived was to seek out Aleathia and thank her for her kindness two seasons before. The following afternoon just before suppertime she knocked on the Parlands' door. Aleathia, looking fit and fine as always, came to the front porch.

"Why, looky here. It's Miss Maggie," she said.

"Just Maggie, please."

"You're a sight for sore eyes, chile. Come in and tell Aleathia how you're doin'."

When she walked into the front room of the house, Page Parland greeted her warmly. "How're you doin', Miss Maggie. It's good to see you back at Jekyl and lookin' so well."

Then he said, "I'll let you ladies talk a spell," and walked out the back door to attend to some unnecessary duty, leaving them alone in the house.

"Aleathia," Maggie began as soon as they were alone, "I came to thank you for your help and kindness when I so badly needed a friend."

"I didn't do much, but I'm mighty glad if I could help a little. It's a blessing to have you back here on Jekyl. I hadn't heard a word since you left, 'cept I did ask Miss Deirdre 'bout you once, and she told me you were doin' fine, but she didn't give me no details."

"Then you don't know about my son?" asked Maggie.

"You had a little boy? How wonderful!" Aleathia beamed.

"Oh, Aleathia. I had the most beautiful baby boy in the world," Maggie smiled sadly.

"Who's lookin' after him now while you're on the island?"

Maggie's eyes clouded. "I wish I knew."

Aleathia's brow furrowed in concern. "What you talkin' 'bout, chile? What's happened?"

"It's a long story, Aleathia."

"Well, set a spell and tell Aleathia 'bout it."

Maggie sat before the fireplace and unfolded her story to her sympathetic listener. When it was over, Aleathia opened her arms to the young mother and held her while they wept together.

"Maggie, Maggie! They're here. The boat's already arrived," called Isabel on the morning of January 30. "Oh, do hurry, and put on the teapot. Mrs. Baker will want a cup of tea first thing."

"I've already put the kettle on." She laughed. "It'll be good to have Cook here again."

The cook, Mrs. Overton, who preferred not to be addressed by her first name, would be arriving on the launch with Mrs. Baker, her daughter, Frances, Abby Steers, Miss Beatty, and Philip, who would serve as Mrs. Baker's coach driver while on the island. Mrs. Overton was an important part of the household, for, even though they took many of their meals at the clubhouse, the Bakers had always preferred breakfast and tea at home and gave occasional dinner parties in their own large dining room.

The rooms for the new arrivals were all ready, and Maggie had placed vases of fresh flowers on their bedside tables. Within the next two weeks, much of the rest of the family would be coming, children and all, and the household would probably be bedlam for the next two months.

In the foyer with the other servants, Maggie waited anxiously for Mrs. Baker. *How hard it must be,* she thought, *for her to come back to Jekyl, which meant so much to Mr. Baker.* They had come here for so many years together. But Maggie was already feeling better and hoped that Mrs. Baker would find comfort here as well.

Alexander opened the front door as the carriage stopped in front of the cottage. Frances Baker was calling gaily, "Hello, hello everyone," as she appeared at the front door and saw the waiting staff lined up in the foyer. "How beautiful everything looks! It's so good to see you all again."

"Annette is not with you?" Isabel asked Mrs. Baker in surprise.

"Her mother took ill, and she had to leave my service for a while to take care of her. Miss Beatty helped me during the voyage, but I thought that perhaps Maggie could take over Annette's duties while we are at Jekyl."

Maggie was thrilled. It was a huge promotion and responsibility, even if it was only temporary. Isabel, she knew, would fill her in on all that was required, which would involve not only cleaning Mrs. Baker's bedchamber, but also helping her select her clothing for the day and perhaps even fixing her hair. Maggie knew from previous observations that there would be at least two different outfits each day, and perhaps more, since everyone dressed splendidly for dinner at the clubhouse and sometimes for other activities as well—such as an afternoon tea at one of the other cottages. She would help Mrs. Baker weave her long hair into the chignon she wore daily, and she would help her with her bath in all probability. She hoped she was up to the task.

"Here, Maggie," said Isabel later that evening, "let me show you which accessories Mrs. Baker requires with each outfit."

She opened a wardrobe filled with drawers of gloves, shawls, and tiny purses. One drawer was locked. "That's where she keeps her jewelry. She wears the key around her neck," Isabel said. "But you'll need to know what's inside, in case you want to recommend the diamond brooch or the emerald necklace or perhaps her favorite cameo. She bought that in Italy some years ago. The others were gifts from Mr. Baker. Perhaps she'll show you one day soon."

"Isabel, you are so kind to help me learn my duties."

"It's my job, dear."

But Isabel was a special sort of housekeeper. Some in her position kept their distance from the rest of the staff, except perhaps for the butler, the manservant who was on an equal rank with the housekeeper. But maids, cooks, and chauffeurs ranked lower on the social scale. Isabel, always more democratic than most in her station, made them all seem more like a family.

"She'll want a fire built every morning to warm the room before she gets up. But do be careful. Sometimes this chimney smokes a bit, and we must be sure the damper is wide open and that the wood is absolutely dry."

Maggie nodded. She had built many a fire back in her parents' cottage near Doolin, even with the wettest of wood. That was one chore for which she did not doubt her ability. The hair and clothes were quite another matter, however, and she was grateful for Isabel's instructions.

The days melted away as the household began to fill with family members. Mrs. Baker's son-in-law and her ten-year-old grandson, Jack, arrived with the boy's tutor in early February. Little Jack was ecstatic. The island was paradise for New York children. They could play outside in the south Georgia air without risk of frostbite. And there was so much to do. The Gould family next door had a swimming pool in the atrium of their house, which caught the winter sun and blocked the wind. They also had a building they called a casino, which held a bowling alley and an indoor tennis court.

When Jack wasn't doing his lessons under the watchful eye of Mrs. Holsey, he was free to run to the back of the clubhouse, where the small cluster of go-carts known as red bugs were parked. Anyone, even children as young as Jack, could drive the little gasoline-powered vehicles, which club members preferred to automobiles on their narrow roads. And it was not unusual to see men with gray beards chugging about the club compound on red bugs. Sometimes they took the little vehicles to the hard, wide beach, where they could race each other like children.

On other days, Jack's father sometimes took him horseback riding in the mornings, or the boy rode a bicycle with other boys on the island all along the many bike paths the millionaires had built beside the marshes and through the woods. Jack's presence cast a cheerfulness on the household that only a child could bring. Maggie knew that Danny would love it here.

The club season was passing with good weather, though even in early March the mornings were still cool, and Mrs. Baker wanted a little fire in the grate before she got out of bed. Maggie stoked the blaze once more, wanting to be sure the room was toasty before her mistress, who was already stirring, arose. Then she hurried down the back stairs to the kitchen to fetch Mrs. Baker's morning tea and toast.

The cook had arranged a little vase of Cherokee roses alongside the plates of toast, butter, jam, a small bowl of mixed fruit, a teapot, and a china teacup and saucer.

"Thank you, Mrs. Overton," Maggie said. "The flowers are lovely. I'll take them right up to Mrs. Baker."

Maggie climbed the steep back stairs from the kitchen to the second floor of the large, rambling house. When she pushed open the door to Mrs. Baker's room, Frances Baker was already up, wearing her warm, flannel wrapper and her bedroom slippers, seated at her dressing table, and brushing her long, gray hair.

"Good morning, Maggie," she said cheerfully. "That tea looks wonderful. Please put it on the table there." She gestured toward the brightest spot in the room, a small alcove surrounded by bay windows that let in the morning light and overlooked Jekyl River. Maggie placed the tray on the table, opened the curtains, curtseyed to Mrs. Baker, and stoked the fire once more.

"Are you warm enough, ma'am? It's a bit chilly today."

"I'm fine, Maggie. Could you hand me my glasses, dear? They're on the bedside table. I'd like to be able to see to butter my toast this morning." She laughed lightly. "It's good to be here, isn't it, Maggie? Jekyl always calms my spirit, and I look forward to the mornings again. I do dread the thought of returning to New York."

"Yes, ma'am," Maggie replied. It was true for her as well. There was something healing about the island and this closeness to nature.

"Send Miss Beatty on down for her breakfast, and then come back in a few minutes and help me decide what to wear this morning. I haven't a single plan all day except to be with my family or perhaps take a carriage ride. I don't need to wear anything fancy. I just want to be comfortable." Frances Baker often preferred to breakfast alone and start the day in tranquility, usually leaving orders with Maggie the night before, so that she would know whether or not to bring up a tray.

Maggie had grown even fonder of the older woman in the weeks they had been at Jekyl. Between her and Isabel Flowers, it was like having her own family about her. Of course, Maggie didn't mistake Mrs. Baker's kindness for motherly love, but she was pleasant to be around, nonjudgmental, and always treated Maggie with courtesy. In turn, Maggie tried hard to please her.

When Maggie returned, Mrs. Baker was seated at the table, finishing her toast and pouring herself a second cup of tea. "Now, what do you think I should wear today? Just lay out whatever you like."

This was the part of the day that Maggie enjoyed most of all—going through Frances Baker's elaborate wardrobe to find just the right combination of fabric and style that she thought would suit her mistress's mood for the day. Color was never an issue, for ever since the day Mr. Baker died, she had put on no color but black, and indeed her entire wardrobe included no other hue. The crepe de chine was much too formal for a casual day. Perhaps the wool henrietta or a simple cotton Viyella. Finally, she chose a soft long-sleeved wool batiste dress with a high collar and a simple two-tiered skirt.

"How's this, ma'am?" she asked, holding up the dress for Mrs. Baker's approval.

"Just perfect, Maggie," she said, setting down her teacup. "Now help me get into it."

As soon as Mrs. Baker was dressed, she handed Maggie the key to her jewelry drawer. "Bring me my pearls, please," she said.

Maggie unlocked the drawer and left the key in the lock, as she fastened the pearls around Frances Baker's neck. Glancing indifferently into the mirror of her vanity table, Mrs. Baker turned toward the door and started down the steps to the parlor, with Maggie at her side to assist her.

"What's that smell?" asked Frances Baker.

"Smell, ma'am?"

"Smells like smoke. Did you open the flue in my bedroom, Maggie?" Mrs. Baker asked. "I've already asked George Cowman to come by to look at it this week. Sometimes the damper sticks."

"Yes, ma'am. I'm sure I did, but I'll go back and check right away."

As soon as Mrs. Baker was safely down the stairs, Maggie rushed back up. When she entered the bedroom, she was surprised to notice a light haze of smoke in the room. Maggie was sure the flue was open, but she knelt beside the fireplace, where the fire had died down, put a handkerchief over her nose and mouth, and peered as best she could up into the fireplace. She rose, coughing. The flue was definitely open. It had to be something else.

Something caught her eye in the back window as she still knelt beside the fireplace. Smoke was pouring out the dormer windows of the attic.

"Oh, no!" she cried.

She raced to the washstand, grabbed the pitcher now only half-full of water, and rushed up the attic stairs. Smoke was seeping from the cracks all around the door. She was hoping that the pitcher of water and the blankets that were kept in the attic trunk could smother the fire. Slowly she opened the door, but flames were leaping everywhere. She dropped the pitcher, closed the door as quickly as she could, and ran down the stairs.

"Fire!" she cried. "The attic is on fire!"

"Oh, good heavens," Mrs. Baker said. "Maggie, hurry, run and ask Mr. Grob to sound the alarm. We'll try to save what we can."

"Mother, you go outside," said Frances Thacher, who had been going over a dinner menu with Mrs. Baker. "We'll take care of it all. Don't exert yourself. Miss Beatty, take her outside." Her nurse-companion was already at Mrs. Baker's side, guiding her by the elbow toward the front door.

Maggie raced to the clubhouse next door and up the brick steps to Ernest Grob's office.

"Mr. Grob! Mr. Grob! Please sound the alarm. Solterra is on fire!" she shrieked.

Julius Falk, who was sitting across the desk from Ernest Grob, leapt to his feet and ran out the door. In a moment Maggie heard the alarm bell. Mr. Grob stood in the clubhouse foyer loudly instructing all staff members. "Rush to Solterra. It's on fire. Do what you can."

By the time Maggie got back to the smoking house, scarlet flames were leaping out the attic windows. Members of Mrs. Baker's staff were hauling tables and chairs, plants, and pictures out on to the lawn. Club employees rushed to help. Some of the braver men raced up the stairs to the second floor, grabbing whatever they could find in the way of furnishings. Cook was running in and out the back door with dishes, pitchers, and whatever she could lay her hands on.

Ignoring the danger, Maggie dashed back into the house and, by some miracle, was able to make it up the stairs to her room and rescue her journal and her photographs of Hector, Danny, and her parents, which she stuffed quickly into her pockets. Then she thought, *her clothes. She will need her clothes.* She hurried to Mrs. Baker's bedroom. The smoke was so thick that she could barely see the other side of the room. Trying to hold her breath, but coughing nonetheless, she snatched all the dresses she could carry from the wardrobe.

Remembering the jewelry, she quickly opened the top drawer where the key was still in the lock, seized the little box that she knew contained Mrs. Baker's best jewelry, including her diamond brooch and cameo. Then she rushed downstairs once more, gasping for breath in the open air. As soon as she was outside again, she laid the clothes across the back of a sofa on the lawn and handed the little box to Frances Baker.

"Oh, my!" said a stunned Mrs. Baker, looking with bewilderment at her dresses. "Do you think I shall ever be able to wear them again?" Tears stood in her eyes. "But thank you, my dear, for rescuing my jewelry box. All of these were gifts from Mr. Baker."

Maggie scarcely heard her, for she had already scurried back into the house for one more thing—the photographs of little Abby and Frederic Baker that stood on the parlor mantle. She knew they were as precious and irreplaceable to Mrs. Baker as her own photographs were to her.

By ten o'clock, the lawn was littered with furniture and bric-a-brac, and the house was a flaming shell. By noon it was a hot bed of glowing cinders. The workers had saved much, but not all of the furnishings.

Sally Gould, Mrs. Baker's next-door neighbor at Jekyl, insisted that Frances Baker and her family come to stay at her cottage, Chichota. They had plenty of room, she insisted, and the clubhouse was almost full at this most popular part of the season. Frances Baker accepted gratefully, with little thought as to what her servants might do, for in the Gould household servants' quarters were much more limited and already full. But Mr. Grob managed quietly to find a place for them all for the few days that Frances Baker would remain on the island.

"We're going home on Friday," Frances Baker announced bravely to her assembled staff the next day. "But I'll rebuild Solterra as soon as possible."

Maggie listened to her words, but she also watched her eyes. She understood better than anyone else that Mrs. Baker did not feel nearly as brave as she sounded.

Chapter Seventeen

5 SEPTEMBER 1915 NEW YORK CITY

Maggie sat on the green bench in Central Park and gently rocked the carriage where the Steers baby was almost asleep. Abby Steers had dropped him off at Mrs. Baker's house for the afternoon to do some shopping with her cousin Franny, knowing that Maggie had eagerly volunteered to watch him any time.

At the moment, however, Maggie's eyes were fastened on the golden-haired little boy racing across the lawn after the red ball he had failed to catch. He brought it back to Suzanne, who tossed it to him once more. This time, to his obvious surprise, he caught it and held it up for her to see, laughing with delight.

Maggie wanted nothing more in life than to run to him, gather him up in her arms, and hold him close. She wanted to brush her cheek against his and feel its softness, to smell that sweet childhood fragrance of soap and young skin, to look deeply into his blue eyes for a flicker of recognition. But she knew that she could not do that and that she would never hold him again as long as Henry Barrett lived. The restraining order still did not allow her anywhere near Danny.

Suzanne never looked at her directly, but she was well aware of Maggie's presence. She had seen her for the first time in more than two years almost a month ago, when Maggie had been baby-sitting the Steers baby and had strolled him to the park. Since that time, she had brought Danny back to the park as often as possible, to this very spot near the pond so that Maggie, on days when she was there, might at least be able to see him. He was almost three now and such an adorable and loving little boy.

Suzanne never acknowledged Maggie's presence, for to do so would mean that she would have to remove the child from her sight. The New York district judge said so. Although the household servants, with the exception of Eloise Fowler, were sympathetic toward Maggie, there was little they could do to alter the situation. But Suzanne could at least give the mother a glimpse of her child, while pretending not to see her, and she had every intention of doing so until Mr. Barrett or his lawyer friends put a stop to it.

The game of catch ended abruptly when the child was suddenly distracted by a yellow butterfly that fluttered past his shoulder. Butterflies were growing rarer in New York, and the boy was enthralled. When it flew away he followed it toward the pond. Suzanne raced toward him, but he had already stopped at the water's edge to watch the butterfly flitter out beyond his reach.

With her eye still on the child, Suzanne, aware that the sun was getting low in the sky, was gathering up the things they had brought with them—the red ball, a boat with white sails for the pond, and Danny's blue sweater, which he had peeled off in the sunshine. She took him by the hand and walked toward the park gate. The path she selected led them by Maggie's bench, where Suzanne paused briefly, never making eye contact with Maggie but saying to the child, "See the baby, Danny. He's taking a nap."

The boy peered with wonder at the sleeping infant, then smiled up at Suzanne and said, "I like the baby."

Maggie, her eyes fixed on her son's face, caught her breath at his beauty, his perfection, the sweetness of his voice. She had not been this near him since that one fateful visit after which she had been barred from the Barrett household, but now at such close range she was able to drink in the perfect innocence of his face and his long silky lashes brushing his cheek as he looked down at the baby. It was all she could do not to reach out and take him in her arms.

The guileless joy she saw in his eyes reminded her of Hector's expression when she had told him that she was expecting a child. She breathed deeply, as though she could smell his presence, and looked gratefully at Suzanne, silently mouthing the words, "Thank you," though the recipient of the words never looked her way.

It was a brief but timeless moment before Suzanne led the boy away. "We'd better go now, Danny, but we'll come back tomorrow to this very same place, if we possibly can," she said, louder than was necessary.

For the first time Danny looked up at Maggie, as though he could feel her eyes on him. She smiled at him, and he smiled shyly back, looking puzzled as though he were not sure whether he might have seen her before. Then, holding Suzanne's hand, he turned away and walked beside her toward the gate. He turned back once to look at Maggie, giving her one final, sweet smile that broke her heart in pieces.

"I don't think Mama will ever rebuild Solterra," Henry Lake said to his sister, Frances. "With all this talk of war, everything is so uncertain." It was early January of 1916, and Frances had been complaining that there were no plans to go to Jekyl Island again this year.

"Perhaps there we could at least forget about it all for a while," Frances said. "Mama may be thinking about going down for a while in February with Miss Beatty, but she plans to stay in the clubhouse. I don't think I would enjoy that so very much with the children."

"I think she's going down to sign her lot lease over to Dick Crane, who has made her a good offer."

"I don't see why they couldn't do that in New York."

"They could, Frances," her brother said with the patient voice one might use in telling the obvious to a child, "but I think she wants to go down one more time to say goodbye. Jekyl was a pretty important part of her life."

War had been raging in Europe ever since Austria had declared war on Serbia after a Serb extremist assassinated Franz Ferdinand, the heir to the Austro-Hungarian throne. His pregnant wife, Sophie, had been shot first, right through the abdomen, killing her and her baby. Her husband's life could not be saved either, and in the aftermath, Europe seemed to have gone mad in a rush to conflict, with Russia declaring war on Austria, Germany declaring war on Russia, France declaring war on Germany, and Germany invading neutral Belgium to get to France. England, which had by treaty guaranteed Belgian neutrality, then declared war on Germany—all this in the months of July and August 1914. It was like a giant line of deadly dominoes standing on end, one knocking over another until all had fallen.

"Insanity, pure insanity," Lake said. "The world has gone crazy."

"We should be in it too," his brother-in-law, John Thacher, said. "After the *Lusitania*, how can we stay neutral?"

The sinking of the *Lusitania* the previous May had reminded many of the sinking of the *Titanic* such a short time before. But this time, there had been no iceberg, only a German U-Boat, and the sinking had been deliberate. While most of the almost twelve hundred passengers had been British, one hundred thirty-eight Americans as well had died on the *Lusitania*, and war fever had been running high ever since.

"Oh, John, let's not even talk of war. It would be just awful if we were to get involved," Frances said.

They were all too young to remember the Civil War, but they had heard tales from their stepfather's friends, old-timers now, who still recalled the piles of dead bodies at Antietam and Gettysburg and the lost limbs of those who had managed to return alive. The younger men, however, could remember only Teddy Roosevelt's "splendid little war" against the Spanish in 1898. And many of them were eager to fight.

"We should be in it, Frances, helping our allies like England and France, not sitting here like scaredy-cats," John argued. Some of his friends were of different minds on the issue, and some, mostly those of German descent, even sided with the Central Powers. John, however, was staunch in his pro-English perspective, and he was adamant in his position. "All we do now is sit by and watch. It's just not right."

"The war is on the other side of the Atlantic," his wife said. "How can we be expected to send troops way over there?"

"We don't live in the Middle Ages," he said. "We have plenty of resources, and we could make a difference."

"We're already making a difference by supplying both France and Germany with weapons and supplies," Frances said. "All it's doing is putting money into American pockets. We shouldn't even be doing that."

"Don't forget, my dear, that we're among those who are benefiting." John referred to their stepfather's chain of warehouses in the port of New York, which were always filled with arms and munitions about to be shipped out to Europe.

"Precisely," Henry broke in. "Let's just profit from the insanity and stay out of it ourselves."

Other members of the household, including their mother, were equally distressed by the war's destruction. After Mrs. Baker had finished with the *New York Times* each day, Isabel brought it to the kitchen, where the servants all sat around the big dining table and listened to Alexander read the war news aloud. Many of them had family still in the old country, and they were horrified at the numbers of war dead and the endless battles.

Although America was not in the war, people took sides, mostly against the Central Powers, and articles began to appear in the newspapers about states banning the teaching of German in public schools.

Alexander Mews hurried into the Baker kitchen just before the noonday meal, waving the *New York Times* of April 7, 1917. "It's finally happened," he said, as the other servants gathered around the table to hear the latest.

"The President has asked Congress to declare war on Germany. I think we're finally in it, whether we like it or not," he told the eager listeners and began to read the article that described America's decision to declare war.

They listened tight-lipped, though no one was really surprised. They had waited anxiously to see what President Wilson would do after German U-boats sank three American merchant ships the previous month. In fact, most were surprised he hadn't acted sooner. It was curious how they no longer thought of themselves as Irish or English or French. They were all Americans now, fervent with patriotism.

Among the men who volunteered almost at once for military service was Alexander's son, Rudy. He appeared at the kitchen door in early May wearing his new uniform to announce that he was to be shipped to France the following day. All the servants gathered around to wish him well.

"Now you take care of yourself, Rudy," said Isabel. "We want you home in one piece." She patted his cheek and gave him an affectionate hug. The boy's mother had been dead since he was twelve, and his father had taken the position as butler in the Baker household, with the provision that his son could live with him. They had for many years shared the chauffeur's quarters over the garage, and she had watched him grow up for almost a decade.

"I promise, Miss Flowers." He grinned, placing on his head his wool felt campaign hat, its round brim tipped slightly forward in a cocky sort of way. He was clearly conscious of how attractive he looked in his uniform and the sense of heroism his impending departure suggested.

"Have you said goodbye to Deirdre yet?" Maggie asked. The two of them had been seeing one another on a fairly regular basis for the past two years. Deirdre was head over heels in love, but Maggie wasn't sure about Rudy. He seemed reluctant to make a firm commitment.

"I'm off to see her as soon as I leave you good folks," he assured her.

"Now, son," Alexander was saying, "you write as soon as you can. You know we'll be worried until we hear from you."

"I promise, Papa," he said again. Alexander walked with him to the gate, and Maggie watched through the window as the two embraced for the last time. She knew that if Hector were still alive, he too would be wearing that uniform and heading for Europe in the near future.

Everyone in the Baker household was eager to help in the war effort. Even Mrs. Baker and Miss Beatty were knitting great piles of wool socks for the troops. Mrs. Baker's personal maid, Annette, responded to General Pershing's call for women who spoke French to serve in the Signal Corps. She was very proud to be accepted, for only three hundred women had been taken, and she too was to be shipped out to France, where she would help with communications.

Once again Maggie took over Annette's role as Mrs. Baker's personal maid. But she also wanted to do her part for the troops. She didn't speak French nor was she a nurse, but at least she could volunteer at the Red Cross office to roll bandages or do whatever else they required.

As the war continued and the wounded began to arrive back in New York, the Red Cross assigned Maggie to go to Bellevue Hospital on her afternoons off to read or write letters for wounded soldiers who had been sent home for treatment. It seemed such a small contribution, but she did as much as she could, and Mrs. Baker was always generous with her time when she knew that Maggie had duties with the Red Cross.

28 AUGUST 1918

On a sweltering summer afternoon Maggie sat beside the bed of a young man with bandaged eyes in one of the wards at Bellevue. His name was Wilber Fendig, and he had been blinded in a battle on the banks of the Marne River when slivers of shrapnel from an exploding shell pierced both his eyes and took off his left ear. He was an emotional wreck, and though he could hear with his remaining ear, he was sure that he would never be of use to anyone again.

Maggie read him letters from home, from his mother, his sister, and a woman named Gladys who wrote every single day and promised to love him always no matter what. But Wilber only turned his face to the wall when he heard these proclamations. Maggie longed to comfort him, but he seemed beyond her reach. All she could do was come twice a week and read to him. She read Mark Twain, which he seemed to enjoy, and sometimes she read from the Psalms, though she had to be careful which ones she chose—none about lifting up one's eyes unto the hills or seeing the light.

Wilber seemed to like the Forty-Sixth Psalm, which began "God is our refuge and strength, a very present help in trouble." He seemed especially to respond to the verse that promised, "He maketh wars to cease unto the end of the earth." But he had not made Wilber's war end, and Maggie knew that his battle within was perhaps his greatest struggle.

She tried to talk with him about people with afflictions who had done wonderful things. Her father had told her that the poet Homer was blind, and she had read somewhere that John Milton was blind when he wrote *Paradise Lost* and that Beethoven was deaf when he wrote his greatest symphony. She tried to share their gifts to the world with Wilber, but he was a country boy from Tennessee, and he had never heard of any of them except Beethoven, and he told her that he didn't plan to write music anyhow.

He just wanted to go back home and farm, and whoever heard of a blind farmer? Finally she just read to him, for it seemed to calm his spirit more than anything else.

A few days later, as Maggie sat silently beside Wilber's bed, realizing that he had fallen asleep as she read, a nurse named Sharon Pickens came over and spoke to her.

"Maggie, there's a soldier on the sun porch that I'd like you to speak to. He saw you come in and asked about you. I told him I'd have you stop by."

"I'll be happy to, Sharon. Just point him out. I think Private Fendig is worn out from my reading anyhow, but if he wakes up and asks about me, tell him I'll be back on Wednesday to finish the story."

Maggie rose and followed Nurse Pickens out to the sun porch, where six or eight young men, some still in their teens, sat in wheelchairs. Some of them had bandaged heads, others arms in casts or legs propped out in front of them, gazing at the greenery outside, playing cards, or reading.

"Sergeant O'Neil, here is Miss O'Brien to speak with you," the nurse said, leaning over the shoulder of a man whose head had slumped forward and whose left arm was missing below the elbow. The stump was swathed in white bandages that had been recently changed, and the upper part of his left leg and groin area were bandaged as well.

The man swiveled his wheelchair around with his good arm.

"Maggie, is it really you?" he said, an uncertain smile breaking across his face.

"Stuart! Stuart O'Neil. I can't believe it!" She bent toward him and placed her hand gently on his shoulder. Then she turned back to Nurse Pickens. "Thank you, Sharon. Stuart and I are old friends." The nurse nodded and pushed forward a chair that was lined up against the wall so that Maggie could sit down.

"I never thought I'd see you again, Maggie, though I looked everywhere. You just disappeared. And I never knew why."

"But here I am again and so glad to see you alive. You have been in the war, I see." She gestured toward his amputated arm. "Are you going to be all right?"

"As all right as a one-armed man can be, I guess. At least it was my left arm. I can still direct traffic, if they'll let me back on the force this way."

"I wish this dreadful war were over," she said.

"A lot of us wish it had never begun."

"But you volunteered?"

"Yes," he said, "I thought I might be able to help. Then this happened in my second big battle—at the Marne—and they sent me home, so I didn't get to help much." He smiled with only a slight twinge of bitterness.

"Enough to become a sergeant, evidently." Maggie smiled encouragingly.

"Field promotion after so many officers in my platoon were killed. A lot of 'em didn't make it back, and a lot of others are worse off than me. I see you've been reading to Private Fendig. He's one I'm truly worried about."

"So am I, Stuart. He seems to have a girl back home who cares about him, but he won't even answer her letters."

"He's luckier than I am then—to have a girl back home, I mean." He hesitated for a moment before asking quietly, "Why did you run away, Maggie?"

"Stuart, I ... perhaps I'll tell you one day, but not today. Today let's just enjoy seeing one another again."

"Are you married?" he asked.

"No. I'm working as a maid to a woman named Frances Baker who lives on Fifth Avenue. She's very good to me, and I enjoy the rest of the staff. My life is as good as can be expected, I suppose."

"Are you promised to anyone?"

"No. I'm only working—not much social life to speak of," she said lightly.

"Perhaps when I'm well enough you would finally consider letting me take you to that picture show we once talked about. There are so many films I want to see."

"I don't go to the pictures much," Maggie said. In fact, she had been to only one since she'd been in New York, when Deirdre had dragged her to see Theda Bara in *Cleopatra*. The film had so shocked her, with her Irish-Catholic upbringing, that she had refused to go back.

"They might take our minds off our problems," he suggested. "I think you'd like some of the Charlie Chaplin films, for instance. They always make me laugh, and that's something I need to do a lot of these days."

"Of course I'll go to the pictures with you, Stuart, if you can find films that can make me laugh. I don't do much of that anymore."

Meeting an old friend like Stuart O'Neil brought color back to Maggie's cheeks. In the days to come, when she went to read to Wilber, she always spent at least half an hour with Stuart. He was getting better every day, and Nurse Pickens said he would be discharged from the hospital soon and probably from the army as well. He was already in the convalescent ward where the soldiers stayed only until they were able to function on their own.

Maggie was pleased, but not surprised, when she returned to the hospital on one of her scheduled afternoons in late September and Stuart greeted her in the lobby dressed in his uniform, the empty lower half of the left sleeve folded and pinned up near the shoulder of his jacket.

"Why, Stuart, how fine you look!" she said.

"I wanted you to see me at least once in my uniform before I have to give it up. I'm being discharged this week."

"Where will you be living?"

"I'm going back to my old room at my boarding house. The landlady never rented it after I left, said she was saving it for me."

"Will you be going back on the police force?"

"I don't know yet whether they'll have a place for a one-armed man or not. I'll have to wait and see."

Maggie laid her hand against his cheek, proud of the way he was dealing with his new disability—so unlike Wilber Fendig. But then, she supposed, it was easier to do without an arm than one's eyes. And even Wilber was beginning to take more interest in what was going on around him. He listened more attentively to her readings and had begun to ask about training programs for the blind. She had hope that he would soon find it in his heart to respond to the letters of the woman named Gladys, which still came every day.

"I know there's a lot you can do," she reassured Stuart.

"I can sure go to the pictures, if I can just find a girl who'll go with me."

"Well, I think you've found her, Stuart. Just name the day."

They agreed to the following Saturday afternoon, her full day off. She gave Stuart the Baker address and asked him to come around to the service entrance at two o'clock. "I'll be waiting," she said.

Stuart rewarded her with a broad, happy smile and a quick salute. "I'll be there, come hell or high water."

She watched him as he went down the hospital steps, holding on to the handrail for balance and still limping because of his thigh wound, but even so there seemed to be a bounce in his step.

Chapter Eighteen

MAGGIE NO LONGER WENT TO THE PARK on weekdays in the hope of being able to watch Danny play, for he and Suzanne had not returned for their afternoon visits since the beginning of September. But on their last visit Suzanne had managed to drop a piece of paper in front of Maggie's bench as they left the park. Maggie scooped it up eagerly as soon as they were out of sight. On it were written only the words "St. Bernard's School."

From this and from their subsequent absence from Central Park during the week Maggie had surmised correctly that Henry Barrett had enrolled the child at St. Bernard's, a private and exclusive academy for boys. Maggie had heard of it from Abby Steers, who was thinking of enrolling her own son there as soon as he was old enough. Danny wasn't quite six yet. She wondered if Henry Barrett was trying to get him out from under foot.

Maggie found the address on East 98th Street, and as often as possible she waited across the street from the entrance as classes ended for the day, hoping to catch a glimpse of Danny before the latest model black Packard appeared to pick the boy up and whisk him away. She dared not come too often, lest Friedrich, who was still the Barrett chauffeur, should recognize her and alert his employer, but she tried to be there at least twice a month, wearing a scarf to hide her hair and sometimes a pair of glasses she had bought for a quarter at a thrift shop on Third Avenue.

Occasionally on Saturday afternoons Suzanne and Danny would still come to the park, but such instances were rare. The last time she had seen them, Suzanne had reminded Danny loudly as they passed Maggie's bench that they would be returning to the park to see the autumn leaves on the last Saturday in September.

At exactly two p.m. that Saturday, Stuart O'Neil, this time in civilian clothes—knocked on the back door of the Baker household. Mrs. Overton opened the door, glanced at the folded left sleeve of his jacket, and said, "You must be Stuart. Maggie's told me all about you. She's ready to go, I think. I'll call her. Would you like a cup of tea?"

"No, thank you. Shall I just wait for her here?"

But Mrs. Overton had already gone to the foot of the servants' stairwell and was calling, "Maggie, Mr. O'Neil is here."

Maggie appeared almost at once, wearing a hunter green wool dress that Mrs. Baker had given her, one that her employer no longer wore now that she dressed only in black. Maggie had taken the bodice in for her smaller frame and shortened the skirt to reflect the new wartime fashions that had lifted hemlines above the ankle.

Stuart looked at her in admiration. "My, you look very nice."

"Thank you, Stuart. I see you've met Mrs. Overton." Maggie was putting her shawl around her shoulders."

"Yes, I have, and thank you, Mrs. Overton, for the offer of tea. May I take a rain check?" he asked.

The cook beamed at him. "Anytime, Mr. O'Neil. Anytime for a hero like yourself."

Stuart laughed with embarrassment. "You're too generous, ma'am." Then he turned to Maggie and asked, "Shall we go? The film starts at three."

"Yes, I'm ready."

Once they had passed through the gate onto the sidewalk of Fifth Avenue, Maggie hesitated for a moment. Then she turned to Stuart and said, "Could we go to a later film? There's something I want to show you."

He looked at her with curiosity, but the film ran every hour, and it would be no problem to go at four o'clock instead. "Sure," he said.

She turned south on the avenue. "It's this way," she said.

Stuart flushed slightly and hesitated. "I'm sorry, Maggie," he said, "I can't walk on the outside and give you my arm as well," he said, gesturing helplessly toward his empty sleeve. "I guess you'll have to choose."

"I can't see that it's a very great problem," she said, smiling. "Let's just cross the street."

"Now why didn't I think of that?" he asked. "I can see that I've still got a bit of adjusting to do."

They crossed over Fifth Avenue to the park side of the street, and Stuart, walking on the side nearest the gutter, held out his good arm to Maggie. "Now where do you want to take me?"

Maggie headed toward the south end of the park. "I have something important to show you," she repeated, leading him through the gate into Central Park and to the bench she usually occupied, overlooking the pond. As they sat down Stuart gazed about, looking puzzled. Her brow was furrowed in concentration as she cast her eyes about the park. He sat quietly and waited.

Finally she turned to him and said, "Stuart, you asked me once why I ran away. Now I want to show you. It's only fair that you know, for once you learn the truth, you may want to change your mind about squiring me to the films or anywhere else for that matter."

He looked at her, bewildered, still waiting. She gestured with her head toward a small figure bent over the edge of the pond, about to launch the sailboat in his hand.

"Do you see that little boy?"

Stuart nodded, watching her face.

"Well, he's mine."

"Yours?" he asked.

"Yes. He's my son. I was expecting him when I came back from Jekyl Island the time you met me at the wharf."

"I don't understand. Why doesn't he live with you? Where is his father?"

Maggie could see the puzzlement in his eyes and thought she discerned disappointment as well. "It's a long story," she said.

Silent for a moment, she watched the child playing under Suzanne's watchful eye. Danny had grown taller, and his pale blond hair had darkened a bit, almost to the color of her own. He was still beautiful, though the innocent smile that had so enchanted his mother was no longer so readily on his lips. He seemed more serious and thoughtful now, less carefree at almost six than he had been at three. But when he seemed to think no one was watching, she could still catch an occasional glimpse of his unbounded joy, so like his father's, at watching a soaring bird or just running free through the grass.

"I met his father at the Jekyl Island Club. He was a waiter there. We were to be married. He drowned trying to save a friend's life."

"Oh, Maggie," said Stuart. "I'm so sorry." He took her right hand in his own. "I wish you had told me then. Perhaps I could have helped. I know it must have been difficult for you, going through all that alone." He watched her face, as she lifted her chin in a gesture of defiance. She didn't want his pity any more than he wanted hers.

"There was nothing you could have done, Stuart. And I won't say that I'm sorry or ashamed—or claim to feel any of those things I should perhaps feel. I loved his father very much, and I love Danny. I have no regrets. But I thought you should know."

"Why doesn't he live with you?"

"That's the other part of this very long story." Again she sat silent, fighting tears and trying to bring forth the words to tell Stuart the whole truth. "A guest at the club, a young man, was very kind to me after Hector's death. He gave me an address of a place I could go in New York to have my baby, and he promised me a position in his family's household where I could keep Danny. But then, when I went there, he too had died ... on the *Titanic.*"

"My God," said Stuart. "Poor Maggie." He squeezed her hand and looked into her eyes as she poured out the rest of her story.

"I've had to watch him grow up from a distance," she said in conclusion, and then sat, silent, waiting for his reaction.

"Good Lord, Maggie, how awful it must have been—must be—for you."

"I suppose I'm luckier than some. At least I have a friend in the household—Suzanne, she's the woman standing off to the left—who brings him here so I can see him from time to time."

"He's a beautiful little boy, almost as beautiful as his mother, and he's got a strong pitching arm," Stuart said, almost wistfully, watching the child who had just thrown his ball to Suzanne. Losing interest in the game of pitch, he was running beside the water as the wind caught the sails of his little boat on the pond. "Isn't there anything we can do to help you get him back?"

"I've tried everything I can think of. Now I just come here. Or sometimes I wait outside his school to watch him when I can. It's torture knowing that he lives with the man who claims to be his grandfather only twelve blocks from where I work. But at least I know he's alive, he's nearby, and he seems to be happy. He's just started to school," she said proudly, "at St. Bernard's. I know he'll get a fine education there. And I get to see him once in a while, though he doesn't know who I am."

Stuart watched her face, and she felt tears well up in her eyes under his close scrutiny. She did not let them fall.

"Did you imagine that I would care for you less knowing about your child, Maggie?"

She didn't know what she had expected, only that she wanted him to know. She felt she owed it to him to explain her sudden disappearance that spring in 1912. He had been her friend then as he was now, and she wished she had trusted him more. But it had been just too soon after Hector's death.

She needed to work it all out in her own mind and heart.

"I didn't know, Stuart. It was certainly possible, but I just needed to be alone. I wanted Danny more than anything, but I didn't want my problems to hurt anyone else."

"Your disappearance hurt more than anything."

"I know. It was a cruel thing to do, and I'm sorry, but I was thinking only of myself and my baby at that point. I hope you can forgive me someday. For everything."

"Well," he said, "I guess a part of both of us is missing now. Maybe we can make a new beginning with that as common ground."

"I hope so, Stuart." She looked at his gentle face, realizing it was true that they had more in common now than they had ever had before. They had shared each other's losses and grief. Perhaps it would be enough.

"Do you care for me less because of a missing arm?"

"No, of course not. You're still the same person."

"And so are you, Maggie. We've both learned a bit more about the unfairness of life, but then that's part of living, I guess."

She thought about his words, remembering Mrs. Baker's losing her husband and then her house at Jekyl in such a brief time. She thought about Wilber Fendig and how his self-pity could keep him from ever knowing happiness again. *Don't give in to the pain, Maggie,* her cousin Eleanor had said to her once.

Stuart was a perfect model of the kind of courage she needed. She could see that he had already forgiven her that selfish act of abandoning his kindness without explanation. She was glad that she had told him the reason at long last, that she had shown him Danny, and that he understood. There was a depth and strength in Stuart O'Neil that she hadn't realized before.

"You know," he said, "we could skip the picture show this afternoon and just sit here and watch that fine-looking boy over there."

"Oh, Stuart, I'd like that very much. We have a lot of catching up to do, and we could do it right here."

He smiled his acquiescence and turned his attention to the little boy with the sailboat, as though he were trying to memorize his features. Maggie had not felt this happy for a long time. She began to relax as the two of them sat on the Central Park bench, watching her son play and unfolding for each other the story of their lives over the past six years.

The New York Police Department, after several appeals, finally allowed Stuart to come back to work, but only at a desk job, filling out reports and doing other types of paperwork. His old friends on the force were happy to see him again and did whatever they could to ease the transition, but it was difficult for him not to be out on the streets. It would take some getting used to.

Seeing Maggie again helped his sagging spirits. He had been surprised to learn about her little boy, for he would never have supposed Maggie to be the kind of woman who would lose her virginity before marriage. It bothered him more than he let on, but in the end he supposed they both were damaged in a way. He knew above all that he still loved her in spite of everything.

She seemed content to spend time with him again, much more so than she had seemed six years ago, when he had the impression that she liked him, but only in a sisterly sort of way. Now, at least, she let him hold her hand whenever they went to the picture show, and she allowed him to kiss her good night when he brought her home. He had not dared try to touch her in any other way, nor would he, unless someday she would consent to be his wife.

Making love to a woman would be awkward with only one arm, but he would manage somehow, and Maggie tolerated with a light spirit their little moments of awkwardness when there was no arm to give her at the appropriate moment. They laughed together on these occasions, and she always found some way to overcome his embarrassment.

He wanted to take her to Newark to meet his brother, but he did not plan to tell his brother and sister-in-law about her child. In a way, it was easier that Danny did not live with her. It was one less difficulty for them to overcome or explain. But then, he felt ashamed of his own reaction, telling himself he would do anything he could to help her get the child back. He knew though that without money it would be an uphill battle, particularly when Henry Barrett seemed to have unlimited resources. Stuart had done some checking on him to see what weaknesses he might have, where he might be vulnerable, but so far he had come up with nothing useful.

Perhaps if he and Maggie were married and had a child of their own, her heart would heal. It was a joy he could only dream of for now—being a father and Maggie's husband. He was sure she must know how much he wanted that, though he had said nothing to her so far about marriage for fear of frightening her away again. For the moment he was happy just to be with her, to have her smile at him, and to see the genuine affection in her eyes when she spoke to him.

Chapter Nineteen

"ARMISTICE SIGNED. END OF THE WAR," the morning *Times* announced in large bold headlines on November 11, 1918. It had finally ended. Triumphant renditions of "Over There" played on the radio and reverberated in the streets of New York.

That evening Stuart appeared at the back door of the Baker home and asked for Maggie. She was not surprised to see him and greeted him with a smile.

"You've heard the news, I assume?" he said.

"Of course. Isn't it wonderful?"

"Do you have time for a walk?"

"I do. Let me get my coat."

The streets were alive with laughter and music and happy couples. The autumn air was invigorating, and Maggie felt young and hopeful.

"Our country did well on the world stage, didn't it?" He reached for her hand.

"It makes me proud to be an American."

"It makes me want to think of the future—" he began.

"But right now," Maggie smiled, not wanting to get into any kind of serious discussion on such a glorious night, "let's just enjoy the present."

18 DECEMBER 1918, SOUTHAMPTON, LONG ISLAND

Frances Baker had not been feeling well since Thanksgiving. She had decided that getting out of the city and into the fresher air of Southampton, where she had a summer home, would help, at least for the holidays. Both Maggie and Miss Beatty had come with her, as had Mrs. Overton, who knew all her favorite dishes and was always prepared with chicken soup whenever Mrs. Baker felt under the weather.

"Nothing like chicken soup and an apple to ward off whatever's troubling you," Mrs. Overton repeated to anyone who would listen.

Three days before Christmas they put up a small fir tree in the parlor and decorated it. Mrs. Baker sat before the fireplace, gazing at it in admiration. Maggie herself did not feel in a festive mood. She was concerned that Mrs. Baker seemed to be growing paler and thinner and to have no appetite. Franny and her husband John had come to the house early for Christmas this year, so that she could assess her mother's condition.

"I'm worried about her, Maggie," Franny confided the morning after they had arrived. "I've never seen her so listless—not even when Papa Baker died and Solterra burned. Not even after she and Miss Beatty came back from Jekyl when she signed her lot there over to Dick Crane. I know all those things depressed her, but her spirits have always bounced back. I'm concerned, because this time she seems reconciled to old age. Or worse."

"Yes, ma'am, I can't seem to interest her in anything. Nor can Miss Beatty. They're both still knitting socks for the soldiers. Mrs. Baker can't seem to realize the war is over, but she rips out more than she knits and starts the same sock over and over again. She complains that she can't see the stitches anymore."

"She never used to look at them at all. It was so automatic—knit one, purl two—and she could do it for hours and carry on a full conversation at the same time."

Maggie nodded in concern. "Is there anything you think I could be doing to help?"

"Oh, I don't think there's a thing you could do, Maggie. You've been wonderful. Just tend to her needs and be here for her."

After the holidays ended, Frances Thacher took her children back to the city where the new school term was about to begin, and the house in Southampton seemed suddenly very still and lonely. Mrs. Baker would sit for hours beside the window, looking out at the leafless trees, resting her head on her left hand. By the end of January she no longer got out of bed in the morning, but asked Maggie to bring her trays to her room.

Finally one Sunday morning in early February when Maggie went to her bedroom to open the curtains, she found Mrs. Baker in bed, her eyes staring straight ahead, her long braid over her left shoulder and resting on her nightgown, and her head leaning back on her pillow. Maggie touched her hand. It was cold. She crossed herself, closed Mrs. Baker's eyes, and brushed away her tears for this noble woman before she went to fetch Miss Beatty.

After the funeral, the house on Fifth Avenue seemed suspended, without a past, without a future. None of the staff had been dismissed, but they knew it was only a matter of time. Frances Thacher and Henry Lake had not yet decided what to do with the house and how best to settle their mother's considerable estate. They were also trying to determine which members of the staff they would invite to be a part of their own households and which ones they must let go.

Frances had already approached Maggie to ask her, on behalf of her cousin Abby, if she would be willing to take over as nursemaid to the Steers children. Their oldest son, the one Maggie had taken to the park so many times, was almost four now, and his little sister was still a toddler. Her salary would remain the same, Frances assured her; perhaps even be a bit higher.

Maggie had no other prospects at the moment, and it seemed a good solution. It would provide her with room and board and a small income. Besides, she liked the Steers children, and it would give her a good excuse to go to the park on Saturdays and perhaps catch a glimpse of Danny.

Stuart did not share her enthusiasm for the new position she had been offered. The care of children would allow her less free time to spend with him, and she would always be expected to be there in the evenings, except for her days off.

"I had hoped, Maggie, that you would have talked with me about it first."

"Talked with you about it? Why on earth would I do that? I must make a living, Stuart." She felt that old sense of annoyance at his presumption that she should consult him before taking actions about her own life.

"I had hoped ..." He hesitated for a moment, and then he said, "I had hoped we could be married in the spring."

"Married? But you hadn't mentioned it before. I had no idea you had such hopes. How could I? You haven't asked me."

"Well, I'm askin' you now, Maggie. Will you marry me?"

She hesitated. Her mouth opened, but no words came.

"If you don't want to, Maggie—"

"It's not that. It's just so sudden. I need to think about it. Where would we live? How would we live?"

"I've saved back a good bit of money over the years. I've got enough to make a down payment on a little house in Brooklyn, and then there's a disability check from the army. And my salary with the force."

"Stuart, let's not rush into it. Couldn't we wait until next spring? The Steers are counting on me, and I've already said yes. In the meantime we could save even more and ..." She could see that he was not pleased.

"Don't make excuses, Maggie. If you don't want to marry me, just say so."

"I do want to marry you, Stuart." The words rushed out, and she hoped they were true. She was twenty-six years old, and Stuart was thirty-five, both of them well past the age when most people had married and begun a family. She was fond of him, and she knew this might be the best offer, perhaps the only one, she would ever have. Still, she hesitated. "I want to meet this obligation, at least for a little while. Can't we delay it just a bit?"

"If you are saying yes, I will wait for you until doomsday if I have to. But I need a firm answer."

"Yes, Stuart." She put her arms around his neck. "Yes. I will marry you. You set the date. Just give me a little time."

He broke into a joyful smile and drew her closer. "Take the job with the Steers and meet your commitment until the end of the year or until six months after the peace treaty is signed, whichever comes first. That way I can pray fervently for the politicians to work diligently and get their act together."

The treaty negotiations had already begun in mid-January. At least she would have half a year to work for the Steers. Perhaps longer.

She laughed. "Fair enough. The end of the year or six months to the day after the peace treaty. That way we'll have a lot to celebrate."

"I love you, Maggie," he said intently.

"And I you, Stuart." She just couldn't bring herself to add the verb. But she was committed to marrying him and to spending the rest of her life trying to make him happy.

There was no need to tell the Steers her plans just yet, particularly with all the squabbling that was going on in Europe, and she enjoyed her time with their children. In the meantime Stuart occupied his time happily in beginning to look for a little house in Brooklyn.

He had selected Brooklyn because of the BRT, the transit system that ran between Brooklyn and Manhattan and was part of the subway system. He could still get to the police station fairly quickly in the mornings by riding the subway. Or perhaps he could get a transfer to a post in Brooklyn itself. Either way it was less expensive to live in Brooklyn than to rent a Manhattan apartment, since he knew they could not afford to buy a decent house in Manhattan itself.

He had begun to read the ads and circle anything that lay between Fourth Avenue and 86th Street where the subway ran. He liked the area on the slope between Fourth Avenue and Prospect Park or in East Flatbush on the other side of the park. The subway crossed the East River over the Manhattan Bridge and connected with the Centre Street Loop, which would take him within an easy walk of the station.

It was always Stuart who took care of these pragmatic details. Maggie was reluctant to move so far away from St. Bernard's and Central Park, the two places where she might be able to see her little boy from time to time. But she knew that she, too, could always take the subway into Manhattan.

When the time came she would have to find some way to communicate with Suzanne, which she knew would not be easy since Danny's nursemaid would never speak openly with her for fear of jeopardizing her position. Perhaps once they were married Maggie could risk writing one letter to Suzanne, listing herself only as M. O'Neil or Mrs. S. O'Neil, which would surely get the letter past the watchful eye of Eloise Fowler. But Maggie dared not try to communicate now, for fear that she would frighten Suzanne away and deprive her of the only glimpses she had of her son.

She thought of her marriage to Stuart. He was a decent, good man. She had grown increasingly fond of him as she learned to admire his strength and appreciate his devotion. Perhaps this time her luck would be better. If she did not feel for him the same mystical connection she had felt with Hector, perhaps it was best. He asked little of her, and their relationship seemed so easy, so simple, so natural. Perhaps this was always the way it was intended to be. Perhaps. But how she missed the wild, sweet completeness she had known with Hector.

Peace negotiations dragged on and on. Finally, on June 28 the treaty, such as it was, was signed in the great hall of mirrors at Versailles. Maggie was already expecting Stuart when he appeared at the back door of the Steers' home the following morning.

"Do we still have plans for December 28?" he asked Maggie, as the sun beat down its summer warmth.

"It would seem that we do," she laughed. But she could still wait a bit longer before she told Abby Steers. She had six months, after all.

Chapter Twenty

15 NOVEMBER 1919

"GETTING MARRIED?" CRIED ABBY STEERS. "How wonderful!" She reached out to hug Maggie. "I'm so happy for you."

"Thank you, ma'am," said Maggie, blushing.

"Oh, but you don't *have* to quit your job, do you? We could work it out so that you wouldn't have to spend the night. You could go home to your husband and just mind the children during the day."

"But it would limit your activities, ma'am," Maggie protested, "not to be free in the evenings."

"Perhaps," said Abby, "but we would miss you so much, Maggie—all of us and especially the children. Do think about it."

She *did* think about it, but Stuart was adamant that she should not work. "It would reflect badly on me as a provider to have a working wife," he insisted.

"But, Stuart, it would give me something to do during the day and the income would certainly be helpful."

"I'd rather you didn't, Maggie. In fact," he said, smiling hopefully, "one day soon I hope we'll have our own children for you to look after."

She too longed for another child, though she knew that no one could replace Danny. Still she had hoped to be able to work at least for a while. Most men, she suspected, would agree with Stuart, feeling their masculinity threatened by a working wife. And she didn't want to do anything to make Stuart feel inadequate. He already felt so depressed at being tied to his desk job. She sighed in disappointment and informed Abby Steers that she would stay only until the day before her wedding or until the Steers could find someone suitable.

"Losing you because you agreed to marry six months after some silly treaty almost makes me wish they had never settled the matter," Abby said, a despondent furrow between her eyebrows.

"You don't really mean that, ma'am," Maggie said, remembering all the wounded boys she had read to at the hospital. She fervently hoped that President Wilson would succeed with his League of Nations, which was part of the treaty, and that it would end war forever.

"No, of course I don't. Not really, but it is certainly a mixed blessing in the Steers household."

When she finally realized that she could not change Maggie's mind, Abby assured her that if she ever needed a job, she should contact them. "The children love you so. You will come to see them from time to time, won't you?"

"Of course I will," said Maggie. "Of course."

Since December 28 fell on a Sunday, Maggie and Stuart decided to push their wedding to the first Saturday of the new year. It was the beginning not only of a new year, but also a new decade. It would symbolize their new beginning.

3 JANUARY 1920, MANHATTAN, NEW YORK

The afternoon was overcast as the wedding party arrived at St. Brigid's Roman Catholic Church in Manhattan's East Village. The little church, built by Irish immigrants in the late 1840s, felt and even smelled like a part of Ireland. The oak pews were occupied by a few of their friends from the Hibernian Society, a couple of off-duty policemen, and Maggie's fellow servants from the Steers household. Rudy Mews was there, mostly to see Deirdre walk down the aisle in her kelly-green satin dress as maid of honor. Waiting in front of the altar stood a nervous-looking Stuart and his brother Robert, his best man.

"You are a vision," Stuart leaned over and whispered to his bride as the little ceremony was about to begin.

Her wedding dress was the one her cousin Kate had worn when she married Patrick Fitzgerald. Cousin Eleanor had sent it to her with Kate's consent, on the condition that she return it immediately after the wedding. She fingered the cascading flowers that Eleanor had embroidered onto the bodice and hem of the dress and the high ruffled neckline, remembering the sad and angry stitches she herself had sewn after her mother's death and how gentle but firm Eleanor had been with her.

She wished with all her heart that her mother were here for her wedding and that her father could walk her down the aisle. But Alexander Mews had been quite flattered to take on that task. She had written to her father to tell him she planned to marry Stuart. He sent back, scrawled in a shaky hand, a four-word reply that she knew came from his heart. "Be happy. Love, Papa." Cousin Eleanor had sent a telegram wishing her and Stuart much happiness as well. But Deirdre and Mrs. Callaghan were the closest thing to family she had here in New York.

It was Deirdre who helped her to take in the seams of the bodice of the wedding dress and find affordable flowers for her hair, not an easy task in New York in January. She had wanted a wreath of wildflowers, which were of course impossible in this weather, but she had finally settled on two hothouse gardenias Maggie knew would turn brown before evening. But now, they perfumed the air and anchored the lace veil that Mollie Callaghan had loaned her. For a bouquet Deirdre had painted a horseshoe white for luck, decorated it with three more gardenias, and wrapped it with festive white ribbons.

"Now be sure to hold it like this," she reminded Maggie, turning the horseshoe so that the rounded side was down, "so the luck won't spill out." Maggie felt a bit awkward about the horseshoe, but everyone seemed so eager to have it a typical Irish wedding that she agreed, provided most of the metal was covered by ribbon and flowers.

After the brief ceremony, Stuart's brother and his wife, Ellen, along with Deirdre, Mrs. Callaghan, and Alexander and Rudy Mews all joined Maggie and Stuart for a small wedding dinner. Rudy, back from the war hale and hearty, had evidently learned the value of a good woman's love during his military service and had recently asked Deirdre to be his wife. They were planning their own wedding in early June.

"Not May, to be sure. 'Marry in May and rue the day,'" Deirdre reminded them all as they hurried toward Paddy's, the little restaurant that was hosting the wedding dinner.

Everyone nodded, resuming their cheerful banter, laughing and teasing the newlyweds, as they walked along, still in their nuptial finery, through a light snow that had been falling like powder since morning.

The warmth of the little restaurant embraced them after the cold of the streets. Savory smells of the Irish fare that was the specialty of the house hung in the air. Paddy had set aside a private room for the wedding party, and, as they entered, rubbing their hands and brushing the salting of snowflakes from their shoulders, he welcomed them warmly and ushered them personally into the back room, offering them glasses of hot mulled wine. Everyone was grateful that that new prohibition law did not go into effect for two more weeks. But it would have made no difference to Paddy. He had already stocked up and stashed away plenty of wine before the law could be enacted. Under no circumstances, law or no law, would he deny an Irishman his glass of toddy on his wedding day.

"*Sláinte!*" Stuart lifted his glass to the guests. "Health!"

Once the wedding party was settled and warm, Paddy replaced the mulled wine with generous bottles of red and white wine for the table. Robert O'Neil rose for the first toast: "May the Lord keep you in his hand and never close his fist too tight." Everyone laughed loudly, cheered and raised their glasses in response.

Then Rudy Mews was on his feet. "I'd like to make an Irish toast that Deirdre taught me," he said. "May you have warm words on a cold evening, a full moon on a dark night, and the road downhill all the way to your door." Once again they cheered appreciatively.

As though on cue, a waitress and Paddy brought in copious dishes of smoked salmon and roasted lamb with piles of potatoes, baked parsnips, and *beacon bruithe*, a special dish of baked mushrooms that Maggie's mother used to prepare. The guests mounded their plates and ate with relish.

When the meal ended, Paddy, with great ceremony, brought in the wedding cake—two ample tiers with white fondue icing and pink sugar rosebuds—baked by Deirdre's mother as a gift to the bride and groom. The revelers lifted their glasses once again to toast the cake's baker.

"I needed the practice," said Mrs. Callaghan, her face reddening at the attention, "if I'm going to bake Deirdre's in June." Once again the little party cheered and lifted their glasses to the newly engaged couple. Any excuse sufficed for a toast.

The party did not end until nearly ten o'clock, when Stuart finally announced with a slightly inebriated smile, "I think it's time to take my bride home."

Everyone cheered again and lifted their glasses once more. "I hope this time next year I'll be bouncing my first nephew on my knee," said Robert. A chorus of "hear, hear" resounded in the room.

"Well, then, if you're in such a hurry to be an uncle, I know it's past time to take my bride home," Stuart said and laughed.

Maggie could feel herself blushing as she accepted kisses all around. Stuart hurried outside to hail a cab for the long ride to their new house in Brooklyn.

25 DECEMBER 1922, BROOKLYN, NEW YORK

How can time pass so quickly? Maggie wondered as she basted the goose she was preparing for Christmas dinner. She had been married to Stuart for almost three years. It had gone by in a rush. The peacetime world seemed so much busier than it had before the war. New automobiles crowded the Brooklyn streets. Telephones rang and radios blared in people's homes. Airplanes flew about the skies. Everyone was obsessed with going faster and communicating across the miles, and the world seemed smaller than it ever had before.

Maggie thought about how much had changed over the early years of the decade—for women especially. The war years, when so many women took on men's jobs in factories, transportation, communications, and businesses had taught the country enough about the capabilities of women that Congress had finally given them the right to vote. Maggie, who had sworn her oath as an American citizen in 1916, had been proud to vote for the first time in the presidential election of 1920, when she cast her ballot for James Cox, the Democratic candidate who had lost to Warren Harding. She and Deirdre had celebrated together when the nineteenth amendment to the Constitution was ratified in August 1920, just a few months after Deirdre and Rudy's wedding.

"It was the country's wedding present to me," Deirdre laughed, admitting sheepishly in answer to Maggie's question that it had indeed been her picture on the front page of the New York *Times* marching for women's suffrage all those years ago.

Maggie was disappointed that Deirdre and Rudy weren't coming for Christmas dinner and bringing their toddler Alex. She had invited everyone who had been in their wedding to join them for their Christmas feast in Brooklyn, but Deirdre and Rudy had declined. Deirdre was eight months pregnant with their second child, and Rudy was protective of her—*overprotective*, Deirdre protested—refusing to allow her to bump over the rough streets between their apartment in Manhattan, where they still lived with Deirdre's mother, and the O'Neils' Brooklyn neighborhood.

Only Robert and Ellen were coming. Although Maggie was fond of Ellen, she had grown a bit wary of gatherings that included Robert. He tended to be abrasive and tactless at times, and he often made Ellen cry, even in front of them. But he *was* Stuart's brother, and she would always include him. It was important in a family to try to get along.

Maggie sighed as she squeezed the basting bulb once more over the carcass of the roasting goose. *One can't choose one's relatives. I should be grateful to have a family here at all,* she reminded herself. She thought about her brother Brendan's letter of the previous May telling her that their father's health was declining and that he'd finally persuaded him to move to Lochrea. Maggie was glad that he would no longer be alone, but she knew how difficult it must have been for him to leave Doolin.

How she missed him and her brother. *Will I ever see them again?* she wondered. She thought of the many times her mother had cooked a Christmas goose. Her face would be red from the heat as she basted it, as Maggie was doing now. She put the goose back in the oven and brushed away a warm tear.

Robert and Ellen were waiting with Stuart at the round dining room table for Maggie to bring in the goose. She had sliced it in the kitchen into succulent pieces to spare Stuart the embarrassment he always felt at her having to be the one to carve the meat at the table.

Maggie lifted the goose, surrounded with braised onions, mushrooms, and celery all decorously arranged on a large platter, and carried it with fanfare to the table.

"Ta da!" she chorused.

They applauded, with Stuart slapping his hand on the table. As she set the platter down, Stuart rose dramatically and lifted his glass of cider, which had replaced their usual wine now that Prohibition was fully in force. "Before we begin our Christmas dinner, I have an announcement to make."

Maggie smiled proudly, for she knew this was an important moment for Stuart. Robert and Ellen turned toward him expectantly.

"I have," he said after a slight pause, "once again been assigned to a police beat in Manhattan and am no longer confined to a desk job."

"Why, Stuart, that's wonderful news! Where is it?" asked his sister-in-law.

"It's a quiet neighborhood in the upper West side. Very nice," he explained.

Everyone nodded thoughtfully. He was no longer in the Irish sector, which teemed with street life and where a policeman needed two good arms to break up a fight or pinch a sneak thief. His new, affluent neighborhood had little crime and few people on the streets besides nursemaids pushing baby carriages and elderly couples strolling in the afternoon. But still, it meant a lot to Stuart to be out of doors once more. He had chafed at being chained to a desk, doing little more than keeping records and filling out forms. At least now, he could walk the streets, tip his hat to the strollers, and bask in the admiration of children who looked up to him and who, seeing his folded sleeve, were candid enough to ask about it and then listen in rapt attention as Stuart told them about his war experiences.

Robert nodded appreciatively. Then he said, "I had hoped it was finally going to be an announcement of the expected arrival of a wee bairn in the family." He emphasized the "finally."

Maggie froze at his words. She and Stuart were both already anxious that she had not become pregnant in their nearly three years of years of marriage. Maggie would be thirty on her next birthday, and she worried about whether or not she was even still able to conceive.

Her mother had gone through the change before she was forty, and both her children had been born in her early twenties. That there had been no more children after that, and knowing her Catholic father as she did, Maggie was sure it hadn't been for lack of trying. She had explained that to Stuart, taking full responsibility herself. She did not ever want him to think it might be some inadequacy on his part, even though the doctor had carefully questioned her about Stuart's war wound and had confided to her that it was most likely the trauma to his groin area that was causing the problem.

Stuart looked at Maggie thoughtfully, then said soberly to his brother, "I, too, wish it had been such an announcement."

In fact, Robert and Ellen had no children either. It was a sore fact of life for them all that there were no second-generation O'Neils in America. Maggie wasn't sure why Robert and Ellen had no little ones, but she knew it broke Ellen's heart every time her monthly flow began. She was older than Maggie by nearly two years and was self-conscious about the sprinkle of gray hairs already evident in her soft, brown bob. She had all but given up and had begun to talk in confidence to Maggie of adopting a child. So far Robert refused even to discuss it.

"I'm so proud of Stuart." Maggie said with a bright smile, changing the subject. "He talked the sergeant into giving him a beat once more. He's a persuasive one, he is."

"Hear, hear," said Ellen, and she raised her glass to Stuart.

Maggie wondered whether Ellen's cheerful demeanor concealed thoughts as painful as her own. But she smiled and joined her sister-in-law and Robert in a toast, while Stuart grinned with satisfaction, spearing a chunk of goose with his fork.

Despite their outward celebration, Robert's comment had cast a pall over the childless table, which did not abate with the gaiety of their words. They all knew how much happier Christmas would be with little ones toddling about, opening gifts, and laughing with delight.

Life grew no easier for Maggie as the months passed. More and more she confided her thoughts to her journal, for, even though the world outside seemed so busy, time hung heavy on her hands. She cleaned the house each day, swept the sidewalk, cooked whatever she thought Stuart might enjoy, and generally tried to occupy her time. But her friends were all in Manhattan. Deirdre had given birth in early February to a baby girl, named Maureen for Rudy's mother, and she had little time for anything else.

How I miss the days Deirdre and I spent together before we were both married, Maggie wrote in her journal. *The world seemed so simple, and we were so young, though hardly carefree. How I misjudged her. She has been my most loyal friend. I only wish I lived closer now and could visit with her and little Alex and Maureen more often. But Manhattan seems so far away. Stuart is gone all day, and I sit here thinking that I should learn to knit or something. Instead I write these words and worry about what the future holds.*

I haven't seen Danny for almost four months now. I wrote to Suzanne not long after my marriage, putting the Brooklyn address on the envelope, with the name Mrs. S. McNeil so that no one would recognize me as the sender. She responded only once—telling me that Danny was well and seemed happy enough, but that I should not try to contact her again. It was too dangerous. Perhaps I should have left well enough alone.

I try to write my dad in Ireland at least once a week, but I rarely hear anything from him. I had hoped Stuart and I could save enough money to bring him to New York. I would be so happy to see him again. But he refuses to leave Ireland. Brendan wrote how he moped about after leaving Doolin. He says Papa misses the sea and is simply wilting away from longing. But at least I know he is safe. He still does not know about Danny, though I know he would love him as I do. But if he can never know him, why break his heart by telling him?

For a brief time in March I thought I might be pregnant again, but it was a false alarm. Deirdre says I should just relax and stop worrying about it, and then maybe Stuart and I could have a baby. But I fear it may not be that simple. Besides, how can I relax when I am so tense? I will never understand the ways of God— giving me a baby before marriage only to take him away, and putting Stuart and me together only to leave us childless. Is this my punishment for loving Hector with such abandon?

She knew that she should not question God's ways, but she was nonetheless bewildered by them. Maggie wrote almost every day in her little notebooks but was careful to hide them from Stuart. She would not want anyone to read her private thoughts, even though he knew most of them already. But she knew he would never invade her privacy in such a way. She loved Stuart—not with that wild, sweet, irrepressible desire she had felt for Hector, but in a calm and gentle way. She needed his abiding love and gentleness. *Love,* she wrote, *can shape itself into many forms, and there is always enough to go around.*

If she had another baby, she knew that it would never diminish her love for Danny, and yet she would love another child just as much. That was the amazing thing about love. It came from a bottomless well, drawn from the deepness of God. As soon as a bucket was used up, it filled once more again and again for as many times as it was needed. A well that would never run dry.

There was no question within her that she cared deeply for Stuart, his welfare and his spirit. She took comfort when he reached out for her, and she accepted his kisses with gratitude. She felt at home beside him at night. She savored, like loaves of warm bread, the sweetness of his love-making, and she was grateful to God that she had not driven away this good man with her self-absorption.

She had even learned to like baseball, which had become Stuart's greatest enthusiasm. Living in Brooklyn where he could attend the games of the

Brooklyn Robins was a boon. Sometimes they both enjoyed the games on warm summer afternoons at the stadium not far from their home, but most often Stuart went alone, while she stayed home to work in her garden. Life had settled into a quiet routine that suited them both, though in her heart of hearts Maggie knew there was still a dark empty place she longed to fill.

Chapter Twenty-One

3 JANUARY 1932 BROOKLYN, NEW YORK

AS SHE ARRANGED THE SMALL BOWL of gardenias for the table, one of the popular songs of the day kept running through Maggie's mind. She couldn't remember all the words but sang and hummed intermittently as she worked. "You must remember this ... A kiss is still a kiss ..."

She stepped back and cocked her head to admire her flower arrangement. The gardenias had been a great extravagance on her part, but this was a memento of their wedding twelve years ago, and she hoped Stuart would also remember the gardenias she had worn in her hair. They had been hard to find. Few people wasted money on such things as flowers anymore in these bad economic times, especially during the winter when they were so expensive, but she had finally located a flower shop on Flatbush Avenue that had a few in stock. They would be so special.

She could hardly wait for Stuart to come home. She had made his favorite dishes—some of the same ones they had on their wedding day, roasted lamb and *beacon bruithe*, with potatoes, a fine salad, homemade rolls, and apple pie. It was a feast, and she had planned it for months.

Stuart's brother and his wife were unable to come, to Maggie's relief, but Deirdre and Rudy would be there with Alex and Maureen. They planned to leave the three little ones with her mother.

"I'm afraid their table manners aren't yet up to public display," Deirdre had said with a laugh. Maggie adored the children and would have loved her to bring them all, but she knew that five children in one model A Ford must be too much to handle.

Rudy had his own garage now and two other mechanics to help him. He was busy all the time and had a reputation as one of the best mechanics in Manhattan. Maggie and Stuart had never bought a car. There never seemed to be enough money, and Stuart argued that they didn't really need an automobile with the subway so close by. Still, Maggie thought, it would be nice to be able drive into the countryside once in a while.

Even after all these years she missed the wild sweet hills of Ireland and the long walks on the paths and beach at Jekyl Island. Even though she had spent only two seasons there, she had never forgotten the sounds of birdcalls, the smells of the salt marshes, and the clove-like fragrance of the Cherokee roses that bloomed in early spring. But, as Stuart pointed out, she had only a short walk to Prospect Park, and, if she wanted variety or more space, she could always take the subway to Central Park.

He was right, of course. Besides, there wasn't money for both a car and a house. And in 1927, before the stock-market crash, they had made a down payment on a small brownstone on Garfield Place, and now it took much of Stuart's salary to make the payment.

After a dozen years of marriage, they had given up on their expectations of one day having a child together. Maggie had finally accepted it as God's will. And Stuart consoled himself with his obsession with baseball. He went to Ebbets Field every chance he got and could afford to watch the games of the Brooklyn team, which had changed its name the year before from the Robins to the Dodgers.

Maggie rarely went to the games anymore, preferring instead to work in her little garden. Stuart didn't seem to mind and used the games to get together and relax with some of his police buddies. It freed up the money for her ticket for something else. Her small plot of earth behind the brownstone was warm and sunny for at least part of the day. It had become a tiny haven of color, with lilacs, daffodils, and azaleas in the spring, and roses and hydrangeas in summer months. She loved the smell of the fresh-dug soil and the fragrance of her flowers. And when her work was done for the day, she could sit on her garden bench for hours and read the poetry she had always loved, write in her journals, or mend the socks that Stuart wore out on his beat with constant regularity.

She no longer took trips into Manhattan to see Danny, for he had finished his education at St. Bernard's years ago and gone on to Philips Academy in Andover, Massachusetts. After his graduation there, she learned that Danny had enrolled at Harvard where he was now a sophomore. All the news came from Henry Barrett's chauffeur, Friedrich, who had first taken the Packard to Rudy's garage for a brake repair at the recommendation of Rudy's old mentor, the Baker chauffeur, Philip Malloy, and had become a steady customer ever since.

A mutual interest in automobiles and a friend in common drew Rudy and Friedrich together. Rudy took a special interest in the jobs and did them all himself, even though he now had several assistant mechanics. As a consequence, Friedrich often came by the shop, even when the Packard needed no attention. The older man loved to talk, and Rudy liked to listen as he tinkered with spark plugs and pistons.

When Deirdre heard about the friendship and recognized Friedrich's name from Maggie's story of the Barrett household, she urged Rudy to ask about Danny. Everything she learned, she passed eagerly on to Maggie. Rudy must have wondered why she was so curious or how she even knew about the boy, but Maggie was sure that Deirdre would never betray her secret, not even to her husband, without asking her first.

As a consequence of the men's garage talk, Maggie learned not only about Danny, but also about Henry Barrett's steady decline. He rarely left the house anymore, and his chauffeur had little to do and much time on his hands. He enjoyed coming by Rudy's garage to take a look at the motors of the different vehicles Rudy might be working on. Maggie worried, when she learned of this burgeoning friendship, that Friedrich might reveal her story to Rudy, but he never did. And she was thrilled with this more or less direct pipeline into the Barrett household that brought her news of her son.

Friedrich liked Danny, Rudy said. Everyone in the Barrett household did, and the old mausoleum, as Friedrich called the Fifth Avenue house, really came to life when the young master was at home. But he came all too rarely, Maggie gathered, having gotten involved in all sorts of activities at Harvard that kept him busy.

Henry Barrett was already pressuring him to go to Harvard Law School and enter his New York firm as soon as he could, but Maggie gathered that Danny was putting up considerable resistance—whether to the profession of law or to entering Mr. Barrett's old firm, she wasn't sure. She just wished that he could choose his own path in the world. Someday, she thought, someday after Henry Barrett had left this mortal coil, she would find Danny and tell him who she was. Someday, she hoped, they could be reunited.

She had just finished setting the table when she heard the front door open and Stuart's voice call out, "I'm home!"

"Stuart, you're early."

"It's our anniversary," he grinned, drawing from behind his back a little box. "This is for you." He held it out to her.

"Oh, Stuart," she smiled, as she opened the box. "What a perfect gift. You remembered." It was a white gardenia corsage. She led him into the dining room and pointed to the table decoration. "It will match our centerpiece. How perfect."

Stuart drew her to him and kissed her gently on the lips. "You're perfect," he said. "I love you, Maggie."

"And I love you, Stuart. Do you realize we've been married already twelve years?"

"Indeed I do. Twelve rapid, wonderful years. I hope they're just the beginning of a hundred more."

"So do I, Stuart. So do I."

She thought about the years they had spent together and how much they had come to depend on one another, how they could sometimes read each other's thoughts and how one could often finish the other's sentences. Perhaps it was that way with all married couples, she thought, at least couples who shared both their joys and sorrows. Anyone could share joys, but sharing their sorrows had brought them closer together.

Stuart let her talk about Danny whenever she wanted. He commiserated with her on her son's birthday, which she could not spend with Danny, now a young man she had not seen for almost seven years. And sometimes he confided in her as well, about how he could still feel his lost hand and how tortured he had been when she disappeared that day in 1912. Then they would hold each other and feel safe.

Their mutual sadness at not having a child of their own never completely abated, and on occasions such as this, when Deirdre and Rudy came with their happy, irrepressible children, they felt it even more sharply. But they had learned slowly over the years to love and nourish one another. It was enough. It had to be. Maggie had also learned to enjoy life again. She took pleasure in long walks in Prospect Park with Stuart on Sunday afternoons and in their evenings at home together, just listening to the radio and watching dusk turn into night.

Sometimes she read to him some of the poetry she so enjoyed, as she did this evening, after their festive anniversary dinner shared with the Mews family had ended. They had cleared the table and their guests had departed to get their children home to bed.

Now they sat together, looking out over the chilly garden, wrapped in blankets and sharing one last cup of coffee. Maggie read aloud in her soft voice the words of a new poet she had recently discovered, Edna St. Vincent Millay, who expressed so well many of her own feelings, especially this renewal of life she had begun to experience so keenly—like a fern uncoiling its fronds to receive the rain.

The world was good and God's creation an unending source of renewal, as Maggie had learned, in spite of whatever unhappiness she and Stuart had experienced. She held the world as close as she dared, as she clasped Stuart's hand and read to him that night, *"O world, I cannot hold thee close enough!"*

Two weeks later, Stuart came home early again. This time he looked gray and weary.

"Twice in one month!" Maggie exclaimed. "They're going to think you come home for a romantic tryst or something." She laughed, but Stuart smiled grimly.

"I felt sick, Maggie, and the sergeant found someone to cover the beat for me."

"Oh, darling, I'm so sorry," she said. "Let's get you to bed right away and I'll call Dr. Randolph."

"No need to bother him. I'm sure it's just the meat pies I bought from a street vendor for lunch. I ate two of 'em, and they just didn't agree with me. I'm going to take some Pepto-Bismol and lie down for a while."

"You do that, and I'll make your lunches from now on. You never know where street food was made or under what conditions." Maggie preceded him to the bedroom and was peeling back the bedcovers. "Shall I turn on the radio for you?"

"No, thanks, I just want to rest and let my stomach settle," he called from the bathroom where he was already pouring thick pink liquid into a small glass. Maggie made him a cup of hot tea, which grew cold on his bedside table as he slept.

By the following Monday he was feeling fine again and set out in high spirits, carrying a brown paper sack filled with a corned beef sandwich, an apple, and a small tea cake Maggie had made.

They thought little of his gastric attack until the end of the summer, when it happened again. This time he went to see Dr. Randolph, who could find nothing wrong with him.

Then on the first of September Sergeant McNair called Maggie from the station.

"Mrs. O'Neil, I'm sorry to be the bearer of bad news, but—"

"Is Stuart all right?" she asked quickly, as her heart lurched. "He hasn't been shot, has he?"

"No, nothing like that, Mrs. O'Neil. But he did collapse on the beat this afternoon. We had him taken to Saint Luke's. It was the closest hospital. I thought you'd want to know."

"Of course, Sergeant. I'll go right over. Do you know the subway stop?"

"I think the closest is West 116th Street."

"Thank you so much, Sergeant. I'm leaving right now."

Maggie fought down her sense of panic, as she quickly found her hat and purse and dashed out to find the nearest subway stop. Stuart had wanted to have the telephone taken out of the house to save money. She knew that times were tight, but she had insisted on keeping it for just such emergencies. When one's husband is a policeman, anything can happen. She knew that Stuart had been given a beat with little crime, but New York was such an unpredictable city. Thank God she had insisted.

The train ride seemed endless, though she knew the subway, even with the stops and changes between Brooklyn and the upper west side, was the quickest way to get to him. *Dear God, please let him be all right*, she begged silently as the subway stopped yet again to disgorge passengers and let new ones board.

When she finally reached her stop, she hurried out of the subway and up the steep steps to the sidewalk that led to the hospital. The woman at the reception desk, with a sympathetic look in her eye, told her that Stuart had been admitted and was in room 222.

The door to the room was closed. She tapped lightly before entering. The man in the first bed was sleeping, and a curtain was pulled between the two patients. Maggie peeked around the curtain to make sure the person in the other bed was Stuart. He was lying there with his eyes closed, his face gray, and his lips grayer still.

She touched his hand, and he opened his eyes. "Hello, darling," she said.

"Maggie, I'm sorry you had to come all this way."

"Well, I'm sorry that you're in the hospital, but I'd have gone to the other side of the country if you needed me. Tell me, what does the doctor say?"

"Not much, I'm afraid. They want to keep me here 'for observation,' whatever that means."

At that moment a woman in white, with a stiff nurse's cap on her head, strode into the room. "I'm afraid visiting hours ended at five p.m., ma'am," she said imperiously.

"Oh, but I just got here—all the way from Brooklyn. My husband was admitted to the emergency room this afternoon. He's a city policeman. Can't I just stay a little while longer?"

"I understand, ma'am, but rules are rules. I don't make them." The nurse hesitated for a moment, then said quietly, "On the other hand, maybe I didn't notice you come in. As long as the man in the next bed doesn't complain."

"Thank you so much," said Maggie. "We'll be very quiet."

She couldn't leave. She wouldn't. Stuart needed her, and she needed to be here for him. She needed to know what was happening to cause these spells. She would stay the night, even if she had to sleep on a stiff sofa in one of the waiting rooms. She sat down in the upright chair beside his bed and reached for his hand.

"Maggie, you need to go home where you can rest. This is no place for you."

"Don't be silly. I wouldn't leave no matter what. I can sleep right here, if they'll let me."

At eight o'clock the stiff-capped nurse returned.

"Ma'am, I'm afraid you'll have to leave now. We need to make sure the patients are settled down for the night. I've overlooked your visit for as long as I can. You can come back at ten o'clock tomorrow morning."

"Oh, dear," said Maggie, but she was in no position to argue. The nurse had been generous to let her stay this long. She kissed Stuart good night and left to look for a waiting room with a sofa that would allow her to stretch out a bit.

The next morning at ten Maggie was back in the room, rumpled and a bit bleary eyed. When she got there a man in a white jacket, whom she took to be a doctor, was leaning over Stuart, listening to his chest with a stethoscope.

"Hello," she said. "I'm Mrs. O'Neil. Can you tell me what's wrong with my husband, Doctor …?"

"Doctor Roberts. It may be nothing but fatigue, but I'd suggest that we keep an eye on his heart. There's a crackling sound in his chest I don't like, though I don't think it's pneumonia. He was suffering from shortness of breath and chest pains when they brought him in. There are no signs he's had a heart attack, Mrs. O'Neil, but I don't think his heart is strong."

"How serious—" Maggie began, her brow furrowed.

"Your husband seems to be very tired," the doctor interrupted, "and he tells me that he suffers from swollen feet when he's on the beat. I'm prescribing a medication called theocalcin that he's to take three times a day. He should limit his intake of fluids and elevate his feet when he sits for a long time. Most of all, he needs a good rest. You can take him home today, but see that he doesn't do anything strenuous until he's back on his feet. And if his feet swell a good bit, you need to see a doctor as soon as possible."

He didn't sound very encouraging, but the good news was that he planned to release Stuart today.

At twelve o'clock a nurse's aide wheeled Stuart to the hospital entrance and released him into Maggie's care. They could not afford an ambulance or a cab to take them all the way back to Brooklyn. Maggie suggested calling Rudy Mews to see if he could drive them home, but Stuart would have none of it.

"I'm perfectly capable of getting there by subway," he insisted. "No need to take Rudy away from his work and his family."

"I'm sure he wouldn't mind, Stuart."

"No," he replied adamantly. "I'm the one who chose not to have an automobile. I don't want to bother him. We'll make it on the subway. I'm fine."

Maggie could see there was no use arguing. She took his arm and they began their slow walk toward the nearest subway station that would take them back to Brooklyn.

Chapter Twenty-Two

24 APRIL 1933 BROOKLYN, NEW YORK

MAGGIE SAT IN HER GARDEN ONE LAST TIME, counting the blooms on her lilac bush and drinking in their fragrance. It was the only place she could be alone and still feel Stuart's presence. Although she had spent many hours working by herself in the garden while he cheered on the Dodgers, she had lost count of their candlelight dinners under the rose trellis and lemonade on the wooden bench on late summer afternoons. They had often talked here until dark as Stuart shared the adventures of his day and where he had kissed her for the last time.

She was sorry her family back in Ireland had never had a chance to meet her husband. She and Stuart had saved for more than six years to make a trip back to their homeland. She had so wanted to see her father again, but when the bank failed in December of '29, they lost all their savings. Two months later Brendan had written of their father's death. They had buried him in the little church cemetery at Doolin beside his wife. Brendan had his own life, his growing family of six children, and a pleasant home in Lochrea, Maggie knew. Even if she wanted to go back, there was no way she could afford it. And she was a part of this country now. It was her home.

It had been hard during Stuart's illness. Paying the medical bills had been more important than making the payments on the brownstone. He had worked for as long as he possibly could, but he grew weaker and weaker. Sergeant McNair had tried to help by putting him once again at a desk job that took less stamina, but in the last months, he had been unable to work at all. With the slightest exertion his legs and feet would swell until he was finally forced to retire for good and draw the pension to which he was entitled after his more than eighteen years of service on the force. But it was far less than he had earned as an active policeman and simply not enough to buy groceries, pay utilities and medical bills, and make their house payments.

After they had missed three mortgage payments in a row, the bank foreclosed, just one month before Stuart's death. A sympathetic bank officer, learning of his condition, had allowed them to occupy the house until it could be sold at auction. Maggie was grateful for that, for it had allowed Stuart, after he collapsed in the hallway while she was helping him in from the garden, to die in his own bed at home, and Maggie had a few weeks to mourn before she was compelled to vacate.

Stuart's brother had paid the funeral expenses and buried him in Newark, not far from his home. Maggie had protested. She thought he should remain in New York, a city he had grown to love, and where she could visit his grave more frequently. But Robert had become more imperious over the years, and, though Ellen sided with Maggie, he insisted that he knew best. Burial plots were cheaper in Jersey, and he was certain that Stuart wouldn't have wanted him wasting any more money than necessary in such hard times on something that, in his view, would do no one any good. He had found a single burial plot that had been long overlooked by the cemetery overseer, and since no one could buy plots for an entire family in the vicinity, Robert was able to get it for a song.

"But what about Maggie?" Ellen asked. "Might she not want to be buried beside him?"

"Ellen, we have to be practical," Robert insisted. "Money doesn't grow on trees these days."

Maggie said nothing. It was his money, and she didn't feel up to debating with him. Besides, she was sure that she did not want to spend eternity in Newark.

After the funeral, even before she began to sell the furniture and pack her things, Maggie called Abby Steers. She knew that the Steers children were far too old to need a nursemaid, but perhaps Mrs. Steers would be willing to serve as a reference. As it happened, Abby had a young acquaintance who was thrilled to hire Maggie to look after her children, a little girl almost two and a boy of three. Maggie was relieved to have a place to go, and the sale of the furniture would help her settle their final bills. All she kept were her clothes, her books, her photographs, and her journals, which had by now taken up six notebooks.

Stuart had worried about leaving her with so little, but she'd reassured him that she would manage. "Perhaps you will marry again," he said. "You're still a fine looking woman, Maggie."

She gave him the look he had come to recognize as one that dismissed utter nonsense. "Not likely," she said with a laugh. "I think your eyesight has been affected. Besides, you're going to live a lot longer," she added with determination in her voice.

He shook his head sadly. "We both know better, dearest." He gazed at her face as though he were memorizing it, and touched her hair. "I'm glad you married me, Maggie. These have been the best years of my life, these years with you. I'm just sorry—"

"There's nothing to be sorry about," she said quickly. "They've been wonderful years. I thank you for being such a good husband. I'm so proud of you." She was proud of the way he had not let his disability keep him down as so many other veterans had. Stuart wore his missing arm as a badge of honor, knowing he had been of use to this country that had adopted him and that he had learned to love. At his funeral, six uniformed policemen from Manhattan came all the way to Newark to carry his coffin, and he was buried with the dignity of one who had served his country well in war and peace.

Maggie pondered all these things as the light began to fade. She would miss this tiny garden, she knew, for it was the one thing she had created from scratch. When she and Stuart had first moved to Garfield Place, the small fenced area behind the brownstone had been a barren junk pile. The previous owner had obviously taken no interest in beautifying the place, which was one reason they were able to buy it so cheap. Little by little Maggie had cleared the ground of debris, old bottles, a worn tire, parts of various gadgets the owner had bought and then discarded. She tilled the soil and fertilized it from her compost pile until it was rich and ready to receive her plants.

Neighbors had given her bulbs and cuttings, and she had found a little neighborhood nursery where she could buy inexpensive small bushes that had not sold while they were in bloom and that the nurseryman wanted to get rid of before winter set in. That's how she had bought the lilac. It had been scraggly at first, but Maggie had been rewarded the second year with three magnificent purple blooms. Since then it had bloomed profusely every spring. She was very proud of it.

The late April afternoon was warm, but she could feel an undercurrent of briskness in the air, which would chill quickly after the sun sank behind the buildings across the alley. She tugged her sweater a little tighter and looked around once more. The daffodil blooms had faded, but she had learned not to cut the green stalks until they had yellowed and died away if she wanted to have blooms the following year. It was amazing how much one could learn from such a small piece of earth, such a tiny Eden.

Now, once again, she felt that she was being turned out of her garden, banished from the joy she had so longed to find in this country. Yet she knew she would manage somehow. Somehow she would survive.

"Maggie," Deirdre's voice called from the back door. "Rudy's here with the car. He says we can get everything in one trip."

"Coming, Deirdre. I just wanted to say goodbye to my garden."

"I know it's hard to leave a place where you've been happy."

"You're right, Deirdre. I have been happy here, happier than I ever expected to be again."

"Life has been hard for you, hasn't it, Maggie, but you are so strong. You amaze me. I think I'd just die if anything happened to Rudy."

Maggie smiled sadly. "You would bear it, Deirdre, for the sake of your children. And perhaps you would find another happiness … in time." Deirdre looked at her soberly, but she did not nod.

Maggie gathered up her two suitcases, while Deirdre picked up the single box that contained the notebooks, books, and photographs. As she left her home for the last time, Maggie locked the brownstone's front door behind her and dropped the key in the mail slot. Together she and Deirdre descended the stone steps. Rudy awaited them on the sidewalk, holding open the back door of the Ford.

Chapter Twenty-Three

"LUCY, PUT YOUR NAPKIN IN YOUR LAP," Maggie prompted the two-year-old, who began to gobble her food as soon as the blessing was said. The little girl did as she was told for once, and Maggie smiled her approval.

It was good to be with young children again. Little Lucy was for the most part a joy, loving tea parties and baby dolls as she did. But she could also be stubborn and wanted her own way most of the time, like most children her age. The only person who could calm her down when she stamped her foot in defiance or began to cry uncontrollably, the only person to whom she would always acquiesce, was her older brother, Matthew, who was her idol.

Matthew himself was quite the little gentleman and could be reasoned with in ways that Lucy could not. He could be a help, even though he was only a year and a half older. But he could be a handful too, particularly when Maggie took them to the park.

There was no sitting on the bench to watch them play, as some of the other nursemaids did. Matthew insisted that she play as well. He had become quite proficient in catching his small blue ball, and he preferred to play with Maggie rather than Lucy, who seldom caught the ball and who was all too easily distracted by a passing dragonfly or a soaring bird. It was amazing to Maggie to realize how different the children were. When they were in the nursery, Matthew liked to listen to her read aloud, but Lucy would wander off into a corner by herself and sing to her doll. She had little interest in the stories, but she enjoyed the nursery rhymes and Irish folk songs Maggie sang at bedtime.

Myra Woodruff, Maggie's employer, came upstairs every night at seven-thirty, just before she and her husband took their dinner, to say good night to the children. Matthew and Lucy were allowed to stay up until eight o'clock, but they had to be in the nursery, fed, bathed, and in their pajamas by seven-thirty. The nightly ritual began with Mrs. Woodruff peeking in at the door and watching them play until they saw her and ran toward the nursery entrance shouting, "Mommy, Mommy!"

At that point Mrs. Woodruff would fling the door wide and open her arms to gather in both children for a shower of goodnight kisses. Maggie felt a sting of envy as she watched the three of them their enthusiastic embraces. She had seen that unbounded affection between Deirdre and her children, and it was something Maggie had longed for since the day Danny was torn from her arms and she was ousted from the Barrett home for the last time.

Maggie knew the rituals would change as the children grew older, but for now, they followed a comfortable routine, and her young charges knew what to expect, which always made life with youngsters easier. They played learning games in the mornings, and then took naps and went to the park in the afternoons, if weather permitted. Maggie had her supper with the children in the kitchen at six o'clock, well before their parents dined. She slept in a small room adjacent to the nursery, where she could hear their every move and whimper in the night.

They were good children, and she felt lucky to have this post, though she would have liked more privacy. That would be possible, Mrs. Woodruff assured her, when the children were older and each of them had moved into his or her own room. Maggie did not complain. At least she had a home, a job, and no financial worries anymore.

Her tiny room was like so many she had known before her marriage to

Stuart. It contained only the essentials, a single bed, a dresser, a small desk and chair. There was, however, one difference. She had a closet for the first time, and it managed to hold all the clothes and shoes, not many to be sure, she had acquired over the years and brought from Garfield Place.

Once the children were in bed each night, though she never closed the door to the nursery, she would go into her own room to read or write. Her reading was sometimes the poetry she loved or sometimes the newspaper, which Mr. Woodruff discarded every afternoon. Maggie would retrieve it from the trash and bring it to her room to catch up on whatever news the *Times* reported. She followed Mr. Roosevelt's administration with great interest, and she had voted for him with enthusiasm. So far she was not disappointed. He seemed to be trying to address the economic issues that were ravaging the country, and she was hopeful that he would help solve the nation's problems.

After she had scanned the front section of the newspaper, she always turned directly to the society section, in the hope of seeing something there about Danny. There had been a brief notice when he graduated *cum laude* from Harvard, and she felt very proud of him. She hadn't seen him now for many years, but she still heard news occasionally from Deirdre that filtered through Rudy. That was how she discovered that Danny had succumbed to Mr. Barrett's pressures to attend Harvard Law School.

Deirdre repeated all the details Friedrich had described to Rudy of the rousing argument between Danny and his "grandfather" during a ride home from the celebration dinner Mr. Barrett had given at the Union Club after the boy's graduation.

In the rear view mirror Friedrich had glimpsed Mr. Barrett leaning toward Danny and saying, "You probably wondered why I invited my old law partners to the dinner tonight." His voice sounded as though he was about to reveal a happy surprise. "You'll be pleased to know ..." He paused, as though to give Danny time to appreciate the moment. "I've made arrangements for your admission to Harvard Law School in the fall. It's all taken care of." He smiled with satisfaction.

Friedrich, listening from the driver's seat, expected effusive gratitude from the young man. But there was only silence for a long moment. Finally he heard Danny say, "But, Grandfather, I've already been accepted for graduate work at Cornell's College of Architecture. That's what I'm really interested in doing."

"Instead of Harvard Law? Don't be ridiculous. There's no real money or prestige in architecture these days. Look around you. The city is all built up." He pointed to the Empire State Building. "Look at that! How do you expect to top that?"

"It's only the beginning, Grandfather. Cities have just begun to develop."

"Bosh!" Henry Barrett dismissed the comment. "There hasn't been a decent architect in New York since Stanford White. And look what happened to him. He was nothing but a disreputable philanderer who came to no good."

"I don't see how his profession as an architect had anything to do with his affair with Mrs. Thaw or his murder by her husband," Danny replied, referring to a well-known New York scandal. "Anyhow, that was a long time ago."

"I haven't forgotten," said Mr. Barrett.

"That hasn't got anything to do with me. I'm interested in designing houses, domestic architecture, not skyscrapers like the Empire State Building. It's my lifelong dream, Grandfather, and I have some wonderful ideas I want to try out. I've told you that before."

"And I've told you it's a childish dream. You'll go to law school and be an attorney, just as I was. Otherwise, you're on your own. You'll pay your own way," Henry Barrett shouted.

The argument went on, according to Friedrich, until they arrived at the Barrett residence, but in the end, Danny, who had never learned to make a living on his own, gave in. As Friedrich had explained it to Rudy, "I don't think he had any other choice. What do those Harvard boys know about earning an honest wage?"

"Old man Barrett," as Friedrich called him, was trying to influence the boy's social life as well, Rudy had told his wife, and was doing everything he could to interest him in the daughter of Roger Steele, one of his associates in the firm. So far Danny had resisted and chosen his own social path.

None of the news came as a great surprise to Maggie, but she grieved nonetheless for her son's lack of determination in confronting Henry Barrett about his choice of profession. *He is still young,* she reasoned, *and, as time goes on, he will learn to make his own way.*

She just hoped it wouldn't be too late.

Two years later, toward the end of June, the front page of the Sunday *Times* society section, which Maggie began to read as soon as the children were tucked in, caught her attention at once. A photograph of a slender young woman in three-quarters profile dominated the upper right side of the page. Her face was tilted upward as though she were staring into a bright, assured future. Her blond hair hung to her shoulders in a well-coiffed pageboy, and her lips turned up only slightly at the corners, as though she was resisting the photographer's attempt to tease a real smile from her. The caption beneath the photo read: "Engagement of Miss Helen Morgan Steele to Daniel Hector Barrett announced Saturday."

The article below the image identified the young woman as "the attractive daughter of Mr. and Mrs. Roger Erlich Steele" and announced her betrothal to "the son of the late David Barrett, who died in the sinking of the *Titanic.* Since his recent graduation from Harvard Law School, Mr. Barrett has entered the firm of Bingham, Swathmore, and Steele, of which his grandfather, Henry Barrett, is a former partner." The wedding was to take place at the Steele's country home in Tuxedo Park on Saturday, July 18.

Well, thought Maggie, *it looks as though Henry Barrett got his way one more time.* The bride-to-be, the daughter of the law partner who had replaced Mr. Barrett at the firm after his retirement, was pretty, but something in her expression seemed artificial to Maggie. A haughtiness about the eyes perhaps? *But one can't tell much from a single photograph,* Maggie reminded herself. *She's probably a very nice girl.* Maggie gazed at the image a long time, memorizing the face, and wishing that the newspapers would print photographs of the groom-to-be as well. Then at least she could have a picture of her son as he looked today.

It was hard to imagine her little Danny as a grown man about to be married. As a child he had Hector's face, his sweet smile and sensitive mouth, but the coloring of her own family, with his blond hair and blue eyes. It was a charming combination. But then, she thought, *I'm his mother. I would have thought he was beautiful no matter what.* She tried to imagine his face as it would look today, but all she saw was the face of Hector in her mind.

She rested her head against the back of the chair and let her mind drift to the man who had raised her son. Henry Barrett—the man she had so hated. *He must have loved his son as much as I love Danny,* she thought. He must have thought him just as beautiful. It must have grieved him to fear his son would never marry and never have children. *Perhaps that's why he fought so hard to keep Danny.* He wanted so badly to believe that Danny was his grandson that it had affected his reason.

She realized, to her surprise, that she was actually feeling something akin to compassion for the old man. In time, perhaps, she could even forgive him for what he had done. Until now she had thought only about herself, her loss, her deprivation of the thing she loved most in the entire world. But she was weary of hating him, weary of the darkness he had planted in her. Now, for the first time, she felt the hard black place within her begin to soften. For the first time in a long time, she began to pray: "Oh God, give Danny the happiness he deserves, and help Henry Barrett find peace in his heart."

She prayed for Danny on his wedding day as well. And the following day she read a description of the extravagant event in the *Times.* The bride had worn a white silk dress with puffed sleeves and a bell skirt that widened into a train. "Her head was covered by a white French lace veil," it said, "and her grandmother's pearl necklace and earrings adorned her lovely countenance." She carried an "elaborate bouquet of white orchids." The lengthy article concluded with the couple's honeymoon plans—a month-long trip to Capri.

Maggie reread the article three times before she cut it out of the newspaper and tucked it into one of her journals hidden in a drawer of her desk. Danny was scarcely mentioned in the write-up, except to remind readers once again that he had recently completed his law degree at Harvard and had been taken into the firm of Bingham, Swathmore, and Steele—as though that were all that mattered. How she longed to see him again and meet the woman he had married.

When she fell asleep that night, she dreamed of Hector for the first time in a long while. She was standing with him at the door of Faith Chapel on Jekyl Island, waiting, a bouquet of daisies in her hands. As the wedding march began, she walked down the aisle of an empty church toward the altar, wearing a white silk dress. As she waited there, she realized she was alone, watched her dress turned to tatters, and felt the flowers wilting in her hands. The church was suddenly filled with people, and in her place at the altar was a coffin. In the coffin lay the body of a little blond boy wearing Hector's face. She woke with dry sobs catching in her throat.

Almost six months later Maggie clipped from the *Times* the obituary of Henry Barrett and tucked it too inside one of the notebooks in her desk drawer. Although Mr. Barrett was no longer an obstacle to Danny's happiness, somehow she felt no elation at reading of his death.

It was no doubt a significant event in her son's life, for Danny was the sole heir, according to the newspaper, of his considerable fortune as well as his responsibilities. Henry Barrett, the article stated, had made a sizeable investment in a South Dakota company called Homestake Mining just before the crash of 1929 and, while, like everyone else, he suffered losses in his other investments, Homestake Mining had continued to grow and more than compensated for his other losses. He had been luckier than most.

Danny was back in New York now, practicing law, and married—a man making his own way and significantly more wealthy than many other young men his age. *Clearly he's no longer my little boy, if he ever really was,* she confided to her journal. *Now that Mr. Barrett is gone, perhaps I can find Danny and tell him that I am his mother. But who knows how he might react? Henry Barrett has had so much influence on his life that he might turn me away. Who knows what he has been told about me—if anything?* As she wrote those words, it occurred to her all at once that Danny's wealth had become a new obstacle.

I can't just show up in his life now, after all these years, and announce 'I'm your mother.' He might think I am contacting him now only because he is suddenly very rich. I would never want him to think such a thing. I care nothing for his money, but how could he know that? I am to him an utter stranger. If he turned me away, I couldn't bear it. Perhaps I should leave well enough alone. At least he has a good wife, and I know he is safe. All mothers must let their children go sooner or later.

After she wrote those words, Maggie felt a new heaviness in her heart. She knew she could never let him go, never just erase him from her life. She put down her pen and gazed out over the street, watching the vehicles scurry up and down the avenue outside her window. It was so hard to know what to do. Nothing had turned out as it was supposed to, she thought. In some ways, she was just where she had started, living in someone else's home. Danny might well consider her an embarrassment, and she didn't think she could survive his rejection. At least she was no longer a chambermaid, but rather a nursemaid, a nanny as they called them in England. It was a position of higher status to be entrusted with someone's children. But still she was a servant—a servant who felt closer to someone else's children than she did to her own son.

Matthew was seven now and had a room of his own. Lucy, not yet six, was still in the nursery, but probably not for long. Matthew had started the second grade. Lucy would not begin first grade until the fall. Maggie would miss her during the day, just as she already missed Matthew. Letting go of one's children was a process, she thought, a process she had never had with Danny—except for the wrenching void of his abduction. It was a process that should begin only with sending a child off to school. She suspected she would miss the Woodruff children even more than their parents would. They would be away most of the day, leaving much of her time empty of their presence, whereas earlier she had been with them twenty-four hours a day.

She wondered if Suzanne had missed Danny when he had started at St. Bernard's. Probably so. But had Henry Barrett missed him at all? She thought about Mr. Barrett many times in the days to come. Had he ever found the happiness he sought when he took Danny? Had he ever been able to forgive himself for losing his own son the way he did? She doubted it, for only a tormented man could do the things he had done. Taking her son against her will. Forcing Danny into a profession, and perhaps even into a marriage he had not sought, only compounded the guilt Henry Barrett had to bear. Or perhaps he didn't care. Either way, she found herself almost feeling sorry for the old man, who seemed never to have found the love and happiness he so desperately needed.

And yet she suspected it had been within his reach all along, if he had only opened his eyes and heart to it. But his rigid social standards blocked his way to comprehending a devotion, however misguided, like that of Eloise Fowler. He never saw her as a woman, only as his housekeeper. Maggie thought about Mrs. Fowler and wondered what had happened to her now that Mr. Barrett was dead. She knew from Deirdre that Friedrich had retired with an annuity that Danny provided from the Barrett estate.

No doubt Eloise Fowler had also retired to some quiet corner of the universe where she could remember her hopeless love and the sacrifice of any principles she may have had for a man who never deserved her loyalty. *Such sad lives.* Both of them, locked within convention, blinded by their own needs, and never able to realize the possibilities that might have been, if only they had been able to reach out a hand in affection and selflessness. She realized, to her surprise, that she felt only pity and a grudging sense of forgiveness for them both. And she was glad that she had not made the same mistake by refusing to marry Stuart. She was grateful for the years of quiet happiness they had known.

In the days that followed, she tried to write Danny several letters, but ended by tearing them all up and throwing them away. What if he didn't want her in his life? What if he didn't believe her? There were still so many questions, so many uncertainties. Perhaps some day God would show her the way, if there was one. For now she would bide her time and wait.

Chapter Twenty-Four

"MAGGIE, PLEASE CHANGE YOUR MIND. We want you to go with us. The children need you."

"I'm sorry, Mrs. Woodruff. I really wish I could, but it is impossible for me to leave New York."

"But why? You have no family here and only a few friends. You'll meet new people in California. It's a very progressive state, and George says that San Diego is very beautiful."

"I'm sure it is, Mrs. Woodruff, and I will surely miss the children and you and Mr. Woodruff as well. But I just can't leave New York."

"But you won't give me your reasons." Myra Woodruff hesitated, then said, "I suppose they're personal, and I can respect that. But in California, with George's new job, we'll be able to raise your salary quite a bit. Do think about it, Maggie."

"I'm sorry, ma'am, but it's just not possible."

"What will you do here, Maggie?"

"I hope to find a job with another family, if you will be willing to provide references for me."

"Of course, Maggie, but only with the greatest reluctance. The children

258

love you as much as they do George and me. You're part of our family."

Maggie smiled. "When will you be leaving, Mrs. Woodruff?"

"We plan to be settled into the new house by Christmas, but we won't leave until after Thanksgiving. Perhaps you'll be able to find a new post by then. If you're sure you won't change your mind."

"I'm sure."

It was true she would miss Lucy and Matthew. But they were getting too old to need a nursemaid at seven and almost nine. Besides, they were at school most of the day, and their mother was perfectly capable of supervising their homework and after-school activities. They would require a baby-sitter for social occasions, but otherwise they no longer really needed her.

The Woodruffs had set their moving date for Tuesday, December 3, and Maggie planned to remain with the household until the day they left and help them with the packing. She wanted to be standing on the front porch of their house, smiling and waving goodbye to the children as they drove away for the last time. She hoped it would leave them a good memory to take with them. It seemed in some ways that her whole life had been one of saying goodbye to people she loved.

But she would not leave New York. Even if she never saw her son again, at least she knew that he was nearby with his family. He and Helen had a child now—a little girl named Morgan, she had heard. Although Friedrich was no longer in contact with Danny on a daily basis, he heard news through the servant grapevine from time to time and passed it along to Rudy. But there were fewer servants now, and the news was sporadic.

Maggie contacted Abby Steers once again for references, as well as Mrs. Baker's daughter, Frances Thacher. With their letters and one from the Woodruffs, something appropriate would surely turn up. She read the want ads each day and placed one of her own. "Mature lady with excellent references and experience seeks position as nursemaid in Manhattan." She had debated over the wording. "Mature lady" sounded so awfully stuffy and rather old-fashioned, but it was the sort of thing that seemed to appeal to New York couples looking for someone reliable to care for their children. At age forty-eight she felt qualified for the description. Still she was in good health and felt young for her years.

It did not take long before she began to receive invitations for interviews. By November 12th she had chosen three that sounded most promising and set up interview times beginning on the following Monday during the children's school hours, when Mrs. Woodruff had assured her she could spare her for a few hours from the seemingly endless chore of packing. The first interview was scheduled for ten a.m. on Thursday, November 14, a week before Thanksgiving.

All of the interviews seemed to go well, Maggie thought. However, at the end of each one, the person doing the interviewing, in one case the husband, in another the wife, and once the two together, which she liked best, indicated that they had other candidates to interview and would let her know when they had made a decision. That suited Maggie fine, because she wanted a chance to consider all three positions and select the one she preferred in the event that she received more than one offer. Mrs. Woodruff assured her that she was "a gem" and that many offers would be forthcoming.

Still it was an unsettling period, particularly since the time left before the Woodruffs' departure was growing short now. She knew she could always stay for a while with Deirdre and Rudy if she needed to, but she hated to impose on them. And their house was already crowded with Deirdre's mother and the children.

On the Monday before Thanksgiving Maggie returned from the park with Lucy and Matthew. As she opened the front door, she heard, despite their noisy laughter, the ringing of the telephone in the parlor. She was helping the children take off their coats and hanging them on the hall tree when she heard Myra Woodruff saying, "No, I don't think so." Mrs. Woodruff listened silently for a moment. Then she said, "Well, I know she's had several interviews and at least one offer already, but I don't think she has accepted anything definite yet."

She listened for a moment and then said, "Of course." She picked up a pen from the hall table and jotted something on the writing pad beside the telephone. Looking up from her scribbling, Mrs. Woodruff gave Maggie a conspiratorial smile as she listened to the voice at the other end of the line.

"Well, I will certainly tell her when she comes in and, if she's at all interested and not already committed, I'll have her telephone you at her earliest convenience." She stood silent for a moment, listening. "Yes, indeed, the very best, absolutely the best, as I told you earlier. We're just sorry she can't move with us to California ... Yes, well, you're very welcome, and I'll tell her you called."

As Mrs. Woodruff put the telephone back on its hook, she turned to Maggie, her eyes twinkling with amusement. "Well, Maggie, word is getting out that the best nursemaid in New York will be available very shortly for a new position. I told you there would be a lot of offers, but they need to know they've got competition. There have been several calls today. That was a gentleman I don't know personally, though I know of him. He's very interested in talking with you."

"Do you know anything about the family, ma'am?" Maggie asked.

"They live on Fifth Avenue, so I expect the salary would be quite acceptable. He's a lawyer, I believe. I've met his wife once or twice. She's a real gadabout, from what I've observed. They have only one child, but, unfortunately, I've heard that she's something of a holy terror, so you might not be interested. Their previous nursemaid just quit without notice. Not a good sign." She chattered on briefly before bending down to embrace her children.

"What's their name?" Maggie asked.

"Whose name?" asked Mrs. Woodruff, having already turned her mind from the conversation.

"The family who needs a nursemaid. The man who just called."

"Oh, him. It's Barrett. Daniel and Helen Barrett," Mrs. Woodruff said over her shoulder as she hugged Matthew.

At the mention of Danny's name, Maggie felt the blood drain from her face and her mouth go dry. *This can't be happening. It's not real. It's just a dream, and I will soon wake up. It's nothing but a dream.*

"Maggie, are you all right?" Mrs. Woodruff asked, rising to face her. "You look pale as a ghost."

"I'm fine." She was taking deep breaths and fighting hot tears that unexpectedly filled her eyes.

"Maggie, tell me, what's wrong."

"It's nothing, just ..." she thought furiously, "just so many changes to absorb. I ..." She hesitated. "I will miss Lucy and Matthew so much." It was true, though the thought of seeing Danny again was a joyful, yet anxious, shock.

"Oh, Maggie, you dear, not nearly so much as they will miss you. I just dread the thought of having to find someone to take your place. It's just impossible."

By this time, the two children, who had been listening intently, were beginning to sniffle. Lucy, especially, was sobbing quietly. "I don't want to move to Ca'fornia," she moaned. "I want to stay here with Maggie."

"Oh, now, you will just love California," her mother cooed. "The sun shines all the time, and there are all sorts of wonderful things to see and do there."

"I don't want to go either," Matthew echoed. "Not without Maggie."

"Oh, dear, now look what I've done," said Mrs. Woodruff, pulling out her handkerchief to wipe her own eyes. "You two run into the kitchen, I think cook has some fresh-baked cookies and hot chocolate ready for you."

Their faces brightened, tears forgotten, and they started to skip off toward the kitchen. Then Matthew stopped and turned around.

"You come too, Maggie."

"I'm on my way," she said, feeling light and unreal as she tried to absorb all that was happening.

Two days later, Maggie stood in front of the Italian Renaissance façade of the Fifth Avenue mansion, remembering the first time she had seen it and the apprehensive hope she had felt at the time. Only the color of the front door had changed. It was now a regal, magnificent red, which provided a splendid background for the burnished brass knocker. She mounted the steps, trying to keep her heart from pounding out of her chest, then hesitated only a moment before she knocked. Three blows. Like the blows of fate.

The door swung open, and the face of Hector, the same strong chin and chiseled nose, smiled at her in welcome. Only the blue eyes and dark blond hair were different, more like her brother Brendan's. She caught her breath.

"You must be Mrs. O'Neil," the man said warmly. "I'm Daniel Barrett; please come in."

She couldn't take her eyes off him as he led her into the study to the left of the foyer. She was only dimly aware of the changes that surrounded her. The dark paint had been replaced by a warm pale yellow. A semi-round Italian marble table topped by a large mirror stood in the foyer, in lieu of the heavy Victorian chest that had once occupied the same spot. But all she truly noticed was a lighter, brighter atmosphere, which could have radiated from her heart as well as from her surroundings.

"Thank you so much for coming on such short notice," Daniel said. "Please sit down." He gestured toward one of the sofas that faced each other in front of the fireplace. He sat across from her, leaning forward. "I assume you have brought your letters of reference, Mrs. O'Neil."

"Please call me Maggie," she said, falling into the depths of his eyes before she looked down to reach into her purse for the three envelopes that contained her references. She thought she saw an odd reaction on his face, a flicker of recognition perhaps, but she was probably only imagining things. Or perhaps he thought her rude to stare at him so.

He opened the three envelopes and read the letters quickly. "All glowing references, I see. Just as I expected. Mrs. Woodruff was highly complimentary about your work, and I know she regrets that you don't want to accompany the family to California. Any chance you will change your mind about that?"

"None at all … Mr. Barrett." It felt strange to call him by the same name she had used for Henry Barrett. But she knew that she couldn't call him Danny or Daniel, the name he seemed to prefer now that he was an adult. "I will stay in New York," she said, hesitating only slightly before adding, "for family reasons."

"Oh? Mrs. Woodruff said she didn't think you had any family in New York. We talked a good bit about you when she called to set up this interview."

Maggie was silent for a moment. Then she said, "Distant family … but the only real family I have here. I don't see them often."

"I see," he replied.

"I understand from Mrs. Woodruff you have one little girl," she said.

"Yes. My daughter, Morgan. She's three and a half now. She'll be four in June, and she's quite a handful, I'm afraid. An active child and quite headstrong."

"All children are a handful, Mr. Barrett. I look forward to meeting her."

"She's in the park right now with the cook, who's been looking after her until we can find a new nursemaid. I'm afraid we're eating a lot of sandwiches for lunch these days." He chuckled.

Maggie liked his laugh. It was warm and natural, and she was afraid that all the love she had held inside for so long was on the verge of spilling over into the room like a great viscous pool of melted butter. She struggled to keep her composure.

"Tell me about her," she said. Anything to keep him talking. She wanted the chance just to look at him, listen to him, as he told her about her granddaughter.

"Well, she's rather spoiled, I'm afraid. Both her mother and I are to blame for that. But her mother is particularly indulgent."

"Will I be meeting your wife?" Maggie was surprised that she was not here to participate in the interview.

"I'm afraid not. At least not today. She is not home a great deal of the time. She's involved in a great many activities. Today, I believe, she's at a meeting of the Junior League or maybe it's the Colony Club. Anyhow, they're planning some kind of Christmas ball, I think. Or this may be the day for her luncheon at the River Club. She's so busy I can hardly keep up with her. You will, of course, meet her if you accept a position with us."

"Does she spend very much time with Morgan?"

"Not as much as she should, I suppose, which is why she's so indulgent when she's with her. But enough of this. Let me tell you about the position. I'm sure you're interested in knowing the terms."

The terms. For Maggie there were no terms too small, too limited, or too difficult to keep her from accepting a place in her son's household. She couldn't say that, of course, and she tried to listen with interest, though she found herself rapt, lost in the sound of his voice, which she had longed to hear for so many years.

"You will have your own room, of course, and meals and a salary of forty dollars a month. You will be free every Sunday and we'll provide a week's paid vacation after you have been with us for a year. Do these terms sound acceptable, Mrs. O'Neil?"

"Maggie," she corrected. "Quite acceptable, Mr. Barrett." She could hear the beating of her heart.

"I suppose I should ask you a lot of questions, but the fact is, I've made up my mind. After meeting you and based on what I heard from Mrs. Woodruff, I think you'll be perfect, Maggie. I would be happy to meet any other offers you may already have."

"The terms you've set are quite satisfactory. And I accept your offer," she said.

A look of relief came over him. "Well, then, when can you start?"

"The Woodruffs leave New York December 3rd. Will December 4th be suitable?"

"Absolutely, Maggie. And welcome to the Barrett household. I have a feeling we're going to get along very well."

"I hope so sincerely, Mr. Barrett. And I am eager to meet Morgan and Mrs. Barrett."

Suddenly they heard the front door open and a childish whine complaining about the cold.

"Morgan!" Daniel Barrett called. "Come and meet your new nursemaid." A pretty blond child appeared at the door, but a scowl marred the sweetness of her features. Standing beside her was a woman, her hair twisted on top of her head in a thick brown braid, her frowning face giving way to a broad smile of relief at Daniel's words.

"Then you won't be needing me any more, Mr. Barrett," she said eagerly. "May I go to the kitchen and get started on dinner?"

"Yes, Mabel." He laughed. "Go ahead while I show Maggie around. But she won't be starting until December 4th, so you're not off the hook just yet. But it won't be long now. This, by the way, is Maggie O'Neil." He introduced the two women.

Mabel nodded. "Pleased to meet you."

Maggie smiled. "Good to meet you as well."

"I don't like her." Morgan pouted, pointing at Maggie. "Make her go away. I want Flossie back." In a final gesture of disapproval the child flung her coat to the floor. Mabel picked it up, hung it on a hall rack, shrugged, and slipped away toward the kitchen.

"Flossie doesn't want to come back," Daniel said. "She's already taken another job. Now be a good girl and be nice to Maggie."

"I don't like her," Morgan said again, frowning in Maggie's direction, pressing her lips together, and turning down the corners of her mouth.

"Now don't say that, darling. You don't even know her yet."

"I don't like her. I don't like her," she said over and over, stamping her tiny foot. "Make her go away."

Maggie ignored what she recognized as a burgeoning tantrum and turned to Daniel. "Could you show me Morgan's room as well as my own now?"

"Yes, of course. Would you like to come, Morgan?"

"She can't see my room. No. No." She was beginning to howl now, trying to block their progress toward the stairs.

"Mabel! Mabel!" Daniel called. When the woman appeared at the hallway door that led to the dining room, he pleaded, "Could you take her to the kitchen with you while I show Maggie around?"

She nodded with obvious reluctance. "Come on, Morgan, let's go and make some cocoa." She took the child's hand and dragged her toward the kitchen, with Morgan screaming, "No, no," at the top of her lungs.

Once the door had closed again, Daniel said, "Well, you see what you're getting into. I couldn't blame you if you changed your mind about the position, now that you've met Morgan. She can be very sweet at times. But she likes to have her own way, as you've observed."

"I haven't changed my mind, Mr. Barrett. Most children want their own way until they discover other people have feelings as well. May I see the rooms now?"

The unforgettable meeting with her granddaughter made Maggie realize that there were serious problems in the household and that she would have her work cut out for her. She smiled inwardly at the welcome challenge as she mounted the familiar staircase.

Chapter Twenty-Five

IT WAS MAGGIE'S FIRST FREE SUNDAY afternoon since she had become a part of the Barrett household. She still had trouble believing that she was actually living in her son's home. Danny's home. And that she was indeed taking care of her own granddaughter.

She had spent a happy Thanksgiving the week before coming here. She had chosen not to go out, but rather to spend time in her room meditating on her good luck, reading, writing, and thinking about how to make the best of the situation and all its uncertainties.

It was true that Morgan was a handful. Even little Lucy as a three-year-old couldn't hold a candle to Morgan in terms of temper tantrums. Maggie had long ago learned that the best way to break a child of a tantrum was to ignore it until the child wore herself out and could be reasoned with, insofar as one could ever reason with a three-year-old. However, it didn't always work when Morgan's parents were around. And she didn't have a big brother to help calm her down.

Maggie had discovered what may have been the source of the problem her very first day in the Barrett residence. A tantrum was frequently the only way the child could get her mother's complete attention. And Morgan had learned full well she could always get what she wanted from her mother by such tactics. Maggie did not meet Helen Barrett until late afternoon on December

4. Danny had taken the morning off from his office to help Maggie get settled and answer any questions she might have, but Helen, who was out all day at one of her clubs, did not return until about four o'clock. When Morgan heard her, she shrieked with excitement.

"Mommy's home!" She bounded down the stairs, with Maggie hurrying behind as best she could, fearing that the child would fall.

Helen had put down her purse and shopping bag on the marble hall table in the foyer, taken off her hat, and was gazing at her reflection in the mirror, her little finger tracing the outline of her lips. Morgan flew to her with open arms.

"Hello, sweetie," her mother said, leaning down to give her a quick peck on the cheek before picking up the hall telephone.

"Mommy, Mommy," the child shouted, jumping up and down as her mother dialed a number. She shushed her daughter when she heard her party answer at the other end of the line.

"I had the most fabulous idea on my way home, Liz," Helen gushed into the telephone. "We could focus the theme of the ball on the first ballet of the season—Swan Lake. What do you think of that?"

As she listened to the response, Morgan was pulling at her skirt.

"Mommy, Mommy, come see my picture," she urged.

Helen didn't seem to hear her. "Just think of the colors we could use—white, blue, silver, and swan motifs for the table arrangements. Perhaps an ice sculpture ..." she rambled on. "It could be glorious."

"Mommy!" Morgan's voice was becoming strident, and she had begun to pound on her mother's hip.

"Just a minute, Morgan. I'm busy now!"

But the child didn't let up. She was starting to whine now. "Come on, Mommy, come upstairs to my room."

"Not now, Morgan," Helen said sharply to the child. "I'm on the telephone!"

Maggie, who had stood in the background so that Morgan could greet her mother undisturbed, stepped forward and tried to take the little girl's hand. "No!" she screamed. "I don't want you! I want my mommy!"

"I'd better hang up now, Liz. Morgan's having a fit. Think about it, and I'll telephone you tomorrow."

She laid the telephone receiver in its cradle, then turned to Morgan with narrowed eyes and said through clenched teeth, "I have told you not to bother me while I am on the phone!"

Morgan burst into tears. "Make her go away," she screamed at her mother and pointed to Maggie. "And come see my picture," she demanded.

"Are you the new nursemaid my husband hired?" Helen asked shortly.

"Yes, ma'am. I'm Maggie O'Neil."

"Well, is this the best you can do with her?" Helen's voice rose in anger.

"She's been quite good all day," Maggie said, "but she's just waked up from her nap. She was excited that you were coming home so she could show you the picture she drew. We just came downstairs to greet you. I'm sorry if she disturbed you, ma'am."

"Well, you should be." Helen looked at Maggie coldly. "Always keep her upstairs until I have a moment to catch my breath at least."

"Yes, ma'am, I'll try."

"Now, come, my little darling," Helen said, picking up her screaming daughter. "Calm your sweet self down, and let's go see your picture. And, guess what? Mommy brought you a present."

Morgan's tears stopped abruptly. "A present? What is it?"

"You'll just have to wait until Daddy comes home so he can see it too."

The screams began again. "I want it now! I don't want to wait."

"Oh, all right. I suppose you can show it to Daddy when he gets here." Helen Barrett set her daughter down, turned to the shopping bag she had brought home, and pulled out a large package, carefully boxed and wrapped. As she helped Morgan unwrap the package, she child rocked with excitement.

"A tea set!!" she shouted. "A real tea set!"

"And not just any tea set. This is an antique Spode tea set. You can have wonderful tea parties for your dolls. Look, it has four cups and saucers, a teapot, a little china platter, and cream and sugar dishes."

"Oh, Mommy, thank you, thank you. Come and have a tea party with me."

"Oh, dear, I'm much too tired this afternoon. You have a tea party with Maggie."

"I want you—not her!"

"Not today, Morgan," Helen said sternly. "I have a headache."

The child began to cry again. "Oh, for God's sake, take her upstairs, will you," she said to Maggie. "I'm going to lie down for a while."

"Yes, ma'am," Maggie said. She bent down to Morgan. "Let's go to the nursery and set your little table with the new tea set."

Morgan picked up one of the saucers and threw it against the wall, where it shattered into a dozen pieces.

"See if you ever get another tea set from me, young lady," Helen said angrily. "That was a special set imported from England. Just deal with her, Meggie or Maggie, or whatever your name is. I can't stand it," Helen shouted as she went to her own bedroom and slammed the door.

"I'm sorry, Morgan, your mommy doesn't feel well this afternoon," Maggie said, squatting down beside the child. "I have a very good idea. Why don't we take your tea set into the garden and have tea together."

"I don't want to," Morgan said. "I don't want to have tea with you."

Maggie picked up the shards of the china saucer and wrapped them in her handkerchief. "Well, then, we'll just sit here," she said, sitting down beside Morgan on the bottom step of the stairwell. The child stamped her feet and crossed her arms, hugging herself and sobbing. When she had worn herself out, Maggie put her arm around the little girl and kissed the top of her head. Then she stood up, rewrapped the remaining items of the tea set and started to carry them upstairs.

"Where are you going?" Morgan asked.

"I'm going to ask your Shirley Temple doll whether she would like to have tea with Teddy Bear. You can come if you'd like."

Morgan, her face still stained with tears and her bottom lip extended, sat still for a moment, as though thinking it over. Then she rose, sniffing, and followed Maggie slowly up the stairs.

Since that first afternoon Maggie made a special effort to reward the child's occasional good behavior with attention and praise. Her biggest problem with Morgan, she knew, would be her mother's inconsistency, although she wasn't home most of the time. Already Morgan's tantrums were becoming less frequent during the day. They only began at night when her parents came home. Maggie knew it was not going to be easy, but she believed that any child would respond to love and consistent behavior, and she intended to provide her with both in abundance.

Usually Helen was the first to come home, though sometimes not more than half and hour before Danny, and she usually wanted to rest and change clothes before he arrived. Unfortunately, it was the time when Morgan most wanted her mother's attention, and the difficult times happened during that portion of the day, between four and five. But when Danny opened the front door, the first thing he did was call out, "Where's my girl?" Morgan would usually be listening from the nursery, and Maggie knew she must move quickly at such moments.

"I hear Daddy!" the child would shriek, dropping whatever she was doing and running for the door. "Daddy, Daddy!" Maggie followed the child down the stairs to watch her throw herself into her father's arms.

He was waiting for her at the foot of the stairs, his arms held out for that little leap she gave from the second or third step.

"Hello, darling," he would say, "tell me what you and Maggie did today."

Morgan would regale him with stories of their adventures, occasional trips to the park, but the weather was cold and rainy now, so Maggie tried to find adventures within the house—learning to make cookies when Mabel could provide free space for them in the kitchen, drawing pictures with crayons on old newspapers or wrapping paper, putting together puzzles, having tea parties, and reading or making up stories. During the day Morgan, while never docile, could at least be interested in a project, provided she was the one to decide what it would be. Maggie tried to give her limited choices. "Would you like to read a story now or pick out an outfit for Shirley Temple?" It seemed to work better than trying to impose an activity on the child.

Despite Morgan's bad temper, Maggie was impressed with her intelligence. Already at three she was beginning to pick out words in her books, and she thought about the stories she and Maggie read and asked questions about them. There was one book she liked above all others. It was called *Clarinda*, a story about a naughty little girl who would slide down the drain as she let out her bath water, only to come up *somewhere else* in a happy pond filled with frogs and fish and surrounded by a field of butterflies and wild daisies. There Clarinda escaped her frustrating world and her naughty self. Maggie could see that Morgan identified with the little girl in the story, which seemed amazing for one so young. At the end of bath time she would watch the water longingly as it went down the drain.

"Where does it go?" she asked.

"Into the East River, I expect," Maggie replied honestly. The child looked disappointed. In the spring, Maggie thought, we will find that perfect pond in Central Park. There might not be many butterflies or wild daisies, but there will be other children to play with and little boats to sail, boats that can take her imagination far away. She looked forward to their first April together.

But visits to Central Park in the spring didn't always go as Maggie had anticipated. In fact, they rarely did. Morgan could still be petulant at times, though she seemed to enjoy being outside. Maggie tried to encourage her to play with other children. She desperately needed to learn to interact with others her own age, Maggie thought, and the park seemed the best place to begin. But the child hung back.

"Why don't you ask that little girl to play with you?" Maggie suggested, pointing to a dark-haired child with olive skin about Morgan's age whose mother was blowing bubbles that the child gleefully chased.

The mother, whom Maggie recognized as the wife of the grocer a few blocks from the Barrett household, was sitting on an adjacent park bench. The woman, whose dark braided hair was pinned neatly at the back of her head, smiled and made a gesture for Morgan to join her daughter. But Morgan shook her head.

"Why don't you want to play with her, Morgan?"

"Mommy told me not to."

"What do you mean? Your mother's not even here."

"Mommy doesn't like me to play with children like her. She says they're cath'lic or 'talian or something." Morgan, who was almost four now, clearly had no idea what those terms meant, but she was adamant.

"She's just a little girl like you. You might hurt her feelings if you don't want to play with her."

"I don't care," Morgan poked out her bottom lip. "I won't play with her."

"Well, I think I will," Maggie said, jumping up to chase a bubble that had drifted by her bench. She held out her hand to catch it, and for just a moment, the bubble perched on the palm of her hand before bursting into almost invisible droplets. Maggie and the other little girl both laughed.

"That tickles," Maggie said.

Morgan sat pouting on the bench, her arms folded as she watched Maggie and the dark-haired child reach for the bubbles as far as they could as they rose into the sky. Sometimes they drifted down again, sometimes not. Their rainbow colors glowed like nacre before they popped, making the little girl giggle. Soon their play attracted the attention of another child, a sandy-haired boy with a small white dog of no particular breed, who barked at the bubbles and leaped upward, popping one on his nose. The boy, taking his cue from the dog, was not interested in catching the glassy bubbles, but in popping as many as he could reach.

Finally Maggie, breathless from her effort to spur her granddaughter's interest, sat down on the bench beside her to watch the other children play.

"They're having fun, aren't they?" she said to Morgan.

Morgan was staring at the two children through narrowed eyes. "My mommy says those people aren't clean."

"They look fine to me. I can't see that they're any different from you and me."

"I'll tell Mommy what you did."

"That's up to you, darling," Maggie replied, though she knew Helen would be furious that she even suggested that Morgan play with the grocer's little girl.

Maggie smiled sadly at her granddaughter and put her hand around the child's shoulder. She had given up the idea of revealing her own identity to Danny, for Helen's attitude toward anyone who had not gone to an Ivy League school and who did not move in their social circles was one of utter disdain. She knew that, if Helen learned that Danny's mother was an Irish immigrant, a nursemaid, a former chambermaid, the tensions of the household would only increase. She understood that she would never be accepted with dignity as Danny's mother, and she had decided that she would just let herself be close to her family in any way she could.

Morgan watched the grocer's daughter and the boy with the dog intently, as though memorizing their movements, their easy interaction. But she never budged from her stolid place on the bench, until finally, she sighed and said, "Let's go home, Maggie. I'm bored."

Persistent in her efforts, little by little Maggie began to gain the child's confidence. Morgan loved the Irish folk tales Maggie told her at bedtime and asked all kinds of questions about Ireland. The child was lonely with no siblings and no one nearby her mother considered good enough for her to play with. Occasionally Helen would invite the child of one of her friends over for a play session, but the afternoons were so highly structured and formal, centering around all sorts of planned activities, that the children never really got to know one another or use their imaginations in play. Morgan seemed more relaxed when she was with Maggie than with anyone else.

When the child turned four on June 8, Helen gave a lavish party for her, inviting her society friends' children from ages three to seven to attend. There were an even dozen of them, the little girls all in elegant dresses of silk and satin ornamented with bows and frills, and the boys in miniature suits and ties like tiny men.

Helen had hired a professional French puppeteer who had once worked with the Guignol in Paris to entertain the children. The cake was provided by the best bakery in New York—a multi-layered birthday cake coated with pink fondue icing and decorated with sugar clowns and balloons. The children took home as favors imported French hand puppets, specially ordered from the company that supplied puppets to the Guignol. A pile of presents lay on the marble table in the hall, and Morgan opened them one by one. As her mother had instructed her, she oohed and aahed at first over each one and thanked the giver profusely. There was a gold locket, a silver bracelet, a Lady Alexander doll, and a tiny string of pearls.

When she grew tired of opening the gifts, she became more petulant and critical of each one." I already have a tea set," she said, opening a Wedgewood tea set bordered in lime green. "And I don't like the color."

"Oh, but it's beautiful," Morgan's mother coaxed. "We can have such delightful tea parties." Morgan looked at her quizzically.

"Really?" she asked hopefully.

"Really," said Helen.

"Then I like it very much. Thank you, Harriet," she said to the little girl who had brought it.

When the gifts were finally all opened and the children had gone, Morgan picked up the lime-green tea set. "Can we have our tea party now, Mommy?"

"Not now, darling. We're all tired out from your birthday party. Why don't you go upstairs with Maggie and rest a while."

Tears welled up in the weary child's eyes, but she let Maggie take her hand and lead her upstairs. Once the nursery door was closed, Maggie took the little girl in her arms.

"Happy birthday, Morgan," she said, handing the child one more gift. Morgan, who was beginning to yawn, opened it and smiled. It was a tiny music box that played "When You Wish Upon a Star." Maggie wound it for her granddaughter and lay down beside her on the child's bed, as they listened to the hopeful song and fell asleep together.

7 DECEMBER 1941 NEW YORK

It was a typical Sunday afternoon. Everyone had slept late, except for Maggie who had gone to early mass, and they had all stuffed themselves at the noontime meal with Mabel's pork roast, potato soufflé, asparagus with baked red peppers, and chocolate mousse. While Morgan napped, Daniel and Helen sat in the parlor before a blazing fire, listening to a broadcast of the New York Philharmonic playing Brahms's Second Piano Concerto, with Arthur Rubenstein as the featured soloist. They had decided not to attend the concert, even though the Philharmonic was one of the cultural activities Helen supported, because a light snow had begun to fall.

It was nice to have a relaxing Sunday afternoon to themselves for a change and just enjoy the fire and the concert. Daniel was stretched out on the sofa reading the news and business sections of the New York *Times,* while Helen devoured the society pages. The music provided a soothing backdrop to the chilly afternoon.

"We interrupt this broadcast to bring you the following special announcement." The radio announcer's voice was abrupt.

Daniel sat up to listen, and Helen laid the newspaper on her lap. What could be so important that they would interrupt the Rubenstein concert?

The strained voice of announcer John Daly came on the air. "Japan has attacked Pearl Harbor, Hawaii, and Manila, the Philippine Islands, from the air." He promised more information on his regularly scheduled broadcast.

"Oh, Daniel, what do you think it means?" Helen asked quietly when the concert resumed.

"It means, I think, that we can no longer stay out of this war," Danny said quietly. "It means we will fight." The new war had been raging in Europe for two years, ever since Adolf Hitler's invasion of Poland, but so far the United States had remained neutral.

They left the radio on for news the rest of the afternoon and learned that President Roosevelt would speak to a joint session of Congress at twelve-thirty p.m. the following day.

On Monday, Daniel called his secretary to give instructions about various matters that needed to be attended to and telling her that he would be working at home today. He wanted to be with his family when they listened to the President's message.

The entire household, with the exception of Morgan and Maggie, who were sent upstairs so the child would not be upset, huddled tensely around radios from twelve-twenty on, unwilling to miss a single word of what was said, Daniel and Helen in the front parlor, Mabel and the day maid, Phyllis, in the kitchen.

Maggie felt the tension in the household, even though she could not hear the President's words. It was the following day before she read them in the newspaper, the brief eloquent speech lamenting the day "that would live in infamy" and asking Congress to declare war on Japan. Three days later there was a subsequent declaration of war against Germany and Italy—Japan's allies. Even Morgan was quieter than usual, she too evidently sensing that something was amiss.

Before the end of the week Danny presented himself to his five-member draft board to volunteer for service, but he was turned away by a friend of his father-in-law.

"Go home, Daniel," he said. "You have obligations here. We're not drafting married men with children, at least not yet. Go home to your family. We'll get you soon enough."

Although Daniel recognized the logic of what the man said and acknowledged his responsibility to his family, he felt a sense of frustration at the response. He longed to do his part in the war. On the other hand, members of his law firm were delighted he wasn't going. He was the only member of the firm, at twenty-nine, who was young enough for the draft. He would wait impatiently, for more than two years, for his turn to do what he believed was his duty.

As the war dragged on, Daniel was busier than ever, not just with his law practice, but with fund-raising for the Red Cross and following troop movements on a large world map in his study. To Helen's annoyance, he had replaced the tasteful painting by Winslow Homer that she had bought years ago at a Sotheby's auction with that ugly world map. The Homer was now stored in the attic, and each morning, after Daniel read the newspaper, and each evening, as he listened to the radio, he moved little red and blue pins on his map to new strategic points.

When Morgan started to school in the fall of 1943, Maggie held her breath, fearful that her presence would no longer be needed in the household, but nothing could have been further from the truth. The war did nothing to reduce Helen's social activities, though they had taken on a more patriotic flavor and the disguise of wartime efforts. In fact, she seemed to be away from home even more than before.

Maggie's presence was taken for granted, and, when the maid, Phyllis, left to take a job in a munitions factory, Maggie filled her days, while Morgan was at school, dusting and making beds. She was willing to do anything to keep her place in the Barrett household.

There were other changes as well. Although Danny still took time to visit with his daughter when he first came home from the office, Morgan got to see him even more, for she and Maggie now joined the family for dinner each evening. When Helen and Daniel first made the decision that Morgan, at six, should now take her evening meals in the dining room and begin to learn the social skills of entertaining and graceful dining, Helen informed Maggie that she could take her evening meal in the kitchen with Mabel, but Morgan would have none of it.

"I want her with me," the child insisted, using her old whiny voice, so seldom heard these days. Her father didn't seem to mind, and Helen, rather than endure what she foresaw as a tearful tantrum, gave in, though on evenings when there were guests, both of them were still relegated to the kitchen. In fact, Morgan rarely had such tantrums anymore, though Helen had failed to notice. The child had learned from Maggie other ways to deal with her frustrations, and she seemed finally to have grown accustomed to her mother's frequent absences. Her life focused now more on her friends from school and on her playtime activities with Maggie.

Though Maggie had always read stories to Morgan in the evening, the child was beginning now to read to Maggie on occasion. Maggie would never forget the first time it happened. It was the night before her fifth birthday when, at the moment of her bedtime story, the child reached for the book, her favorite, *Clarinda*, and said, "Let me read to you." Morgan took the book and read word for word, with every inflection and special voice that Maggie always used. Maggie was never certain whether she actually read the book or whether she had simply memorized it, but she turned the pages at the appropriate moments and never missed a single word.

Now, a year older, she was beginning to read books she had never heard before, and often, during the afternoons after school, they read aloud to each other, sometimes from *The Wind and the Willows*, sometimes *Heidi*, who at the beginning of the book was about the same age as Morgan, and sometimes even the poems that Maggie so loved and which Morgan had come to enjoy as well. She had even learned one or two of the shorter ones by heart. Those afternoons were precious to them both.

Maggie liked to read to her granddaughter about children from other cultures, to help her understand that everyone, even in America, was not like her, but that everyone had value and needed love. She was thrilled the afternoon Morgan had come home to tell her about her new best friend at school. Her name was Huiking, and she was from China. She had other friends, of course, whose names were Susan and Barbara, but it was Huiking she talked about most, at least to Maggie.

When Daniel's draft notice finally arrived in early October 1943, Maggie's heart sank. She had known since the war began that, sooner or later, he would go to fight, but she had dreaded the day. Like any mother, she was concerned for his safety, but in her case she feared not only the loss of her son, but of her granddaughter as well.

With Daniel gone, she felt insecure in her position in the household. Helen could be so impetuous and unpredictable, and Maggie had always had the feeling that Daniel's wife resented her presence for some reason. All she could do was wait and see and pray.

Chapter Twenty-Six

MORGAN LOST HER FIRST BABY TOOTH the morning her father kissed her goodbye and went off to join the army.

"Take care of Mommy," he said to his daughter as he picked her up and held her in his arms. "You're a big girl now."

He was leaving for Fort Meade, Maryland, where he would begin his basic training. He gave a quick hug and a grin to both Maggie and Mabel, who were standing in the background to see him off as well.

"Look after my girls while I'm gone," he told them.

Maggie nodded, with tears in her eyes. Daniel stooped down to squeeze Morgan one last time before picking up his suitcase, giving Helen one more kiss, and bounding out the door. They all moved out to the front stoop to wave goodbye as the yellow cab taking him to the train station pulled away from the curb. Morgan reached for Maggie's hand after she blew her father a final kiss.

"Well," Helen shrugged and said to no one in particular as the cab turned the corner, "I guess it's all up to us now."

As November and December passed, the house seemed big and empty with Daniel gone. Even though he had been at his office much of the day, knowing that he would come home in the evening always gave a brightness of anticipation to afternoon. Maggie could tell that Morgan missed the times with her father.

"Let's have a tea party," she would say at four o'clock. Or, "Let's read your new book." Anything to occupy her granddaughter during those lonely hours.

Helen, on the other hand, did what she had always done. If she were saddened by her husband's absence, she showed no sign of it. And she wasted little time in finding substitute male escorts to the various charity functions she attended.

Morgan sat on the bottom step watching her mother pat her hair and retouch her lipstick as she waited for her escort of the evening. She looked at herself appraisingly in the mirror.

"Who's coming tonight, Mama?" Morgan asked. There were three or four gentlemen who always seemed willing to accompany Helen to dinners and ceremonies she didn't want to attend alone.

"Mr. King, darling," she said, leaning toward the mirror. "I don't think this dress is quite right for the occasion," she said. "I'd better change." She glanced toward the grandfather clock at the end of the hall. "Oh, my, look at the time. I'd better hurry. He's to be here at seven." She rushed back into her bedroom.

The child sat alone, staring at the front door. Dudley King—a banker reputed to be one of the richest men in New York—came most often now. In fact, Helen hadn't had any other escort for several weeks. He sometimes came to dinner at the Fifth Avenue home, and sometimes he invited Helen to dine with him at a fine restaurant.

Maggie watched the scene from the upstairs balcony. Now she called out to Morgan, "Come on up, dear, and let's pick out your clothes for school tomorrow." The child dutifully got up and trudged up the stairs.

Maggie tried hard not to be judgmental. She knew that many other women of Helen's social set with husbands in the military also had male escorts to such functions. Whenever possible, they went on the arms of brothers or cousins, but Helen had no brothers or cousins in New York, and it would be unseemly to go without a male companion, or so Helen said. One had to attend these functions after all, particularly if it were for a good cause—a charity event or a wartime fund-raiser. And certainly there was no shortage of such affairs in New York.

Whenever Mr. King came to call, he always inquired politely about news from Daniel. Helen chattered away about the latest letter she had received. Her husband was in Officers Candidate School at Fort Benning, Georgia, she said, now that he had finished his basic training. He had been encouraged by his battalion commander to apply for OCS, given his Harvard law degree.

"I will soon be what my buddies call 'a ninety-day wonder,'" Danny had written. "But I'd be just as content to fight alongside the men with whom I did my basic training. They're good people." Helen told Dudley about that letter.

"I dare say he'll be much happier among his own kind." Mr. King chuckled and smoothed his moustache.

"You're probably right. At least I hear the food is better for officers," Helen replied, taking his arm to lead him in to the lobster Newberg dinner Mable had prepared at her request.

Frequently Helen would invite another couple to attend these little dinners, but Maggie and Morgan were never included. Morgan's chattering seemed to annoy Mr. King, who had no children of his own. He and his wife had been divorced three years earlier, and he seemed to enjoy his restored bachelor status.

A letter arrived from Daniel in mid-March 1944, letting them know that he was shipping out the following week to England for further training. That was all the message indicated. Helen wrote him every few days, but she had also given his army address to Maggie and asked her to help Morgan write her father once in a while as well, now that she had learned how to write.

"I expect he'd rather hear from her than me anyhow," Helen said tartly, as she pinned on the white orchid Mr. King had sent over for the Colony Club dance—a charity function to help sell war bonds. "You feel free to write him too, Maggie, and tell him how she's doing in school and that sort of thing. I'm told soldiers like to get a lot of letters, but I just can't write every single day."

"ALLIED ARMIES LAND IN FRANCE...GREAT INVASION IS UNDER WAY," blared the headlines of the *New York Times* on June 6, 1944. Allied troops who had trained in England were storming the beaches of Normandy. For days heavy casualties were reported in the press, and Maggie held her breath for news of Danny. She knew he must be part of the invasion. But when no telegram arrived for the next two weeks, she breathed easier again.

Letters from overseas were scarcer now, and when they came, they seemed to arrive in batches of three or four. They could have been sent from anywhere, and Danny could never tell them where he was. She was sure he was no longer in England, but that would not have been much safer than France or Belgium, considering the German bombardments.

Helen had dutifully hung a blue star in the window of their house to indicate that the family living there had someone in the military. For that, Maggie was grateful. She went every Sunday to early morning mass at St. Patrick's Cathedral, where she could pray for her son and ask God to protect him. Hers were the same prayers as those she heard whispered in the pews around her.

"Can't you at least look after Morgan until I wake up?" Helen asked one Sunday morning, her face scowling over her steaming cup. Sunday was technically Maggie's day off, but Helen usually stayed out past midnight most Saturday evenings and liked to sleep late on Sunday.

"I can't stand Morgan bothering me before I have my coffee," she said.

At noon she usually went out to lunch with friends. Maggie needed to be there to look after Morgan. Her day off was a thing of the past, but she didn't mind so much, except that she was determined to attend mass.

"Ma'am," she said to Helen one Friday evening after dinner, "would it be all right with you if I took Morgan to church with me on Sunday mornings?"

It seemed the perfect solution. Helen hesitated only a moment about letting her daughter go to a Catholic Church. After all, the Barretts and the Steeles were nominally Episcopalians, the group that New Yorkers considered the church for the elite and the wealthy. On the other hand, they rarely went to church at all, so what difference could it possibly make? As long as Morgan didn't hobnob with the other children there. It would keep her occupied on Sunday mornings and let her mother get her much-needed beauty rest.

"I don't think her father would mind, Maggie. If she wants to go," Helen said.

The child had not been to church more than a half dozen times in her life—when she was christened as an infant at Trinity Episcopal Church and on scattered Easter Sundays or Christmas Eve services, and she wasn't sure what to expect. Nevertheless, she agreed to go, at least once. Maggie told her about the liturgy in advance and helped her learn some of the Latin phrases she would hear.

"We can pray for your Daddy to come home safely," Maggie told her.

Morgan smiled eagerly at the possibility. On her first Sunday at morning mass, she was awed as she looked up at the towering structure of St. Patrick's.

"Why did all the people go up to the front of the church and kneel down?" she asked about the Eucharist.

And she talked for days about the "colored windows" that cast such beautiful hues onto the marble floors, asking about the stories and symbols they depicted. Maggie answered all her questions as best she could and told her about her faith, the little church in Doolin where she grew up, and the magnificent Cliffs of Mohr, where God always seemed closest to her.

Morgan listened intently and began to look forward to going to mass with Maggie on Sunday mornings. She seemed hungry for something to believe in. But she was upset that she could not participate in the Eucharist, which was reserved for Catholics only

"Mama, I want to be a Catholic," she said one night at dinner.

"No daughter of mine will ever be Catholic," Helen declared bluntly and without hesitation. Morgan looked at Maggie, whose resolve never to reveal her true identity strengthened at the outspoken prejudice of her son's wife. But she smiled gently at Morgan, whose eyes were filling with tears. At least Helen hadn't forbidden her going to mass.

Maggie and the child spent half an hour or so each day composing letters to Morgan's father. For the most part, Maggie let her granddaughter put things in her own words, though occasionally she would add a little note of explanation. Daniel began to write back, with letters sent especially to his daughter, beautiful letters he thought would appeal to a child, describing the artwork of Jack Frost on window panes of the houses where he sometimes slept or the spring colors he saw from his tent.

Once he wrote a grown-up letter, instructing Morgan to keep it and read it again when she was older, telling her why this war had to be fought, but also revealing his fundamental opposition to war and violence. Maggie made sure that all the letters were tucked away and preserved for Morgan to read again when she could fully understand them.

Everything Morgan and Maggie wrote to him was meant to lift his spirits and make him want to come home safe and sound to those who loved him. Helen's letters, apparently, began to take on a quite different tone, which reflected itself in the increasingly pessimistic letters he sent to Morgan.

"If I don't make it home," he wrote to Morgan once, "you must always know how much I love you." Maggie hated that letter and its equivocal nature. Of course he would make it home. He had to, and he must make his daughter believe that.

Morgan burst into Maggie's room before breakfast on a cold morning in early January 1945. Tears were streaming down her face.

"Morgan, what on earth is wrong?" Maggie reached out to hold the child.

"Mommy's leaving." Her body was wracked with sobs.

"There, there, darling," Maggie knelt down beside the child to kiss her tear-stained face. "What do you mean?"

"Mommy's leaving. She's going away with Mr. King." Morgan could say no more.

Maggie knew that Helen had awakened Morgan earlier that morning and taken her into her bedroom, but she hadn't known why. Her brow furrowed. *How can she do this to her daughter while Danny is away? How can she do it to Danny? What does it all mean?* Maggie wondered. Was she leaving for good? Was it to be a brief vacation?

"Come on, Morgan," Maggie said, rising and taking the child by the hand. "Let's get you some breakfast, and I'll go talk to Mommy and find out what this is all about."

Morgan sniffed hopefully. If anyone could help, she knew Maggie could.

Maggie knocked softly on Helen's door.

"Oh, for heaven's sake, come in," said an exasperated voice from inside the bedroom. Maggie opened the door.

"Ma'am," she said, "Morgan tells me you're leaving. How long do you plan to be away?" She could see three suitcases open on the bed, and all of Helen's toiletries had disappeared from the vanity.

"I don't know that it's really any of your business, Maggie, but I guess you'll have to know since I'm leaving you here to take care of Morgan."

Helen opened her small black purse and took out a cigarette, which she put between her lips and lit with the gold-colored lighter from the night table, a gift from Dudley King. She had taken up smoking after Danny left and seemed to use her cigarettes more as props than for enjoyment.

"I'm weary of this damned war and all the gloominess in this house. Mr. King and I have decided to take a trip to Palm Beach, where I'll spend the duration of the war. I've already contacted a lawyer here in New York—not one from Daniel's firm, of course—to draw up divorce papers. This whole marriage has been a charade for a long time, as you probably know, and enough is enough. I just want to live a little while I'm still young."

"I see," said Maggie, her mouth dry. "And will you be sending for Morgan?" Her heart thudded as she waited for Helen's reply. *Oh, God*, she prayed, *let her say no.* She knew that Morgan loved her mother, but she couldn't bear to see Danny lose his daughter as she had lost him.

"All that isn't decided yet. Dudley doesn't like children very much, and Morgan's used to being here with you. She has school, of course, and I hate to disrupt her life more than I have to. I thought I'd let her stay here, at least for now. When her father comes home, then we'll make some kind of permanent arrangement. And I think that's about all you need to know." Helen studied her fingernails for a moment and then turned back to her packing.

Maggie stood, unmoving, unable to believe what she was hearing. How could Helen want to leave her only child this way? And yet, in spite of her concern for her granddaughter and her son, Maggie was not sorry to see her go.

"Does her father know?" Maggie asked, thinking of Danny's shock and dismay when he learned of his wife's betrayal.

"He will soon enough. I sent him a letter two days ago. Oh, one more thing, Maggie," Helen said, turning around to face her once more. "Daniel's law firm will continue to take care of household expenses as they always have. I'm having my lawyer send them a letter explaining all this. You'll be in charge until Daniel returns."

Maggie nodded, wondering how she could explain all this to Morgan.

"Oh, quit looking at me that way. Morgan's upset right now, but she'll get over it. You've been more of a mother to her than I have anyhow. I never meant to have children. She was just an accident."

Maggie bit her lip and held her own hand to keep from slapping Helen. The urge passed as quickly as it had risen up in her. She pressed her lips together and then forced out the words, "Goodbye, ma'am. I'll take good care of her."

She closed the door softly behind her and went to the kitchen to find her grieving granddaughter.

Maggie and Morgan heard nothing from Daniel for several weeks following Helen's departure. Morgan cried for two days after her mother left, but finally let Maggie dry her tears and help her refocus her attention on writing to her father and talking about what they would do together when the war ended.

Maggie waited a week to be sure that Danny had received Helen's letter before she wrote to him herself. It was the only letter she sent in her own name. Any other news she shared had been attached to Morgan's letters to her father. This time, however, she wanted to send a message she could not send through Morgan.

"You must make a special effort to come home safe and sound," she wrote. "Your daughter needs you more than you can imagine. She misses you, and you are her only anchor in a very uncertain world."

Danny wrote back two weeks later a letter addressed just to Maggie. He thanked her for her words and for helping him to understand why his life must go on. At the same time he wrote to Morgan to tell her how much he loved her and how much he longed to come home to her. "We will have wonderful days together," he wrote, "and we will find adventure and excitement when this war ends, which will be soon, I think."

Morgan loved that letter and kept it in the top drawer of her clothes chest, where she hid all her special treasures. She would go to sleep at night with the music box Maggie had given her alongside her pillow. She wound it tightly so that it would play a long time, and she would fall asleep to the tinkling sounds of "When You Wish Upon a Star." Maggie knew her wish—that her father would come home soon and she would be part of a real family again.

Chapter Twenty-Seven

3 JANUARY 1946 NEW YORK HARBOR

"HOW WILL WE EVER FIND HIM with all those people on board?" Morgan asked. The enormous vessel, the *Queen Mary*, had put in at Manhattan's 42nd Street dock area before noon, but so far none of the troops, who had been on the ship since it sailed from Southampton, England, on December 29, had been allowed to disembark.

"I don't know, but we'll watch the gangplanks as the men come down if nothing else." Maggie eagerly scanned the faces of those waving and calling from the deck.

"He knows we're going to meet the ship, doesn't he?" Morgan asked, apprehension in her voice.

"He does." At least she hoped so. She had tried to get word to him. More than eleven thousand troops were said to be coming home on this ship alone. They had been pouring into New York ever since June, when the war ended in Europe.

Daniel had been shipped back to England from Germany, where his unit had gone after the liberation of France and Belgium. He had been assigned to do legal work in London, helping prepare documents for the Nuremberg war trials that had begun the preceding November. Finally, when his commanding officer had learned about his wife's departure and his little daughter in New York, he had insisted that the young captain, as he now was, be released from his duties and allowed to come back to the States.

Morgan, who would soon be nine years old, had received the telegram in her own name. She was thrilled. Her daddy was coming home.

The docks looked nothing like the one Maggie remembered from her arrival in 1911. These had been shored up for wartime traffic and now teemed with eager faces gazing anxiously up at the ship's decks.

Will we even recognize him in his uniform? Maggie wondered. *I'm sure he won't know Morgan. She has grown so much.*

Suddenly Maggie saw him. He had already spotted them and was frantically waving his service cap high in the air to try to catch their attention. He was standing right beside the gangway.

"Look, Morgan, there he is!"

A smile broke across the face of the little girl who was taller than Maggie's shoulders. She must look so different to her father, Maggie thought, for she had, in his absence, lost almost all her baby teeth, replaced now by straight, even permanent teeth. A few pale freckles, not unlike Maggie's own when she was younger, sprinkled her nose, and her eyes were steady, blue-gray, and wide with wonder. Her hair had darkened to a sandy blond and hung in loose curls to her shoulders. She was no longer the little girl he had left behind, but one who was already well on her way to becoming a poised young lady.

"Daddy, Daddy, Daddy," she called, waving her hand wildly and jumping up and down.

When the uniformed men were finally allowed to come ashore, Danny saluted smartly as he left the ship and rushed down the gangway, bee-lining for his daughter. He dropped his bag and swept her into his arms.

"My beautiful girl, how you've grown," he said. "Let me look at you." He studied her face intently. "What a beauty you're turning into. You have all your teeth again," he teased.

Then he turned to greet Maggie. "Thank God you were with her. I'm not sure I'd have recognized her, she's changed so much, but you haven't changed a bit." He hugged Maggie with genuine affection, and she hugged him back, feeling his strong arms around her.

"I've brought you presents, Morgan," he said. "You too, Maggie. I can't wait to get home and let you see them."

"You're the only present I need, Daddy. I'm so glad you're home." Morgan burst into long pent-up tears.

They would all have to form new habits and get to know one another again in different configurations now that Helen was gone. Uncertain of the protocol, Maggie hung back at dinnertime, even though Mabel had set three places in the dining room.

"I expect you'll want to have dinner with your daughter alone, Mr. Barrett," she said to Daniel. "You have so much catching up to do."

"We do indeed, Maggie, but I'd like to have you join us as well. You have been Morgan's mainstay while I've been away, and I can't tell you how much I appreciate all you've done. I don't know what she would have done without you. You're part of the family now." She smiled gratefully at his words. He seemed cheerful and glad to be home, but Maggie sensed beneath that cheery exterior a profound sadness. She suspected that a part of him had not come home.

Two nights later Maggie was awakened by a crashing noise downstairs. She looked at her clock. It was two-twenty a.m. Slowly she crept from her bed, put on her robe, and cracked her door. A dim light flickered below. *Perhaps someone forgot to turn off a light,* she thought, though the noise had frightened her. *Could someone have broken in?*

She picked up the flashlight she kept on her dresser for emergencies. It would make a good weapon in case she needed one. Then quietly she slipped out her door and began to creep down the stairs.

When she reached the bottom of the stairs she realized that the flickering light was coming from the parlor fireplace, which shouldn't be burning this time of night. She peered around the half-opened pocket door. There, kneeling in front of the fire was Danny, who was burning something in the grate.

As she leaned against the door, it rattled slightly, and he turned around. Although she could see little more than his silhouette outlined against the light of the fire, she could hear a strange catch in his throat when he asked gruffly, "Who's there?"

"I'm sorry to disturb you, Mr. Barrett. I heard a noise downstairs and thought ..."

"I'm sorry if I woke you up," he said. "That was just me crashing into the coffee table in the dark." She could hear tears and alcohol in his voice.

"Are you all right, sir?" She wanted to move toward him and put her arms around him, but she stood gripping the doorway.

"I'm fine, Maggie. Just being a bit self-indulgent and histrionic, that's all. I'm burning Helen's letters—a magnificent gesture, don't you think?" There was self-deprecating sarcasm in his voice.

She took a step toward him. "She must have hurt you very much."

"Not as much as she hurt Morgan, I expect. That's the one thing I can never forgive her for. For deserting her at a time her daughter needed her most." He sounded bitter. Then his voice softened when he said, "Thank you for being a mother to her while I was away."

Or a grandmother, Maggie thought. She noticed a half-empty highball glass on the hearth.

"Let me make you a cup of tea," she said. "That's what my mam always did to make my brother and me feel better."

He turned back to the fire and tossed in the few remaining letters he had in his hand. "A cup of tea," he murmured and then laughed, staring at the flaring blaze of paper. "Sure," he said, a tinge of irony in his voice, "that ought to do it." He hesitated for a moment, then turned toward her and said in a new tone, "Tell you what, Maggie. I'll have that cup of tea if you'll join me."

"Of course," she said. "I'd love to." She moved toward the kitchen, turning on a light in the hallway. The brightness dimmed the dramatic flickering of the fire. "Shall I bring it to you here?" She gestured toward the parlor.

He was standing now, facing her. His eyes reflected the bright light of the hallway. He wiped them with the back of his hand. "No. Let's have it in the kitchen."

He followed her to the kitchen and stood waiting while she put on the kettle, got out the teapot and cups, and found tea bags in the pantry. Finally he sat down at the table and watched her intently. When the water had come to a boil, she prepared the tea in silence. Then she uncovered a plate of sugar cookies Mabel had left on the table covered with aluminum foil, which was plentiful now that the war was over.

He opened his mouth as though to speak, then closed it again. He seemed to want to talk, but no words came.

Finally, to break the silence Maggie said, "You must miss Mrs. Barrett very much."

"I did, or thought I did, at first," he said honestly. "And I guess in a way I do, but I think what I miss most is the habit of her. To tell you the truth, I probably would never have married her except for my grandfather's determination that I bind myself to that damned law firm of his. Her father was once a partner there, though he retired a few years back, thank goodness. Otherwise it might be rather awkward now. Helen was his only child."

"But I know it must have been hard when you received her letter, telling you about …" she hesitated.

"Dud King?" he snorted. "It was a blow to my ego, that's for sure, to be left for a fop like him. I was damned angry and pretty depressed for a while. I really didn't care whether I lived or died, and the war seemed like a convenient escape." He took a swallow of tea.

"Then I got your letter. You'll never know what it meant. You forced me to think about Morgan, not just myself. You helped me grow up, Maggie, and face reality. I've never properly thanked you for that."

"It was presumptuous of me," she said.

"Not really. You had been left to take care of Morgan, and that's what you were doing. When I think about it now, if she had lost her mother and her father, what might have become of her? I guess she would have had to go and live with the Steeles and ended up just like her mother—not a pretty prospect, as I see it. I'm really grateful for what you did."

Maggie wanted to tell him that she was only doing what any grandmother would do for her granddaughter, what any mother would do for her son, but he was dealing with too many other things just now. She didn't want to add to his emotional upheaval. A melodramatic revelation of that sort could only make him wonder why she had remained silent all these years. It was better just to let things remain as they were, she thought, and perhaps as they were meant to be.

The moment passed, and they chatted on for a while about the changes in America that had come about during the war. By the time they had finished their tea, Danny's face had relaxed, and his eyes had taken on a calm and sleepy look.

Such late-night chats in the kitchen would become rather common in the weeks ahead. On many evenings after Morgan was tucked in bed and Mabel had retired to the little apartment over the garage that had once been used by the chauffeur, Maggie and Danny would settle in the kitchen with a hot cup of tea or cocoa. In the weeks it took to finalize his discharge papers and get back into the swing of his law practice, he seemed to need someone to talk to in the evenings. And Maggie was always there. He had come to trust her and ask her advice on all sorts of things, not just those relating to Morgan. He could just be himself, without pretense, knowing that she understood.

He showed little interest in going out with women he had known in his social set before the war, although many of them, now widows or divorcees, constantly invited him to dinner parties where an extra man was always welcome. Although he went occasionally, he always came home early and rarely followed up with anything more than a polite note or a small bouquet of flowers to the hostess.

Then one night near Christmas, as Danny and Maggie shared slices of still-warm banana bread and sipped on cups of hot spiced tea, to her surprise, he brought up the subject of his parents.

"I often wonder," he said, "what it would have been like to have a normal childhood with a mother and father."

"My own childhood was like that," said Maggie, "and it was a happy one with my brother, Brendan. But having two parents doesn't always guarantee that things will stay that way, as Morgan learned the hard way."

"I suppose you're right, and yet, my grandfather was the only role model I had, and he was a bit of a tyrant, I suppose, determined to have his own way most of the time."

"What do you know about your parents?" Maggie asked, fidgeting with the handle of her cup.

"Well, I think you may already know that my father died before I was born—on the *Titanic*. And my mother abandoned me as a baby."

"Abandoned you?" she asked incredulously.

"They weren't married, you see, and according to my grandfather she just showed up one day out of the blue and left me with him."

"No mother would do such a thing, abandon a child like that."

"Helen did."

"True, but not right away. Perhaps your mother had no choice. Perhaps it was never what she wanted. Perhaps—"

"Maggie, you're such a romantic. You'd never have done such a thing, it's true, but then you're not like most women."

"Oh, but I am, Mr. Barrett." She hesitated only a moment, then said softly, "In fact, I'm—"

He interrupted. "Please, you must call me Daniel. I call you Maggie, after all."

"It isn't the same. It wouldn't be seemly."

"I wish I could have had someone like you as my mother, Maggie. Perhaps things would have been different."

She smiled sadly, her courage failing. "Or perhaps not. Your mother was never far away in her heart. Of that I'm sure." She hesitated for a moment. "I think, Mr. Barrett—"

"Daniel," he corrected. "At least here in the kitchen."

"Daniel," she said softly, letting herself savor the word before she continued. "I think that God often works things out as they were meant to be. In the end, it's not your mother or your grandfather who is responsible for your life. It's you. And I think you're a good man, in spite of them both."

He squeezed her hand. "That means a lot to me. You know, Maggie, you've become my very best friend. I'm glad you came into my life. Lord knows, I did nothing to deserve it."

"Nor I," she said. "But I'm glad you invited me in."

He read longingly about all the post-war building going on in New York state—Long Island, Queens, Jackson Heights, Elmhurst—as in so many other parts of the country.

"I once wanted to become an architect," he told his daughter and Maggie one night at dinner. "It was my dream." He had read that morning in the *New York Times* about parcels of land for sale on Long Island. How he had longed to make investments like that and design homes for modern living.

"Why didn't you, Daddy?" Morgan asked.

"My grandfather had my life all planned. He got me admitted to Harvard Law School without even asking me. He was a well-known lawyer himself, you know, and he just wanted me to follow in the family firm."

"Is it too late?" Maggie asked. "To become an architect, I mean?"

Daniel laughed. "It's too late for me to become a licensed architect, I'm afraid. It takes years of training, and I'm pretty well involved in legal cases I can't possibly give up."

"Do you have to be a licensed architect to design your own home?" she asked.

"Well, perhaps not to draw up the initial plans, though I'd certainly want a skilled draftsman to take care of the details. I just don't have the training needed to go beyond the basic concepts."

"Perhaps you should think about it."

Little by little the idea took hold in Daniel's imagination.

One evening he announced at dinner, "I've been thinking. This Fifth Avenue mansion is really too much house in this day and time. And I find it rather gloomy."

Since he returned he had hired a cleaning woman who came in twice a week to do the heavy cleaning, though during the war, it had been Maggie and Mabel who picked up the burden after Phyllis went to work in a munitions factory. Mabel was almost seventy now and had already began talking about the possibility of retiring to move nearer her daughter in Albany.

"What would you say, Morgan," he asked, "to moving into something a little smaller in Manhattan and having a second home on Long Island or in Connecticut or someplace we could go for weekends?"

Morgan didn't hesitate for a moment. "You mean a place in the country? I'd love that, Dad. Maggie would come too, wouldn't she?"

"What about it, Maggie? Would you be willing to make a move as well?"

"'Tis not my decision to make, Mr. Barrett. I would be willing to go wherever you and Morgan choose to go."

"What if we moved to California?" he asked archly, remembering why he had been able to hire her in the first place.

"Even there," she said.

"What about your family here in New York?"

"I would miss my friends, 'tis true, but I don't think my family would mind anymore. Not now."

Morgan chimed in to tell him about meeting Maggie's friends, Deirdre and Rudy, and their children while he was away. "Two of their sons were in the war," she told her father. "They're really nice, and they have grandchildren almost my age. We played together in the park. It was fun."

"I hope you don't mind too much, Mr. Barrett," Maggie said. "Deirdre is my dearest friend from many years ago when I worked at the Jekyl Island Club."

"Of course I don't mind. I wouldn't presume to make judgments about your decisions, Maggie. If she's your friend, she must be a good person." He hesitated, then added, "You know, I remember hearing about that club when I was a kid. It was quite a place in its heyday, they say. I think it closed down when America got into the war. I didn't know you had worked there." Daniel seemed genuinely interested.

"That's how I came to work for Mrs. Baker, whose daughter was one of my references when I came to work for you. The Bakers were club members. But all that was a long time ago. I've lost touch with the people I knew there, except Deirdre once in a while. She's an old and dear friend."

Maggie had not taken Morgan to meet Deirdre until after Helen left, for she knew that the child's mother would never have approved. But the world was changing now, becoming more democratic since the war, when all kinds of men had fought side by side. Those old rigid barriers of breeding, class, and even money seemed to be less important than they once were.

Many young soldiers from poor families were going to college on the G.I. Bill, and, although only time would tell whether they would succeed, education had always been the best way for poor boys to move up in the world. For women, she supposed, it had always been through marriage, but even that was beginning to change, and more young women were going to college as well. It was an exciting world for Morgan to be growing up in.

Daniel warmed to the idea of planning his own house, and he was excited to think of the light he could bring in, the natural views he could incorporate. All would be planned for convenience, more casual living than he had grown up with, and harmonizing the outer world with the inner, both the interior of the house and the inner spirit. He drew his plans over and over until he was sure the proportions were just right. He had found a ten-acre plot in the Great Neck area of Long Island and was negotiating to buy it.

Maggie was glad to see him taking an interest in something creative. He and Morgan pored over his design, and he explained his architectural philosophy to her. She would listen with wide, sparkling eyes, and Maggie rejoiced to see them together. But she knew from their late-night talks in the kitchen that, although Daniel loved his daughter deeply, something was still missing from his life.

Chapter Twenty-Eight

THE SALE OF THE FIFTH AVENUE MANSION had been easier than Daniel thought it would be. The price was right, and a small art gallery and museum were eager to move into the upscale neighborhood. Their offer had been somewhat lower than the asking price, but it was more than enough to cover the cost of the new apartment Daniel had bought in the upper west side of Manhattan as well as the land on Long Island where he planned to build his summer "cottage."

The burden of moving had been eased considerably when Daniel decided that he didn't really want to keep all the heavy antique furniture that had belonged to his grandfather. The oversized armoires and sideboards wouldn't fit into their new apartment anyhow. And they certainly didn't go with the more modern décor Daniel had chosen to enhance the sweeping views of the Hudson River and Riverside Park from their fifth-floor rooms. The antique dealer who came in to appraise the furniture and arrange the auction pranced excitedly from one piece to another. And most of the old furnishings were gone in a flash. Daniel felt as though he were recreating his life.

With Morgan alongside to help make the selections, he reserved some of the smaller pieces that might be useful in the new apartment while a few others were put in storage for whatever sentimental value or future possibilities they might have. Eight of the sixteen dining room chairs were to go to the new apartment, along with the parlor's mahogany coffee table, and the vanity and canopy bed from Morgan's room that were said to have belonged to Matilda Barrett.

Daniel donated his grandfather's papers to the New York Historical Society without bothering to go through them, and they were able to make the move with a single van to their new home at the corner of Riverside Drive and West 116th Street, located in a building that had the rather grand name of The Colosseum.

Once the move was completed, Daniel set to work on plans for the new Great Neck house. Maggie had not seen him so excited since he returned from the war. But his law practice got in his way most of the time, and she could see that he was burdened by the tedium of drawing up wills and trusts for wealthy clients.

"Daniel, have you ever considered taking a legal case just to help someone?" she asked one evening over a cup of hot chocolate.

"The firm doesn't do much *pro bono* work, Maggie. If it doesn't pay, it tends to be put on the back shelf."

"But what if someone really needs a good lawyer and can't afford one?"

"Well, I guess they'd have to go to legal services or find a lawyer who *was* willing to take the case."

"What if a mother had lost her child and there was no one to help her get it back? What if you could really make a difference in someone's life?"

She had been following a newspaper story about a war widow from Memphis, Tennessee, who had almost no financial resources, but whose little girl had been snatched by alleged "authorities" while she played in a city park. The mother, who had seen two men grab her screaming daughter, thrust her into the back seat of a big black car, and drive away, was frantic. She didn't know for weeks what had happened to her child, only that she had been kidnapped. But Memphis police discovered that the little girl had been placed in an orphanage called the Tennessee Children's Home Society, where supposedly abandoned, neglected, or abused children could be put up for adoption. The home produced a document signed by a judge that declared the society's right to take the child from her "unfit" mother, but the woman, Amy Fletcher, had never been brought to court or accused by anyone of being unfit to care for her daughter.

By the time Mrs. Fletcher found out where her daughter was, the child had already been adopted by a wealthy New York couple. She had appealed to Tennessee authorities, but the Children's Home Society kept no records or had destroyed them all, and it was impossible to trace the whereabouts of the child. Mrs. Fletcher had found out only after she befriended an outraged former secretary at the orphanage who by chance remembered the golden-haired three-year-old, as well as the name of the couple who had taken her away.

Even though the Children's Home Society was now under investigation in Tennessee, Amy Fletcher had no money to hire a lawyer to get her daughter back. Her husband's death on Utah Beach in Normandy in 1944 had left her all but destitute, while the couple that had adopted her daughter lived in a Manhattan penthouse and was well known in New York society. Mrs. Fletcher had come to New York to find her daughter and, she hoped, someone who would help her.

As Maggie told Daniel the story, tears welled up in her eyes. She knew the mother's sense of desperation. The little girl would be five years old now, and her mother had not seen her for more than two years. Maggie could imagine her sitting in Central Park hoping for a glimpse of her daughter.

Daniel listened intently, and by the end of her impassioned tale, his throat was tight, and he too was blinking rapidly to hold back tears. He had already heard something through legal channels about the investigation of the Memphis-based society headed by a woman named Georgia Tann. She was well connected in Memphis and had supporters among powerful Tennesseans, the most important of whom was a Shelby County judge named Camille Kelly, in whose court the papers were signed and the adoptions quickly granted.

Daniel thought of Morgan and how he might have felt in Mrs. Fletcher's situation. He couldn't imagine the pain of losing a child in such a way—knowing she was alive and well, but living with someone else.

"Why does this case matter so much to you, Maggie?"

"Because ... I ... I know how the mother feels ... I lost a little boy once."

"Oh, Maggie, I'm so sorry. I can only imagine how awful that must be." He touched her hand, as a tear spilled over onto her cheek. "At least Helen didn't take away my daughter."

Maggie opened her mouth, but no words came. He squeezed her hand.

"I can see that this is really important to you," he said gently. "Okay, Maggie. I'll look into it and, if her case seems legitimate, I'll talk with the partners at the firm to see if they'll consider letting me take it on."

She smiled her thanks, still unable to speak, and wiped her eyes. She had always known that he was a good man, but she had never felt such a sense of pride as she did at this moment. She took a deep breath to calm herself, but once again the moment when she might have told him who she really was had passed. He was already scribbling in his little pocket notebook, jotting down the name of the lost child's mother and the circumstances Maggie had described.

The next day, however, the news he brought from his law firm was not what she had hoped for.

"The partners won't go for it, Maggie," Daniel told her over dinner. "The New York couple in question is quite prominent. They're afraid it will cause too much ill will for the firm."

Maggie's shoulders drooped and a furrow creased her brow. "I'm sorry to hear that."

"But, Maggie," he said. "I've still got enough money from the sale of the house to tide us over for a while. I've already set up a meeting with Amy Fletcher. If it feels right after I've talked with her, I'm going to take a leave of absence from the firm and take on the case."

"Oh, Daniel! Thank you." She suddenly realized it was the first time she had called him by his first name in front of Morgan, but it seemed so natural. With a wide smile, she reached out to squeeze his arm.

On the other side of the table Morgan wagged her head from side to side in bewilderment. "Will someone please tell me what's going on?"

Maggie had never seen Daniel work so intensely, not even when he was drawing up the plans for the new house at Great Neck. Amy Fletcher proved to be a sympathetic woman with mousy brown hair and large, sad eyes. She had once been pretty, no doubt, but now she was thin and drawn in upon herself with worry. Daniel had found her story even more compelling than he thought when Maggie first told him about it.

Amy had been living in a city shelter when Daniel first contacted her, but since then, the social worker assigned to the case, a woman named Jill Meyer, whom Daniel had still not met, had invited her to move into her own apartment until the matter was settled and she could return to Memphis. New York was expensive, and Amy had no resources and no choice but to depend on whatever city or state services were available. The social worker's invitation was a godsend.

On the day after Christmas, Daniel flew to Memphis to talk with the investigators of the Children's Home Society case. The inquiry, they said, had proven beyond a doubt that the society was a front for a black-market adoption ring that used secret bank accounts and questionable accounting practices. Apparently the director, Georgia Tann, skimmed off eighty to ninety percent of the high fees the society charged and used them, not only for her lavish life style, but also to provide regular payments to the judge in question, along with other government officials, for their help in ramming through hundreds of adoptions like that of Amy's daughter or else for looking the other way.

The society had become known nationwide as an easy place to obtain children, and such celebrities as actress Joan Crawford had adopted children from Memphis. Daniel was sure that all of New York would be as outraged as he was when they learned of it.

He had a meeting set up in the early afternoon with Amy Fletcher and Jill Meyer to tell them all he had learned in Tennessee. He had even located the former secretary who had told Amy where she could find her child, and she was willing to testify in court, if it came to that. But he was also negotiating with the New York couple to help them understand that if they turned over the little girl willingly, proclaiming their lack of knowledge about her origins, it would go better for them in the press than would a hard-fought court case that he was certain he could win. He promised them that his client would be willing to allow them to visit the child whom they too had grown to love. But turning her over without a legal battle would earn them the city's good will, and he assured them it was always better for all concerned to settle out of court. He was hopeful that he had persuaded them.

When Daniel came home that night, he was elated. The meeting had gone well. The two women were excited about his investigation, and Jill Meyer was so sure that Amy would soon have her daughter back that they had greeted Daniel as a conquering hero.

He was eager to tell Maggie about the meeting. "I want to thank you for urging me to take this case," he said. "I've never felt so good about legal work in my life. It's made me understand that there might be a reason for my being a lawyer after all."

"God always puts us where we're most needed," she said. "It took me a long time to understand that."

"Well, I'm sure glad He decided we needed you in the Barrett household."

She smiled broadly. "So am I."

As he gave her all the details he legally could about his discussion with the women, she noticed that he mentioned the name of Jill Meyer quite frequently, extolling her generosity in welcoming Amy into her own home and taking such a special interest in the case.

"I want you to meet them both," he said. "Do you think it would be possible to invite them to dinner one night soon?"

He had never before had a client to dinner that she could recall. Sometimes he took clients to lunch, but he did not invite them to his home. This case had obviously become important and very personal to him.

"I don't see why not," she said. "What about next Friday evening? I'll make sure that Morgan won't be spending the night with friends. I have a feeling it would be good if she could be here as well."

"Absolutely. If you'll plan the menu and work it out with the cook, I'll issue the invitation tomorrow."

Daniel fidgeted with his tie as he waited nervously in the living room the following Friday. He put a Mozart symphony on the record player and checked his watch. Morgan swooped into the room as gracefully as possible for a thirteen-year-old. She wore a simple pale blue chiffon dress. Daniel worried that they might all be too dressed up. Amy probably didn't have many clothes.

He checked the table arrangements. It was uncharacteristic for him to worry over such trivial details, but he wanted everything to be just right. He would sit at one end, he decided, with Morgan at the other. He had placed Maggie beside Amy, and Jill would be on the opposite side, where she would be silhouetted against the deep crimsons and blues of the dining room tapestry.

"My, you look elegant, Morgan," Maggie said, coming into the room. Maggie, wearing her black crepe dress, looked quite handsome herself, especially for a woman approaching sixty.

"And so do you, Maggie. Do you think we're too dressed up?"

Before she could answer, the doorbell rang. Daniel bounded to the door before anyone else could move.

He need not have worried. When he opened the door, there stood two attractive women, one pale and thin, the other vibrant with dark flowing hair and dark eyes that sparkled at the sight of Daniel. Both women wore simple but tasteful dresses that blended with the crepe and chiffon that Maggie and Morgan were wearing.

"Welcome, Amy and Jill," Daniel said. "Come in. I want you to meet the two most important women in my life."

The evening could not have gone better. Daniel was the perfect host, and the conversation never flagged. Both Daniel and Jill were confident now that the case they were sharing would end well. Amy was in brighter spirits than usual, but she would never relax completely, Maggie knew, until her little girl was back in her arms.

Daniel had learned during the week that the couple in question had finally agreed to cooperate, but Jill thought it best for the little girl that there be a period of transition during which the adoptive parents and the birth mother would meet together with the child and that she should begin to spend limited periods alone with Amy. Jill would be there to help in case anything went wrong. The little girl, whose birth name was Beth, though the adoptive parents had renamed her Lila, would need time to get to know her birth mother again. Jill was already meeting with the little girl to prepare her for the changes she was about to confront. Maggie was excited for Amy. She knew what she must be going through as a mother, and she encouraged her to talk about her feelings.

Throughout the evening Maggie noticed that Daniel's eyes drifted most frequently to the side of the table where Jill was seated. Morgan, too, seemed to take to the pretty social worker at once. Jill appeared to be in her mid-thirties. She had a ready smile and soft brown eyes that looked at ease with everyone at the table as she listened to all they had to say. More than once she dismissed in a self-deprecating way Amy's effusive expressions of gratitude as she told the little group all that Jill had done for her.

"Even this dress," Amy said, pointing to the well-cut navy shantung outfit she was wearing, "was a gift from Jill. There is no way, if I live to be a hundred, I can ever repay both Jill and Daniel enough for all they've done for me. They're both such good people, and I know rich rewards await them in heaven."

Jill and Daniel looked at each other and exchanged silent smiles. Their eyes held for a long moment. Then Jill said, "Amy, it's just been a pleasure to have you. I can hardly wait until you and Beth are together again, but I'll miss you when you go back to Memphis."

12 FEBRUARY 1951 LA GUARDIA AIRPORT

Amy Fletcher, her hair blowing in the wind, a flush in her cheeks, and a broad grin on her face, paused at the door of the plane. She looked tall and self-assured as she held the hand of her daughter, whose hair, the color of ripe wheat, shone in the sunlight. They both turned back to wave one last time to Jill and Daniel, who stood inside the glass window of the gate area, waving back.

Now that the case was over and had ended with such positive publicity that made New Yorkers feel good about themselves, Daniel's law firm was eager to have him back. He had not sought the publicity. Instead he had simply done what his heart told him was right, with no thought for whether the firm would take him back or not. In the future, he suspected, his requests to do *pro bono* work would not be refused. It had all ended well, thank God, better than he could ever have imagined. Watching Amy and Beth get on that plane together, with Jill here beside him, would always be one of the fullest moments of his life.

Without thinking, Daniel reached out to take Jill's hand as, together, they watched the silver plane take off and vanish into the clouds. When it disappeared from sight, he turned to look into the dark, shining eyes of the woman he had come to love as she opened her heart to someone in need, the woman he knew he would love for the rest of his life.

"Shall we go home?" he asked. She nodded with a smile. Still holding hands, they retraced their steps to the airport parking lot.

When they announced their engagement six months later, following a sumptuous dinner at the Barrett apartment, both Maggie and Morgan applauded vigorously. Maggie had seen their relationship growing from the first night she met Jill. She was so different from Helen, so right for Daniel, and she would make a good mother for Morgan as the girl grew into womanhood. She had hoped Daniel would not delay too long and let her get away.

Once they were married, Maggie wondered, could she finally tell Daniel the truth that she was his mother? She thought about it long and hard, even prayed about the decision she should make. In the end, she decided to let the matter rest once and for all. She had waited too long, she thought, and they deserved to enjoy their happiness without complications.

What difference would it make now anyhow? Her life was better than that of most mothers she knew. They loved her, not out of familial obligation, but for herself alone. What more could she want?

Chapter Twenty-Nine

8 JUNE 1958 TRINITY CHURCH, MANHATTAN

"With the blessing of God and by the power vested in me, I now pronounce you husband and wife."

At the words of the priest, the tuxedoed groom swept the glowing bride into his arms and kissed her with passionate intensity.

As they walked back up the aisle, Morgan, the bride, who was also celebrating her twenty-first birthday, held tightly to her handsome new husband's arm and blew one kiss to her proud father and stepmother and another to Maggie, who sat beside them. This perfect wedding was the best birthday present Morgan's father could ever have given her. He looked as happy as she felt.

Daniel took Jill's hand and whispered, "Does it remind you of our own wedding?"

"Of course, and would you take those vows again?" she whispered back, knowing the answer but loving to hear it from his own lips.

"I'd shout them from the top of the Empire State Building if it would keep you as my wife." They had been married for more than seven years, and he could still hardly believe his good luck to wake up beside her every morning.

Daniel, Jill, and Maggie all liked Morgan's new husband, Mark Hamilton, whom she had met when she was a junior at Barnard and he was a first-year graduate student in architecture at Columbia University. He and Daniel had hit it off right away when Mark admired the sweeping, contemporary design of the Long Island "cottage" Daniel himself had planned. Mark was interested primarily in domestic architecture as Daniel had been, and they shared much of the same philosophy—that homes should be built not for show to the outside world, but for comfort and a contemporary life style, allowing residents to be as close to nature as possible, through varied levels of outdoor patios and decks and large windows that let in the light and brought the outdoors inside. Even more important, they both loved Morgan.

Mark had no impressive family credentials that would gain him entry into elite New York clubs. ("Thank God," Morgan had said.) He came from a poor West Virginia family and had worked his way through Columbia with part time jobs, work scholarships, and an engaging manner. He had finished his graduate work even before Morgan received her B.A. degree, then immediately landed a job at a top architectural firm, thanks to his high honors as a student. As soon as he could afford the rent on a decent Manhattan apartment, he asked her to marry him.

Morgan, her Barnard degree in English in hand, had several upcoming interviews with large publishing houses. She knew she could be nothing more than an editorial assistant for the time being, but it would be good experience. She planned to take time off to have children, but she hoped that when she went back to work, she would be able to move up quickly in the publishing world. Right now, however, all that mattered was Mark. Whatever happened professionally, they were starting their life together with a full measure of love.

24 DECEMBER 1960 NEW YORK

꙰ "The oyster stew is delicious, Maggie," said Morgan. Over the years, it had become one of Maggie's Christmas specialties.

"I have to find some way to justify my existence in the Barrett household, since I do so little around here," she said. Everyone laughed.

She and Jill did most of the cooking now. The last cook had retired shortly after Morgan started college, and Maggie decided to take over the task herself. She wanted to be useful and had become an excellent cook. Jill helped as well with the evening meal unless her social work caseload was too heavy. The two women enjoyed their time together in the kitchen, and they made a good team. But Maggie had made the oyster stew all by herself.

Before the end of the first course, Morgan put down her soup spoon, smiled at each individual around the table, and took Mark's hand.

"We have some news," she said, letting the silence settle before she announced, "We're going to have a baby."

Jill and Maggie reached out to her simultaneously, and Daniel got up and walked to her chair and gave her a kiss on the cheek before shaking Mark's hand.

"Before everyone gets too excited," Morgan said, interrupting their exuberance, "I have a request you may not like so much."

She had everyone's attention again. "When the baby comes, I'd like to ask Maggie to come and live with us. You guys have had her long enough, and Mark and I are really going to need her."

Daniel and Jill exchanged silent glances. Maggie was such an integral part of their household that they couldn't imagine life without her. At the same time they understood that Morgan could use the help. She knew absolutely nothing about babies, and it would give her reassurance to have Maggie there.

"You're asking a pretty big sacrifice, Morgan," her father said solemnly. "But I think we ought to talk it over and let Maggie decide."

Maggie laughed. "Well, whatever the final decision is, it's nice to be wanted, and I thank you, Morgan and Mark, for your confidence."

Maggie knew perfectly well what she would decide, but she wanted to give Daniel and Jill an opportunity to be a part of that decision, or at least to think they were. As much as she loved them both and knew they loved her, they were still like newlyweds in many ways. It would be good, she thought, for them to have their lives all to themselves for a change.

Morgan would really need her. Maggie knew that, and it would be wonderful to have a baby to care for once again. She was sixty-eight years old now, and her usefulness in this world would not last many more years. This would be her final gift to her granddaughter.

Morgan wanted to go back to work as soon as she could, once the baby was born. She loved her job and believed sincerely that she would be a better mother if she felt fulfilled herself. But she was unwilling to entrust her child to a nanny sent over by some agency. Only Maggie would do, which was just fine with Maggie.

By the following June, she had settled into her third-floor bedroom in Morgan and Mark's new brownstone. They told her they planned to install an elevator, but she wouldn't hear of it. Not for her.

"I need to climb those stairs. It will be wonderful exercise." Her room was cozy, not as large as her room in the Colosseum apartment, but bright and sunny and much larger than the rooms she had lived in when she worked for other New York families. Best of all, it had a bay window that overlooked a small garden filled with roses that climbed on a latticework trellis behind the house. She liked it. It reminded her a little of the house in Brooklyn where she had lived with Stuart and learned to be happy again.

Morgan had furnished the room in a charming way, incorporating a few antiques Maggie recognized from the old Fifth Avenue mansion—the inlaid mahogany desk from the room she had occupied so briefly when Henry Barrett was alive, a small rocker, a marble-topped plant stand that held a lush

Boston fern, and an antique Turkish rug. The bed was new and matched the mahogany nightstand and the large chest that stood just outside her bathroom door. Maggie had arranged her most treasured possessions, her box of photographs, her journals that still held newspaper clippings from the old days, and her books of poetry in the little desk.

The framed photograph of her parents sat on the nightstand by her bed. She often looked at the old photographs, especially the two she had of Hector. How much Daniel resembled him—the strong jaw, the intensity of his eyes, his enthusiasm for life—only Daniel was older now than his father had ever been. He looked as Hector would have looked if he had lived.

As Maggie organized her things in the well-appointed room Morgan had prepared, she thought back over her life, her adventure in America, and she considered the happiness she had found here. Even in the most difficult times, she had somehow never felt truly alone. It was as though her path were being guided by an unseen hand, her life taking on a shape she had never planned, but one that seemed destined to help her reach this very spot. It had happened slowly, more gradually than she had first hoped, but it happened all the same.

It was well past midnight when the phone rang beside her bed. Morgan and Mark had gone to the hospital at six p.m. on July 5. Maggie had made them promise to call as soon as the baby came, whatever the time. She had waited anxiously as long as she could keep her eyes open, and she woke immediately at its jangle and reached for the receiver.

"Boy or girl?" she asked, knowing who it had to be.

Mark laughed heartily on the other end of the line, which told her everything was all right. She held her breath, waiting for his words.

"It's a boy, Maggie. We're going to bring you home a beautiful little boy who weighs eight pounds and four ounces. And we're going to call him Danny."

Chapter Thirty

The children were already in bed. Morgan had tucked them in herself at eight o'clock. Their evening routine was briefer now. The children thought they were too old for bedtime stories, and both Danny, who was almost eight, and his little sister Jillian, six, could read for themselves. Morgan was soon back downstairs, and she and Maggie were cleaning up the kitchen together as they did most nights. It was their special time with one another, when they shared their thoughts about the children and the events of the day, about what mattered to them as women, just as Maggie and Jill had done so many years ago.

As the last dish was dried and put away, Maggie lightly touched Morgan's arm.

"Why don't you go on up to bed? You've had a long day at the office, and this is about the only time you and Mark have to spend alone together, without the children and me underfoot. I'll turn out the lights and lock up."

"Thanks, Maggie. You're a gem." Morgan gave her a hug, hung her apron on the closet peg, smoothed back her hair, and started eagerly up the stairs.

Maggie smiled, watching her go. She had grown into such a splendid woman. Who'd have ever thought that headstrong little girl she first met could ever turn into such a fine woman—attractive, even beautiful—and so competent and self-assured in everything she did? In less than seven years Morgan had risen to head of her division at the publishing house. It was she and her team who determined whether a children's book would be published, whether it would be nominated for the Caldecott or Newbery Awards, whether its author would get the support and backing of a best seller.

Morgan's success and rise in her chosen profession had been phenomenal, and Maggie was proud of her. But, in spite of her work, Morgan never neglected Danny and Jillian, always giving them her full attention when she came home in the afternoon. And she spent all her days off with them and their father. Maggie sometimes wondered if Morgan ever thought how she might be compensating for her own mother's shortcomings. She seemed determined to be the antithesis of what her mother had been.

The house darkened as Maggie turned off the kitchen lights and those in the foyer. Only the lights that illuminated the stairs remained on all night. She liked the soft dimness, the shadows, the quiet of the house after everyone had gone to bed. It was when she did her reading and writing.

As always, when she reached the second-floor landing, she tiptoed into the children's room where both were sound asleep. She stood watching their quiet breathing, the abandon of their small bodies, the smooth perfection of their untroubled faces. Danny looked so much like her brother, Brendan, his tousled hair the color of cornsilk against the pillow. His little sister Jillian's hair, curling moistly about her face, was dark like her father's. Their beauty always took Maggie's breath away.

Danny had kicked off his blanket, and she reached down to re-cover him. As she touched his shoulder, he opened his eyes for just a moment and mumbled sleepily, "'Night, Maggie."

"Goodnight, Danny," she replied, smiling in the darkness and planting a gentle kiss on his right cheek. "I love you."

"I love you too," he echoed into his pillow as he turned over to give himself up to sleep once more.

She kissed Jillian's sleeping face as well, breathing in her sweet innocence. Then, with one more look, she slipped quietly out of the room, leaving the door cracked so that she or their parents could hear them if they called out in the night. She turned off the hall light and started to climb the steps to her room on the third floor.

Halfway up, she paused, feeling suddenly weak and a bit dizzy. She gripped the banister tightly to steady herself until the dizziness passed. Then she took one step at a time, fighting off the tightness in her chest, the vagueness of the discomfort between her shoulder blades. One step at a time.

She reached the top of the stairs, her bedroom door, her bed, where she was grateful to sit and rest for a moment. *The pork tenderloin did not agree with me. I hope it wasn't spoiled,* she thought, remembering how carefully she had selected it at the market. It had smelled fresh, and the butcher assured her it had arrived just that morning. She would know soon enough if the meat was bad, she thought, as she washed her face and put on her flannel nightgown. If it was, she knew the entire household might be sick tomorrow.

It felt good to lie down, though she felt the tightness once again and a pain that was sharper now. Surely it would go away if she just lay still and closed her eyes. She lay there for a long, quiet moment, bidding sleep to come.

In the distant dark she could see a watery figure, as though moving through a mirage, coming toward her. She did not see him clearly at first, but then, as she felt herself sinking into sleep, she saw he was not walking, but swimming toward her. His face was shining, as though from a reflected light.

The face seemed at first to be that of her son, but the hair was dark, waving in the current as she stretched out her hand toward him in echo of his own hand stretched toward her. And then she knew. Hector had come for her at last.

The telephone rang sharply in the Barretts' bedroom. Daniel Barrett rolled over sleepily and picked it up.

"Hello?" he said, glancing at the clock. Almost eight. He realized he had slept late, but it was still too early for business calls. The secretaries didn't come in until nine.

"Dad?" It was Morgan, and her voice sounded strained.

"Are you okay? Is something wrong?"

"Dad, it's Maggie. I can't wake her up. I think she may be … Dad, she's not breathing, and I can't find a pulse. I held a mirror in front of her face, but … nothing."

He opened his mouth to reply, but no words came. "Who is it, Daniel?" Jill asked, concern in her voice.

"Morgan," he told her. "It's about Maggie."

"What's wrong?" The tears in his eyes gave her the answer. She sat up, put her arm around him and rested her head on his shoulder as he continued to hold the phone.

"Dad?" He heard Morgan's voice on the other end. "I wanted you to know."

"I can't believe it. What happened? She seemed fine at dinner Sunday night."

"She mentioned a touch of indigestion while we were washing dishes, but it didn't sound like anything serious. And she shooed me up to bed first while she turned out the lights. We all went to bed fairly early. I don't know what happened."

"Where is … her body, Morgan?" he asked. His voice sounded choked. "What can I do to help?"

"Dad, I don't know what to do. I haven't called anyone yet, except you. Do you know anything about her family here?"

"Not really. She hasn't mentioned them in years, and then only in the abstract. Where is … she, Morgan?" he repeated.

"She's still upstairs."

"This will be hard for Danny and Jillian. Where are they now, by the way?"

"Mark dropped them off at school before I knew. I haven't even called him yet."

"I thought she was always up at six-thirty to help see the children off to school. She once mentioned that they kissed her goodbye every morning. It seemed important to her. Why didn't you check sooner? Has she been ill?"

"No, but she's been tired and sometimes sleeping a bit later these recent weeks, so I didn't worry, and I didn't want to disturb her. But when she hadn't come down by seven-forty-five, I went up to check on her and ... Oh, Dad, I'm going to miss her." Daniel heard the tears in her voice.

"We'll all miss her, Morgan. I guess you'd better go ahead and call an undertaker—Campbell's, the same one we used for Grandfather, I guess. I'll be right over. I doubt they'll get there before I do, but please don't let anyone take her away until I've arrived. I'd like a chance to say goodbye. She's been an important part of our lives since you were little."

"I know, Dad. She looks so peaceful and almost seems to be smiling. I had to close her eyes." He could hear Morgan choking back a sob.

"I'll be right over." He hung up and reached for Jill. They held each other for a long moment, remembering the goodness Maggie had brought to their lives and the role she'd played in bringing them together.

When Daniel rang the bell at his daughter's home, Morgan came to the door, her eyes puffy and red.

"Jill's not with you?" she asked.

"She wanted to come, but I wanted to do this alone. She understood, thank God. She always understands."

He followed Morgan up the stairwell to Maggie's room on the third floor. It had become harder in recent years for Maggie to climb these stairs, but she had vehemently refused Mark's plans to install the elevator they had talked about. Maggie always dismissed the idea. "I need the exercise," she'd said. "Otherwise I'll grow old and stiff."

Thus, each day, she had trudged up and down the two flights that connected her room with the first floor. She had not wanted Morgan and Mark to go to any trouble or expense for her.

Standing beside her bed, Daniel gazed down at Maggie's serene face, her eyes closed now in rest. "You're right. She does look peaceful." He studied her face for a long moment, then knelt beside the bed and reached out to hold her cold, still hand. He lifted it to his lips and kissed it.

"She was a wonderful woman, Morgan," he said wistfully. "We were lucky to have found her when we did. And she probably saved my life,"

"She was an important influence for us all."

"I know. I only wish ..." He felt unexpected tears springing to his eyes.

His words were interrupted by the loud chime of the doorbell, and Morgan rushed back down the stairs. It was the undertaker and his assistant. A long, black hearse was parked out front, and the assistant carried a folded stretcher. "We've come for the deceased, ma'am," the undertaker, dressed in a three-piece black business suit, said somberly.

"She's upstairs—on the third floor." Morgan thought she heard a small groan from the undertaker's assistant, but she may have been mistaken.

"Follow me," she said.

After the two men had struggled down the stairs with the stretcher holding Maggie's small, sheet-covered body, loaded it into the hearse, and driven away, Morgan asked, "Would you like some coffee, Dad?"

"Thanks, that would be great."

It was already brewed, and she poured the hot, black liquid into two mugs. As they sat beside the breakfast-room window, Morgan asked again, "Can you think of anything she might have said about her family? Isn't there someone I should contact?"

"You know, in all those years she lived with us, she told us very little about herself. I know she was a widow. I think she had lost a child at birth or something. Her parents were dead, and she had a brother in Ireland, Brendan, I think his name was, but I have no idea about the last name or where he might live. O'Neil was her married name. How could I never have asked her those questions?"

He sat in silence for a moment, staring into his coffee cup. "It's funny, isn't it? How you can know someone so well—or think you do—and then discover that you know nothing at all."

"Except her great capacity for love, her kindness, her joy in living. Only the really important things," his daughter said.

"You're right, Morgan. Those were the important things. Nevertheless, we should try to find her brother. He might want her buried in Ireland."

"I'll look through her things before the kids get home from school and let you know if I find his address."

Jill met Daniel at the funeral home on Madison Avenue to select a casket and try to help him decide what arrangements should be made. They spent much of the afternoon talking with the coroner who had examined the body. It had evidently been a heart attack or a massive stroke, he had concluded without an autopsy, but whatever had happened, it appeared to have been sudden and to have "caused little stress to the deceased," he informed them. Certainly on her face, which seemed younger than it had in years, there was no sign of pain. Only peace.

At six o'clock that evening, Daniel and Jill sat beside the fireplace sipping their cocktails. The weather was still nippy outside, and the fire felt good. Daniel had been quiet all day and was trying to tell Jill about Maggie, how she had come into their lives for such a long time, and been literally his salvation as his marriage to Helen fell apart.

She had been a kind and sympathetic ear when he needed to talk, and she had done wonders for Morgan, taking their spoiled and pampered little daughter in hand and molding her into the fine young woman she was today, a daughter he was truly proud of and a wonderful mother to her own children. Jill had heard it all before, but nonetheless she listened intently, knowing that he needed to tell it all again.

"It's sad she never had children of her own, because she would have been a terrific mother," he said thoughtfully.

"You were lucky to find her when you did," Jill said. "She was the sort of person I would have selected to help raise my children, if I had had any of my own."

He touched her arm. "You have my child and grandchildren now."

"I know, darling, and I am ever so grateful. I just wish they had all been in my life from the beginning."

"You know, it was Maggie who convinced me I'd be a fool if I didn't marry you."

"Really? You never told me that before, and here I thought it was your own idea."

"Well, it was in a way, but I had been so badly burned in my marriage to Helen that I was, quite frankly, scared to take the plunge again. Maggie told me that it was love that made life worth living, and that if I'd found it, I'd be a fool to ever let it go."

"I knew she was an amazing woman," she said, smiling.

"She thought you were amazing," he told her.

"The feeling was quite mutual. It's hard to think of life without her."

The telephone rang in the hallway.

"Why don't you just let it ring and relax a bit?" Jill said, worried that he had been so tense and quiet all day.

"No, I'd better get it. It might be the funeral home. I gave them my number this afternoon so they wouldn't bother Morgan. She's got enough to deal with right now, helping the kids to understand and cope."

He set his glass carefully on the wooden coaster and raised himself wearily from his armchair to move toward the hallway to the nearest telephone.

"Hello?"

"Dad, it's me again." Morgan's voice sounded strange. "I think you need to come over right away. And this time you need to bring Jill."

"Can't it wait until morning? I'm really tired tonight."

"I'm pretty sure you'll want to come now. And I don't think *I* can wait until morning."

Twenty minutes later Daniel and Jill parked their Lincoln in front of Morgan and Mark's brownstone. Before Daniel could even ring the bell, the door flew open, and Morgan, whose eyes were swollen from crying, threw her arms around her father. Then she took his hand and led him into the foyer, with Jill following after.

"Jill, I'm so glad you could come with Dad," she said. "I think he'll need you. I've sent Mark and the kids out for supper so we could have some time alone."

"What on earth ..." Daniel was completely mystified by his daughter's agitation. "Morgan, what's wrong? What's happened?"

"Follow me, both of you." She started up the stairs as quickly as she could.

When they reached Maggie's room on the third floor, Daniel could see that Morgan had laid out most of Maggie's personal articles on the bed— letters, notebooks, poetry books, pressed flowers, framed and unframed photographs.

"Did you find her brother's address?" he asked.

"Yes, I did. And a whole lot more."

She picked up one of the notebooks, its pages yellowed with age, and opened it to a particular page. The ink had browned over the years, and some of the ink on the back sides of the pages had bled through to the front, but one could still read the words.

"Take a look at this, Dad."

He took the notebook into his hand, pulled his glasses case from his jacket pocket, put them on, and began to read aloud. "*Tonight was the second beginning of my life. This time there was no dinner bell, but only the gentle lapping of waves along the shore. Hector held me in his arms and kissed me as though there were no tomorrow—and as we made love, the future stretched out before us like a shining ribbon. I have given myself to him body and soul, and nothing can ever come between us.*"

Daniel looked up. "Morgan, this is private, and I don't think we should be reading Maggie's personal journal, which is clearly what this is."

"Dad, read on. Believe me, you need to read it—all of it."

He began to read again, this time without saying the words aloud. He turned the page and read on, turning the pages quickly. By the tenth page, he caught his breath sat down on the chair beside the bed.

"Oh, my God," he said quietly, reading on.

Morgan took Jill's arm. "Let's go make some tea," she said, leading her toward the stairwell. Jill looked at her curiously but followed her obediently down the stairs.

Half an hour later, Daniel appeared at the kitchen door, his face ashen and his eyes red.

Jill stared at him. Morgan had told her nothing, believing it to be her father's prerogative.

"How could he do such a thing?" Daniel asked his daughter.

"I don't know, Dad. I don't know," she said, reaching out to hold her father.

"Who are you two talking about?" Jill asked.

Daniel handed the notebooks and a handful of letters to Jill, who began to skim the words as quickly as she could to learn the secrets of Maggie O'Neil that had caused her husband and stepdaughter to weep their silent tears and cling to each other as they were doing.

"Jill," Daniel said finally, pulling back from Morgan's embrace. "She was—" His voice broke. He paused for a moment, waiting to collect his emotions and get them under control. "She was ... my mother." With those words any attempt at control was forgotten. He sat down heavily and began to sob. Jill rose from the table and put her arms around both him and Morgan.

Then, she smiled at her husband. "Daniel, darling," she began, trying to find sufficient words. "Thank God you've found out before you shipped her body off to Ireland. You always told me you were sorry you never knew your mother. But you did, Danny, you did," she said with excitement.

"She loved you and you loved her. And she lived with you and your family for almost twenty years. That's more than most of us can ever hope for."

Jill always knew just what to say to calm him, to make him see the truth, to make him understand. He was so lucky to have her, even though they had not found each other in their younger lives. It was now that counted. Now that he needed her most.

If his first wife, Helen, had found out that he was the son of an Irish maid and a Greek waiter, she would probably have left him as a low-life. She had left him anyway for someone with more money, taking as much of his grandfather's money with her as she could possibly manage. And he had not heard from her again.

Jill was so different from Helen. She would understand Maggie's anguish at being sundered from her only child. It was such understanding that had brought them together. She would see not just the pain, but also the beauty, in their stories and make him see it as well. He understood so clearly now why Maggie had wanted him to take the case of Amy Fletcher and her daughter. Why she had felt they needed a champion against the odds of the wealthy and powerful. People like his grandfather.

His *grandfather*! The word reverberated with bitter irony in his mind. How could he ever think of Henry Barrett as his grandfather again? He had crushed the life of his own son by his suspicions, taken Daniel from his mother, and almost destroyed her life.

"You mustn't judge Great-grandfather too harshly, Daddy," Morgan said. "He was doing what he thought was best for you, and he was struggling with his own grief at the time. Let your own emotions settle before you think too badly of him."

Her father looked at her, his eyes softening. "You've become a wonderful woman, Morgan. I'm proud of you."

"I learned a lot from Maggie," she said, "and from you, Jill. I've been lucky." Her stepmother hugged her again, and Daniel smiled at them both through his tears. He understood now how Maggie could sometimes smile and cry at the same time. It was in his genes.

"Well," he said, "at least one problem is solved."

"What's that?" asked Morgan.

"I think I know where Maggie ... where my mother ... will be buried."

Morgan and Jill looked at him, uncomprehending, as he added, "I will send a telegram to Brendan O'Brien tonight, followed by a long, long letter."

He smiled at Jill and reached out for her. "How would you like to take a vacation to Ireland this summer?"

She was holding one of the letters from Maggie's brother in her hand. "I hear there's a wonderful town called Doolin. I think I might like to visit there. What do you say?"

Daniel's heart was full to overflowing. He had a family—an uncle and perhaps cousins. He could only nod his agreement and choke out two words. "Sounds great."

The problem of where Maggie should be buried was, in fact, not so easy a decision as Daniel had first thought. He wanted to bury her in the family plot, where his grandfather lay and where there was a large memorial stone on the grave of his once-supposed father, describing his death on the *Titanic*. It had been Daniel's intent to acknowledge Maggie openly as his mother in this way. And it would serve his grandfather right to be recognized as the tyrant he was.

Although he tried, Daniel couldn't think of Henry Barrett in any other way than as his grandfather. As Jill pointed out, he had been the only grandfather Daniel had ever known. Many people, she argued, don't particularly like the families they are born into. And although he wasn't born into it, it was all he had as a child.

As he considered it further, his first thought about the burial did not seem just right. There were other factors he needed to consider. Where, after all, would *Maggie* want her remains to lie for eternity? Surely not beside Henry Barrett.

Two weeks later, in New York's Trinity Cemetery, Daniel and Jill, along with Morgan, Mark, and their children stood in the shadow of a great tree, as the gray memorial stone, carved with a wild rose symbolizing love, was put into place. They had deliberately put off a formal service until they could have the stone mounted for all the mourners to see, since there was no grave to lay flowers on. The marble works had done an admirable job of getting the stone ready in time.

Daniel had sat, stoic and dry-eyed through the earlier service, while Jill and Morgan wept quietly. At Daniel's request the liturgy was officiated by both a Catholic priest from Saint Patrick's and the Episcopal rector of Trinity. Only family members and special friends attended. John and Frances Thacher were there, as was Abby Steers and a few people Daniel did not know, but who signed the memorial book as Alexander Mews, Deirdre and Rudolph Mews, and Suzanne Lefranc. He thought he recalled Maggie mentioning Deirdre and Rudy. He assumed they must have read the obituary in the newspaper and learned of Maggie's death. There was still so much Daniel had to learn about her life.

As the stone was set in place in the Barrett family plot, everyone who did not already know what it said, widened their eyes in surprise, then nodded at its rightness, for they had all heard Maggie's story.

In Memoriam
Margaret O'Brien O'Neil
Beloved Mother
of Daniel Hector O'Brien Barrett
Widow of Stuart O'Neil

She was a native of Doolin, Ireland
born March 20, 1892
died April 2, 1969
Requiescat in pace.

16 MAY 1969, JACKSONVILLE, FLORIDA

At two-forty-five in the afternoon the plane landed on the Jacksonville runway. Daniel and Jill emerged into bright sunlight and a warm breeze and crossed the tarmac to the terminal. All Daniel had carried on the plane was a small bag, too precious to be trusted to the baggage handlers. He had arranged to have a car waiting. Once they had claimed the rest of their luggage and found the Hertz desk, it was already well past three.

"The drive is only a couple of hours, I think, maybe less," Daniel said to Jill as he loaded the bags into their rented Ford Mustang. "Time enough for you to take a quick nap."

Jill smiled gratefully. She had not slept well the night before, not so much with worry as with excitement. She knew that Daniel shared her excitement, but nothing, she had noticed over the years they had been married, ever kept him awake.

They turned north on U.S. Highway 17 and drove for a time in silence past run-down filling stations and roadside produce stands.

"Mind if I turn on the radio?" he asked.

"No," Jill murmured, already half asleep.

He turned the dial until he heard the voice of Ray Charles singing "I Can't Stop Loving You" and settled there, letting his mind absorb the music and drift wherever it wanted to go.

The landscape was mostly wild as they passed through pine forests followed by snaky-looking swamps dotted with cypress trees and clumps of lily pads. As they reached the northern border of Florida and crossed into Georgia toward Brunswick, marshlands began to stretch out to the east, with early green spartina grass lining the tidal streams. Maggie had written about the marsh grasses in her journal, and Daniel found himself looking for the herons and egrets she had described.

He hoped he had made the right decision. Even though Maggie's life might not have been what she had originally hoped for, it had its complexities that made no decision simple. He had briefly considered taking her ashes back to Ireland and had written to Brendan O'Brien of Maggie's death. Brendan had responded promptly and courteously, though rather cautiously. He was saddened to hear of his sister's death, he wrote, but he had not seen her in many years. He had not known, he said, that Maggie had a son.

The letter was rather guarded and discouraged any consideration that Daniel should bring her remains to Ireland. "She chose America," he wrote, "and if that is where her heart lay, it is where she should stay." If Daniel and his wife did come to Ireland in the summer, Brendan said, they would be most welcome at his home in Lochrea. It was an invitation they hoped someday to accept.

Maggie's husband, Stuart, Daniel learned from one of her journals, had been buried in Newark. But Daniel had heard Maggie many times express her dislike of visiting Newark. He had also discovered from her journals that no burial plot was available beside her husband's grave. That left only one logical choice, and he had decided it was the right one.

Daniel steered the car from Highway 17 onto the causeway that led to Jekyll Island. Maggie had written it "Jekyl," but the signs clearly spelled it with two l's.

"Wake up, darling," he said to Jill. "You don't want to miss this."

The sun was lower in the sky and its light played in the watery passages that divided the marshes on both sides of the causeway.

"These must be the Marshes of Glynn she wrote about," he said.

Jill was sitting upright by now, drinking in the magnificent view, colored by greens and blues and rosy hues already beginning to reflect in the waterways.

"Look," she said, "look at that big white bird with the long legs."

"I think it's an egret," Daniel answered.

They drove for miles across the marshes, insatiable as they took in the ever-changing colors and gaped at the wildlife. In the distance off to the left they could see a small dock and a white round tower rising behind the trees on the island.

A drawbridge separated Jekyll Island from the causeway. They drove straight on, looking for someone to tell them where to go. Finally, as they dead-ended at a street marked Beachview Drive, they saw a small shopping center to the left. Daniel turned the car into the entrance and parked in front of a store with a sign in front that said "Maxwell's."

Inside, a woman with a broad face and lusterless eyes stood behind the counter that held the cash register. She looked bored, but she was keeping an eye on the two customers who were roaming about the store, looking at souvenirs. When the man stepped up to the counter, she brightened a bit and said, "May I help you?"

"I hope so," said Daniel. "I hear there's a cemetery on Jekyll Island, and we're hoping to find it.

"Oh, yeah," she nodded. "There's an old cemetery across from the Horton House. You go back toward the causeway and turn right just before the drawbridge. It's up at the north end of the island, three or four miles, I guess. Or you could go on down Beachview and turn left on Captain Wylly Road, then right again when you get to Riverview. It's not hard to find."

"Thanks, and are there any hotels or motels on the island? I think I once read something about the old Jekyll Island Club being a hotel now."

"Used to be. But it's closed down now. You'll pass it if you go back toward the causeway and turn right. But there's plenty of motels. Turn left on Beachview and you'll find the Wanderer a mile or so down the road on the right. Some others down toward the south end. One of 'em's the Buccaneer," she said, motioning in the opposite direction. "You can't miss 'em." She chuckled now, and her eyes began to sparkle with humor. "It's pretty hard to get lost on Jekyll."

"I'm sure we'll find them. Thanks again."

He backed the car out of the parking place and turned it back toward the causeway.

"Guess what?" he said to Jill. "The old clubhouse is still here, but it's closed now. Why don't we go take a look?"

Once they had turned north onto Riverview Road, they came quickly to a series of once grand old houses.

"Wonder who lives in these? Some pretty neat architecture, don't you think?" Daniel asked, slowing as he drove by. In front of one was a sign proclaiming it "Rockefeller Museum."

Then up ahead he saw what must be the clubhouse. The white tower they had seen from the causeway stood at the south end. The structure was an old frame Queen Anne style building with whimsical balconies and porches. To the right of the clubhouse they could see another large gray building that also appeared deserted. Daniel turned into the driveway and parked the car.

"Wow," he said. "Too bad it's closed now. Want to see if we can find a way in?"

"I wouldn't miss it for the world." Jill was already climbing out of the car.

They mounted the front steps of the building to the wide curved porch. It appeared still sturdy, but Daniel could see that, in places, the wood was beginning to rot and the paint was peeling. The wooden facade of the clubhouse looked neglected and ghostly in the late afternoon light. The heavy front door was locked, but Daniel found a window partially opened. Pushing it up farther, he crawled through and stepped into a parlor.

Moving on into the hallway, he called to Jill, who was climbing in through the window. "Take a look at this!"

She followed him into the wide hall, where a magnificent row of huge mirrors on each side reflected their image a hundred times or more as far as they could see. "Looks like they were trying to compete with Versailles," he said.

They reached what was once the lobby, and they could detect, beneath the scattered rubbish and tawdry modernization that had obviously been attempted, what was once a fine old clubhouse. An elevator shaft had been installed where there had probably been a grand staircase when the club was new.

Ahead of them they saw what they thought must have been the dining room, stacked in the middle with old wicker furniture. The walls were painted a garish pink, and a water leak had caused one part of the ceiling to sag. In spite of its condition, the former elegance of the room was evident from the large fireplace at one end and the eight Ionic columns that supported the ceiling, which was bordered by a graceful frieze.

"So this is where my father worked, in this very room," Daniel said, reaching out for Jill's hand.

"It must have been quite splendid then," she answered. "Should we find a way to go upstairs?"

"The upper floors don't look too reliable." He pointed to the sagging ceiling. "And I don't see a staircase. The elevator won't work, because there's no electricity."

The light was fading, and Daniel caught sight of the setting sun through one of the large windows of the dining room.

"Let's go back outside and watch the sunset."

They had never seen anything like it. The entire horizon was bright orange, but already in the upper regions, the color was fading to a pinkish purple. They sat on the clubhouse steps to watch, as the great ball of sun began to sink behind the marshes. The river that ran in front of the clubhouse was aflame with the molten reflection.

"You know," he said, squeezing his wife's hand, "one could be happy in such a place."

She laid her head on his shoulder. "Yes," she murmured. "I know."

Chapter Thirty-One

❧ THE LIGHT HAD SOFTENED to a gentle gray by the time Daniel and Jill retraced their steps back to the shopping center. They turned right and drove south until they found the Buccaneer Motor Lodge, nestled in a shady grove behind the dunes. They requested an upstairs room facing the beach, where they hoped to get a view of the Atlantic. The room was comfortable and had a tiny kitchenette, so they could make coffee in the morning and sit outside on the balcony to feel the warm breezes that blew in from the ocean.

Both of them slept well. They left the balcony door open to hear the soothing sounds of the waves lapping the shore. When Jill awoke, she smelled coffee already brewing. Daniel had gotten up early, as he often did, and driven to the little shopping center, where he found a Huddle House just behind it. He had picked up a pound of coffee (thanks to a hefty tip to the waitress who at first protested that they did not sell unbrewed coffee), four muffins, a large container of chunked mixed fruit, and a side order of bacon. He had found white plates and cups in the kitchenette's cupboard and laid out their breakfast on a little round table he had pulled up to the edge of the balcony.

"Mmm, that smells good," Jill said, stretching away the stiffness of sleep. "May I join you?"

"Please do, Mrs. Vanderbilt. Your breakfast awaits." A hand towel draped over his arm, he bowed politely, and stood behind her chair while she put on her pink wrapper over her silk nightgown and slid her slender feet into matching slippers.

"My," she said. "The service here is wonderful. Why don't you join me for breakfast, and I'll leave a very nice tip."

He lifted his eyebrows in mock approval and sincere anticipation. "I'll count on that," he said. He gave her a slight, formal bow and added with a grin, "I'm at your service."

After breakfast and the lengthy "tip," they both put on shorts, t-shirts, and sandals and headed out through the dunes to the beach. To the north was an endless strand, littered with shells, sand dollars and an occasional jellyfish. To the south they could see another island in the distance and an even wider stretch of beach. Only three people were visible as far as the eye could see. Obviously there weren't many shell-seekers this time of year.

They walked south in silence for half a mile or so, listening to the sounds of the sea and shrieking gulls and watching the terns and sandpipers enjoying breakfast along the shore.

"This is an amazing place," Jill said finally. "I don't think I've ever seen such an unspoiled stretch of beach, at least not for the past ten or fifteen years." They had given up vacationing in Florida, where most of the beaches they had known had become lined with rising condominiums, thick knots of people everywhere, and even cars driving on the beach. "I can't even see a house or the motel, for that matter."

She pointed to a water tower in the distance. "That's the only visible sign of human habitation. We could be marooned on a desert island."

"But we're not, and that's the best part."

"I can see why Maggie loved the place."

"So can I."

They had not brought bathing suits, assuming the water would still be too cold to swim, but they waded in the warm surf, carrying their shoes and regretting their decision. It seemed pointless to waste time buying swimsuits now, since they would be leaving the next morning, and Daniel was already lamenting that he had made their return reservations for such an early date. He had legal matters in New York that needed his attention, but Jekyll was an extraordinary treat, unlike anything he had ever known.

After they showered and dressed, it was time to attend to the matter for which they had come. The small bag Daniel had carried on the airplane lay on the Mustang's back seat while they drove north up the beach road, turning left on Captain Wylly Road, as the woman in Maxwell's had suggested, and then right again on Riverview.

Finally up ahead they saw the ruins of an old house that looked as though it were made of stucco. As they slowed and drove nearer for closer inspection, they could see that the base of the cement-like material contained oyster shells. Across the road, a wall made of the same substance stood behind a painted, misspelled sign that said "DuBignon Cemetary."

"That must be it." Daniel turned the wheel sharply to the left to veer across the road and pull up beside the wall. But he didn't immediately get out of the car. "Just give me a minute," he said.

"Come whenever you're ready, darling." She opened the car door to slide out and head toward the cemetery gate.

She waited at the entrance, gazing at the various tombstones, but not wanting to enter until he was by her side. Three raised graves with elaborately carved writings stood among large cedar trees. Behind them were two small headstones, but she couldn't make out the writing from where she stood. Beyond the small cemetery, she could see the marshes stretching toward the mainland.

Daniel was at her side now. "Let's go in," he said.

They both looked at the larger raised tombs, which bore the names of Félicité Riffault, Joseph du Bignon, and Ann Amelia du Bignon. Although they were carved in elegant script and looked very old, they were not what had lured Daniel and Jill here.

It was the two small gravestones at the back of the plot, probably ignored by most tourists, that attracted their attention. The small granite markers stood side by side, simple and inconspicuous. The one on the left contained four lines of block letters:

Hector Deliyannis,
A native of Smyrna
drowned at Jekyl Island
March 21, 1912

Daniel stood for a moment, staring down at the grave of his father. It had all happened just as Maggie had written. And thanks to the small collection of photographs they had found with her letters and journals, Daniel knew what his father looked like. One of the snapshots had been taken the day he had first arrived at Jekyll and another the day he had drowned. He was handsome, suntanned in the second shot, sure of himself, muscular, and athletic, as he posed with his friends and fellow waiters on the beach.

Jill had commented on Hector's resemblance to Daniel. "The coloring is different, but there is something about the eyes and the self-assurance—even the way he has his arms folded and the slight tilt of the head—that is so like you," she had said.

Daniel knelt beside the grave. "I should have brought flowers." He felt completely inadequate to the moment.

"You brought him the greatest flower of all," his wife replied, touching his shoulder. "Shall I get the bag?"

"If you don't mind. I'll just stay here for a moment."

As she turned back to the car, Daniel, now alone, touched the gravestone. "I never knew you, and you never knew me. But I think we would have been friends," he said to the granite surface. "We both loved Maggie."

Jill brought the entire bag, not just its contents.

Daniel unzipped the top and pulled out a sealed metal urn. "Do you think I'm doing the right thing, Jill?"

"Absolutely. It's what Maggie would have wanted. I'm sure of it."

Her words added to his resolve. "But what if it's illegal? I probably need permission."

She reassured him. "Forgiveness is sometimes easier than permission in such circumstances, if either one is needed. Besides, who will know?" He nodded and handed her the urn to hold.

Opening the bag again, he pulled out a folded army shovel. Unfolding it, he began to dig the sandy soil about half a foot in front of Hector's tombstone. When the hole was roughly a foot deep, he laid down the shovel.

"Are you ready?" Jill asked.

"I think so." She handed him the urn.

"I have something I want to read," he said. She smiled at him, not surprised.

From his pocket he pulled a small, folded piece of paper.

"There is so much I don't understand about all this," he said to her, "but these words speak to me and, I think, to the moment."

He unfolded the paper carefully and read: "'For now we see in a mirror dimly, but then face to face. Now I know in part; then I shall understand fully, even as I have been fully understood. So faith, hope, love abide, these three; but the greatest of these is love.' Rest in peace, Maggie O'Brien O'Neil, my beloved mother."

At that moment a shaft of silent sunlight pierced the thick cedar branches overhead and fell across the gravestone. Daniel picked up the urn with tenderness and removed the cover. He tilted it to let its contents sift slowly into the hole he had dug. When he had covered the hole again, he patted it firm and smoothed the sand over with his hand, hoping no one would notice it had been disturbed.

"I've brought her back to you, Father. Both of you, together, *requiescat in pace*. Rest in peace."

Danny stood up. Jill was waiting to take him in her arms. Tears were streaming down both their cheeks.

"I love you, Daniel Hector O'Brien Barrett," she said. "I love you."

The next morning they packed up the car with the few things they had brought with them and a few others they were taking home, mostly several carefully wrapped seashells they had found along the beach.

"Do you think we will ever come back?" Jill asked.

"I'm sure of it. The lady at the Huddle House who sold me the ground coffee told me there's an old saying that once you get the sand of Jekyll in your shoes, you'll always come back."

He took off the loafer he was wearing home and turned it upside down. A teaspoonful of sand poured out.

"Well, then," said Jill with a laugh, "I guess that's it. Next time I'll bring a bathing suit."

Who would ever have believed that life would bring me here? Daniel thought, as he drove back across the causeway. It was hard to return to New York, knowing that so much beauty and history, his own personal history, lay on this relatively obscure sea island. He looked with longing over the wide expanse of marshes that were just beginning to take on a hint of summer green. From his office windows in New York City all he could see was concrete, traffic, and tall buildings. Here, nature prevailed.

Jill had settled her head back against the headrest and closed her eyes, a smile playing on her lips. He watched her for a moment. *What have I done,* he wondered, *to deserve these wonderful women in my life?* Jill. Morgan. Maggie. He had been deprived in large measure of female influence for his first two decades. Suzanne had watched over him and taken care of him, but she had never replaced his mother.

It had been his grandfather who had been the greatest influence on his young life. And his schoolmasters at the fancy prep schools where Henry Barrett had sent him—St. Bernard's and then St. Alban's—were all men. Even at Harvard he had had no women teachers and was exposed only to the female students at Radcliffe, who were hardly typical of most women.

When he had met Helen at a fraternity mixer on the Harvard campus, he had practically no experience with women. He didn't have a clue about the grace and wonder that women could bring to life. He had only noticed that Helen was pretty and that she seemed compatible with the "right" social set of which his grandfather approved. It was little wonder that their marriage had not worked out. In fact, it was amazing it had lasted as long as it did.

After their divorce, when he met Jill, she was different from any woman he had ever known, down to earth, committed to social justice, and utterly indifferent to New York society functions—the absolute antithesis of Helen. Jill wasn't merely pretty. She reflected an inner beauty he had not completely understood before. She was like a breath of pure oxygen in his life. She and Maggie had hit it off from the beginning. Under their influence—Maggie's and Jill's—Morgan had become the fine woman she was today. *It's certainly not been my doing,* he thought. *I've just been blessed.*

He looked over at Jill again. Her eyes were open now, and she had raised her head, rapturously watching a gray pelican soaring just over the tidal stream.

"I love you," he whispered.

She smiled back. "I love you too." Her gentle eyes spoke the truth of her words.

Daniel had never felt God's presence more than he did on this Sunday morning, driving through these magnificent marshes, with his soul mate at his side. Happiness flooded over him like warm sunshine.

Yes, he said to himself, *there's no doubt about it. We will come back.*

Author's Note

MANY OF THE CHARACTERS THAT APPEAR in *Almost to Eden* are real people who were a part of the historic Jekyl Island Club during the period in question. (The spelling of *Jekyl* was officially changed to *Jekyll* by the Georgia legislature in 1929.) Hector Deliyannis and George Harvey were, in fact, club waiters who drowned there on March 21, 1912, shortly before the club season ended. Hector was, as he is in the novel, the waiter for the J.P. Morgans while they were at Jekyl that season. He was only twenty-three years old when he died, while George was thirty. Visitors can still find their graves in the du Bignon cemetery on the island, though few who pass by notice their small monuments or know who they were.

Other historical characters in the novel include Ernest Grob and Julius Falk, Page and Aleathia Parland, Captain James Clark and his wife Minnie, Bert Stallman (with his ubiquitous camera), and Frances Baker and her family.

Maggie, my main character, springs entirely from my imagination and my desire to create a story for Hector, whose life was cut so short. Henry and David Barrett, Daniel, Jill, and Morgan, Deirdre and Rudy Mews, along with many other people who weave in and out of the novel, are purely fictional.

The world in which they move, however, is historically accurate, and I have made an effort to authenticate every detail of the times, from the sinking of the *Titanic* to the phases of the moon. Solterra did burn as described in

1914, to be replaced three years later by the elegant Crane Cottage. The Jekyll Island Club did close in 1942 just after America entered World War II, and the island became the property of the state of Georgia in 1947.

The state made an effort to run the clubhouse (then painted white) as a hotel until the late 1960s, when it closed and remained empty and abandoned for almost two decades. It was not until 1986, one hundred years after the founding of the elite club, that it was restored to its original splendor and reopened as the Jekyll Island Club Hotel.

Readers who would like to know more about the island's fascinating history can visit the island today or consult my non-fiction books, *The Jekyll Island Club: Southern Haven for America's Millionaires* (co-authored with my late husband, William Barton McCash), *The Jekyll Island Cottage Colony,* and *Jekyll Island's Early Years: From Prehistory through Reconstruction,* all published by the University of Georgia Press.

Needless to say, I love the island as much as Maggie and Hector did. It has worked its magic on me since my first visit there in 1983, when I had an opportunity to see the faded splendor of the deserted old clubhouse, the future of which at the time was still uncertain. Since then the historic district has come back to life. The drawbridge and the Huddle House are gone now, as are the Buccaneer and the Wanderer (its name at least). The clubhouse has been carefully restored to its original magnificence.

One by one the old houses of the cottage colony have been painstakingly refurbished by the Jekyll Island Museum, and the Jekyll Island Club district has once again become a major attraction on the coast of Georgia, now accessible to all people, not just wealthy club members. I hope that my readers, if they haven't already visited the island, will someday have an opportunity to see it for themselves and will open their hearts to its wonders.

Acknowledgments

I WOULD LIKE TO THANK THE FOLLOWING PEOPLE for their many suggestions. My special appreciation goes to those who have read all or portions of the manuscript and made recommendations for its improvement—Dick Gleaves (my husband), Debbie Conner, Kathleen Ferris, Michelle Adkerson, Margaret Ordoubadian, Pam Davis, and members of the Murfreesboro Writers' Group, especially Mary Jo Bratton, Susan Daniel, and the late Bob Daniel—all of whom provided many insightful comments. I am also grateful to Ron and Emily Messier, who seem to be a part of everything I do and whose ongoing friendship and support mean so much; to Lisa Collins, the lawyer who recommended the Tann/Children's Home Society case when I was looking for an appropriate pro bono case for Daniel Barrett to take on; and to John Hunter of the Jekyll Island Museum for his continued assistance and for finding in the museum's collection the images of the club house that appear on the cover. I would also like to thank novelist Brian Jay Corrigan for his encouragement and especially for the literary award he gave to the book's opening chapter and synopsis at the Southeastern Writers' Association Conference in 2008.

Above all, I am indebted to my editor, Emily Carmain, for her keen eye and always helpful suggestions, as well as to the book's designer, Gwyn Kennedy Snider, for her intriguing cover and overall aesthetic contribution to the work. They have both been a joy to work with.

Reading Groups: Questions and Topics for Discussion

1. What are Maggie's expectations when she first arrives in America? Why do you think she has such expectations? Is hers a typical immigrant experience in any way?

2. What events give her a more realistic view of the new world?

3. Discuss the interactions of the members of the Jekyl Island Club with the various staff members. How does the social hierarchy come into play even among the club's workers?

4. Consider Maggie's friendship with Deirdre. Why does she reveal herself more freely to people of other social backgrounds—Aleathia Parland and David Barrett—than to her close friend?

5. Comment on the differences between Maggie's relationships with Stuart and Hector. Have your own experiences in any way mirrored these two love relationships?

6. In what ways does the parent-child theme reverberate, both positively and negatively, throughout the novel? Compare Henry Barrett's actions to those of Maggie's parents? Compare Helen's "mothering" to that of Myra Woodruff? Do you think Maggie fulfills the role of a parent to her son?

7. Discuss the influence of the various female characters on the development of Morgan as she grows from a child into a young woman and becomes a mother herself.

8. Why does Henry Barrett feel such a strong need to claim Danny as his grandson? In the end, has he learned from his experience with his own son?

9. How does Maggie help Daniel heal the wounds of war and his broken marriage?

10. Compare the relationships of Daniel with his wives, Helen and Jill. How do the two marriages come about, and why is the second more successful than the first?

11. The motif of Eden reverberates in many ways throughout the novel. Explore some of these moments to see how Maggie's hopes and dreams evolve. In your opinion, does she ever find her Eden? If so, how? If not, why not?

12. What lessons does Maggie learn in the course of her life? What in her understanding does she pass on to others?

13. Why and at what point in her life is Maggie finally able to forgive Henry Barrett? Should he be forgiven? What does her willingness to forgive tell us about Maggie's character? Does she change in the course of the novel?

14. Why does Maggie never reveal her true identity to her son? The reasons evolve throughout the book. What opportunities did she have to do so? Do you think she was right or wrong to keep her secret?

15. What do Daniel and Jill discover during their visit to the island at the end? In your opinion, will they really come back? Why or why not?

About the Author

Photo by Richard D. Gleaves

June Hall McCash is the author of three non-fiction books about Jekyll Island, all published by the University of Georgia Press. In addition, she has published three books about the Middle Ages. She holds a doctorate in Comparative Literature from Emory University and has been a fellow of both the National Endowment for the Humanities and the American Council of Education, as well as a trustee of the Jekyll Island Foundation. Not only is she the recipient of awards for teaching, research and career achievement during her tenure at Middle Tennessee State University, she has also won literary awards for her non-fiction, fiction, and poetry. She is now a full-time writer, living in Murfreesboro, Tennessee. *Almost to Eden* is her first novel.

LaVergne, TN USA
06 March 2011
218998LV00002B/91/P